Ian Pattison is a noted TV writer whose credits include *Atletico Partick*, *Naked Video* and writing all ten series of *Rab C. Nesbitt*. He has written three novels, including *Looking at the Stars*. His play *I, Tommy*, toured throughout 2012. He was born and lives in Glasgow. You have been warned.

CANCELLED

IAN PATTISON

Unhappy-Go-Lucky

Tindal
Street
Press

First published in 2013 by Tindal Street Press,
an imprint of Profile Books Ltd
3A Exmouth House
Pine Street
London EC1R 0JH
website: www.serpentstail.com

ISBN 978 1 90699 446 4
eISBN 978 190699 447 1

Designed and typeset by Crow Books

Printed by Clays, Bungay, Suffolk

10 9 8 7 6 5 4 3 2 1

Acknowledgements

I thank my agent Anna Webber at United Agents and Alan Mahar at Tindal Street for their faith in and support with this book

'There are some things one remembers even though they may never have happened'

Harold Pinter

To the present

One

I'll give it to you straight – my mother was ill, another relationship had broken up and I feared I'd lost direction in my work. Throw into the mix that I'd started drinking alone. If you're still with me, relax, you've had all the bad stuff, right up front.

I was sitting in my living room eyeing up a second bottle of Merlot when the phone rang. It was Tom McIninch asking me how I was doing. Tom had heard about my run of bad luck, what with my mother and with Emily, and he wondered if I'd like to shoot the breeze at his house on Saturday night with a few of the guys from the old days. He thought me to have been depressed and had the good intention of cheering me up. But I wasn't depressed – I know me – I was becalmed on the ocean of my own life. What I needed was for a new breeze to spring up and plump my sails.

'Let me get back to you on that,' I said.

'Sure, let me know.'

We talked on, and Tom filled me in on the latest with the boys, which is to say the men, all middle-aged now, all fathers, some grandfathers, anyway these guys I'd hung out with before I had left for London at the age of fifteen.

As we spoke, I looked idly out of the window. It was early

autumn and the streets were freckled with dead leaves, not yet crinkly. Out front, a pregnant neighbour woman with her hair tied back, name of Siobhan, one of those exhausted, endlessly lactating middle-class breeding sows, was trying to coax her small twin daughters into a Jeep Cherokee. Each kid carried a little black violin case and they were wearing matching duffel coats and pink boots. They didn't want to be corralled into the Jeep, I could see that, and were putting up an argument so they could play around the gutters kicking up piles of dead leaves instead of scratching out ropey bits of 'Three Blind Mice' or Beethoven's Late Quartets, whatever.

In the communal gardens, a pair of work experience teenagers were stacking and bagging leaves and grass. In the pale autumn sun, little piles of gold and green-yellow choked the street drains like hair round a bath plug. In a week or two I'd be able to see the shops again through the skeletons of the trees.

The place I owned was a conversion, on the top storey of a B-listed building in the West End of Glasgow. Meandering round the living room with the phone at my ear, I admired the stately confidence of the cornice work. Emily had cajoled me into having it retouched. On top of that, she'd arranged for a company that specialised in sash windows to come in. They'd replaced every cord and fixed all the warps in the frames so that I no longer needed to plug the gaps with scrunched up sheets of old script whenever a wind gathered. Add to that, I'd installed a new fireplace, which was to say an old Victorian fireplace with a matt black stove squatting in the hearth. I'd spent a tidy bundle on the place, for sure. We'd clashed, Emily and me, over the issue of carpeting, but I'd prevailed. With the living-room door open, I could look upon great fields of rolling Axminster, as far as the eye could see. It's not fashionable but I have a thing about carpeting.

If you hang around long enough to know me better, you'll understand why.

'What are you working on?' Tom asked.

'A book,' I lied.

'What's it about?'

'I don't know – I'll tell you when it's finished.'

He pushed me and I prattled on about this so-called book. In fact, I wasn't working hard on anything. I told myself I was 'trusting the process' – holding something in reserve, waiting for that expectant inner tremor for which there is no name but which, for me at least, signals the onset of a prolonged piece of writing work. You can't go into that sort of ethereal guff with old school pals like Tom, these are men who hit things with hammers and sell insurance – real jobs; speaking of nebulous things in Tom's company always made me feel like some sort of flouncing idiot – a feng shui salesman or one of those preening male presenters who give breathless updates about the soaps on breakfast television. Tom did building work – he had palms so rough they could smooth the splinters off a planed door.

'This'll be my fourth novel,' I blustered. 'It's a technical advance on the other three in that . . .'

In London, I'd made good money from the television racket. When I'd come back to Glasgow, I'd headed straight for the chic West End but the boys were still mostly on the other side of the river, scattered around Paisley, very few having moved far from the vicinity of Dreichstane, my old town, our old town.

The boys, the men, were all long married and though nobody said so, I knew they had always been puzzled by my solitary ways and stubborn resistance to the idea of marriage or even of living with someone. With Emily things had started to turn sour the moment she'd moved in with me.

'But enough about me – how are you, Tom?'

It still seemed strange calling him Tom. He was 'Tonga' in the old days. But we were mature and whiskery now and while nicknames don't exactly fall away with time, there is a natural statute of limitation in force and after a while you tend only to apply them with scurrilous affection when the owner isn't present.

'I'm doing a homer over Erskine,' Tom said. 'I'm knocking out a fitted robe, putting in an en-suite.'

'Great – so still busy?'

I was bored already. I was hoping Tom wouldn't tell me any more about Erskine; or the dreary mechanics of installing en-suite bathrooms. I didn't like reality. I lived in the attic of my imagination. I'd pulled up the rope ladder to the real world years ago and waved everybody down below goodbye.

Tom, Tonga, said something that hit me.

'You remember Bo Divney?'

'Sure, what about him?'

'Got the Bengal.'

'What?'

'Bengal Lancer. Cancer. Pancreas and spreading.'

'Jesus. Bo Divney? Poor guy.'

'Exactly.'

'Give him my best if you see him.'

'He's in hospital – you can visit and give him your own best.'

'You do it for me – you'll give my best better than I ever could.'

'You don't want to see him?'

'My mother is ill. I'm on compassion overload.'

'That's a first,' said Tom. He changed tack. 'Okay. What about the other thing? Saturday night, over at my house?'

'I'll let you know.'

'You can't just say yes or no?'

'No.'

'No, you can't say yes or no, or no you're not coming?'

'The first one.'

He was growing impatient. He said, 'Why are you being so slippery?'

'I'm not being slippery. If I was being slippery I'd say yes. Then I'd cancel at the last minute.'

'That's what you did last time.'

'Exactly. I was being slippery last time. This time, I'm not.'

'I get it – you're stalling for a better offer. If you don't get one, you'll come.'

'I have no further comment at this time.'

Tom forced a chuckle as he said, 'Ivan, you're a selfish bastard.'

'Don't knock it – it's been good to me.'

I put the phone down. I wasn't troubled over the Saturday night thing. It was legitimate, in my opinion, to prevaricate on a Wednesday as to one's arrangements for the coming weekend. All the same I still felt unsettled by the Bo Divney thing. I hadn't seen Bo in over thirty years – I needed time to mull, mulling time, before sitting at anybody's sick bed, offering matey encouragement. It's dangerous to meddle with the deep, dark past – you start shaking up the sediment from that stuff and it might never settle again. Then what are you stuck with from here to the grave? Grey hair, a paunch and unsettled sediment; that's what.

I sat down in my armchair and picked up my glass. I couldn't help myself; I started thinking about the old days. Back then, Bo Divney was known as Bob, but we'd knocked off the second 'b' when he'd appeared one day in a light grey coat with a black velvet collar trim and we'd decided he looked like Beau Brummel – so right then, at the tender age of thirteen, the matter of his future nomenclature was forever fatefully sealed.

I poured myself a big glug of the Merlot. Dusk was gathering but I didn't bother turning on a light. About halfway down the second bottle I noticed I had started singing. It was an old song, a thing from the sixties – 'You've Got Your Troubles' by the Fortunes. To shut myself up, I poured another glass. I downed it and weaved to the bathroom. I grimaced into the mirror. I looked old. My teeth were pink but they were still in my head, which was a bonus.

I tottered toward the bed.

I woke in the dark with the glass in my hand.

Next day, walking along Byres Road, trying to look purposeful, I bumped into a theatre director, name of Vaughan Tetley.

'Hello, Vaughan.'

'Hey, Ivan, how's the book coming?'

Nobody ever enquired about your wellbeing on Byres Road – just what you were working on. To our West End minds, it was the same thing. In a minute he'd ask whether it was commissioned work, which it wasn't.

'Oh, you know, what with one thing and another . . .'

I did pain-in-the-eyes acting, followed by a touch of silence. I was hoping Vaughan would feed me a get out of jail card. He did.

'I'm sorry to hear about your mother. How's she doing?'

'Ah, it's a difficult time.'

'I understand.' Vaughan's own mother had died. He understood.

'It's pulled the stuffing right out of me,' I said.

'Knocked you out of your stride, uh?'

'Yes, the stuffing and the stride – both kicked to hell.' I mulled reflectively for effect. 'And now I'm behind schedule with the book.'

'Don't worry. You'll catch up. Suffering enriches our work.'

'Not our own suffering though – other people's, preferably.'

Vaughan seemed a little taken aback by my apparent heartlessness. 'I'm blessed,' I said, trying to claw back lost spiritual ground, 'she's blessed me.'

We stood there nodding at each other, me slurping up the sympathy. Actually, I had contributed very little thus far to the run of the illness show and had left things as much as possible to Stan, my younger brother. He was busily eating up all his annual leave from the Department of Employment in order to take care of the care business. Karma being what it is, Vaughan hit me in the solar plexus.

'So, if the book's behind schedule it must be a commissioned work, right?'

He gave me an expectant smile. I smiled back but didn't answer.

'You still with the same publisher?'

I wasn't with a publisher any more. I had to tell him. I told him.

'It's a speculative work.'

'Not a commissioned work?'

'No.'

Vaughan's smile dropped from his lips. A sweeper-up outside Thorntons clattered a broom into his yellow dust cart. He could have swept up Vaughan's smile and bagged it with the rest of the autumn waste.

'Ah,' Vaughan said.

I affected a resolute air. 'This way I'm free to do my own deal once I've written it.'

'Of course,' he said.

On I blundered. 'I've been stung by producers and publishers too many times in the past,' I explained. 'It's the power, you see, I'm retaining it.'

He nodded. It was easy, my retaining all this power over me, since no one else appeared to want it.

'I admire your stance,' Vaughan said, playing up generously to the role in which I'd cast myself. I was the vagabond genius, the unworldly artist trapped in a morass of rapacious fools. I caught a glimpse of my reflection in the window of Phones 4u. I was wearing one of those long scarves with horizontal stripes, the sort you knot in an artful way around your black-coated neck – the type of scarf which, once on, puts you in resolute denial that you are a bogus, pretentious prick, until you can finally take it off again in the congenial misery of your own home. On top of that, I was aware I still had pink teeth and stank of last night's Merlot.

Vaughan said, 'Look, we're having a few people over the house on Saturday night – why don't you come?'

'Saturday night?'

'Yes, have you something else on?'

I thought of Tom, Tonga's, party. 'Well . . .'

'You'll like it. There'll be people – fun people, interesting people.'

I thought of how Vaughan's party might be. Then I thought of how Tom's party *would* be. Picturing Tom's party, I saw a gathering of middle-aged relics from the school room, all scrunched together on a leatherette settee in a Paisley Barratt home, eating cold pizza and downing tins of chilly Tennent's.

I looked at Vaughan. 'Interesting people, you say?'

He nodded. He lowered his voice so that I could hardly hear him above the abrasive rumble of the traffic.

'*People who might be useful to you.*'

I felt my face flush. My soul scorned his pity. My mouth didn't though. My mouth said, 'Okay – what time?'

'About eight o'clock,' Vaughan said. 'See you then?'

'Sure.'

He gave my elbow a supportive squeeze before disappearing like a pointillist's dot into the teeming clutter of grungy students, myopic visionaries, unemployed Falstaffs and beggar collectives who tramp the café-strewn banks of Byres Road.

It was settled then. I would go to Vaughan's party. I would not go to Tom's party, because there was nothing in it for me at Tom's party. Vaughan's party, on the other hand, would be good for my career. There would be movers and shakers at Vaughan's party – theatre people, television people, publishers; people in whose eyeline I might stand, in my striped shirt looking, once more, relevant.

At Tinderbox café, I wheeled right into Hyndland Road. I would schmooze them all, I decided, I would grease the wheels. I'd seen wheels greased, I could do it too – that modest yet confident air, the ready smile, the wine glass held tastefully by the stem, the trick of always remembering the little wife's name or increasingly, since this was media, the little husband's. I would join the club. I would insinuate myself into that vapid clique of couthie mediocrity; those self-important home-based dregs left in the permanently leaking bottle of Scottish talent; those chest-poking, hairy-kneed dullards, forever punching the air at regional award bashes, endlessly trumpeting the cause of Independence from atop sturdy Munros of state funding. Okay, you see now why I was rarely invited to dinner parties. Come Saturday night I'd be stoic and sober. I would be ready. I would wow them.

Two

Saturday came. I wowed them. Not in a good way.

'Wow, what a mess!'

'Christ almighty!'

'He'll be fine – give him space. Bring it up, Ivan, it'll do you good.'

'I can't, there's nothing left to—'

'Aoowoo – aa.'

I heaved. My stomach lining seemed snagged like a coat on a nail. I could see bits of vol-au-vent clinging to the porcelain. Shutting one eye, I brought the other into woozy focus. The porcelain had dimples.

'He's vomiting into your Jacuzzi.'

Jill took it well. 'It's social comment – he's an iconoclast.'

Tittering ensued.

Vaughan and Jill owned one of the new duplexes in Partick, on the site of the old Meadowside Granary, overlooking the Clyde. I let my good eye rove around their bathroom. People came and went, looking at once thrilled and gleefully disgusted by my conduct. I didn't disappoint them.

'Aoowoo – aa.'

'Give him air!'

'It's all right, Ivan. Don't worry.'

'How'd he get a name like Ivan? Is he Welsh?'

'His father was a reader. He liked the Russian romantics.'

I groaned. My head, a spinning plate, teetered on the wobbling jelly of my boneless neck. People backed away from me, just in case. Jill leaned toward me, just in case.

'Don't worry,' she said again. She guided my aim discreetly from her fleecy bath mat.

I could feel her soft hand caressing my forehead. There hadn't been much caressing in my life of late. As a token of gratitude, I groped her thigh.

'Hey, now,' I heard Vaughan's gently scolding voice say. 'Josh, help me.'

I was lifted up and escorted by the armpits from the room. Vaughan and Josh flopped me across a bed, my body a dishevelled lumpy throw.

I shut my eyes. I heard Vaughan say, 'Go easy – he's having a bad time.'

'I'm having a bad time,' I agreed, mumbling.

Waking, I could hear the low mutter of voices from the living room. It was the stage of the party when a few favoured close friends linger on into the small hours for coffee and confessional talk. Only the occasional jagged laugh spoke of the night's earlier revelry. With the paranoia of the practised drunk, I wondered if they were talking about me. Sitting up in bed, I realised someone had removed my shoes. I had the intention of putting my ear to the door and listening but first I had to find those shoes, I felt vulnerable without them. I strained my eyes and scoured the floor, searching.

From across the river, a welding torch sparked off the night's tinder. Vaughan's house was right across the Clyde from the BAE shipbuilding plant in Govan; a working-class ghetto. This had never made sense to me. Vaughan's house was chic and stylish; which meant if he looked out of his living-room window he'd see unhappy, socially deprived faces staring back at him out of theirs. Vaughan's window then was a picture frame hosting a living construct: a glowering, howling, Govan version of the Bayeux tapestry; I knew this because generations of my own family had helped to people its fabric down the years.

Across the rippled darkness of the water lay the shipyard. Shafts of moonlight showed the silhouettes of the night shift busying to and fro on an unfinished deck. The ghostly grey hull of a naval frigate spoke of temporarily full wage packets and swing shifts. From the innards of the vessel I could hear the muffled buzz and clang of the workmen – platers maybe or old-style riveters. On the bare deck, with the moon snuffed by the drifting clouds, sharp fissures of torch light composed little tableaux of crouching figures stowing tools or brushing slag from hot fresh welds.

When I was a boy, that shipyard was called Fairfield's. Every morning, hundreds of stunted workmen with grimy caps and brown grooves on their lower lips where their roll-ups sat, would answer the banshee wail of the work siren. Even then, it didn't escape my attention that it was the same sound you heard in old black-and-white movies when Humphrey Bogart would bust out of the State Pen. Down the years the yard seemed to change hands over and over. Company names came and went, but this shipyard clung to the riverbank like a drowning man to the side of a cliff. Maybe next time it wouldn't be so lucky. Maybe the money market would jump up and down on its straining fingers. Maybe it would let go to become a casino, or a multiplex or a heritage museum with interactive software where paid actors would pretend to be welders while real welders were signing on, unemployed, round the corner on McKechnie Street. That's if people still signed on there; or anywhere. Luckily, I was out of touch and hoped to keep it that way.

From the living room came a blast of laughter. Someone had muttered a punch line. Jill shushed the voices. On the ancient tom-tom of memory, my own platers and riveters beat out a long forgotten ditty in my head; a song my mother used to sing when I was a kid in Govan.

'*Olé . . . I am the bandit . . . Olé . . . of ooold Brazil . . .!*'

The toilet flushed.

'Ivan is . . .'

Hearing my name spoken aloud sent me hurrying to the bedroom door to eavesdrop. 'Yeh, he's still asleep,' said a man's voice, the guy from the bathroom. He shut the living-room door and the voices withdrew to a low muffle.

I spotted my shoes, sitting primly together by the bedside cabinet. They had wide mouths, mute screams, dying to be heard. I looped and knotted my ridiculous scarf around my ridiculous neck, picked up my coat from the hallstand and tiptoed out of the house. I stunk of stale, boozer's sweat. Outside, I wore the darkness like a hood; the robe of a shamed boxer leaving the ring.

Back home, I sat in the dining room. This was a sparsely furnished room I rarely entered let alone used. On a cane-backed Windsor armchair sat a shiny black bin bag full of Emily's unwanted clothes. 'Now you'll be able to live your life exactly as you want,' were her parting words. I picked up a card Stan had recently sent me. It read: 'To a dear brother.' I opened it. Stan had written: 'This is what it feels like, you cunt, to receive a birthday card.' I closed the card. So other people disliked me too. It was cheering to have my low opinion of myself endorsed.

On the mahogany dining table stood a bowl of fruit, long dried up, almost papery. It was how I imagined my mother's insides to be; shrunken and desiccated, retaining shape but not vitality.

I hunkered down in my coat. It was a relief to escape from

the real world. Who needs words when you can slip in through the mind's open door, take a seat in the stalls of your own imagination and ghost back to the flickering residue of your own earliest memories? To answer my own question, I needed words. Words are good things to have around. I opened my laptop and started to write; to remember . . .

Post-war austerity was ending – a working man could buy a Ford Popular, a three-piece suite and have a holiday on the Ayrshire coast all for, oh, what; one pound ten. If you went to Saltcoats, you wouldn't even need to buy the armchairs, there'd be at least six of them dumped on the beach – and a drunk couple slumped on every one, clutching the table lamps they'd won at the bingo and singing 'Three Coins in a Fountain'.

I'd gone to Saltcoats when I was six as the guest of my aunt Tina, uncle Con and two unruly cousins. The cousins caught tadpoles, I caught head lice. When I came back, my mother drew the blinds for a week. We pretended there'd been a death in the family but really she'd be going through my hair night and day with one of those tiny combs that had a million teeth, rooting for beige nits to crack between her thumbnails.

My parents were typically Scottish; my father was bipolar and my mother was a martyr. Father would come home from work every day and inspect my mother's palms, looking for stigmata. It was his wry way of saying, 'Cut the crap, lady, and get the fucking tea on.' I hold them both in high regard. Though they could not afford to give me a public school education, my parents strove to give me an unhappy childhood which, for my trade, is a far more useful thing.

Not that my father didn't have his own cross to bear. We neither of us respected him, my mother nor me – she because he drank, me because he wore a tie to work. All the other kids had fathers with calloused hands – they wore grimy boiler suits and marched off every morning to Fairfield's or Stephen's, or Harland and Woolf's, singing welding shanties – at least that's how I imagined them. Not my father. He was stuck behind the counter at Dunne's grocery store on Langlands Road, weighing out corned beef to pensioners. About five hundred times a day he'd say, 'It's just over the quarter, will that do?'

Though I brushed over my father's unmanly occupation, it did yield the odd erratic bonus. Once a month, he'd be allowed to take home a small quantity of bashed tins with no labels to feed our greedy mouths. Tea time became a game of Russian roulette. Take it from me, kidney beans and custard* is an acquired taste. Like all Govan families, we'd eat anything except what was good for us. We believed vegetables to be the devil's work because they made you live longer. What kind of twisted bastards would inflict longevity on the suffering poor?

I was resentful of my father. I'd sit at the table, his table, under his roof, eating his food and wearing clothes that he had paid for out of his pitiful wage packet and proceed to put him wise about his lowly place in the universe. Sometimes Mother would pitch in too, which meant that Father was the lucky recipient of a double dose of wisdom. He was ungrateful, oddly enough, and never once did he utter so much as a 'Thank 'ee, young master, for putting an old sea dog right'. How would I sum up our family? We were desperate but unruly – in a phrase, unhappy-go-lucky.

From around the age of nine, I assumed the role of my parents' confessor. If my father was out on the ran-dan, Mother would pour us each a mug of tea from the pot that sat stewing endlessly in the fireplace. Chain-smoking from a packet of Embassy, she would treat me to an embittered litany of her woes and my old man's shortcomings that would last from supper time to the wee small hours.

* peas v frankfurter sausages is slightly better.

'He's away to hell with the drink,' or 'I'm up the pole with worry,' that kind of stuff. Occasionally, if she felt my interest to be waning, she'd lob in a nugget of flattery. 'You've more responsibility in your little finger than he has in his entire body.' This endorsement would keep me going through yet another pot of over-ripe Typhoo.

Conversely, if my mother had upped and gone to live with my maternal grandparents, so as to gain temporary reprieve from his allegedly scandalous behaviour, Father might serve up his side of the drama over mince and dough balls at Mac's Restaurant on Elder Street.

'There are two sides to every story,' he'd state sagely, dribbling gravy down his crumpled polyester tie. 'Women are insecure. Your mother's no angel.'

'You're right. Can I have cake and custard?'

'Not so fast. Whose side are you on?'

'Yours, Father.'

'Good boy – waiter!'

I'm paraphrasing, but that's the way it worked. If I'd been a sensitive child, I'd have been bent double with the weight of their combined miseries, but luckily, being an aloof and de-tached individual, or selfish prick – you choose – any lasting damage has been containable.

That was back then, of course, in the different time of which I speak. As the song says, 'Who knows where the time goes?' These two people were young and hopeful when they met and married. They were middle-aged and disillusioned by the time, as intimate strangers, they parted. What happened to them in between? Were they doomed from the start? Or maybe, as Orson Welles put it, 'Unless it's an unhappy ending, you haven't heard the whole story.'

Three

The bleep from my mobile phone brought me back to the present and the chill early hours of the morning. I was still at the dining-room table, my laptop before me, and my crossed leg was dead of feeling. I hadn't taken off my coat or ridiculous scarf. I had a new text message. It read:

Hope you're okay. Forget the Jacuzzi incident. Jill & Vaughan x

I remembered the Jacuzzi incident they were urging me to forget. As my face flushed, the landline phone rang.

'Hello?'

'Callous bastard,' said a whining voice.

I thought for a moment. 'Hello, Stan.' My brother wore his name like a hair shirt. 'Stan', unlike Ivan, bore no hint of bookish allure, neither Russian nor Joycean, being short not for Stanislaus but Stanley. By the time of Stan's birth, Father's interest in all things literary or child-related had waned. The naming of his second child had degenerated into a matter of humdrum family genealogy rather than the handing on of any flaming idealistic torch. There had been other Mosses called Stanley, the defeated, sluggish logic seemed to say, why not more? As he grew up Stan ascribed this change in outlook to Father's debilitating experience with me and he had thereafter borne me a grudge.

'What've I done?'

'Turn it around – what didn't you do?'

'Tell me.'

There was a pause. I could hear Stan's indignant breath quiver down the line. 'You didn't get our mother's prescription.'

'Ah.'

'She's been without medication all day.'

'Oh.'

Stan left a conversational hole, tempting me to topple in. I thought about mentioning my own pain; that of the artist who struggles to create, but I demurred. But neither did I topple. Any toppling to be done let him do it. My brother obliged.

'You promised you'd see to it. I can't do everything,' he said in a cracked and pleading whimper.

'I had meetings,' I said, for show. 'I'll do my bit in future.'

'You will?'

'Definitely,' I heard my voice say. The future seemed an agreeably distant and nebulous entity.

My brother saw his chance and pounced with haste. 'She has an appointment with Dr Semple at ten o'clock on Friday.'

'So?'

'You can take her. I have a meeting in Harrogate.'

'What's happening in Harrogate?'

'It has to do with my job. Do you really want to know about my job?'

'No.'

'Then just take our mother to see Dr Semple. Will you do that?'

'Yes.'

'About time. I tell you, you are one selfish . . .' There was more, much more in this vein. Having grovelled for my help, my brother now unsheathed the chainsaw of his resentment.

I remained silent while he listed an inventory of my shortcomings. Soon, we were in the peaceful land of Overkill. When we have the same nerve hit often enough our pain, once keen, fades then dulls.

Finally, the whining engine of his voice puttered to silence. But not before one last startling backfire. 'This is the big one.'

I felt my eyebrows shoot up. 'What do you mean, the big one?'

'You'll see.'

My brother put the phone down. I sensed his gloating, victorious smile as he pictured me left holding the receiver like a dumbass, in a cold sweat, as I now did. Once again, I felt Real Life sucking me back into its thick, glutinous quicksand.

Come the Friday, I stood at the wardrobe mirror, wondering whether or not to wear my ridiculous scarf. If I wore it, I'd feel a fool but a distinctive one. If I didn't, I'd feel mundane and depressed. I wore the scarf.

'What's that around your neck?' my mother asked, standing at the door.

'A scarf.'

'That's a big knot.'

'It's my tribute to Albert Pierrepoint.'

'Come in,' she said, with a tone.

She was annoyed because I was early. I was early because I knew she'd have been annoyed if I'd been late.

'I'm not making tea,' she said, warningly, as we entered her small living room, her queendom.

'I didn't ask for tea.'

'Just as well.' She had the fags out from under her cardigan sleeve and was lighting up before her ass had hit the settee.

'How are you?'

She gave me her familiar answer when annoyed, which was to ignore my question.

Finally, she said, 'Today's the day.'

'What day?'

She looked shocked. 'The day I get my scan results. You mean you don't know?'

'Stan didn't tell me.'

'I didn't tell Stan. He took the trouble to ring the doctor. Did you ring the doctor?'

'No.'

'Then that's why you don't know, not because of Stan.'

'Okay, I know now.'

I picked up a newspaper and turned to the sports. The paper smelled of smoke. Everything in the place smelled of smoke, including the smoke. I tossed the paper down.

'You ready?'

'I'll just finish this cigarette.'

'Yeh, that's what you need right now, another fag.' I was rattled because of her reprimand so I gave her that one back.

She took a deep drag and blew a grey bellow into the air. She caught my look.

'Don't judge me,' she said. 'I don't inhale.' This was always her mitigating boast. She was impervious to ailment because she didn't inhale. She sat there with brow furrowed, elbows tucked in, knees locked, looking isolated.

I tried to lighten the mood. 'At least today you'll find out the worst,' I said.

She looked up, sharply.

'The worst?

'The best,' I corrected.

'Do you know something I don't?' She was edgy. 'I don't want people lying to me.'

'I don't know anything. I don't even know enough to lie to you.' I went into the kitchen to make the tea that neither of us wanted.

It wasn't a good start. I felt bad about reprimanding her. I also felt irked. I felt more irked than bad, which was usually the case with my mother. If she hadn't smoked, she wouldn't have needed to be taken to the doctor for the results of her scan. And I wouldn't have been irked.

I took through some digestives and offered her one, like a dutiful son.

She ignored the plate and took another draw. 'Your father will be dead ten years in June,' she announced.

I saw what was on her mind. 'Relax,' I said, 'you won't be joining him any time soon.' It was what she needed to hear. Only with her grim little laugh, did I realise how tense she'd been.

Her face tightened again. 'What time is it?'

'There's plenty of time. I've put the kettle on.'

She gave me another accusing look, like kettle boiling was one more damning act of cavalier indifference.

She picked up a half-finished cup from a side table. I wondered, idly, how many times in my life I'd seen her nursing a cup in one hand and a cigarette in the other. The thin coil of smoke rose up to spread into a messy fan then a cloud blanket that hovered above our heads.

'I didn't hate him, you know.'

'Who?'

'Your father.'

I don't know why she said that; guilt perhaps. Maybe she thought the old man was hanging around in her Embassy Regal ether, or at God's right hand, saying 'That's her – that bitch is why I'm dead. Go get her, Jehovah.'

'I should've gone to the funeral,' she said. 'They asked me to go but I didn't. I should have though.'

'You didn't want to go, remember?'

'Don't tell me to remember. I'll remember when I'm good and ready.'

I thought back to the funeral. My parents had long since divorced and my father had remarried. As my mother had said at the time to show up would have seemed somehow 'wrong'. I'd gone though. To me it had only felt 'half wrong' and therefore 'half right', and on that basis I'd chosen the path of least resistance rather than spend the rest of my life justifying myself to myself for electing, in some set-jawed fundamentalist way, not to attend my own father's funeral. The way I saw it, Father was safely in his casket and would be then, and for ever, twenty-one grams short of the half pound and as such unlikely to provoke any untoward soulful scenes. Mother had spent that evening reiterating to me why she thought she'd done the right thing and therefore had 'No regrets, none'. But if you have no regrets, none, why keep bothering to mention it? I'd inherited Father's Fiat Punto that day and had driven it home from the crematorium in Ayr with his jaunty feathered trilby still on the rear shelf.

'What time is it now?' She was still on edge.

'It's a five-minute drive to Dr Semple's surgery. Relax.'

'Relax, he says. That's easy for you to say.' She treated herself to another doleful chuckle. To divert her mind, I asked her again about how she'd first met Father.

'You really want to know?'

'Sure,' I said. I vaguely figured that putting her in touch with her past might help give her strength to deal with the present. Also, if I'm more honest, the need to keep her upbeat and reassured was proving something of a strain. Luckily, like most people, my mother couldn't pass up the opportunity to talk about herself.

'Well . . .'

It was a tale I'd heard so often when growing up that on occasion I'd correct her on its details, as though I'd lived it myself, not just provided an audience. As she spoke, I realised it had been years since I'd last talked with her. We sat in the living room clutching our mugs of thin, dusty-tasting tea. To the stultifying, hissing pibroch from the gas miser, Mother told me of her and Father's early courtship . . .

In the beginning, it seemed, was the word. And the word was 'No'.

But my aunt Celia persisted and the word became softened to 'maybe'. At the time, Mother worked with Aunt Celia at Skirling Jock's biscuit factory in Hillington. Mother was wary of Celia, even though they both stole biscuits. Usually these would be the inexpensive 'Skirling Jock's Crofter's Rich Tea' but on occasion, say if Old Mr Jock was tight with the overtime, some of the more luxuriant, chocolate-coated 'Sir Jock's Superior Assortment' might find themselves slipped into the slack of a green cotton overall. Mother thought Celia fancied herself a sniff above the other girls. There wasn't a natural kinship, and Mother was uneasy.

'I know he'll like you,' pressed Celia, in a simpering voice.

The war was four years over and Celia's younger brother Ivan, my father to be, was home from the sea. A dutiful sister, Celia was trying to find her favourite sibling a match.

Mother said nothing. To her, looks weren't the issue. Not her own, at least. She was uncertain of many things in life but secure about her own attractiveness. In their black wellies and work turbans most of the women looked as ugly as Ali Baba's forty thieves, but Mother could always be assured of running a flattering gauntlet of verbal molestation as she pulled her laden biscuit trolley through the sweaty gangs of machine-room men on into the dispatch area.

The real question, which Mother found too awkward to pose was – how could she be sure she might like Father? After all, the signs hadn't been good. Aunt Celia had played the sympathy card right up front, citing a romantic upset Father had recently suffered at the hands of Maria Tomlin, a heartless siren from Polmadie. As a result, Father's propensity for mood swings had increased.

Against her will, this had touched Mother. She too had known romantic disappointment. Hadn't Tommy Fintry, short and cocky, who drove a delivery van for the Co-op and was the very spit of the young Sinatra, not taken her for a highly expensive ride? Three dates, one new raincoat, a half-crown cut and bob at Vallee's and for what? To be wrestled to the floor among the square sliced sausage and grinning pigs' heads and groped with mincey fingers? She'd told him off in no uncertain terms. To test his mettle, she'd avoided him. Tommy's mettle had proved as strong as hers though and he'd upped and left and was now driving a different Co-op van round Coventry. Mother was hurt and piqued. All Tommy had been required to do was perform the accepted lovers' minuet – to apologise and perform a modest spot of grovelling. Was that too much to expect? Apparently, it was. So yes, Mother knew well of love's sweet brutality. Unlike Celia's brother Ivan, however, she'd kept her own counsel and allowed her bruised feelings to heal privately.

And wasn't there a further complication? Why, hadn't young Mr Jock himself shown an interest in her? Not overtly, of course, but he had helped Mother to her feet when she'd slipped on a soggy oatcake and insisted on escorting her personally to the treatment room. They'd sat waiting patiently while Nurse Duff dressed another labourer's macaroon burn and he had talked openly and passionately of his future plans for the factory.

As he had spoken, scales had dropped from Mother's eyes. Young Mr Jock presented the world of luxurious sweetmeats to her. The heady scents of life's possibilities opened up in a way she had never before considered. Young Mr Jock had been to Paris as a student and described radical new movements in confection styles and crumb density. In a Montmartre café he'd witnessed Otto Stollen, the self-styled 'High Priest of Pastry Chaos', take an ordinary stick of bread, skin the crust, ply the soft flesh with currants and dust the carcass with icing sugar he'd badgered from a cowed kitchen porter.

'If you want to create a sweet loaf,' Stollen had declared, 'Then I say – *why not!*'

Stollen was an unhinged showman, of course, but his ideas had begun to inspire others. Now young Mr Jock had returned to Scotland fired by the same pioneering zeal – eager to break the stranglehold of the past. Yes, he admired Scotland's old master, Thomas Tunnock, and had studied the fine classical pillars of his Caramel Wafer and, true, the fibrous majesty of the Coconut Log, garnished with its daring innovatory slivers, had been a nod in the direction of the modernists, but there was more, so very much more, that might be achieved with artistic and commercial courage.

Mother eyed him coyly as she listened. With his gruff tweed suit and sturdy black brogues, young Mr Jock looked every inch the dour custodian of upright Calvinistic values. Only his soft, clean hands and the exotic yellow beret he wore instead of a sober brimmed hat hinted at a nature held hostage to fortune.

'What is it, Kathleen?'

'You were shouting, Mr Jock.'

'Was I? How embarrassing!'

They shared a self-conscious laugh.

With rueful eloquence he went on to explain how his dreams might never be realised. His father, old Mr Jock, would not be persuaded of these daring new ideas and continued to serve steadfast allegiance to the trusted methods on which he had founded the family success. He had informed his son that he would never – repeat never – in his lifetime brook any change of biscuit direction. Now a robust seventy, the old man might easily clump along his blinkered path for another decade, perhaps longer.

'By then,' explained young Mr Jock gloomily, 'our products will be passé; our shortbread fingers dreary and old fashioned; our oatcakes the sport of young buck satirists and iconoclasts.'

Mother had felt strangely elated. She heard herself say, 'Don't worry. Scotland will always be a nation of biscuit munchers.'

Young Mr Jock had looked at her. Was it a trick of the light, or was that the glint of empathy in his shining eyes?

'I see you every day, young lady, yet I don't even know your name.'

Young Mr Jock laid his hand on hers.

Yes, young Mr Jock, heir to the Skirling empire, had held Kathleen's small chapped hand, albeit briefly, while looking her full in the face. As their eyes met so the smell of TCP antiseptic scented the air, like Chanel No. 5. Nurse Duff appeared in the doorway. By her side the machine-room labourer stood with a fat white bandage on his hand. The labourer was trying to look chirpy, Mother remembered, but his face was pale from shock.

'Next,' said Nurse Duff, all business.

Young Mister Jock gave an encouraging nod and Kathleen had risen. At the office door she'd looked back to smile, but he was already gone.

On the way home, her head still swimming, Kathleen had gone into Bray's chemist near the corner of Elder Street and bought a bottle of TCP . . .

Now, fifty years later, thinking back, she felt foolish. After all, she had just been a common floor girl, one of dozens, and he a graduate of Glasgow University, the owner's son and heir.

Two sons, a husband, a divorce and three score and ten foam-filled sofas later, I watched her pick up her tea mug and peel off the plastic coaster that had stuck to its base.

'So you had hopes with young Mr Jock?'

'No!' said Mother, stamping out the word as though it was a small but dangerous blaze.

'All the same . . .' I said.

'All the same . . .' she agreed. Mother confessed that for weeks, and against her will, she'd sniff the TCP bottle and feel a wistful pang for that exhilarating moment in which the door of life had creaked briefly open, only to slam shut in her face. After her slip on the floor, young Mr Jock had smiled at her only once and spoken to her not at all. Mother had begun to hear rumours of a fine lady from Ralston, a young woman of good breeding, whose family traded in whipped fondant.

I tried to bring her back on track. 'Well, what did you say?'

'To what?'

'Celia's question. When she asked you if you'd go out with my father?'

My mother was silent, a pursed smile playing about her lips. She leaned forward and took a light from the safely caged, puttering yellow gas jets of the fire. She was in no hurry to answer. I was no longer her son and she had ceased to be my mother. She was Kathleen now and her mind was drifting back; she was a girl again among the clang, the grinding whirl, the scented, slopping yarns of dough in the factory. I pictured Aunt Celia's face beaming expectantly, hanging on her reply, as I now did. I imagined my mother, Kathleen, thinking of the fine lady from Ralston, and of her own evenings at home, spent sneaking off to her room in melancholy fashion to sniff antiseptic.

'Why not,' she said.

'You'll meet him?' asked Celia

'Yes,' said Mother. 'I'll meet him.'

Three nights later, Ivan Moss, peacocking to good effect in his radio officer's uniform, met Kathleen Cairns at Cessnock Underground station. He was on shore leave. His pockets were stuffed with money and he was anxious to make a good impression. And lo, these two unwitting youngsters, my future mother and father, did sit and speak of many things.

But not now they didn't. Reality, the present, their future, had interrupted. I looked up at the clock.

My mother saw me looking, knew what was coming next. She sat there, sucking on the comforting nipple of her cigarette, reluctant to let it go.

I jiggled the car keys in my pocket. She nodded.

It was time.

Four

We sat in the waiting area. She was nervy, uncommunicative. She was fiddling with the belt of her beige raincoat. She had a thing about belts; and beige raincoats. Starting the car, I noticed she'd nearly throttled herself trying to fasten the safety belt and I had to reach over and disentangle her. Luckily, this produced a rare bout of mutual mirth. It was late morning. I looked out of the slatted blinds onto Paisley Road. The windows were full length so there was plenty of light to take the weight off the human gloom. I kept the chit-chat coming as best I could but it wasn't appreciated or approved and she started up a conversation with an elderly woman, seated opposite, another member of the beige raincoat club. They spoke to each other with exaggerated old people politeness, ladling on the pleasantness. Listening to pensioners, it's easy to convince yourself that they're a different breed, chivalrous, courteous, custodians of all that's finest in human nature. But let a bus driver refuse their concession ticket a minute before the appointed hour and he gets a mouthful of wheezing abuse. I congratulated myself on the job I'd done of damping down her worried hysteria. If I could run down the clock until Dr Semple saw her, I'd be off the hook. I likened it to an effective Man United performance in Europe where they

29

draw the early passion of the opposition then systematically bore them into drab submission. I was mentally checking the amount of injury time left when a swift breakaway resulted in a freakish goal.

'I'm not too late?'

Aunt Tina was breathless. Fresh air clung to her and she'd brought along her sense of drama. 'I wasn't going to come but then I thought – I've got to, I can't let you down.'

Seeing her, my mother became agitated. She dragged herself back to reality, the other beige raincoat woman suddenly invisible and forgotten. A receptionist behind the desk leaned on her bosoms and called out, 'Mrs Moss?'

I stood self-consciously to help up my mother, Mrs Moss. Tina had beaten me to it and had her by the elbow.

'I was going to go in with her,' I said.

'It's better if I go,' Tina said. I looked to my mother.

'Tina will come in with me,' said my mother.

In they went, Mother first, leading her little sister, all their nerve summoned. My mother's raincoat belt was straight, her shopping bag at her side, like a soldier with rifle sloped. She was ready. I picked up my ridiculous scarf and felt comforted by its splash of colour.

An hour later I had the kettle on again; her house, another brew.

'It isn't cancer,' my mother said. 'Tina's got it wrong. Dr Semple was only told the shadow on my lung *might* be malignant.' She was vehement. To prove her point she lit another cigarette.

'You sure you should be doing that?'

'I wouldn't do it if it was cancer but it isn't, so I will.'

'How can you be sure?'

'You saying you're unsure?'

'No,' I said.

'Then stop putting doubt in my mind. I have to be positive if I'm going to beat this thing.'

'What thing?'

'You know.'

'The not-cancer?'

'Exactly. Pass that ash tray.'

I passed the ashtray. I picked up my tea mug and snapped a digestive, catching the crumbs in my palm to avoid rebuke. I'd spent lavishly from my fund of sympathy and now felt tetchy and eager to be home. Well, not home, but away from her, my mother, and the atmosphere of stern foreboding. Something made me stay though, duty maybe, or just an obstinate desire to chisel away at the great mound of gloom until I'd carved it into something like a happy face, then I could lose myself back in the normal world, the privileged home of the blimpish, blissful, uncaring, able bodied.

'Son?'

'What?' I was alarmed. She never called me 'son'.

'Would you stay the night here?'

I looked at her. She looked wretched at having asked.

'Just tonight.'

My heart ached. It also sank. If I'm honest it more sank than ached. I had no choice. I took off my scarf.

The TV was bellowing out the *Emmerdale* theme. The noise, the oppressive smoke in the small room, made me feel like screaming. To divert myself and hopefully her, I took up the subject of her and Father again.

'What did you talk about?'

'What?'

'Can I turn down the sound?'

'What?'

I put the set on mute. 'If you want me to stay then at least talk to me.'

'I wasn't watching it.'

'Then why have it on?'

'It's always on.'

'It's not the law. They go off too.' I turned the TV right off with the remote, blacking the screen for emphasis.

'I like a noise in the house.'

'I'm a noise in the house – speak to me.'

'What about?'

I left a pause then I said, 'You.'

'What about me?'

'Your story.'

She blinked, looked surprised, like I'd reminded her she existed.

'Why are you so interested in the past?'

'If you're scared about the future and blocking out the present what the hell is there left?'

She looked wanly toward the television set.

'It's off,' I said. 'Let's keep it that way.'

She didn't argue. She reached for her cup. 'What do you want to know?'

'Tell me about the pub.'

'What pub?'

'The pub. The one you went to on your first date.'

'It wasn't a date.'

'If it looks like a date and sounds like a date . . .'

'Okay, it was a date.'

'So what did you talk about?'

I was inviting her to dredge up then polish a bit of family history. After all, it wasn't just her history, it was mine and Stan's too.

'Nothing.'

'Didn't he ask you any questions?'

'He asked me how my drink was.'

'And what did you say?'

'Fine.'

'Fascinating. That must have really clinched the deal.'

'It got us started, smart arse.'

'Then what?'

'He said: "You're drinking port. A lot of girls like sherry."'

'So you were drinking port. What else?'

'I said, "I like sherry but I like port too."'

I looked at her.

'I know,' she explained, looking sheepish. 'But we were young.' Her face brightened. 'I remember there was a storm.'

'A big storm?'

'The pub door blew open. It was big all right.'

'Which way was the wind blowing?'

'What difference does it make?'

'East or west. I like details.'

'I don't know.'

'Yes, you do,' I told her. 'You just haven't asked yourself.'

She considered. 'Wait a minute. On the way there a newspaper flew into my face, I remember now. Right up off the street. I was worried it had smudged my make-up.'

'Did you catch the headline?'

'What?'

'Doesn't matter. Where were you? Which way were you going?'

'I'd just turned into Elder Street, Woolworths corner; full in the face, I kid you not.'

'So it was an east wind.'

'What does that matter?'

'It matters to me.'

I pictured their aching awkwardness, sensed the racing pulses and fluttering stomachs. Outside, the bawling gale would whip up and bully a tide of rain across the North Atlantic, would clip the Ulster hills, would batter Arran and wee Cumbrae before marauding down the Firth of Clyde to menace washing lines and harass Glasgow's chimney pots. At Paisley Road Toll and the soot-blackened Angel statue the gale would fork; half its force would wheel westward to Ayrshire; the other stem would probe inward, through Plantation and Wine Alley into the dingy rump of Govan, its rooting ebb and flow tossing up and toying with the familiar Govan night sounds – the batter and grind of the shipyards and factories: the all-night rattle of Harland and Wolff, of Fairfield and Stephen's; three working yards in less than a mile of the Clyde's south line, from the dry dock by the Town Hall, down past Elder Park to Linthouse. Finally, across the street from the Lyceum cinema, the gale would beat its fists against the heavy swing doors of the Harmony Bar, where sat Ivan and Kathleen.

'Was it a scary storm?'

My mother shook her head. 'It made us feel cosy. We had another drink.'

I pictured Kathleen laughing, throwing back her head to show dazzling teeth, fashionably false.

I hit her with the big one.

'Did you fancy him?'

'What kind of question is that?'

'A nosy one.'

'Back off.'

'Don't tell me then. What's it to me? I know the answer anyway.'

'I was fed up with men,' she said at last. 'Every last one. I'd had enough.'

'Right.' I wet my finger, dabbed a crumb off a side plate.

My mother leaned forward. Lighting a cigarette through the grille of the gas fire, she got ready to justify herself.

'Go ahead,' I said. 'You don't inhale.'

The message wasn't lost on her but did she stop? Stop she did not. She puffed on heartily.

I thought about my mother and father in the pub. What she said made sense. In the tangled euphoria of the drink she'd feel again the keen edge of her own foolishness with men. She would teach them a lesson, every last one, from that swaggering Tommy Fintry to that la-di-da young Mister Jock, she'd show them both – even if neither of them was looking. She'd take another sip of port, making her lips shine cherry red in the smoky fug.

'You say you'd finished with men. But if you stayed, there must have been something you liked about him.'

'He was generous.'

'I'm sure he was.' He would be, I thought, thinking he was on, the horny bastard.

'And he was a good listener.'

'Like me?'

'No. Your father was emotional. He was less of a vulture than you.'

I felt wounded over this insult, this bird of prey slur. I could have pecked her eyes out where she sat. But it was late, my chair was comfortable and I was lulled by the rolling pageant of memory.

'What happened after the second drink?'

'We stayed till closing time.'

I pictured Mother and Father giggling as the drink kicked in, two fresh-faced young people convinced they're starting to get along famously. Kathleen, being leery, would know it was really the drink at work, maybe laughing with her, maybe at her, but either one would do, hell, anything would be better than skulking in the bedroom sniffing TCP like a weirdo. Yes, as the port slipped down, Kathleen would open her heart to Ivan Moss. She would tell him of her dreams, her aspirations; she'd sweep back a bob of dark hair from time to time and him being observant he'd notice the scabbing ear lobe that had never taken to piercing.

And Ivan would listen, edging closer, nodding in sympathetic fashion while flashing the single line of braid on his uniformed cuff as the smoke snaked up from his Player's Navy Cut to lick the tainted ceiling.

Maybe he tried it on, later; in the close mouth and was mollified with a kiss. Perhaps he considered trying for a grope but probably not. Mother was a pretty prize, and Father was, behind the braid, a frail vessel newly broken on love's unpredictable currents, eager for the relief of a safe harbour. As he held Kathleen in his arms, he may already have seen himself buying two return bus tickets to Polmadie, so that he might saunter back and forth outside Marie Tomlin's house, parading his new love exultantly like she was the Scottish Cup, and she, that heartless Tomlin bitch, the vanquished opposition.

I took a bitter slurp of cold tea. 'How did you leave it with him?'

'He asked to see me again.'

'What did he say?'

She gave me a look. 'What do you think? He said, "Can I see you again?"'

'So you said yes?'

She feigned impatience, like I was nosy, which I was, and she was reluctant to speak, which she wasn't. She said, 'If you must know, the words I spoke were: "Jesus God. It's still raining."'

I looked at her. She shrugged, defensively.

'You asked what I said, that's what I said . . . I was stalling.'

I could fathom that. She hadn't wanted to decide. In fact, she didn't much care whether or not she saw this sailor again.

She'd been in the lobby, she said, taking off her coat when he'd rattled the flap of the letterbox.

'Next thing I know he's shouting, "I'm sailing tomorrow for Helsinki!" He's calling out, "I'll be back in a fortnight – I'll be back, I promise!"'

That had been enough to bring her mother, Big Dora, my granny, busying into the lobby.

'Who's that shouting?'

The mouth of the letterbox flapped again.

'I'll take you out anywhere you like – just name it!'

Dora, taking Ivan for a lost drunk with belligerent tendencies, had seized a brush and poked the pole through the slot.

'Bugger off, you drunken article!'

Ivan Moss, the drunken article, retired aggrieved but without protest.

'That's the way you deal with men at night,' said my mother, repeating Dora's words.

I was tickled by the phrase 'men at night' and said so.

Mother allowed herself a smile. She admitted she had been troubled by the letterbox antics. She was unable to decide if Ivan's action had been bold or desperate. She couldn't be doing with any flawed individuals, weakness in a man made her blood run cold; like that feeling you got in the mornings when you'd cleaned and set the fire and your hands were dry from the ash and you were putting your nylons on for work.

Big Dora had swept a few granules of coal soot from around the bunker, so as not to have wasted the trip to the lobby. She was still muttering. In the scullery, Kathleen was already hunkered down, selecting potatoes from the string bag under the sink, getting them ready for a peel and a wash and a plate of chips because she was ravenous after the drink.

'Are you seeing him again?' asked Dora.

'Who knows?'

'He didn't even buy you chips and you're seeing him again?'

'I haven't decided.'

'Some men have the cheek of the devil,' mused Dora. 'God forgive me.'

Kathleen felt a glow of sentiment blush her cheeks, or maybe it was the port, or the prospect of chips. So it had been cheek then, not desperation? Well now, a wee touch of devilment put a different complexion on things. She liked a bit of spirit in a man. Maybe she would see him again after all, this sailor, this Ivan.

On careless whims are worlds turned and lives altered . . .

I slept on the couch. I woke a few times through the night, my head pounding from the tobacco fug. Whenever I did, I would hear the squeak of the bedroom floorboards and the muffled hum of talk radio through the wall.

She was scared.

The following morning I threw back the kitchen curtains with a jaunty flick. I'd forgotten about the cemetery below. The Jewish quarter overlooked, or rather underlooked, my mother's window. The grass was shiny wet and the earth luscious with robust good health. It was raining, of course, heavily, incessantly; a grim downpour, drenching streets and spirits. It rains most days, all through the year in Glasgow and we've done our best to adapt physiologically; few of us grow taller than five foot seven. This is because the cloud layer starts at five foot eight. Mentally, though, we have never adapted. People can't, you see. The human animal, even in Glasgow, craves vitamin D. Watch us on rare days when the sun shines; we're transformed. 'Isn't this lovely?' 'What a beauty!' But the smiles are never wholly open or full. We can't trust life, you see, for rain lies just around the corner. In Glasgow we have many corners. Consequently, we drink to defy time and to suspend the moment. Outside, the typhoon may rage, but inside our hearts and kidneys are aglow with the cheery despair of fuddled respite.

Thus deprived, the sober citizen copes as best he can: he feels resentful, acquires rheumatic limbs, brews endless tea, smokes and talks about the past, or present, which, at a certain age, becomes the same thing.

'How did you sleep?' Mother asked. She was already at table, pouring a second cup. My eyes squinted against the smoky plume from the cigarette that dangled from the corner of her mouth. On the electric cooker, the frying pan sizzled. She looked, so to speak, in her element. She placed a bread roll clamping two fangs of bacon before me. Margarine ran and grease solidified on my side plate.

'It's good to have somebody to cook for,' she said, shovelling a dripping sausage from the spatula onto my plate. The residue of last night's conversation was still in her head.

'About your father's funeral.'

'Yes?'

'Was *she* there?'

'Who?'

'Old Maidie?'

'You've never asked about the funeral. What's made you bring it up now?'

'Same thing that made you bring it up last night.'

'Yes,' I said, 'she was there.'

My mother nodded, gave a little grunt. 'I had no time for her,' she said. 'But two sons gone before her. I hope you and Stan last longer than your father and Rolf.'

'Moss men are built for the sprint not the marathon.'

'Say that again.'

'Sons.' It felt somehow significant, hearing Mother attribute the masculine gender to Father instead of the neutral 'that'.

Mother saw me measuring my paunch between thumb and forefinger.

'Don't worry. There's as much of my family's side in you as there is of his.'

I thought of Mother's side: Grandpa Evan, Uncle Hughie, her cousins Lenny and George; all dead or chair bound, wheezing.

'How does that help?'

She avoided an answer by busying herself with lighting one cigarette from the smouldering end of the other. I felt my teeth clench. Like I've said, everything in the house, including me and the food I was eating, smelled of stale smoke.

I put down the roll. I stood up.

She looked alarmed.

'You're not going?'

'I have to work,' I said. I tried to make it sound masculine, like I'd a hard day ahead of me at the word mine, hacking out adjectives and similes with a pick. I'd done my shift at the compassion factory and wanted home.

'I have the specialist next week at the hospital.'

'Yes. Stan's going to take you.'

'I want you to take me.'

I fumbled in my mind for a plausible excuse. While I was fumbling she nipped in quick.

'Stan has too much to do. Will you take me or won't you?'

I looked at her; the skin smoke-grey, the old woman mauve cardigan pristine but reeking like the upstairs of a fifties bus. I nodded.

'Okay.'

Five

A week later, we were in the hospital waiting room, queuing to see a specialist. I'd driven her over and on the way she'd gone through her whole repertoire of irritating habits, culminating with the belt antics, both raincoat and car seat. I tried to stay patient; spoke to her.

'You know what day it is today, don't you? It's special.'

'Yes,' she said. But she wasn't listening.

The hospital building felt hot; fetid and unhealthy like the crotch heat from an over-friendly uncle. People sat silently in lines, trying not to look at each other. Nobody appeared obviously ill, though a number must have been. The law of averages would dictate that some, according to the specialist's report, would leave this place turning mental cartwheels while others would shuffle out to begin their very own personal and bespoke long or short, quick or slow, helter-skelter ride to oblivion. There's no spiritual element to hospitals, no ambient music, no ceremonial shite and onions to prissily camouflage the fact that we're soft machines in motion making pit stops for maintenance, repair, or, in extreme cases, the scrap heap. God, bells and candles just don't enter into it.

We were in the waiting room. My mother was fidgeting with

her belt again. I felt trapped. I should have been in my West End apartment, wearing a cravat and caressing fine porcelain objects.

'Is this belt twisted?'

'No. Leave it.'

'Could you straighten it for me?'

'I can't; it's not twisted. How about if I twist it and then straighten it again?'

My voice was cold and scraped the air harshly. People gave me sly looks, relieved to find an uncaring brigand they could self-righteously tear asunder on the bus home.

She was miffed. I bought her a cup of tea from the vending machine and she cheered up. After one sip, she wanted to go outside for a cigarette. She had just stood up when the receptionist called her name.

'Mrs Moss?'

She sort of froze. I felt the belt about to be given another going over so I took the plastic cup from her hand and binned it. I took her by the arm along the corridor. In a few minutes she would know for sure.

People knock the Health Service, but you speak as you find. I found the young Malaysian doctor to be caring and sympathetic. Maybe they learn it these days on empathy courses and at compassion seminars, but so what; people crave the human touch. My mother sat with her hands clasped and her message bag at her side while he explained in a soft voice what was going on inside her body. He then outlined the courses of treatment available to her. I didn't interject. At the end, he didn't rush her; just let her rise to her feet in her own time.

We didn't speak till we were outside the building.

'What a lovely man,' she said. 'I feel I'm in good hands. He's so thoughtful.'

'Yes,' I said.

We were in the car. I fixed the seat belt for her without waiting to be asked.

'I can't get over how nice he was,' she said again, while I struggled to hear the click of the buckle hitting lock.

'I agree,' I said. 'That's the nicest confirmation of cancer I've ever heard.'

She looked at me.

I handed her a card and a cardigan in an M&S bag with the receipt still inside.

'Happy birthday,' I said.

It was her birthday. She had forgotten.

The phone rang while I was having dinner. It was Stan. I rattled the cutlery and made unpleasant chomping noises to show him he was inconveniencing me.

'It's confirmed,' I told him.

'What did the specialist say?'

'I just told you. The diagnosis was confirmed. She has lung cancer.'

'No, what words did he actually use? Was he hopeful?'

'Hopeful? You know how those guys sound. He was practically wearing a black cap.'

Stan was frightened. It came out as pique. 'You're not helping me. This is a terrible blow. I may lose my mother here.'

'She's my mother too.'

'Yes, but you're . . .'

'What?'

'You're you.'

I felt stung. There were too many people out there in the world accusing me of being me.

'I'll be an orphan,' my brother whined.

'Relax,' I said. 'There are still options, the doctor told us; treatments.'

'Have you discussed the options, the treatments, with her yet?'

'No.'

'Why not?'

I didn't like his tone but kept my cool. 'I'm going over there tomorrow to do just that.'

'Okay,' he said reluctantly. 'Let me know.'

'I will,' I said and left a pause. 'How's Harrogate?'

'Harrogate's fine. Was that a tone?'

'No. Why should there be a tone?'

'You know why: because I'm down here and not up there.'

'You've been up here. Now you're down there. I'm up here now.'

'I'll take over when I get back,' my brother said. 'It would be completely unfair on me if there's a tone.'

'Take your time in Harrogate. There's no hurry.'

'Yes, there is. She has another meeting with the specialist. About the treatments; her decision.'

'I know,' I said. 'I'm taking her to that meeting.'

He was taken aback. 'You took her to today's meeting,' he said.

'Yes.'

'I'd rather I took her to the next meeting.'

'You're always complaining you do too much.'

'I'd rather take her.'

'Tough titty, brother,' I said. 'She's asked me.'

I couldn't help myself. I held the mouthpiece close. 'Mother always loved me best, Stan. You know that, don't you? And Daddy too. You know what his last words were?'

'No.'

'Ivan, you're my favourite.'

Stan was silent.

'Stan?'

'Yes?'

'That was a tone.'

'Cunt,' my brother said. And hung up.

We were sitting in my mother's living room. She had been diagnosed with lung cancer. We were discussing possible treatments. She was lighting up a cigarette.

'What about chemotherapy?'

'I don't know.'

'Radiotherapy?'

'I'm not keen.'

'French polishing?'

'It's all right for you.'

'What then?'

She took a long draw and sent a flare of grey smoke out into what was left of the air.

'I need to think about it.'

'There's not much time. We have to let the specialist know.'

'Dr Jaffar.'

'What?'

'The specialist,' she said. 'That's his name.'

'Yes. We have to tell Dr Jaffar what you've decided.'

'I know I do.'

I let it go. I knew I would get nowhere. And, in truth, where was there to go? What was the end game in this situation? What would that be, despite any and all of the available treatments? It occurred to me that my mother wasn't only putting off making a decision; she was deferring being a patient; that's to say, a person who would henceforth be defined by their illness. She was clinging to the last vestiges of what now passed in her life for normality. An enormous load of worry was building up minute by minute to fill her every waking hour. I had no idea how I might cope in her situation. Of course, life being what it is, whatever it is, we'll most of us have a chance to find out.

'What happened after Helsinki?'

She looked at me. I wanted to drag her away from the here and now.

'You and the old man; I assume you must have gone out with him again?'

'You're too nosy.'

'You like me being nosy. Who else would ask about your life if I didn't?'

This miffed her. But we were alike. I was prickly about my need to hide my private world and she was prickly over her eagerness to reveal her own.

'Well . . .'

Six months later at the Plaza on Govan Road, after the wee picture but before the big picture, Ivan Moss had made an important announcement. He informed Kathleen, his girlfriend, my mother to be, that he was due to take a three-month-long voyage to New Zealand. He wanted to be certain that she would wait for him.

When she had failed to give her ready assurance an argument had erupted, a row so serious it had caused Kathleen to quit her seat and stomp off up the centre aisle of the cinema, even though she had been only a spoonful into her vanilla cup. Faced with a choice between remaining to watch *The Man on the Eiffel Tower*, or enduring a second dumping, Ivan had opted for the path of emotional prudence and had pursued Kathleen. Over coffee in glass cups at the Lyceum Café, he attempted to rescue their relationship.

He could not quite bring himself to say 'I love you' but

instead undid the tinfoil wrapper of her tea cake for her which, in Scotland, is the next best thing.

After due deliberation, a compromise was brokered. A form of words was agreed that would permit either party the opportunity, upon the date of Ivan's return, to end the relationship, hereinafter known as 'The Relationship'. This could be done without reproach or recrimination from he or she, the abandoned party, should this prove to be his or her accorded desire upon the date of termination of the agreement, hereinafter known as 'The Agreement'.

Kathleen opened out the tinfoil wrapper, so that it became a tiny place mat for an imaginary tea cake ornament. She thought of young Mr Jock. Thinking of young Mr Jock made her think of Tommy Fintry. Thinking of Tommy gave her a sharp pang of panic.

'Well?'

At that moment she made a resolution. She would make a point of bumping into Tommy's sister Maureen as she crossed on the ferry to her early morning cleaning job at the Kelvin Hall. On the trip across, Kathleen would stress her own current state of ecstatic happiness then enquire, in an off-hand casual way, about Maureen's full-of-himself younger brother. She was a good sort, Maureen; she had a withered arm and a tender soul and could be trusted. After all, Kathleen thought, I'm twenty-two and getting no younger. I need my future settled.

Across the table, Kathleen was aware of Ivan watching her hands. She looked at them. Her fingers had toyed absently with the tinfoil, curling it into a question mark.

Being a man of experience, Ivan would have known full well what she was thinking. When a woman shouts at you, that's good. If she throws stuff at you, even better – she's revealed her hand and showed you she cares. But when she withdraws, says nothing and clams coldly up, it's time then for a man to do some serious worrying.

'I want you to wait for me,' he implored. 'Another three months isn't a long time.'

But even while he was busy imploring, holding her hand and uttering that soulful, dewy-eyed shite and onions men did to convey sincerity he was very possibly planning his diplomatic retreat. It was quite likely he didn't think she'd stay. He lacked the confident indifference that made women wait for a man; well, a man like him anyway. He'd think of sweet Maria Tomlin, no longer his. All flimsy defiance gone, he could doubtless have wept where he sat but instead he would have steeled himself. No point crying onto the Formica. Kathleen was his last ticket in the girlfriend raffle, a slim chance being better than none. So he'd reached into his pocket and placed the small velvet box on the table before her.

'What's this?'

'Open it,' he said.

Kathleen didn't open it, though; she just sat there horrified, as if it might contain a tiny shrunken head or heart, not some tender token of devotion; so he opened it for her himself.

'Well, what do you think?'

He felt relieved. The ring looked nice, sitting there on the quilted silk, its little cluster of garnets circling the clear sparkling stone in the middle, not at all the midget gem he'd feared it might turn into when viewed outside the confines of the shop.

'Aren't you going to try it on?'

Kathleen felt her insides ice over. Her face creaked into the parody of a smile and she offered her finger hesitantly, as if he might be intending to bite it off. The ring didn't fit, of course, Ivan wasn't lucky that way, and when it dropped, he had to pluck it out of the sugar bowl.

'You can take it back into H. Samuel's in the Arcade,' he said. 'They'll size it for you.' He made his voice assume a hopeful tone. 'Maybe you and Celia could go together at the weekend?'

'No,' said Kathleen, a little too quickly, 'it's all right. It'll keep till you come back.'

'Will you wear it while I'm away?'

She noticed his eyes had an unattractive, imploring look. She made herself nod. What harm could a nod do?

'I'll put it on a chain around my neck,' she told him.

My mother took a reflective drag at her cigarette. I took a sip of lukewarm tea.

'And did you?'

'What?'

'Did you put it on a chain around your neck? More details. I want accuracy.'

'Yes,' she said. 'I wore it.'

'I'll bet you did,' I said. 'But behind high-necked sweaters and fully buttoned blouses, am I right?'

She didn't reply, which was, of course, her reply.

'Do you want to hear this story or don't you?'

I leaned back, rested my cup on the arm of my chair. 'Go on.'

'I can't, I've lost my place.'

'The ring. What was he like when you said yes?'

'I didn't say yes.'

'Okay. What was he like when you didn't say no?'

'Well . . .'

This is what Ivan was like: seemingly he perked up. On the stroll home to Burndyke Street he even danced a showy little hornpipe to demonstrate his lovably daft side to his new fiancée. Trapped by the ring in her pocket and the dancing fool at her side, Kathleen quickened her step and at the mouth of number 14, bade Ivan a brisk farewell lest sexual liberties be sought as an advance withdrawal against their joint account of marital bliss to come.

In the room, she found her father Evan, standing poised, on a single foot, clutching a trailing *Daily Record*. Big Dora sat darning his missing sock. Dora didn't care for chores – cooking, darning, sex. When Evan ventured a mild query about when he might be able to redeem his sock, Dora threw it at him and told him to mend it himself. Evan sat down without a peep, took the thick needle and fumbled.

Kathleen knew that neither of her parents approved of her current boyfriend. Ivan Moss had visited only twice and on each occasion had failed to bring the ritual offering of chips or chocolates, which was a failure of tribal etiquette that had not passed unnoticed. More tellingly, he seemed aloof and, though polite, Dora would catch his sly, surly, judgemental look as Evan, ears prematurely dulled by decades of shipyard clanging, sat straining at the wireless to guffaw at Tommy Handley, or at the Crazy Gang's approximation of Marx Brothers anarchy.

No, Dora had tried but she could not stick Ivan. There he went, swanking about Govan like fucking Horatio Nelson, God forgive me, and the best of it was he only lived in Plantation and his da worked up at Shieldhall for the cleansing, trying to make shite smell like roses – just like the rest of his la-di-da family. If only Kathleen could meet a down-to-earth Govan man, like her wee sister Tina had. Though two years younger than Kathleen, Tina was married and already had two daughters to Con, a rough diamond, well maybe not diamond, a garnet, who liked the drink and would neither work nor want. Con sang songs of Irish Independence while drawing British dole and was always fighting with the polis, but he had great stories, you could wet yourself; anyway Tina was happy and had the scars to prove it, that was the main thing, you could take the odd battering for the weans' sake so long as there are a few chuckles along the way. Dora resented Evan Cairns for never having choked or slapped her, just for the gesture of it, he didn't need to mean it, at least then she'd have known him passionate and red blooded, not just this dreary automaton who loved her, unconditionally.

Dora told her daughter straight that Ivan Moss wouldn't make her happy. Only once could she recall Kathleen returning home flushed and laughing from a date with him and that was when Lonny from the Clyde Vaults had sat the pub parrot on Ivan's peaked Merchant Navy cap when he wasn't looking. Ivan had sat there with his big snobby graveyard face and the fucking parrot on his head, God forgive me, wondering what all the sniggering was about.

Dora Cairns could not easily draw a bead on what held her daughter to him. But what could you say, your children had their own lives to lead, their own mistakes to make, the wise course was to stand back, say nothing, then gloat about how right you were after it all turned sour. All the same, you might offer some gentle guidance along the way.

'You're early,' said Dora. 'I thought you were going to the pictures with the bam?'

Evan looked up from his darning. He risked giving Dora a look. 'Even bams need girlfriends,' he said. 'A bam's a bam for aw that.'

'There's no need to take her side,' said Dora. 'She ignores me anyway.'

Kathleen ignored her mother's remark about how she ignored her mother.

She hung her raincoat on the living-room door hook. It was a powder blue raincoat, the one she'd bought for Tommy Fintry, and she didn't want to risk coal dust from the lobby bunker smudging it. Evan was still fumbling with the thread and needle.

Dora watched, with mounting irritation. With his weak eyes and calloused fingers her man was no match for the loose thread ends.

'You know who I liked?' she said, suddenly, to divert herself.

Kathleen knew what was coming. She would stay silent.

'Tommy Fintry.'

Kathleen felt her stomach lurch.

'You thought him a bam too,' reminded Evan. He was an authority on bams, his wife having judged him, he felt, to be an exemplar of the breed.

'I didn't know what a real bam was till I met Ivan Moss.'

'It's my business,' said Kathleen.

'Don't get serious with him, that's all I'm saying. That boy's strictly a DFN.'

Evan Cairns looked puzzled. Dora enlightened him.

'A do for now. Until she gets a better offer.'

Kathleen couldn't help herself. 'What if I never get a better offer?'

Dora didn't answer.

'Was I a do for now?' asked Evan.

'You still are,' said Dora.

She snatched the sock from her husband, knotted the thread ends with quick movements and slung it back at him.

Despite herself, Dora had been relieved to have married Evan and found in him everything she'd wanted in a man: he was teetotal, unattractive to other women, had a low sex drive and always handed over a full pay packet.

The radio beeped, signalling the top of the hour.

'There's your time, mister,' said Dora.

Evan rose, crossed to the mantelpiece clock, opened the glass and with his finger nudged the minute hand forward. He did this every night at the same time. It made Kathleen's teeth grind.

'Dad, why don't you buy a new cl—'

'Shh!'

Kathleen and her mother remained dutifully silent until the clock had chimed nine times.

Satisfied, Evan turned to them. 'Ah well,' he announced, 'I'm done in. That's me for the Land of Nod.'

Evan Cairns worked six and a half days a week. He went to bed at nine o'clock every night. He rose at five o'clock each morning, except for Saturdays, when he would luxuriate till five thirty.

When her husband was finally tucked up in the bed recess, rasping and asleep, Dora pressed her daughter for her intentions about the future.

'Will you marry him?'

Kathleen looked up, startled, from her *Tit-Bits*. She'd managed to forget she'd become engaged that night.

'It depends,' she said.

'On what? Either it's a love match or it isn't.'

Kathleen wouldn't say. Sure, it was a love match all right between her and Ivan. The only trouble was, they were both in love with other people.

That night Kathleen couldn't sleep. As her bedside clock struck midnight, she was still awake.

She knew that at the same moment, from the Prince's dry dock at the scrag end of Govan, the *Placebo*, a patched up, Liverpool-registered merchant vessel, would be sliding along the oily, slurping waters of the Clyde. She looked out through the chink in the curtains. It was a heavy, damp night and Ivan Moss should have been below, listening on his headphones for weather updates. But she knew he'd have stolen on deck, as he'd promised, and would be thinking of her as the ship slid out toward the Firth. He'd button up his dark greatcoat to the collar against the night cold. As the *Placebo* ghosted past Fairfield's, quiet as a hearse, he would see the firefly studs of the welding torches slur the smog into pale grey streaks on the night air and as he watched he would think of her, as promised.

And as she thought of him watching her, she felt the ripple wash of panic steer her thoughts to Tommy Fintry.

Next morning Kathleen Cairns stood near the wooden jetty at the foot of McKechnie Street, where the Govan ferry docked. On the other side of the river they called it the Partick ferry. The jetty smelled of rotting wood and tarred rope. The ferry was a small, single-deck vessel. It was busiest early on because even though the Underground ran under the river, the first trains didn't start till later in the morning. A queue had already begun to assemble but Kathleen didn't join it, and she stood back a little, by the railings, watching.

The river troubled her. Its rolling silence had the power to unnerve. Everything in life changed: boyfriends, opinions, hemlines, hairstyles, but the river remained constant, an all-seeing mirror held up to a person's nature, as close as your mother's cooking smells, as sleek as a wet rat. Wherever you went in life, whatever you did, it made no difference – the Clyde was always there, changeless, whenever you came back, ready to confer its silent judgement. Whenever she looked in this river mirror, she felt small and confused. Now she came to think of it, this was why she did not like the river.

'Kathleen!'

Maureen Fintry, Tommy's sister, was walking toward her. Maureen was smiling self-consciously because she'd forgotten herself and shouted out loud and people had turned to look at her. Her message bag was in her good hand and her withered arm leaned at its familiar angle across her midriff, the hand seeming to taper away to a point like a stick of well-sucked seaside rock.

'What are you doing here?'

'I've a wee message to run in Partick for my mother,' said Kathleen, lightly. She felt her face tinge red as she lied.

The ferry docked, shuddering the ancient timbers of the jetty. The relief ferryman, a surly figure who only brightened when making racy remarks to young girls, clambered out and tethered his vessel to a slimy post. Busy people in overcoats, with bags and haversacks, were already galloping up the greasy steps while he secured the knot. As she and Maureen chatted, Kathleen felt the nerves flutter in her entrails. She watched the ferryman from the corner of her eye. He took a fresh roll-up and tapped it against the tin. He was eyeing the steps, maybe spotting for glimpses of suspender. After a two-match struggle against a river breeze, he looked around. The last stragglers were safely away. He pursed his wizened lips and sucked on his fag.

Kathleen made a quick calculation; it would take at most five minutes to cross the Clyde. She would then walk Maureen up the winding cobbled bank on the other side. At the top of Dumbarton Road, she'd turn left and Maureen right. She had ten minutes, at most, to try to change her life.

'Right,' grunted the ferryman and gestured everybody aboard.

The wind flecked faces with river water and the younger women knotted their headscarves tighter against the wayward breeze.

'How are you liking Skirling Jock's?' Maureen asked.

'Oh, great. The lassies are nice, the money's good and you can eat rich tea digestives till your mouth feels like cardboard.'

'A job is only as good as the people you meet, Kathleen.'

'Very true. Are you still cleaning at the Kelvin Hall?'

'Oh, I love it, except when the circus comes. Elephants are the worst, they're honking.'

'In more ways than one, says you.'

Maureen chuckled politely at this limp witticism, allowing Kathleen to move the conversation forward.

'And are you winching these days?'

Maureen affected a perky air and shrugged in an off-hand manner. 'Ach, you know me, free and easy.'

But she was not free or easy. She was achingly self-conscious about her gammy arm and, because of it, wretchedly timid with men. Kathleen knew this, and felt ashamed to be trampling over Maureen's feelings, but they were nearly halfway across the river and the time for niceties was over.

'Sure, that's the best way,' Kathleen said and shut abruptly up. Having dug a cunning pit of silence, she gambled that Maureen, being nice, would topple into it, gammy arm and all, God willing.

God obliged.

'How about yourself, Kathleen, are you seeing anybody?'

'Me? Oh, yes.' Kathleen smiled exultantly, showing teeth. 'I'm very happy. Wonderfully happy. Yes, happiness is great, I'd thoroughly recommend it.'

'I think I saw you out with him,' said Maureen. 'Was that him that had the parrot on his head in the Clyde Vaults?'

Kathleen beamed relentlessly on. 'Yes,' she said, from behind clenched teeth.

'That's good. In that case, it looks like everything's worked out for the best.'

Kathleen didn't understand. 'How do you mean?'

'You know Tommy's in Coventry?'

'Yes.'

'Well, he's just got engaged.'

Engaged. The word, a falling meteor, crashed through Kathleen's skull and thudded into the pit of her stomach.

'I wasn't sure if I should tell you. But I see it's all right now, because you're happy. And so is he.'

They were halfway across the Clyde. The cross currents were at their worst here. The ferryman made the wheel spin with forceful wrenches, so that the boat trembled. Kathleen gripped the hand rail. Among other, far stronger feelings, she felt inconvenienced. She knew her life had changed and that, from this moment on, she would always be obliged to take detours in order to avoid the river, because the river would forever now remind her of this moment and this place, where she'd learned that Tommy Fintry, the man she loved, had become engaged to be married to another girl.

The ferryman loomed into Kathleen's face. 'We're here, hen,' he said, with a twinkling leer. 'Do you want to toot the funnel?'

'Not today, thank you,' said Kathleen.

She and Maureen climbed the steps and walked together up the hill onto Dumbarton Road. Kathleen made herself talk a lot and laugh, urging a vow from Maureen that they would meet up more often, perhaps to hit the Flamingo on Paisley Road together for a great laugh and a dance; it was a long time since they'd had a great laugh and a dance together, in fact, now she came to think of it, they never had.

'Yes, I've never been happier.' Kathleen smiled again, desperate to stamp upon Tommy Fintry's sister a lasting image of her never-ending personal bliss.

With Maureen out of sight, Kathleen peeled off her smile, threw it in the gutter and walked down to Merkland Street to wait for the Underground back to Govan Cross.

If she was to avoid the river, she might as well start now . . .

My leg had gone to sleep. I uncrossed it and kneaded some life into it. 'Why'd you marry a man you didn't love?'

'I did love him. You grow to love people.'

'Not as much as the other fella.'

'I couldn't get the other fella. Anyway, Tommy was all looks, just looks, that's all, he'd have bored me in no time flat.'

'He'd have made you happy.'

'It's the same thing.'

I nodded. It could have been me talking. Except if Tommy Fintry had been my father, I wouldn't have been talking. Not like this anyway. Timing and circumstance, they're what decide it. I stood up. She looked alarmed.

'Don't go. Stay for another cup of tea.'

'I only came to talk about the treatment, remember?'

'I haven't forgotten about the treatment,' my mother said. 'Put the kettle on.'

'What have you decided?'

'That's between me and Dr Jaffar.'

'Suit yourself.'

'I intend to, believe me.'

'What's that supposed to mean?'

'Never mind. You'll find out.'

'When?'

'When we see Dr Jaffar.'

I wanted to argue, which is to say to meddle. I was keen to make sure she did the right thing regarding her treatment. Except that it dawned on me I had no idea what the right thing might be.

There was the chemo approach and/or the radiotherapy approach. Then green tea and crystal stones if you wanted the alternative approach. In other words, my mother knew as much or as little as I did. She saw my resolve weaken.

'Now will you put the kettle on?'

I nodded, stomped some life into my dead leg then headed for the kitchen.

From somewhere, out of something, she'd decided to take charge.

When I arrived home there was a message from Stan. I rang him back.

'Stan?'

'What's the word?'

'About what?'

'The treatment. What did you tell her about the treatment?'

'I didn't tell her anything.'

'You told her nothing? Why not?'

'I'm not a doctor. She trusts her specialist, her doctor, Dr Jaffar.'

'Dr Jaffar?'

'Her specialist.'

'You mean you didn't look for a second opinion? Did you pursue information via the internet?'

'No.'

'You didn't Google?'

'No. I didn't via and I didn't Google.'

'I see, I see.' He was doing baffled incredulity to push me into a corner. He was going to pepper my face with his jab, as always. I was rattled. I should have Googled. I barged my way back into the centre of the ring. 'I prefer a real person to tell me about the cancer, the treatments, not Jimmy Wales, MD.' I swung with a haymaker. 'And besides, she's made her mind up.'

'She's made her mind up?' He'd slowed down his voice and made it sound astonished to rub in my dereliction of duty. 'Without a second opinion?'

'Yes. No.'

'What's she decided?'

'I don't know.'

There was a pause. 'My, you're really on the ball, aren't you?'

'Stan . . .'

'Our mother's really lucky to have somebody as capable as you around to not know things for her. It must be a great comfort.'

He was thudding my kidneys with his right; it was payback for the 'Mother loves me better' routine last time we'd spoken.

'Tell me something,' my brother said. 'What do you do when you go there?'

'Where?'

'To our mother's house, where else? What exactly is your contribution to the situation?'

'I get her to tell me stories.'

'She tells you stories?'

'About her past. Our past. Who we are.'

It sounded limp, I know. My brother's voice was flat yet contemptuous. 'I know who we are,' he said, stringing the words out. 'We're her sons.'

It was his *coup de théâtre*.

I put the phone down.

Six

We were in the hospital again. It was early. There was no one else in the waiting room. There was an uneasy, distant calm about her and she hadn't even done the fidgeting routine with the belt of her coat.

I took the opportunity to ask her a dramatic question.

'Was I illegitimate?'

'What?'

'It's a straight question. If the answer's yes, it makes no difference.'

'The answer's no.'

'Oh.'

'You sound disappointed.'

'You can tell me the truth. I wouldn't think the worse of you.'

'That's big of you.'

'You're welcome.'

'What made you ask a thing like that?'

I looked at her.

'I see,' she said. 'It's a now or never conversation? Well, you're not illegitimate.' She smiled, grimly. 'It was a close run thing, though.'

'I had to ask,' I said.

'You didn't have to, you wanted to.'

We talked some more. I raised the cancer subject, the object of the meeting. I strove for a note of reassurance and quiet optimism but she wasn't in the mood for any of that. To support a person at times of perilous illness you have to be sensitive to their bullshit threshold: too much BS and they despise you and become irritated by your presence; too little and they feel you're a gloomy Jeremiah and they despise you and become irritated by your presence. Also, you have to be careful that they don't begin to associate you with the illness, since your escorting them to consultations concerning its development are the only times they see you.

If that happens and you and the illness become inextricably interlinked then they begin to despise you and become, well, you know the rest . . .

'Kathleen Moss?' It was the receptionist.

'Let's go in,' my mother said.

Dr Jaffar spoke softly. He reprised the narrow range of treatment possibilities he'd outlined at our previous meeting. When he'd done this he stopped talking and listened. My mother folded her hands across her lap, opened her mouth to speak, unfolded her hands, fiddled with her belt, coughed, looked to me.

'What do you think, Ivan?'

I was startled. Caught cold, I panicked. Who was I to know what I thought? Besides, hadn't she told me she had already made up her mind which treatments she would be undertaking? I'd taken it to be a done deal.

'It's your tumour,' I found myself blurting out. 'You do what you want with it.' Dr Jaffar blinked, like a man who thought he'd heard it all, until then.

My mother composed herself. He probed a little more, asked

her again. They had a civilised conversation. I didn't join in. I didn't feel very civilised. I stood at the door while my mother offered effusive thanks, holding Jaffar's hand in both of hers, gripping it like he was a saintly guru. But thanks for what? She'd have had as much chance under Dr Crippen as him. He was just a waiter offering her a menu of ghastly horrors. Sometimes it's all in the presentation.

We walked back up the corridor.

'Well, you blew that one,' I said.

'I know,' she agreed. 'I'm sorry; I'll be ready next time.'

Only next time, she wouldn't be seeing nice, sweet-natured, scented-candled Dr Jaffar. She'd be moving on, going hard core. She was on a hospital conveyor belt that didn't stop for anyone. She'd be taking a step nearer the roaring furnace that dwelt at the heart of the Oncology department. She would see the chief stoker himself, Dr Ryford. This time there could be no back-sliding or prevarication. We walked across the car park.

'You're all I've got to lean on now,' she said and climbed stiffly into the car.

'And Stan,' I reminded her, for selfish reasons. 'I'm not very good at this.'

She looked at me. 'Me neither,' she said and smiled.

I unwound the seat belt from around her neck and made it secure.

'You're doing fine,' I said, and meant it.

When people die, their memories die with them. But their memories are not their exclusive domain, encompassing as they must, the lives of others. Contained within our memorabilia, other people walk and speak, inhabiting our dreams and anecdotes. The only person one never sees in a memory is one's self, since we are otherwise engaged, crouched behind our mental camera. Memories, therefore, are not only a personal but a social history. One of the things Vaughan had said to me that day on Byres Road was: 'I wish I'd got it all down before she died.' He was talking about his own mother. I'd heard that same utterance several times from different people. But why didn't anyone ever take their own advice? The reason, in my case, was simple: who the hell ever listens to their mother? Like a Facebook home page, they talk in an ever-flowing, unedited stream of trivia, gossip, local news, repetition, received opinion, stale myth, whimsy and spite. To listen out for items of true interest amid the babble is to risk turning oneself into a crazed prospector panning for decades through murky silt in the hope of turning over a golden nugget or two.

I tried though.

I found out that in Tradeston Church, Kathleen Cairns had married Ivan Moss. The bride wore a white dress with match-ing white skin, patent black shoes and a discreetly visible foetus. *No* Father looked dashing in his naval uniform with its braided cuffs and faint reek of engine oil. Father's brother Rolf was granted shore leave to attend as best man. Father was overjoyed at the prospect of fatherhood.

'Are you sure it's mine?'

'Of course it's yours,' protested Mother. 'Who else's would it be?'

'I was away for months, anything could've happened.'

'That cuts both ways – do you want to swap separation stories?'

Father demurred. Though back on dry land, my guess was that he would have felt himself all at sea – things were changing too quickly, too decisively, for him to keep a telling grip on life's rudder.

Mother was close to tears. Father tried to put her at her ease,

↳ she was X-rayed ?

with silken words.

'If it's backward, we can always bung it into an orphanage.'

Mother grew alarmed. 'Why would it be backward?'

'It's a precaution. A first child's either the pick of the bunch or the worst.'

'You're a middle child,' observed Mother.

'I know,' mused Father, darkly.

So it was that Mother became a housewife and Father left the sea to join Dunne's grocery chain, as an assistant manager. There was great rejoicing in the house, followed by depression and recrimination. For two footloose single people, each with discretionary income, had come together to form one hastily married couple who would henceforth muster but a solitary pay packet between them from which to worship God, buy fags and put down outrageous key money for a grubby single end in Garmouth Street: which is where I now come in – a snivelling, unformed wretch, yes; but a sentient presence nonetheless and henceforth an active contributor to the creation of this, the Moss living tapestry.

My earliest recollections of life are housed in that single end. On the screen of memory, my own memory that is, I see myself toddling at high speed across bare linoleum. I am wearing only a vest and crying. It's an unedifying portrait to present to you, and for that matter, to me, and had I a choice I would have proffered you, and me, something that would have cut a more metaphoric and less literal dash. But choice have we none – I've been stuck to that dismal first image of myself, the running, whining wretch, these many years now and it has adhered to my brain like gum to the sole of a shoe. If our lives are a journey, then memory is forever peering into private windows as we speed past in our darkened carriage. Memory is a tart that knows neither restraint nor decorum. Memory does not know when to avert her eyes, discreetly. She is untouched by the finger of taste. Therein is her seductiveness and power.

Whining then. And running, as stated, across bare linoleum with my mother in anxious pursuit. But where is my father? Ah yes, it's daylight, or the Scottish equivalent thereof, so he'll be hard at work around the corner on Langlands Road, wrapping slices of corned beef in greaseproof paper.

Gripping the windowsill with my fingertips, I see me press my nose to the glass. Perhaps I am looking for him, my father. The sights and sounds of Govan distract and mesmerise me: the screech and rattle of tram cars; the shouts from outside; an open-topped lorry, laden with filthy coal bags, puttering along the grey street, ruining the street drawings of red-kneed brats. The blackened driver leaning out to cry with the flinty gruffness of a New Orleans blues singer, 'Co-al briqu – eeettes.'

By the pavement stands a battered white van, with drooping balloons tethered, like unwanted pets, to its open rear doors. The van's custodian, a runtish individual draped in an overlarge brown dust coat, trumpets a harsh business cry. His neck twists in a peculiar nervous spasm as he too calls out, more or less melodically . . . 'Toays furrags . . . Toays furrags.'

Toys for rags. The untutored melancholy of his cry to this day claws at my entrails. At three, I had never heard of country music, or Bill Monroe's high lonesome, but already I knew, by racial memory, that the ragman was our Hank Williams. The catch in his voice caressed the boundaries of our street and lives, his heartfelt words beat their fists uselessly against the prison walls of our grimy tenement slabs. 'Toays furrags, henny old kinda raaags . . .'

I saw a snarling boy once, bug eyes set in a face of scrubbed potato, holding a man's suit under his arm. 'Toys furr . . .' sounded the ragman's voice, blue as a freight train whistle at midnight.

He broke off abruptly to offer the boy a brown ten-shilling note in exchange for the suit.

The boy accepted the money but declined the whimsical embellishment of a balloon. When his father rounded the corner yelling, 'My fucking good suit, I'll kill you,' the boy took to his heels.

A row erupted and the ragman was chided. 'You twitching freak,' accused the furious, suit-less father.

A blow was struck. Blood decorated the lapel of the ragman's dust coat like a garish state honour from a tin pot republic. I watched curiously as the blow was returned. There was grappling of a clumsy nature. A small crowd gathered.

The street pageant ceased abruptly, for I found myself hoisted aloft in large confident hands before being set down on a flannelled knee.

'Look at his stomach,' declared Dr Shapiro, lifting my vest. 'It's measles all right.'

'Oh my God!'

Mother seized the drama of the moment, clutching her throat, in the accustomed female fashion. When she did so, a fag packet peeked out from under the sleeve of her cardigan.

I squiggled for freedom. Dr Shapiro fixed me by the head with the skull cap of his splayed fingers. The mighty battering ram of a large digit prodded at my pink belly. *spotty all over, twit.*

'Keep him in bed,' counselled the doctor. I was passed from hand to hand, like a china ornament of sentimental value – a present frae bonnie Scotland.

'He's awful young for the measles,' fretted Mother, cradling me. 'Is it dangerous?'

'No, no,' said the healer dismissively but he paused nonetheless to consider. 'Best cover that bulb,' he cautioned. 'His eyes, you see – the brightness.'

Through the stultifying gloom of a Scottish afternoon in late autumn, my mother peered at the doctor.

'What brightness?'

'For the best. Precaution.'

With the doctor gone, Mother fixed the bulb in the recommended fashion. I lay under the covers in my parents' big saggy bed and watched her. A dishcloth muted the thin dazzle of the bulb and obscured the bowl's familiar mottled flooring of frazzled dead flies. Outside, as drizzle distressed the windows and the street cries faded, I discovered the delight of easy slippage into passive gloom. As if to consolidate the mood of the moment, Mother sang to me my favourite song.

'*Olé, I am the ban-dit,*' she crooned, with grand delicious misery. '*Olé, from old Bra-zil . . .*'

My mother always sang with feeling. Her songs were songs of loss – lost love or youth. Sometimes she'd make up her own words. These would speak of empty purses or of the passage of small items from personal ownership once the pawnbroker's pledge ticket had expired. Father's naval uniform had gone the way of the pawn shop. With its surrender had gone Father's worldly mystique, until Granny Moss rescued it out of the window for three times what Mother had received for it.

A tapping noise sounded above us; too rhythmical, too lacking in angry insistence to be a complaining neighbour.

I had become drowsy from the crooning and the darkness, but mustered enough curiosity in my expression to elicit an explanation from Mother.

'What's up, wee Ivan, are you hearing that funny noise?'

In the curious way adults do, she vibrated my lip with her pinky. She continued. 'That's the man up the stairs, Mr Fredericks, back from the pub. He loves dancing. Daddy doesn't like Mr Fredericks. Daddy calls him "Fred-Up-the-Stair".'

Mother looked at me, smiling gamely. 'It's a witty pun, you see,' she explained. 'Fred Astaire is a famous dancer.'

I was slow to learn the art of speech and though I possessed several words in my repertoire, I was not generous with them. Something held me back. Presbyterian reserve possibly, or a precocious desire to create an enigmatic air – difficult, when one is covered in measles spots, dribbling, and naked from the waist down. I stared back at her, blankly.

Mother looked disappointed. She gazed up at the muffled light bulb and sang:

'Once I robbed a big ranchero, he was rich beyond compare,
And to ransom held his daughter, she was young and she was fair . . .'

My mother, then, was of low character. Only people of low character sang at their toddlers while chain-smoking. My father, on the other hand, was strictly abstemious. In our culture, this meant that he drank heavily but only at weekends. Father gulped down the stuff in swift, no-nonsense draughts, like medicine, in pints and quarter gills to be taken relentlessly between meals.

So long as one did not drink for enjoyment, but merely for the approved purposes of blotting out reality, between the prescribed hours of Friday tea time and Sunday night before the Inchinnan Hotel called 'Time', one could be regarded as a man of respectable character and sober habit.

Thus, drink was not a source of recreation to men like my father, more a cultural duty.

'Measles?' he queried.

'That's what Dr Shapiro said.'

She bared me where I lay for Father's inspection. Grim-faced, he perused the pimply evidence.

'I wouldn't trust that quack. If he was any good, he wouldn't be in Govan.'

'If you were any good, *we* wouldn't be in Govan,' countered my mother. 'Anyway, I thought you were a socialist?'

Momentarily wrong-footed, Father waved an imperious hand in lieu of further argument. With this gesture he dismissed all suggestions of elitism.

I tried to talk to him.

'What was that?'

'What?'

'He made a noise with his mouth.'

'He's speaking. Aren't you, my wee man?' She leaned over me, beaming.

'Coo coo coo,' she said.

'Don't do the baby thing, it makes me queasy,' reproached Father.

The harshness of his tone made me whimper. Father looked at me. By a freak mischance, our eyes connected. I held his gaze with the steely confidence of the imbecile. Father blinked first. Instead of taking it off, my father buttoned again his coat. I saw my mother open her purse. My father put his hand inside.

'Just a loan,' he said.

When Father left, Mother threw her purse at the wall.

That evening, when he returned, father stooped over my bed. In his hands was a gift and he spoke to me. I cannot recall the conversation but it probably went something like this:

'This came from a shop on Langlands Road,' he said. 'The shop is called the Modern Book Shop.'

My reply, I suspect, was limited.

'Do you want to know what it is? It's a book!' Father's presentation always lacked the magic of surprise.

What I recall is the smell of freshly opened pages and how the stiff red spine of the volume creaked as Father read aloud to me.

I looked at him, dumbly. I knew only that his sour breath tickled my nose and made my eyes water.

Mother called to him. 'Ivan?'

'Yes?'

'What's that you're reading to the wean?'

'*Letters from the Underworld* by Fyodor Dostoevsky.'

'Jesus Christ.'

Father continued reading in defiant fashion. '*Indeed, what man of sensibility could even possess self-respect . . .*'

'Ivan.'

'What now?'

'He doesn't like Fyodor Dostoevsky. He likes *Billy and the Puff Puff Train.*'

'I'm not filling his head with that rubbish,' declared Father, with finality. He cleared his throat by way of punctuation and ground on with his instructive tale.

'*Offending the laws of nature has been the chief, the constant concern of my life . . .*'

'Uff-uff.'

'There, you see!'

'See what?'

'He said "Uff-uff". That means "Puff Puff". He wants *Billy and the Puff Puff Train.*'

'No he doesn't; he's only parroting what you said.'

'Yes, because he likes it. You said "Fyodor Dostoevsky", but you don't hear him asking for any of that stuff, do you?'

At a loss for a cogent riposte, Father's mouth flapped silently. Desperate for signs of literary appreciation, he scrutinised my face.

'Uff-uff,' I said again.

My father drew away sharply, in a disappointed fashion.

'Ivan, please,' coaxed Mother.

'This is for his benefit. Education is the passport to a better life.'

IAN PATTISON

'He's only two. He can have a better life later on.'

Father was duly convinced, but it was a marginal decision.

'You win.'

He threw the book down. Mother handed him the worn out copy of *Billy and the Puff Puff Train*, already open at the place.

My father read, grim-faced.

'*Once upon a time there was a little boy called Billy who wanted his very own puff puff train.*'

'Uff-uff,' I said again, obligingly.

Disappointment and disgust jostled for possession of my father's features.

Upstairs, Fred's feet broke into a fresh and gleeful rash of rhythm, invading Father's concentration and causing the light bowl to vibrate on its chain.

'Ach, what's the fucking use!'

Father skimmed the book in anger along the table, making a fallen skittle of the sauce bottle. I tensed, frightened.

'I'll go upstairs and ask him to stop,' offered my mother, sensing a mood.

'He'd better, or there'll be trouble.'

When she had gone, Father moaned and rubbed his forehead. He was muttering to himself. He stared at me. In lieu of throwing me out the window, he jabbed my stomach with the meaty pole of his finger.

'You're hopeless.'

'Uff-uff,' I replied, just to watch him grind his teeth.

At that age, you can get away with murder.

The editor of memory discards several scenes thereafter and I next find myself heading for Golspie Street to visit Granny Moss. I know time must have passed for I was walking or, to be more accurate, trotting. Contrary to popular belief, children

72

must learn to run before they can walk. Small children have poor balance and the momentum of propulsion is necessary for remaining upright. As with a bicycle, so with feet: in both instances, one discovers early on in the learning process that one may hurtle unopposed for considerable distances before a lamp-post, stranger's arse, or other item of street furniture brings forward trajectory to a calamitous conclusion. As a robust metaphor for the trials of living, learning to walk is the dibs: if we go too fast we run into things; if too slow, we wobble then fall. For added safety I wore, like a small wayward animal, a harness. To a child, restraint is a hair shirt and by way of useless protest, I would cry. Not just any old cry. I had created a custom-built, hand-tooled whine, all of my own; a wheedling, needling torment of a cry, cunningly designed simultaneously to both antagonise and dispirit.

'Please stop it,' begged my mother, her hair frizzled from drizzle, her strength exhausted from tugging my recalcitrant form behind her. '*Please.*'

Heartened by her weakened state, I refuelled my lungs with sooty air and increased my volume to a confident and sustained howl. Sustained, that is, until it was prematurely severed. It is a strange thing to have one's howl cut off. It is as if one's ears have popped. The world is restored upon the instant to all its noisy, incoherent bustle and diversity. What had happened was this – my mother had given a shriek, a sort of '*Hchaagh!*' The sound had caused both of us, myself and she, to stop in our different tracks, startled. Perhaps '*Hchaagh*' is too constrained a replication of the sound my mother used; why not try '*Achaagh!*' Yes, the addition of a trilling vowel plays the note of truth upon the scale of my mother's anguish. I knew by instinct that this sound, unlike my own, was an authentic utterance, born of the unrelenting burdens of adulthood. Life had become, at that moment, simply too much for her to bear; the empty purse, the torn stockings, the sheer misery of the joy of motherhood, too much and too heavy a load.

Upon hearing this rival cry, I did what any competent infant would have done in the circumstances: I lay face down on the pavement and began to flail in the gutter. Moral rectitude, I felt, was on my side. My mother had upstaged me which, under the unwritten contractual agreement that exists between mother and child, was not permitted. In the rolling, solipsistic drama that is the life of a toddler, no one is allowed to upstage the star. A mother is literally and metaphorically a 'feed' and must never attempt to build her part. I screamed and flailed till my toes ached from hacking the pavement concrete – to no avail. When I looked up, my mother was gone.

'Mammy?'

Nothing.

I tried sucking the thumb. I added the whiny custom-built cry, even a couple of 'uff-uffs'.

Not a blind, blessed thing.

Seven

Till I followed my nose.

The door of the Harmony Bar swung open. I could smell
Father's familiar stink of warm beer and stale cigarettes.

But it was my mother who was standing at the bar.

And the man standing with her was not Father . . .

'You're late,' said Granny Moss, Father's mother, in her nippy
fashion, helping my own mother off with her coat.

'Sorry, Maidie, but the wee one took sick. We had to turn
back to change his romper suit.'

'Oh, dear,' said Granny M, with smiling mouth and cold eyes,
not entirely convinced. I was at the table, eyeing up the jam pot.
Granny Moss came over and did that clucking, hair-smoothing
thing on me, but I wasn't fooled. She was sniffing on the quiet
for signs of vomit. Within the family circle, Granny M was re-
nowned for the sensitivity of her nasal apparatus. This ought
to have made her life with Grandpa Moss a source of exquisite
agony, since he worked at the Shieldhall sewage plant. But it did
not.

'Hmm,' said Granny, her eyes two slits, glinting.

She snatched the jam spoon from my hand and in a swift,

flowing movement draped Mother's coat over a side chair.

'What's this?'

'Sorry?'

'Sticking out of your coat pocket. This.'

Granny Moss held up an emaciated, ravaged-looking flower and awaited explanation.

Mother had none.

Colour drained from her face; she was demonstrating a new cosmetic range, Guilty as Sin by John Calvin.

'I've no idea how it got there,' said Mother. 'We passed some gypsies on Burleigh Street, maybe they . . .'

'Tinkers,' interjected Granny Moss. 'Not gypsies. Low-life Irish. They camp on that bombsite by the car ferry, back of the Water Row. A tinker will steal the purse from your pocket or the eyes from your head. They're not known for making flowery gestures.'

'It wasn't a flowery gesture.'

'It's a flower.'

'Yes, but it wasn't a gesture.'

'If you don't know who put it there, how can you say?'

Mother was at a loss. 'I can't,' she admitted.

As a full stop to the interrogation, Granny Moss gave Mother her gimlet stare. 'Put the kettle on,' she instructed.

While Mother obeyed, Granny Moss wiped some margarine across a slice of bread.

I could see she was building up to something. It was Father's let down.

'It's happened to Ivan before, you know.'

'What?'

'That one before you – Marie Tomlin – she threw him over.'

This touched a nerve with Mother. 'I know what that's like,' she said. 'I had someone else too – once.'

'Did he let you down?'

'I was too young. Pride got in the way. I didn't know any better.'

'Is that a yes or a no?'

'Yes.'

'That's all I asked,' said Granny Moss. She dragged a smear of jam across the yellowed slice. 'Have you got your name down yet on the Corporation housing list like I told you?'

'You know I have,' said Mother, adopting a chirpy tone. 'You frog-marched me up to Bath Street and sat with me till I'd done it.'

'And have you heard anything?'

'No.'

'You need more kiddies. Kiddies mean housing points.'

'We're thinking about it,' said Mother to shut her up. Mother held the handle of the kettle on the gas, as if somehow that would make it boil quicker.

'Why don't you get pregnant?'

Mother's grip tightened on the handle.

'I've been pregnant. I didn't like it. I tore, badly.'

'I tore too,' said Granny Moss. 'But I knew what to do. Maybe that's why Ivan doesn't come near you now.'

'He does come near me.'

'Men like it tight. Didn't you ask the surgeon for the extra stitch like I told you?'

'No.'

Granny looked shocked. 'You didn't you ask for the husband's stitch?'

'No,' Mother said. 'The very thought of asking for something like that. It makes me feel sick.'

'You can't be selfish, think of Ivan. It's good sense for a woman. Believe me, the tighter his wife, the less likely is a man to stray.'

'He hasn't strayed.'

'Neither has his father. And you know why? I'm fifty-six but down below I'm as tight as the crease in that tablecloth.'

Mother's pink face reddened.

'Do you know what Ivan's father calls me? Over there, in the corner?'

Each, in their differing ways, eyed the bed recess.

'No.'

'The hairline crack.' Outwardly prim, privately a slut, Granny Moss gave a short, ghastly cackle. 'He's a terrible man! He comes in here, stinking like sin! And he throws me down, he throws me!'

'Maidie, please.'

The kettle spout puffed steam. My mother poured its contents into the teapot. She looked hotter than the kettle.

'Don't say things like that.'

'I'm only thinking what's best for you and Ivan. Glasgow's changing, there's redevelopment ahead; you can read about it in the *Govan Press*. Here, I've saved you a copy.'

Granny Moss unzipped my mother's message bag and dropped in the folded newspaper. I watched her sly eyes have a quick flick round the bag while she did so. She continued.

'My sister Tessie's in Edinburgh, they redeveloped there. They do it street by street, Tessie said, moving the bigger families out first. The more kiddies you have, the better your offer. With five or more, you'll get a terrace row with back and front garden, automatic.'

'Who'd want five children?'

'Catholics,' said Granny Moss at once, 'tinkers all. They have a head start, so get cracking. Believe you me, the pick of the council schemes will be riddled with them and you young ones will only have yourselves to blame.'

'My father is Catholic,' reminded Mother.

Granny Moss halted in her flow. Deftly she lifted her mental skirts, leapt the puddle of her faux pas and pressed on. 'Anyway, with two or three you'll get a flat with a balcony. With one, well, what good is one child to anyone?'

The two of them eyed me in the corner, where I squatted, listening.

'I'll take my chances,' said Mother. She put down two tea cups on the table. 'And what about yourself?'

'Me?' Granny Moss shook her head. 'I'll never move from this close, they'll need to burn it down. They'll have to carry me out like a well-fired roll on a bread board.' She lifted a digestive biscuit and took a nibble. I watched tiny crumb boulders cascade down the valley of her blouse front.

'Did I ever tell you about when I first moved in?'

'No,' my mother lied, breezily.

'Well . . .' Granny Moss settled to her tale:

'In those days, old Mrs Elphinstone was downstairs. She'd make my life a misery if the kids so much as crossed the floor.'

'You and me both,' said Mother. 'That old witch Mrs Doherty's never away from my door.'

Granny Moss gave Mother a look. This was a non-stop express monologue. There could be no impediments on the line, halting its scheduled progress. She continued.

'Elphinstone would bump the ceiling with her stick, then she'd—'

'So does old Doherty,' enthused Mother, grimly.

I watched Granny Moss give an inward harrumph before changing trains.

Her voice assumed a rasping tone. 'Then there was Stumpy Scanlan from over the lobby.'

Granny M narrowed her eyes across the table. Mother looked

awkward. She had taken the hint. She was to be the guard on this conversation, not the driver.

'Why did they call him Stumpy?'

'You mean I've never told you about Stumpy Scanlan?'

'No.'

Mother waved the green flag, Granny's train pulled away from the station.

'Well . . .'

And she was off. Resigned to her role, Mother assumed a fixed bright smile. All she'd wanted was to body swerve the subjects of sex, babies and houses. Granny Moss must have known that too, but when nostalgia opened its arms she could never resist rushing headlong into its embrace.

'Stumpy had a wooden leg from the war,' said Granny M. 'He had a handcart and he'd clump around the streets buying rags. The kids would follow him on his rounds, clapping and singing. They had their own wee song, it went like this: "*Stumpy Scanlan, dearie me, half a man and half a tree!*"' Granny gave an indulgent chuckle. 'They were happy days.'

'What happened to Stumpy?'

'He hanged himself. Help yourself to a chocolate finger.'

'I'm fine, thanks.'

Granny M continued. 'Stumpy's son Michael took over the business. You'll see him about the streets to this day in his van.'

My ears pricked up. I pictured that brown dust coat, heard that melancholy cry.

'*Toays furrags* . . .'

Maybe young Michael would end up jerking from a rope like his father. He already had his own twitch, he was halfway there.

'Uff-uff.'

'What's that he's saying?'

'Puff puff train. He says it all the time.'

Granny Moss made a wailing sound. 'Oh, don't talk to me about that phase. His father used to say "tee tees" for "sweeties". It drove me demented. Every time we were in a shop. "Tee tees, Mammy, tee tees." I'd wait till nobody was looking and nip him on the wee podgy leg with my fingers. He'd howl the place down, but it was a warning to him and a consolation to me. Every child brings out something different from you. Ivan was good at drawing. He'd bring his pictures home from school and expect me to say lovely things.'

'That's nice.'

'No it wasn't. I'd make him put them in the coal bunker and tell them I was posting them up to Jesus. It was all I could do not to wet myself laughing! I don't know why.'

Mother held her tea cup in both hands, for comfort.

Granny Moss attempted a good-natured chortle. 'Times were different then,' she said. 'There's too much mollycoddling now.' She gave me a strange, smiling look. The look said, 'Go on, wee man, try saying your cutesy little "Uff-uff" baby thing. See what you get soon as your mammy's back's turned.'

Avoiding Granny's gaze, I chewed ruminatively at my slimy bread. My card was marked. First Father had seen through me, now Granny M. It was time to broaden my linguistic horizons.

'Mark my words. The housing plans are set. Within five years, Govan will be—'

Granny stopped in mid-sentence. Her nose twitched.

'Here's his lordship, back for his dinner.'

It is a rare thing for individuals to feel heartened by the whiff of industrial cleanser. At that moment, myself and my mother were two such souls.

'Hello, Kathleen,' said Grandpa, radiating gruff good cheer. 'My, Ivan, you're getting big.'

'He is that.'

81

Grandpa loosened off the straps of his boiler suit. He gave Granny's waist its dinner-time tickle. 'He he – you're a terrible man,' said Granny, squirming deliciously.

Grandpa M washed his hands at the sink.

'I was just talking to Kathleen about this overspill housing programme.'

Grandpa M frowned, waxed stern. 'It's progress but it'll come at a social cost,' he said. 'It'll mark the death of working-class solidarity and set neighbour against neighbour in a consumer frenzy.'

Grandpa M dried his hands on a 'Visit Lovely Ayrshire' tea towel. I watched the face of Robert Burns take a mashing.

'I fought Fascism in two world wars,' continued Grandpa. 'I say this to the establishment – keep your medals! Just give me an inside toilet and a hot water tap.' He winked at Granny. 'And a real bath wouldn't go amiss either, eh?'

'He he, sit down, I'll get your dinner.'

Grandpa draped his cap over his chair. A fine coating of smooth, beige slurry covered its entirety. I fought an urge to lick it off.

'What's this? Is it for me?'

Grandpa had seen the flower on the table. He held it up in its plastic sheath.

The frying pan sizzled. Granny peered over her shoulder as she cracked an egg.

'Oh, that,' she said, all innocence. 'It was in Kathleen's pocket. It's a mystery how it got there – apparently.'

Granny whisked her attention back to the egg before Mother could deliver a steely stare.

'I'd better be going,' Mother said, rising.

'Don't forget about the overspill.'

'I won't. Come on, you.' Mother helped me off my chair.

'Is that you away, big fella?'

In accordance with the custom of the time, Grandpa Moss reached into his trouser pocket. I heard the thrilling jingle of change. He handed me a shiny sixpence.

Outside on the landing, Mother zipped me into my romper suit. Her hands were shaking.

'All that palaver over a wee flower,' she said. 'And there was nothing to it.'

But there had been something to it. And if my grandparents had asked me, I could have told them – Fred-Up-the-Stair had slipped that flower into Mother's pocket.

Just as they'd kissed and said goodbye.

Forty years later, I recalled the subject.

'Whatever happened to Fred-Up-the-Stair?'

'What do you mean?'

My hair was matted from the rain. I'd been to the chemist across the street on Paisley Road and had returned with a bagful of groceries and her prescription. Unpacking in the kitchen, I felt I was in good enough odour to tackle the thorny topic of my early memory.

'I was wondering.'

'Here we go. Give it a rest.'

'One of my first memories is of you and Fred. You were in the Harmony Bar.'

There was a pause. 'How could it be your first memory? You wouldn't be allowed into the Harmony Bar.'

'I notice you're not denying it.'

'What?'

'You and him.'

'You're as bad as your father.'

'So I imagined it then?'

'What?'

I took a breath. I'd been doing waggish cheeky chap acting to give myself the licence I needed. 'You kissing Fred-Up-the-Stair,' I said. 'As you came out of the Harmony Bar.'

She pulled a face, shook her head. 'You're mistaken.'

Maybe she was right. But this memory was deep rooted. If I couldn't trust the images on my mental hard drive, what could I trust? Then again, who was I to question my own memories? Which in turn begged the question 'Who indeed, am I?' My sense of self trundled like a ball bearing in a child's puzzle, looking for the hole called Home.

'You sure?' I asked, clutching at straws.

'Absolutely.' She looked up at me. 'It was Watson's Bar.'

'Ah,' I said.

'I'll take a co-codamol.'

I handed her the packet.

She fumbled to open a fresh sachet, struggled to break the tin-foil seal with her thumbnail to release a pill. I stood before her, holding a glass of water. It was true then; my mother had loins and desires. I tried not to think about her loins, even though, evidently, I had sprung from them.

I asked her if she felt like talking. No, she said, she was heading early to bed.

She did just that, leaving me to finish the tea I'd just made. I was about to head home when she shuffled back into the living room in her slippers. She was minus her teeth and clutching a hot water bottle.

'Yes,' she said.

'Yes, what?'

'I'd like to talk.'

I unbuttoned my coat.

* * *

Time passed. After the flower incident Fred stopped dancing and mother stopped singing. Father, alone, seemed happier.

'Man is born free but is everywhere in chains,' he announced, perkily, one day.

He was laid low with flu but high on Friars' Balsam. He felt expansive.

'Nice words,' said Mother. 'But the wean needs a uniform for starting school. I'm not having a boy of mine looking scabby.' Hearing my name invoked, I raised my head from the table where I'd stored it for convenience.

'Everybody round here's scabby,' countered Father. 'You think if we buy him a new blazer folk are going to think he commutes every day from Balmoral? Or Immoral, as I prefer to call it.'

Father twitched proudly at this rebellious extravagance. Mother was not impressed.

'That'll bring the monarchy down. A three-pound-a-week shop assistant calling them names.' Frustration had seen her lapse into the occasional unseemly outburst.

'You're getting very lippy these days.'

'Lippy my arse,' said Mother.

'That's being lippy,' I observed, helpfully.

'Shuttit!'

I took a whack to the head from Mother and mused on the contrariness of adults. A couple of years before she would have had everybody clustered around, cooing, to hear me say 'Uff-uff' – but having taken the trouble to utter a fully formed sentence, all I earned these days was a cuff on the cranium for cheek. A sore one it was too, the wee swine of a diamond on the engagement ring catching me above the ear. I'd considered an orgy of self-righteous tears – always an emotional delicacy – but resisted as it would only have caused a rumpus and I'd have missed *The Woodentops* on Children's Hour.

'I could take out a Provvy and we'll get him kitted out at Arnott's.'

'A Provident line,' sneered Father. He was the only man in Govan who used all three syllables in 'Provident'.

'If you don't like it, Carnegie,' sneered Mother, 'then show us your wallet.'

Father was silent. He could not oblige. His wallet consisted of a trouser pocket, lightly weighted with fluff, loose change and a pawn ticket for two minor medals, awarded for the Atlantic crossings.

'A Provident line it is,' he conceded, 'but I'm not happy about it.'

Eight

So it was that, clad in grey gabardine and an overlong blazer, I commenced my education.

'Are you nervous, wee Ivan?'

'No. And stop calling me wee.'

'Do you want to blow your nose?'

'Do I have a cold?'

'No.'

'Then why would I want to blow my nose?'

'You're not nervous? I'm nervous.'

'Then blow your own nose.'

Thus, according to the stopped clock of memory, went our conversation as we stood by the open gates of Fairfield Primary. We were waiting for the headmistress, Miss Highgate, to toll her hand bell, signalling the first day of my ten-year custodial sentence. As the exchange above indicates, I was, like many a five-year-old, already a keen student of loathsome unpleasantness.

'Ach, it's just bravado,' opined a female voice, loudly, next to Mother. I looked up to see a Fat Article give a slobbering laugh. 'I've had five weans and sure they're all the same – on the first day, nothing but cheek! But he'll be blubbing away for his mammy, soon as your back's turned, you mark my words!'

I looked the Article up and down. Great loose dugs flapped under her cardigan as she gave my carefully plastered hair a senseless ruffle. *in Glesca? No.*

'Isn't that right, Mr Pucker Chops? Look at his wee chops pucker!' A great pink face hovered before me. I stood firm against the onslaught of flesh.

The Article turned to my mother. 'Is he always like that?'

'Always,' conceded my mother. 'Never a smile out of him.'

The two beamed down at me, with their cloying maternal grins. Myself, Mr Pucker Chops, gazed resolutely back.

Miss Highgate tolled the bell in a brisk fashion. Swift downward strokes, like whipping a donkey.

The many mothers looked one to another. Each pulled her own personal 'well, this is it' expression.

'Fair takes you back, doesn't it?'

'It does that.'

'Seems like only yesterday it was us.'

'I wish, says you.'

'Ha ha!'

'He he!'

The hand bell pealed again – time to muster.

The mothers choked back tears and stooped to administer last hugs and reassuring words to their lost-looking, cherished issue.

Mine too.

But I was already up and away on my spiteful infant toes, heading for the straggling queues of fellow inmates. Once in line, a backward glance gave me the conclusion I craved. I saw Mother standing alone, looking gratifyingly wretched, my Fry's Chocolate Cream play piece held pathetically in her grasp.

It was, of course, a hard sacrifice on my part to refuse it. But a principle was a principle.

Siding with that Fat Article indeed; and on her wee man's first day of school.

Let that be a lesson.

Each partitioned classroom held around fifty pupils, and to infant eyes the chief impression was of a sea of dull brown desks, horizoned by forbidding walls. Those occupying desks near at hand became instant friends whereas others who dwelt in distant lands over by the radiator or toward the window facing Fairfield Street were as remote as the Inuit in their igloos. Everyone looked poor – we all wore darned jumpers and defeated expressions but, as in everything, there were varying levels. Broadly speaking, there were three categories of urban deprivation – Respectable Poverty, Pathetic Poverty and Christ, Would You Look at That, Poverty.

On the first morning, Miss Wren, our teacher, introduced herself. Then she introduced us to the Almighty. This was the first time I'd ever prayed. It seemed a peculiarly one-sided and grovelling conversation, consisting of sustained and unremitting flattery on our part and blind indifference on the Almighty's. No matter how lengthily we extolled his virtues, he refused to offer as much as a 'well thanks very much' or 'half of that would've done' in return.

Looking back, I do not blame him, as sycophancy encourages bad character traits on both sides and is best resisted.

Intelligence, strikingly, appeared to have been allotted by the Silent One according to income. Although we'd all started out together, the Respectable Poor held a near monopoly of ignorance. I was comfortably located in the Pathetically Poor section and could be relied upon to thrust my snotty sleeve into the air and answer questions incorrectly but not laughably so. Mirth lay in the gifts of the Christ, Would You Look at That, Poverty freak show and they were to brighten many a dreary afternoon of simple grammar or elementary geography with their entertaining repertoire of muttering, bawling and crass stupidities.

God being Love, as well as Silence, he would toss us the odd anomalous human wreck to prove his ways were not only mysterious but brutally unfair. One such was Harry Crawgie. Harry was one of nature's finest examples of Christ, Would You Look at Thatness. To compound his misfortune, Harry's intelligence was of the higher grade Pathetic Poverty standard, which meant that he would be forever cursed with an unhelpful measure of self-awareness.

Harry in his rags was a heart-rending sight to behold – at first. After a while, he became a great big laugh and I tell you this, some of the concoctions he came in wearing would have had Mother Teresa, St Francis of Assisi, and the Pope and all his cardinals pitching forward for a good old thigh-slapping guffaw. If you think this an inappropriate response to the misfortunes of another, I give you three words – net curtain underpants.

I kid you not, a charity worker with a misguided sense of priorities, or perhaps a keen sense of humour, had passed some old netting to Harry's mother. No doubt the Crawgie *mère* had tugged a dutiful forelock then, with her benefactor safely away, had looked up at the wooden boards on her broken windows, thought 'fuck that' and promptly adapted the net for more pressing purposes. Harry denied that his underpants were curtains, strenuously and to the point of tears. But it was the days of short trousers and well, when he ran around the gym they'd peek out like a wee border from under his breeks and by the time we started doing tumbles on the rush matting they'd be halfway down his thighs. These were curtains and no mistake. On cold days, you'd tell him to close them to cut the draught.

Harry's life was bad but, because every little helps, I did my part by making it worse. Not out of naked malevolence, just simple pique.

It happened like this: the subject was arithmetic. The practice of Miss Wren was to write out sums on the blackboard. We would then copy the sums into our exercise books and attempt to solve them. Having grappled to the best of our ability, or inability, with these conundrums, we would exchange exercise books with the person seated to our right. Miss Wren would then demonstrate the correct answers on the board. Each pupil would thus mark his peer's efforts. Harry Crawgie at that time sat across the aisle from me. So I exchanged with Harry. As his social superior, it was my confident expectation that my intelligence would prove in advance of his and that he would not disturb the natural harmony of the universe by recording any correct answers to questions I may, inadvertently, have answered wrongly. But that is what happened. And when it did, I upheld the honour of the status quo by working my pencil furtively over Harry's work so that his solution to the fractional problem under discussion became not the correct 'one quarter' but the incorrect 'three quarters'. When his book was returned to him, Harry perused it before leaping to his feet in protest.

'Miss! Please, miss! Miss Wren!'

'What is it, Crawgie?'

'Miss, Ivan Moss changed one of my answers!'

'Sit down, boy.'

'But he did, miss, he did!'

As tears of injustice smarted at his eyes, I sat with my hands clasped in wounded dignity, letting Harry Crawgie rail on.

'He's a cheat, miss!'

I looked away, with the restrained contempt of superior breeding.

'That's enough, Crawgie!' shouted Miss Wren. 'Sit down!'

'I know why he did it, miss, I know!'

'Sit down now!' warned Miss Wren, her voice crackling with menace.

Crawgie sat.

'Now tell me, Ivan, what was Harry's mark?'

'Eleven out of twenty, miss,' I said evenly, inviting her to make her own assessment. Which was to say, my assessment.

'There, Crawgie, you see? Eleven! What would Moss have stood to gain by changing your answer by a single point? Scoring twelve instead of eleven would hardly have made you a mathematical genius, would it?'

A wave of licensed laughter washed around the room. The wave drenched Harry Crawgie where he sat, looking dejected. He gave a whimper. It sprang from exasperation not self-pity. He knew he couldn't win, though right was on his side. He had been shown his place in life. The whimper was acceptance of that place. When he muttered, 'It's because of my pants,' I pretended not to hear.

At playtime, I received the sympathy that was my due from several of my fellows.

One or two, the mean-minded, gave me suspicious looks, which I rose above, through natural grace.

I was a bad boy, it's true, sneaky and cruel, but I discovered an ability to dismiss these failings with surprising ease. When you win at anything, even through foul means, you can't help feeling blessed, as if it's God's reward for enterprise. On such delusions are great empires founded; small ones, too. I scored twelve, incidentally. One more than Crawgie, which proved God must have loved me better.

So there.

Other life lessons followed, in quick succession.

'You see him?' asked Shivram Singh, one dull afternoon in the playground. 'That's Bannon, the best fighter in the school.'

For something to do, I had formed a queue, on my own, and Shivram had joined it. Even in those days, Govan was a haven of harmonious integration and we, its citizens, blind to racial prejudice. Thus, as a result of post-war complexity, we had Pakis, Tallys, Yids, Polaks, you name it, all under our broad Proddy roof. No Catholics, though: charity ends at home.

We watched in awe as Bannon swaggered past, trailed by swarthy hench-boys. All hard men love to be looked at, so that they can grunt 'What are you looking at?' as they pass. And we, the weaker members of the herd, would glance prudently away, fearful of a mauling. This, though, is not one of the life lessons to which I alluded. Bear with me while I draw a red pen through the unedited scroll of memory.

There now, it's done, and we are back in the playground perhaps a year later. In our class was a boy called Hutton. I do not know his first name. Since his parents were Christ, Would You Look at That poor, perhaps they could not afford one. I will call him Alec. But his family, collectively, were not known by any individual names. If you saw them in the street, mother, father, the seven or so children, you'd just say, 'There go the Huttons.' When I say they were Christ, Would You Look at That poor, I do not exaggerate. Here is an example.

I once observed a small-to-medium Hutton returning with his mother from the shops. The mother was negotiating a dented pram that had a wheel missing and there were four other Huttons of assorted sizes trailing behind her at regular intervals. The small-to-medium Hutton was skipping by the pram and clapping his hands as he went. As we closed on each other I heard his small-to-medium voice chant in gleeful rhythm to his own clapping. The chant went like this – '*We've got jam . . . We've got jam . . . We've got . . .*'

To any right-thinking person, the poignancy of that utterance is undeniable. The seismic rumble of its social message is strong enough to stir the most lethargic breast and stop every clock in Britain.

But my reaction was not edifying. I laughed helplessly. In fact, to be frank, I pissed myself. For the moment was hilarious. The highest aspiration in Huttondom, it seemed, wasn't for an Oxbridge scholarship, or a sumptuous semi-detached villa in Ralston, but to possess a pot of ten-penny jam from Galbraith's store. Ah, such piquant ludicrousness. And then the look on those Hutton faces at seeing me chortle. Hurt, they glowered like wounded beasts. Their fragile joy had been crumpled to dust. The family jailer, Poverty, had for a moment rattled the key in the lock, only for me to snatch it from his hand and hang it back on the hook.

'*We've got jam . . . We've got . . .*' Ha ha, what larks!

My laughter echoes down the corridors of time to haunt me.

I am mature now and shamed by my younger self. Tempered by experience, my reaction would these days be different – I'd wait till they were round the corner, then I'd piss myself. If this seems heartless, bear in mind that the key word in the above description is 'helplessly'. What could I have done about it? In Govan, sarcasm was our blues. I use the collective term 'our' because the Huttons, too, had been conditioned by want. As the school hard man Bannon was to discover in the playground, on the fateful day he confronted Alec, the eldest Hutton.

Alec was a typical example of the Hutton breed in that he rarely spoke and seldom mingled.

I do not recall what personal sleight or breach of honour had prompted Bannon to demand the satisfaction of fisticuffs. What I do retain is a picture of Hutton standing with his back to the wall, being cheeked and lipped by the usual Bannon minions. I recall the dourness of the Hutton demeanour, his lack, as he was taunted, of any nervous movement. Hutton's hands were at his sides, still. Or, more accurately, ready. I see Bannon, construing this stillness, as I had done, for frozen fear and becoming emboldened enough to lunge forward and throw the opening punch at Hutton. I then see Bannon's closed fist glance from its target, grazing hair, and he, the feared Bannon, the bully, the puncher, suddenly pinned against the wall by the lapels of his jerkin. And the change in Bannon's expression from surprise to apprehension – not fear, there wasn't time for that – because his white face had become quickly spattered with red as first his nose burst, then his mouth while Hutton, with his free hand, thudded blow upon ferocious blow into the undefended features of his opponent, knocking teeth clean, or more specifically, messily, out. 'Help . . . help me . . .'

I recall Bannon's unseemly shouts for his minions as he kneeled on the ground on all fours being kicked in his face with his head jerking backwards spraying blood, his neck a twanging spring. But the minions didn't help. Not even when we saw the pulp of Bannon's nose being rubbed against the rough of the asphalt in the playground gutter did any of us attempt to assist him. Even when the shout became a wail and the wail became a gurgling howl of 'Mammy, Daddy, stop . . . Please stop . . .'

I blushed with reflected shame when I heard Bannon cry 'Please'. It was a word which, in all my years of polite schoolboy society, I'd never heard uttered. It told me I was now in a place beyond the familiar playground scrap. Beyond fear, lay curiosity and we watched, mesmerised. For the first time, I was in the Land-Behind-the-Laugh, a strange, unsettling, oddly sexual country to which Alec Hutton, the poorest of the poor, had provided a chartered jet.

It took two teachers to dislodge Hutton from his prey; one of whom, Mr Mullen, required a half-moon of stitches to his palm, following a chomp.

A special meeting was convened at which Miss Highgate and her staff debated how best they might deal with this savage force of nature that had erupted in their midst. Approved school was discussed as was psychiatric counselling. In the end they made Hutton a milk monitor. It was an effective move. From that day forward, bottles were always returned on time to the crate. Many were still half full and warm from terror. And the lesson I learned? Simple; if you loose a tiger, better kill it before it kills you.

There was light relief also. Not long afterwards our elderly neighbour, Mrs Doherty, was found rigid in her armchair. Nowadays, with the sad demise of community values, the mortal remains of old persons can lie in their homes undiscovered for months. But I speak of a more social time and Mrs Doherty was missing for a mere three days before the police broke the door down to discover her sitting upright, teacup on her lap, forever fixed in the act of dunking a bourbon biscuit.

Mother pretended to be grave but her woe seemed to me somewhat on the exuberant side.

This impression was given substance by the fact that I was allowed to skip across the floor, bang a saucepan drum and bounce up and down on my parents' bed; all without reproach.

On the morning of the funeral, I looked out to see all the blinds in the street drawn in homage.

In the fifties a death was the next best thing to Christmas, providing an unexpected bonus of glee to children. A funeral was more fun than a wedding since the bounty it conferred was richer in texture. For a wedding, you waited for the cars to depart then you fought over the fistful of coins, or 'scramble' that the guests would throw out for good luck en route to the church or registry office. The benefits of bereavement were not fiscal but nonetheless material.

'What time is Mrs Doherty's funeral?' I asked Mother, over the morning porridge.

'Three o'clock, why?'

'No reason,' I said.

The cortège slid into the street. Neighbours huddled around the close mouth, pretending to weep, presumably to take the bad look off their nosiness. I and a gang of like-minded seven-year-olds looted the midden area for the more entertaining of the deceased Mrs Doherty's former possessions.

Among the spoils was a set of false teeth wrapped in newspaper, which I took out and wore instantly, out of showmanship. There were old letters and saved cards from forgotten Christmases, also bits of elderly person's jewellery – heavy dull brooches and the like, necklaces that looked like horse harnesses and those earrings with tiny paste jewels which to a boy's eyes look like scabs. The girls fought over such dainties while we males hauled out Mrs Doherty's folded mattress and undid the old window sash cord with which it had been carefully tied.

Joan Hebbie, who lived up the stairs, and was always lucky, found a bag with big granny specs inside, then Margaret Cogan with the lazy eye shrieked out 'Yes!' on uncovering an umbrella. Until then I had never seen an umbrella in the wild, far less touched or stroked one and believed them to exist only in the rarefied atmosphere of film or television. While we were grouped in a circle, fondling it respectfully, Joan, a tomboy who a year later would be showing you it for threepence, approached from Margaret's blind side and made a grab for the brolly. But I was slyer and faster than her. 'You'll get your turn,' I told Joan, shielding the umbrella behind my back.

We positioned the mattress on the ground below the roof of the midden shed. I put on Old Doherty's big specs and, making an approximate parachute of the umbrella, took a flying leap off the roof onto the mattress below. Not to be outdone, Joan dredged from the bin a black Sunday hat with a broken feather and was about to put it on her head before discovering it reeked of cat piss, so planted the hat on my head instead. What with the false teeth, the big specs and the Sunday hat with the broken feather, I fancied that I cut a dashing figure around the Govan back courts. I quickly became a sort of human maypole around which everybody danced and yelled.

Inside the entrance, I could see black-clad mourners carrying the coffin in shuffling reverence round the awkward bevel of the lower stairwell. They had to step over a drunken man to do so. Every dunny held a drunk man in those days, as a sort of non-paying guest. We children became charged with hysteria. Such was our rackety glee that Father appeared in the back court looking severe and demanding calm.

'Cut that noise now. Show some respect for the dead!'

I tried to reply but was afflicted by a paralysing speech disorder. I removed the false teeth and was cured.

'But, Father,' I pleaded, 'we've found an umbrella!'

Father grimaced, signifying imminent wisdom.

'Let me see.' Father looked the umbrella over. A sophisticated man of the world, he handled it confidently, without trepidation.

We clustered around him. I felt proud. 'This is a man's umbrella,' he explained, expertly. 'Observe the thickness of the handle; the length of the shaft. It must have belonged to old Mr Doherty before he died.'

I removed the cat-piss hat and fingered the brim, reverently. I had been a paratrooper when jumping off the shed roof but now I was a cowboy at Boot Hill. 'Dust to dust,' I said, having seen them say it often on *Wyatt Earp*. Everybody mumbled, 'Dust to dust,' including Joan Hebbie in the big specs. I made a vulgar fluttering noise through my lips and made my legs wobble.

People looked at me, puzzled.

'It's my horse,' I explained. 'He's hungry. He ain't eaten since Abilene. Guess I'll have to stop at the Feed and Grain store then I best be moseying up to El Paso.'

There was a brief lull in the conversation while I trotted my non-existent horse around in a little circle. I didn't reach El Paso, though.

'Ivan,' warned Father.

I nodded. I had a tendency to take a thing too far.

Father fixed two thin chrome spokes that had dislodged in flight and, raising the umbrella to its intended purpose, created a fine unbroken circle, no longer approximate. We gasped, as though it was a firework display.

Father was pleased. He smiled his rare smile at us and looked for once young. A moment later, a shout rang out from above our heads.

'Hey, Gene fucking Kelly!'

Father looked up. His brow darkened. A ragged tongue of glinting water poked rudely from a white pail, splashing Father's head and spraying the rest of us with droplets.

'Now give us "Singing in the Rain"!' yelled Fred-Up-the-Stair. His eyes were glinting madly; his face was flushed with drink.

Though damp of head, Father met Fred's gaze steadily. Fred lost his nerve and shut the window with a bang.

With my child's instinct, I knew Fred wished he hadn't done the water thing. With hindsight, I'd guess he still missed Mother and couldn't help himself.

'Look everybody.'

Father stepped apart to let us see him better. Though dripping, he began flashing the umbrella in and out, in short staccato bursts.

'Morse code,' I informed the group.

'This is what we called on ship "sight signalling". Does anybody know what I'm saying with this umbrella?'

'SOS, Father,' I said, proudly. 'Three dots, three dashes, three dots.'

'That is correct,' said Father. 'I am sending out the international distress signal.'

'Why?' Joan Hebbie asked, not unreasonably.

Father had no answer. He was just soaked and internationally distressed. He lowered the umbrella, then his head. For some reason, I took his hand.

To cheer ourselves up we stood at the close mouth and watched the funeral cortège depart.

As a mark of respect, I wore the teeth.

One day, Miss Wren was handing out marks. I was in a daydream, or 'dwam' as they're known popularly in Glasgow, and paying scant attention. Outside, open lorries laden with tenement rubble lumbered up and down Fairfield Street. A gauze of dust on the windows accentuated our hemmed horizons. The homing bird of melancholy settled in my soul. Miss Wren droned on.

'The silver star goes to Margaret Cogan. And the gold star to . . .'

A rude elbow nudged my gloom to one side. 'Get up,' said Rory McGrath who sat next me.

'What?'

I looked around. Everyone was looking at me, looking at them.

'You've won the gold star.'

Impelled by the demands of the occasion, I stood up.

'A very good essay,' said Miss Wren.

She peeled a dot of gold from a backing sheet and jabbed it onto the top corner of my A4 page. when was this? Anachronism.

Upon Miss Wren's instruction, my peers applauded. Some

with mimed fakery, others with reluctance, true, but I soaked it up, nonetheless.

I felt walls collapse; my swimming head adjusted to a strange new vista. What was this glittering new planet whose seductive orbit I had just entered?

I'd call it 'Approval'.

Granny Moss felt walls collapse too. Where mine were inner, hers were outer.

Govan was changing. True to her word, Granny stood firm against the council's entreaties to quit her home. When they served her a writ, she lit the fire with it. But progress was not to be thwarted and when Corporation workmen knocked down her house in Golspie Street, Granny found herself inconvenienced since she was still in it at the time. Once the huge mechanical swing ball and scraping claw had done their appointed business, and the gritty billow of choking dust had risen then settled, she found herself minus a living-room wall and occupying centre stage in the unexpected proscenium arch of her own front room.

Summoned by the noise, an audience of children, of whom I was one, gathered hastily below and waited to be entertained. I see Granny M yet, in the theatre of my mind's eye, clutching a pan at the cooker, forever frozen in the attitude of shaking the grease from chips. There was a bottle of brown sauce on the table, I remember, and a flop of pink Spam hung over the rim of my grandfather's plate, pending his arrival.

Granny Moss being what she was, whatever she was, it did not take her long to recover her composure. Abandoning Grandpa's chips to the hiss and sizzle of the still-hot fat, she fetched a brush from the lobby and began sweeping debris from the room out onto the mighty blocks of tumbled sandstone below.

'What are you all looking at?'

We shuffled. Being products of the fifties, we had never seen a house with its front off and had no vocabulary for the occasion. In the hiatus, we attempted to make a withdrawal from the memory bank of shared experience. Finding little deposited therein, I found myself speaking for my fellows.

'We don't know what we're looking at, Granny Moss! We've never seen this before!'

Granny M narrowed her eyes and scanned the growing throng. 'Is that you, Ivan?'

I slid behind the gnarled monolith of big Mrs Boyd, a large, conveniently stooped arthritis victim, and peeked out in a skulking fashion.

'Ivan?'

A loosened lump of wall dropped lazily from the arch framing the remains of the living room. We gasped as it hit the ground in a puffing cloud of magician's dust.

'Stop hiding,' yelled Granny M, 'and get help!'

I did not get help. Instead, we squatted down, we boys, on our hunkers.

Though we had not experienced war, we were acquainted with its peacetime equivalent – pantomime. Many of us were Life Boys, and had already survived several harrowing tours of duty to the Glasgow Empire where the enemy, Walter Carr, the Joseph Goebbels of Scottish comedy, had attempted to crush our collective will with his relentless onslaught of morale-sapping jests.

As a result of our stern training, we knew that where there was a plate of food upon a table, a major character would swell a progress by coming in to eat it. So it was, on hearing the cistern on the lobby landing flush, we tensed in anticipation. When Grandpa Moss made his entrance, braces at waist, paper in hand, we cheered wildly. He obliged us at once by reeling back in astonished horror as he surveyed, through the picture window where his living-room wall had once been, the small but appreciative audience huddled down below. Raising his eyes, he confronted the breezy vista of the Elder Park, and further still the hunched shoulders of the Campsie hills. It was all too much for Grandpa Moss. He swayed from the slippers up. His newspaper fluttered to what was left of the floor. Granny swept on, oblivious.

'Behind you!' we grizzled panto veterans cried.

Granny gazed back at us, baffled. 'Eh?'

'Behind you, Granny, behind you!'

Granny Moss looked behind her. But Grandpa Moss was now staggering about in front of her.

Unable to comprehend the magnitude of what had happened to his house, Grandpa inched toward the non-existent wall, feeling with groping hands, as if the new and inexplicable view might reveal itself as some enormous painted mural.

'What's happened?' His mouth was agape and his speech breathless. 'Where's the wall gone?'

It was at that moment I saw Grandpa swoon, lose his footing and topple headlong onto the rubble many feet below. The audience drew a sharp collective breath as he hit the stony ground.

We boys sped forward for a better view. Grandpa was motionless. His *Daily Worker* flapped at his head. 'Look – blood.'

The man with the swing ball jumped down from his cabin. Snapping into decisive action, he lit up a fag.

'It's your own fault, missus,' he said, tapping the roll-up on his shag tin. He was feigning indifference but his voice trembled with the fear of litigation. 'You were warned what would happen if you stayed,' he said. 'Everybody else moved out last month.' Feeling the authority of this phrase on his lips, he turned to the crowd. 'Everybody else moved out last month,' he repeated.

Granny Moss looked at Grandpa then narrowed her angry eyes. 'You've murdered him!'

'Rubbish.'

All the same, the swing ball man balled Grandpa's *Daily Worker* and tucked it under his head, doubtless feeling the gesture of concern would play well at any trial.

The moving of his head made Grandpa stir slightly.

'Ivan – get an ambulance,' shouted Granny Moss. 'Run!'

I ran, obediently, aimlessly, this way and that. As I did, I remember wondering where they kept the ambulances.

Grandpa Moss was in hospital for a month.

Mother cried on the day she took me to see him. I cried for being obliged to go. I'd wanted to stay home and watch Robert Shaw as Captain Dan Tempest in *The Buccaneers*. So we walked, crying for our different reasons, along the corridors of the hospital, slaloming our way through the two-way traffic of cleaners, porters and laden trolleys bearing the hollow-cheeked and helpless victims of the healing arts.

Before we entered the ward, Mother made a corkscrew from the corner of a hanky and probed my drizzling nostrils with it. While doing so, she warned me that Grandpa was no longer as I had known him and that I should prepare myself for a shock. I felt a small firework of hopeful glee create a sunburst in my soul.

'How bad is he?'

'You'll see.'

Disappointingly, we found Grandpa sitting upright in bed, albeit looking slightly bewildered. The scrape of our chairs roused him from his waking trance and he turned woozily to my mother.

'Is that you, Maidie?'

I heard my mother's voice give a little catch before she answered. 'No, it's me, Kathleen.'

'Kathleen? I don't know any Kathleen.'

'Yes you do. I'm Ivan's wife.' Mother's lower lip trembled.

'Your daughter-in-law.' Mother clutched her throat at the aching poignancy of Grandpa's bewildered look.

I scrutinised my grandfather for signs of fraudulence. People are always playing to the gallery. The only visible evidence of an altered state was that Grandpa's rude mane of coarse grey hair had been shaved to the pink from the middle of his head out to the left ear, whereas the right side retained intact its former follicular glory. Half a head of hair may have been an indicator of mental aberration but it hardly offered conclusive proof.

'What did the doctors say?' Mother pressed, gently.

'They say I'll make a full . . . They say there won't be any . . .'

'Any what?'

'Change. Except that I . . .'

'Yes?'

'Except that I . . .'

'Go on,' pressed Mother, still gently.

'Except that I canny finish a . . .' His voice trailed off.

Mother and I looked at each other.

'Can't finish a what?' she asked.

She gave Grandpa's hand a helpful squeeze lest he retreat again into Trance Castle and pull up the drawbridge.

'Sandwich?' I provided, helpfully.

Grandpa shook his head. The remaining half of his cow's lick haircut jiggled on his forehead.

'I canny finish a . . .'

Mother tried. 'Cigarette?'

Again, a sad shake of Grandpa's grey head.

This was turning into fun. I sensed opportunities for anarchy.

'Gazelle?'

Mother, on flippancy alert, nipped insurrection in the bud with a hostile look.

'Take your time,' she said.

Which he did. Ours too.

'Sentence,' said Grandpa at last.

'What?'

'Kathleen, sweetheart, I canny finish a . . .'

'He can't finish a sentence!'

I roared it out victoriously, like we were playing a parlour game. I sat back in my chair, swinging my legs, looking pleased with myself. Here was us, too poor to own a parlour, yet here was me, born to lowly menial stock, guessing it all the same.

'Be quiet, Ivan.'

So it was that Grandpa made a full recovery from his head knock, except that he could no longer finish a.

On the day Granny M collected Grandpa M from hospital, the wrecking crew seized the opportunity to knock down what remained of their home. Granny was compelled at last to uti-lise the keys of the two-bedroom retirement flat in Penilee into which the Housing Corporation had hitherto and without suc-cess been trying to corral her.

Grandpa hated the isolation of the new flat but loved the nov-elty of having a balcony. He would climb onto the parapet and threaten to fling himself off. Then Granny M would bring out a nice bacon sandwich and place it on the wee table by the french windows and Grandpa would forget he was unhappy and climb down to eat. Embracing his reduced status, he threw himself into the role of invalid. A taciturn man, his conversation be-came terser – that's if a short speech can grow longer by the interposing of silences. Should the silences be said to be part of the conversation or did they stand independently from it? It depended how you measured sentences and the spaces between the words. Granny's conversation suffered too. Thus, Sunday evening tea became a nightmare of tedium.

'Maidie, pass me a.'

Granny would stare at him. 'A what?'

'Pass me a.'

Granny did her best, but her impatience would soon explode. You could see it coming. With each incorrect suggestion she would rock back and forth on her chair, muttering with growing agitation, until finally she could take no more. She'd slap her palms down hard onto her knees, shoot to her feet and yell, 'For God's sake, everybody – help me out!'

Suffering a ban of silence, I'd be condemned to watch the adults grope in their minds until the floodgates of suggestion were thrown open wide.

'Slice of bread?'

'No.'

'Newspaper?'

'No.'

'What then?'

'A fork.'

'You've got a fork. It's in your hand.'

'That's a . . .'

'Knife. Yes. But the other one's a fork. You're holding your cutlery in the wrong hands.'

'Ah.'

Respect for Grandpa's revised status was tested, and only narrowly prevailed.

'Call yourself a man?' Granny would chide. 'When I ask you a question, answer me!'

'I can't answer you, Maidie, I can't finish a . . .'

'Sentence, I know. But all I need is one word.'

'That's no help, some sentences are only one.'

'One what? Word?'

'Yes. You see, that was an.'

'Example?'

'Yes.'

Miserable in her new abode, with a dented stranger for a husband, Granny could not rest until she had made those around her miserable too. Mother grew to dread visiting.

'Kathleen, have you heard anything yet from the Housing Corporation?'

'No, Maidie.'

'Have you written to them?'

'Yes, Maidie.'

'I'll give them a call myself.'

'There's no need.'

'I'll get you living out here beside me, you mark my words. You'd like that, wouldn't you? We would be neighbours.'

I'd watch Mother's forced smile. If I listened closely, I could almost hear the brass band playing 'Abide With Me' as her heart sank below the waterline.

Nine

One day we were on Clachan Drive, Mother and I, having visited Granny and Grandpa Moss. We were walking home, as usual, to save bus fares.

'You don't want to move from Govan, do you, Mother?' I said.

'I never said that. Anyhow, you shouldn't have been listening.'

'How could I have been listening if you didn't say it?'

'Shut up. Any more cheek and you'll get a whack.'

To entertain me, Mother started talking about her old job at Skirling Jock's. She told me how much she missed it. I had heard all her stories many times. On Langlands Road, a bus pulled up beside us. It seemed like providence. That's in so far as providence ever bothered with people like us.

'That's a fifty-five,' I said. 'It goes to Hillington.'

'So?'

'Skirling Jock's is in Hillington. You could go there.'

'Why would I want to go there?'

'Because you never shut up about it.'

Mother gave me an incredulous look. I recoiled, anticipating a whack.

The conductor tinged the bell. On an impulse, Mother

yanked my hand, firmly. We found ourselves on the bus, sitting on the long seat, by the door.

'I meant you could go, not me. I want to go home.'

'Quiet, Ivan. One and a half, please.'

So it was, after ten long years, Mother found herself standing again outside Skirling Jock's biscuit factory. 'This is where Mammy used to work,' she explained.

'Yes,' I said.

I gazed up at this place of myth, a nondescript building of red brick, with latticed steel barring its squat windows. I looked at Mother. I could see that Skirling Jock's remained a haunt of yearning reverence in her mind. A sweet aroma, thicker than women's scent, filled the air. 'What's that smell?' I asked.

'Caramel.'

Saying the word made Mother give a little heartfelt gasp. She looked all around; anywhere but into my eyes.

'I was happy here,' she said. 'And I didn't know it.'

A hooter sounded its tinny racket, splitting our souls like an axe through wood. Women in turbans and black welly boots cascaded onto the street, chattering and reaching for cigarettes. I watched Mother. Everything about her, her thrilled smile, her fixed and shiny eye, told me she yearned to rush forward and greet these women. Her actions, though, were in open contradiction to her feelings and she even took a sideways step, yanking us both under the canopy of a tree shadow where she might remain unseen, to lurk and look.

Perhaps not quite unseen.

'Kathleen? Kathleen!'

One of the turbans was waving at us. I heard Mother mutter, 'Hell.'

'Who's that?'

'Your aunt Celia.'

I had seen Celia before, of course. Transformed by the miracles of permed hair, lipstick, make-up and heels, she'd looked exotically attractive. Now, bare of face and with a curled green rag on her head, she looked as ugly as everyone else. She hurried over.

'Hello, wee Ivan.'

'Hello, Auntie Celia.'

'My, he's getting big. Isn't he getting big, Kathleen?'

'Then why do you call me wee?'

Mother gave me one of her looks. It would mean a whack later, but I couldn't have let it pass.

'Wait till you hear the latest, Kathleen – Maureen Bain's married.'

'No? Maureen Bain?'

'Yes! And Sandra McCaskill. And Alice Middleton. And Lorna Black's engaged.'

'Not wee Lorna!'

'To a lathe operator at Babcock's. They met at—'

Having performed my social duty with Aunt Celia, I allowed my eyes to wander up and down the street. Brick factory bunker followed bunker, with from each the spill of anonymous worker drones in their grimy boiler suits on allotted ten-minute tea breaks. I peered through one of the darkened doorways and heard a cacophonous world, mottled with silent, scuttling worker shadows.

'You miss the factory, don't you, Kathleen?'

Mother nodded, reluctantly. 'Life was simple then.'

Aunt Celia permitted the implied criticism of her own brother, Kathleen's husband, to elude her mental grasp. 'There's a rumour Mr Jock might be taking on workers for night shift,' she said. 'Why don't you apply?'

'I can't. Nights are out of the question.' She gave a nod in my direction, indicating the nature of the obstacle.

'How about evenings?'

'Ivan likes his tea on the table.'

While they were mulling over the weighty matter of Father's tea, a sleek sedan car slid past the raised shutter gates of the factory and stopped by the office doorway. A uniformed chauffeur appeared and held open the rear door.

I watched, startled, as a lady's shapely legs were followed by the no less shapely rest of her. She was wearing a pale blue dress with white spots. She had blonde hair and a hat and, when a little breeze blew, she held the hat down with her hand. Holding her hat down meant she forgot to hold her dress down too and, thanks to that little breeze, I saw more of the lady's legs than she might have wished. I felt a lump of desire spring to my throat.

The lady was like ice cream and not just any old ice cream, the most select and sumptuous ice cream – a Strawberry Mivvi. I wanted to lick all the strawberry off the lady, right down to her Mivvi, slowly, voluptuously, then bite through her cream and deep down into her to suck till her Mivvi melted on my tongue and dribbled.

I was not alone in my desire. A row of sweaty machine-room men, sitting on the wall like boiler-suited crows, grinned silently as the lady approached. They, too, had contemplated her Mivviness. One of them, the most confident, with a tattooed forearm and a stiff Ed 'Cookie' Byrne quiff, sniffed the air exaggeratedly as the lady passed by. His mates grinned as he made a comment and the lady gave the faintest of ladylike smirks before turning her head back to the car. A young man, the same age as the quiff fellow, but smaller and softer, much smaller, much softer, and better dressed, had climbed out of the car. Obviously, this was the lady's escort. The chauffeur was stacking the escort's hands with bags from posh shops, House of

Fraser and Dunn and Company. Common stores, Galbraith's or Nicholl's, weren't in it, not for those sorts of hands. The soft-handed man wore a tweed suit and brown brogues. He stumbled as he stepped onto the pavement, dropping a bag into the gutter. Something pale and feminine, some underwear perhaps, peeked out from a folded square of tissue paper.

As the man squatted on his hunkers, the workmen crows did not snigger. A veteran of playground psychology myself, I realised that the men did not resist sniggering through kindness or empathy toward the man, rather the reverse. They resisted from cruelty. To have laughed would have broken the tension of the moment. And they wanted the tension of the moment taut and intact, as a judgement on the soft-handed man. And they wanted the lady to know their silent, scornful judgement. 'We have no money,' that silent judgement said, 'but we can suck your Mivvi, lady, much better than he ever will, that's if he even sucks it at all . . . Let me,' each pair of eyes seemed to say, 'be the one to taste your essence.'

I was so engaged with watching all the watching eyes that I failed to see my mother spring forward to help the man with his bags. With the soft feminine thing safely scooped and hidden in the tissue paper, the man bid Mother, 'Thank you.'

'You're welcome,' said Mother.

Speaking made their eyes meet. It was a day for the meeting of eyes. But these two sets of eyes held a tender mutual message unlike those others.

'Hello,' these kinder eyes seemed to say. 'Let me drink you in. It's been the longest time since we met each other's gaze and so much has happened, so much troubled water has passed below our different bridges.' That's what these eyes said. But their mouths didn't say that. Their mouths said:

'Goodness gracious. Kathleen?'

'Yes. Hello, Mr Jock.'

I watched Mother blush, demurely, a young girl again for a moment, not a mother.

'Johnny!' The lady was calling after her man, her escort, young Mr Jock.

'A moment, my dear,' called young Mr Jock.

The workmen crows sniggered now. It was the 'my dear' that did it. Calling your woman a thing like that. Totally stupid, I ask you; and wet, a wet wick. All the same, it took a sort of confidence to stand there and sing out a thing like that – 'My dear!' When they realised it took a confidence of a rare type which they did not possess, not even the one who tried to be Ed 'Cookie' Byrne, the workmen crows began to shamble away, dispersing.

'I'd better get back,' said Aunt Celia, for show. But Aunt Celia didn't move and young Mr Jock did not seem to notice her. It was the eyes thing again.

'You're married now, I hear,' said young Mr Jock. 'You must be very happy.'

Mother nodded. 'Yes, I must be,' she agreed.

Out of awkwardness, Aunt Celia guided me close, smoothed my hair. 'This is Ivan, Mr Jock, sir, Kathleen's son. Her husband is my brother.'

'Really?' said young Mr Jock.

He looked. He kneeled, so he could speak on my level. His trousers were tweedy and he smelled of girl.

'How old are you, Ivan?' asked young Mr Jock.

'He's eight,' provided Mother, instantly, fearing one of my moody silences.

'Listen to me, Ivan,' began young Mr Jock. He took my hand for emphasis. 'Never let anyone live your life for you. Be whatever you want to be, no matter what that is. Do you understand?'

I nodded respectfully. He deserved respect. He hadn't called me 'wee'.

'John-ny!'

The lady again. A harsher, more exasperated tone. We turned to look. For the benefit of any worker drones who might still be hanging around gawping, she'd assumed a good-natured 'what in heaven's name is he like' smile. But there was only us left. And we didn't know what he was like. Only young Mr Jock knew that. And he wasn't telling.

'Coming, dear!'

Young Mr Jock rose to his feet and looked again at Mother. He spoke earnestly, quickly. 'If you want to come back, Kathleen, let me know. So long as I'm at Skirling Jock's, there'll always be a job for you here.'

He hitched his expensive packages under his arm. His fine lady was holding the office door open for him. Young Mr Jock started off walking and then, being a gentleman, speeded up to a hasty trot. The door shut behind him and they were gone.

'Did you hear that,' thrilled Aunt Celia. 'You could walk back into your old job tomorrow.'

'Do you think I could?'

'Of course! Ask Ivan – how can he say no?'

The hooter jeered.

'I'd better go,' said Aunt Celia, 'or I'll be quartered.' She folded her arms, into the sleeves of her overall and ran in that dainty, scuttling way that welly-booted women did. At the gate, she turned back. 'You will ask Ivan, won't you?'

'I will,' Mother called back. 'I'll ask him.'

Mother was elated. Seizing the moment, I coaxed an Aero out of her at a nearby paper shop.

We'd barely reached the stop when a bus pulled up. It was our day; hers and mine.

* * *

Father was already home, seated at the table.

Mother took off her coat and gripped the back of a chair. She was breathing hard, barely able to contain her excitement.

'Ivan?'

Father looked up.

'I was out at Skirling Jock's today. I've some news.'

'So have I – you first.'

'I've been offered my old job back.'

A smile was frozen expectantly to Mother's lips. I don't know what her expectant smile expected of Father. Perhaps a grateful burst of Italian light opera.

He didn't speak. He dipped his hand into the fruit bowl on the table, took out a letter, a letter fruit and handed it to Mother.

'What's this?'

Father's face twisted into a grimace, signifying joy.

'Read it,' he said. 'It's from the Corporation.'

Mother eyed the brown envelope. She unpeeled the letter and read, silently.

'What is it, Mammy? What's up?' I was alarmed.

'Shush, Ivan!' She looked at Father.

'Dreichstane? Where the hell is Dreichstane?'

'In Renfrewshire. It's a lovely picturesque wee town by the arse end of Paisley. The offer is a flat, but it has two bedrooms and an inside toilet.' Rising quickly, Father pointed to the offer. 'We'd be mad to turn it down.'

'But, Ivan, I can have my old job back.' She tried to squeeze the hint of joy out of her voice. 'It'll mean extra money.'

'You're too late,' said Father. 'I've accepted.'

Mother gave him a hard stare. Father shifted his weight on his slipper-clad feet, hitched his crumpled trousers.

'Why did you do that?'

'Because.'

'Because isn't an answer,' I said. Father glowered. That was another one stored up for the whack drawer and no mistake.

'He's right,' protested Mother. 'Why didn't you ask me first?'

As if on cue, Fred-Up-the-Stair did a rapid, rhythmic toe tap on our ceiling, his floor. We could hear him singing 'Begin the Beguine'. The light shade did a jiggle dance on its chain.

'I have my reasons,' said Father, darkly.

On the appointed day, a crew of removal men uplifted our possessions, rumbled the thirteen miles to Dreichstane, then dumped them in a heap on the floor of our new home. Their feet clumped on the bare, clean boards and the sound echoed around the fresh walls which we were forbidden to paper for nine months till the new plaster dried properly out. Our battered furniture was deposited, more or less, into the rooms that accorded with function. Some smaller items went missing, never again to be seen – at least by us. Thus the Day of the Great Removal passed into family infamy. For decades afterwards my mother, under the mildest of promptings, would rage against those callous, gum-chewing crooks, those dust-sheet pirates, who had spirited away the tea chest containing her china ornaments, each one of which had been individually wrapped in its loving newspaper shawl of *Evening Times* or *Govan Press*. Depending on mood, I might remind her of the other chest that vanished that legendary day, the one that had held my collection of American comics – dozens of *Archies*, *Sad Sacks* and *Casper the Friendly Ghosts*, ruthlessly abducted and destined for the shady underworld of comicbook trading, forced to parade themselves luridly in lowlife bric-a-brac stalls, next to the broken hairdryers and bent toasting forks.

As a small child, I'd strained on tiptoes, my hands gripping the windowsill, to gaze out gloomily from the incarceration of our cramped Govan apartment. Life had changed; I now stood gazing out gloomily from the incarceration of our Dreichstane apartment. Back then, I had been too young to play outside. Now I was old enough but had no one to play with. There were no kids in our street. In fact, the estate was so new that there was no street in our street. The surface was of layered ash and stone, the workmen having barely begun the spreading of tarmac from the faraway sloping end of the crescent. Across our street with no street, lay a playground with no play area, a rough oblong of wilderness with weeds too long for ball games but too short for hiding in.

'Look, Ivan – come see your bedroom.'

I didn't respond to my mother's call. My short unhappy life had worsened and for ever. In Govan, I had enjoyed a certain status, was held in esteem by my peers. Had I not been the Wee Commander, organiser of bin raids, starter of meaningless queues? In Dreichstane, I didn't even have peers. 'No peers Moss,' that's what they'd call me. That's if collective misfortune ever gathered enough lost souls to this dust-strewn, weed-infested nowhere ever to comprise a 'they'.

'Kathleen?'

'What?'

'What kind of beds shall we get when the time comes? Single or bunk?'

'Bunk. We'd never squeeze two singles in there.'

My ears pricked up. By 'in there' my parents meant my room.

'I'm only me,' I said. 'Why would I need two beds?'

'You don't know?' Father replied, affecting astonishment. 'Then it's time you did – tell him.'

Mother sighed and patted her stomach. 'You're going to have company.'

Brainwashed by Hollywood protocol, Father gave Mother a clumsy hug. My parents smiled at each other, like people did in films. I feigned retching and father swung a leisurely boot in the direction of my rump. He sauntered to the door, clutching a hoe.

'Best make a start on the garden,' he said.

'Our garden,' said Mother.

I watched them squeeze each other's hands. They were absorbed in their roles of Nathan and Betsy, wholesome Midwest prairie couple, working the land together and praising the Lord for his bounty. An hour later Mother, which is to say Betsy the prairie wife, took Nathan out a tray of tea and Abernethy digestives. Nathan was nowhere to be seen, of course, having fucked off to the nearest boozer. The hoe stuck out at a limp angle from the earth. It pointed down the hill at the road to town.

It had plumb gone supper time when Nathan finally pitched up.

'Where have you been?'

'Wetting the baby's head.'

'It doesn't have a head yet, it's barely a foetus.'

'Don't split hairs.'

Mother ran into the bathroom and slammed the door in her rage, shattering its mottled glass panel. It was to cost eighteen and sixpence to replace that panel and as a result we had no fig rolls, newspapers or cornflakes for a fortnight.

I didn't see Nathan and Betsy around too often after that.

Ten

One day, tramping bored and alone through the plot of wood that skirted Elm Drive, I spied a boy hanging a dog from a tree. Having no pressing engagements, I decided to stop and watch. 'What's its name?' I asked, in a spirit of audience participation.

'Black Blob,' answered the boy.

I thought I had misheard. 'You mean Black Bob?' There was a famous collie dog character in the cartoons. His name was Black Bob. His owner and co-star, a dull, nondescript shepherd in a bunnet, was strictly a feed, in both senses.

'No, I mean blob.'

'Why did you call it that?'

'Because it's black and it stinks. Look, its belly's all swollen up.' The boy jabbed his forefingers into the bouncy bed of the dog's bloated stomach. This made the ligaments in Black Blob's hind legs attempt propulsion – but the paws were locked solid with rigor mortis and refused to jiggle.

'I think it's been dead a while,' said the boy, authoritatively. 'Come and sniff it.'

I approached with apprehension, fearing the dog might spring to life and start biting, or worse, licking me. I did not like animals, except in tins. Luckily, the dog was not up to shenanigans of either sort, and in truth looked quite poorly.

I saw for myself how poorly when I got close and spun it gently on its taut leather lead. Intestines spilled from its mangy fur and dead maggots fought with shrivelled live ones for the prize of its putrid flesh. A little red dog tongue drooped from between two rows of brown pointed teeth. Drops of dried, foamy spit still flecked the chin whiskers. I noted the frozen front paws. They were forever set at a poignant, expectant angle, awaiting a Pedigree Chum tin that was never to arrive.

The boy turned to me for my opinion.

'He's minging all right,' I attested.

'What's your name?' the boy asked.

'Ivan Moss.'

'Mine's Arthur Run-with-the-Buffalo McDonald.' He looked me boldly in the face. 'I was raised by Apaches.'

I nodded, accommodatingly.

Oh dear, I thought, he's still at that stage. I had been raised by Apaches myself, in my head at least. I had been obliged to abandon that particular fantasy when challenged by Joan Hebbie to display the ceremonial eagle-feathered headdress belonging to my father, Ivan Run-with-the-Bacon-Slicer. I was laughed to scorn when I told them it was at the cleaners.

Sensing my scepticism, Arthur Run-with-the-Buffalo recanted, swiftly.

'Just call me Arthur.'

We stood back and regarded the hanging dog, as though he were on display at an exhibition. All in all, Black Blob looked at peace with the world, notwithstanding he had been dragged, beaten and strung up by his own choke chain.

'I wonder who did it?'

'The Mad Jappa, likely,' said the boy. 'They're a gang. They run wild in the streets at all hours, except from four in the morning till seven.'

'Why is that?'

'The leader does a milk round.' Arthur was silent. Then he said, 'Do you ever wonder – you know, about life and death and all that kind of thing?'

My heart leapt joyously at the mention of death.

'Yes!' I exclaimed. 'Death and the stars and all that kind of thing! Where do the stars end? What lies beyond the planets?' I found myself growing animated. 'We live in a universe – it must end somewhere! But where?'

'I don't know,' admitted Arthur, shrugging. 'I can't even do compound fractions.'

I stopped worrying about the universe and started worrying about compound fractions.

Arthur looked the same age as me and yet he had heard of these strange new arithmetical puzzles and I hadn't. I was alarmed by my own ignorance. I would be a daftie at the new school. They'd sit me in the front row and I'd be obliged to drool and to hold my pencil like a fork. I'd be cast down into the 'Christ, will you look at that' lower depths.

Arthur noted my troubled frown and sought to cheer me up. 'Do you fancy doing a dance of death?' he asked.

'How'd you mean?'

'To worship the dog and that.'

'I don't know, what time is it?'

'Two o'clock.'

I don't know why I asked the time. Perhaps in the drawing room of my mind, I had somehow decided that dancing round a disembowelled hound before noon marked a vague breach of polite social etiquette. I watched as Arthur improvised a gauche and untidy skipping movement around the carcass. He began making soulful moans and warlike yelps in the approximate manner of American Indians in Westerns. I felt disinclined to contribute.

Arthur stopped dancing. 'What's up?'

'I don't know the steps,' I lied.

He thought for a moment. 'What dances *do* you know?'

'Only the St Bernard's Waltz,' I said. 'I learned it in the school gym.'

'Me too,' said Arthur. He considered. 'Okay, we'll do that then.'

So it was that the two Apaches, one lapsed, one current, joined hands and performed the St Bernard's Waltz of Death, in honour of Black Blob, the dog who had been killed by the Mad Jappa who ran amok, but only between appointed hours because their leader did a milk round. Indeed, our clumping rhythm and joyous, sing-along style induced in us a mildly euphoric, not to say hysterical state, so that we did not see the Panda car pull up, nor two uniformed policemen tread toward us looking suitably grave, while we laughed like drains.

'Youse!'

We looked at them. Then at each other. We were 'Youse'.

'Whose is that dog?' demanded the senior policeman.

'Nobody's,' said Arthur, boldly. 'You can have it!'

'Walkies were hard work,' I said, picking up his mood. 'And he's a bit slow at fetching sticks.'

We collapsed laughing on the ground.

'Oh,' said the junior policeman, dryly, 'a comedian.'

'Come with us,' instructed the senior policeman.

And we stopped laughing.

When I had not returned home by seven that evening, Father was dispatched to find me. He was thorough in his search and tried every pub in Dreichstane before returning empty-handed. Empty of me, that is. In a crumpled flower of newspaper, the ravaged pollen of a pie supper nestled in his palm.

'I didn't see hide or hair of him,' he growled, swaying. Focusing, he noticed me seated at the table.

'He was held in police custody,' said Mother.

'What?'

'The custody of police,' I supplied, helpfully.

'A son of mine, held?'

Father was white-faced. He still hadn't managed the leap from assistant manager to manager. As his worldly authority had diminished, so his domestic tyranny had increased. Life, which is to say me, his only begotten son, had extended a glorious opportunity for a licensed bellow against the trapped disappointment of his futile existence.

'They took him down to the station in the square,' said Mother, 'and questioned him for hours.'

'Concerning what?'

'He hanged a dog.'

'I did not.'

'He hanged it. A Scotch terrier.'

Father assumed a grave tone. 'The breed is immaterial.'

'I did not hang it!' My voice was shrill from injustice.

'Then what did you do?'

'We did a waltz around it,' I explained. 'Me and another boy.'

My parents looked at each other.

'The St Bernard,' I added, feebly.

'Appropriate for a dog,' admitted Mother. We watched Father's lip begin to twist. He limbered up with some righteous indignation. 'A boy of mine caught . . .' He fumbled for the words, 'dog waltzing!'

I did head hanging, for effect. He was in full voice.

'I've done everything for you! Books! Haircuts! The Morse code! But what's been the bloody point, eh?'

I shrugged. I did not know the point, either.

'A waste of time.'

Father gripped the table and banged it for emphasis. He was swaying, like a man stricken by moral outrage. Really, it was the several pints along the high street that were causing him to bend and buckle, like a poplar in the breeze.

'You're useless, what are you?'

'Useless.'

'He's just slow.'

'He's hopeless. Get to your bed.'

I gave a wounded glower.

'Go on!'

I rose and left the room.

I was useless. And slow.

So be it.

In my room, I picked up my Frido football and inked my name and address on it. After the postcode, I added 'Europe, Planet Earth, The Cosmos'.

I would be useless on my own terms.

This interest in football was new. It stemmed from a yearning to impress my father by becoming a Proper Boy. I had seen pictures of these superior beings in comics. Proper boys were always jolly. They had freckled faces and upturned noses and wore their school cap at carelessly squinty angles and had catapults sticking out of their back pockets. Proper boys had good-natured dogs called Patch that ran gladly at their heels and followed their young masters faithfully all the way home from school. Proper boys seldom hanged their pets, as I had done. Above all, at an open cottage door, a proper boy's father would be standing in his shirt sleeves, hands on the hips of his cavalry twill slacks, his legs sturdily astride, his brogue shoes hugging the wholesome loam, a confident smile on his face, his glowing pipe clamped between even white teeth. Behind him, his beautiful but wholesome wife, the proper boy's mother, would be carrying a freshly baked apple pie to the gingham-covered table, while wearing shiny high heels and a pinafore over her smart evening gown.

Above all, proper boys played football and not rugger. There were, of course, no proper boys in Dreichstane, only improper boys like myself. The likes of myself being all there was to play with, then they would have to do.

I had seen the likes of me playing, a few evenings before, down at the cricket pitch. This was a sprawling expanse of grass, bounded by a mesh fence with council houses on three sides and on the fourth a small stream that meandered down from the bluebell woods skirting the steep end of Maple Drive.

Here I had stood, on the fringes of the game, deliberately conspicuous among the bordering of tall weeds, hoping to be asked to contribute my skills. The invitation having been forthcoming, I had then promptly disgraced myself. I had displayed neither defensive bravery nor attacking prowess. Indeed, in an unusual tactical move, I had been asked to play deep, so deep that I was no longer on the pitch and was in fact sitting on a swing, among the small girls and the more docile boys, where I could not impede the progress of others, team mate or opponent alike, with my pointless, irritating presence. This was a sore ignominy for the former Wee Commander and I had watched in a spirit of desolation, as the players ran about in a bonded herd, dribbling and gesticulating, their smarting oaths drifting up on the night air, serving to emphasise my solitude.

At around 7 p.m. a curious thing happened. The ball was lifted and the players trooped away as one, toward the gate. The game had been prematurely abandoned. On enquiry, I learned that this was so the players could return to their homes to watch a specially televised screening of the Real Madrid versus Eintracht European cup final, from Hampden Park in Glasgow.

Curious, I returned home to do likewise.

The evening being balmy, Father had withdrawn to the sanctuary of our still-uncultivated garden. Mother followed quickly with the hoe, pre-empting further pub business.

Alone and intrigued, I noted the football skills on view, especially from the team in white.

Cocky showmanship was allied to their technical mastery. We have a word for that in our country: 'gallus'. Forget 'Real', for me they were Gallus Madrid, the Harlem Globetrotters with shin guards. In my enthusiasm, I looked for a player on whom I might model my style – a dashing forward, naturally. Puskás, I decided, was too portly, Di Stéfano too bald, while Canário bore the doubtful Christian name of D'arcy. There was nothing else for it – henceforth I would be a speedy left-winger, just like Francisco Gento.

So it was a few evenings later, having practised incessantly with my Frido ball – knocking it for hour upon inexpert hour against the wire fence that skirted the stream at the end of Vine Crescent – I returned to the cricket pitch and stood again in the unkempt rough, awaiting the chance to redeem myself on the playing field.

The same boys gathered; sides were selected with the more skilful players being quickly snapped up by the rival captains. By the end of this Darwinian process, two players remained unselected – myself and a boy called Chalfont who wore a surgical boot. Damningly, Limpy Chalfont was picked before me, on the optimistic grounds that since he had a club foot, he might prove a hidden wonder, like the legendary, lopsided Garrincha of Brazil. For myself, I felt my tardy selection to be a short-sighted and cowardly decision based on a failure to see beyond my total lack of ability. I rose above the insult and steeled myself. I had learned a trick or two in the interim and would show them all.

To be accurate, I had learned a trick or one – the back heel. My first attempt at this manoeuvre drew applause and shouts of surprised admiration from my team mates. Heady with the unaccustomed perfume of praise, and anxious to prove it no fluke, I did it again. Once more, appreciation was audible. A third time too. By the fourth, however, the appreciation had dwindled and by the fifth and sixth demonstrations, my back heel was the subject of outright scorn. This hardened into collective team anger when, clean through, head down and galloping toward our opponent's goal line, I executed yet another stunning halt and dainty pirouette. This time the truth dawned on my peers.

'He's a clueless bastard – he's just running about like a dick,' an opponent opined. The said clueless bastard, myself, could do little more than concur with this verdict. For, in my haste, and unlike my mentor Francisco Gento, I had not actually taken the trouble to learn the rules of football. Consequently, I ran about enthusiastically, in various directions, performing indiscriminate back heels, to no advantage. Showmanship, to me, was all – winning a mere adjunct to the obligation to entertain. It was as though Mr Bojangles had inexplicably signed for Brechin City. As my fellows mocked, I did a fortunate thing. On an impulse, I exaggerated my solitary trick. I took it up to and beyond the point of grotesqueness, so that my legs turned to wayward rubber and my arms flailed in ludicrous abandonment. The lesser players stopped to watch this exhibition. Others joined them, lured by the gleeful prospect of watching someone making an arse of himself in public. By degrees, the game dissolved into anarchy. The older players watched, frowning, as idiot juveniles mimicked my garish spastic motions. Oh, how my heart sang with joy! Before long all but Malcolm 'The Elk' Muncie, a majestic player, with ears like antlers, had joined the unedifying, tasteless farce. The Mighty Elk waited patiently, foot on ball, until eventually the hysteria was spent and the game could be resumed. With order restored, he looked at me.

'You,' he said, and jerked his thumb behind him – 'in goal.'

It was a routine punishment which failed to dampen my spirits. A week before, I had been ordered to the swings. Now I was again at the periphery of the game, but at least this time I was still on the field. I had made some new and timely friends. I'd be starting my new school in a matter of weeks. I walked home weary, yet glad of heart, eager to inform my parents of my good fortune.

On Vine Crescent, I saw Father awaiting me at the door of our home. His legs were astride and his hands were on his hips, just like a proper boy's father. Euphoric from the success of my evening, I ran toward him gladly, the way decent fellows did in *The Hotspur*. I made my young face glow with open-hearted proper boy wholesomeness.

'Good evening, Daddy, how's Mummy?'

My father's eyes did not flicker. 'Get fucking in,' he hissed through razored lips.

In the living room, Mother was seated, ashen-faced, on the couch. A newspaper lay open before her on the old tool bench – Grandpa Moss's – that now served as our coffee table.

'You told us you didn't do it,' she said.

'Do what?'

Father gripped me by the neck. 'That dog!' he screamed. 'You said you didn't hang that fucking dog!'

He hauled me across the floor. My head was rammed down toward the tool-bench coffee table until I could smell cold newsprint.

'That's the weekly paper,' my father said. 'The *Dreichstane Gazette.*'

My anxious, frightened face discerned a picture of my smug, jovial face beaming back at me.

'If you didn't do it – explain that headline!'

'I can't read the headline, my head's too close to the paper.'

'Let me oblige,' said Father. Which he did, pointing to each word and spitting them out in a staccato fashion, for emphasis.

'Monster – Boy – Warned – Over – Sick – Attack.'

'You see, Monster, singular,' said Mother. 'And you swore there was another boy.'

'There was. I'd just met him.'

'Liar!'

Father gave my head a shake. It was a vigorous shake that made my teeth rattle, like coconut halves faking horses' hooves.

'I can check,' warned Mother. 'I'll look his parents up in the phone book.'

'He's not in the phone book.'

'How do you know?'

'He's an Apache.'

'What's his name?'

'Arthur Run-with-the-Buffalo McDonald.'

Father rattled my chops again.

'I'm not lying.'

'Then why isn't he in the picture with you?'

I didn't answer. The truth would only have inflamed my parents further. Arthur wasn't in the picture because, knowing better, he'd slunk away when the photographer had approached us. I, on the other hand, had proved a willing convert to the bad faith of notoriety.

'The man from the paper asked me,' I explained. 'I did it because I felt sorry for the dog.'

'There's the photograph – you don't look sorry.'

I perused the picture. My father had a point. I was miming a throttling motion while grinning cheerily to the camera.

'The photographer told me to do that,' I pleaded. 'He said if it was a boring picture then it wouldn't make the paper – he told me to do monster boy acting.'

Mother, a moth to the damning flame, picked up the *Gazette* and read: '*Swaggering defiantly for the camera, alleged canine killer Ivan Moss, aged ten* . . .' She could read no further. The paper fluttered to the floor.

'Oh my God!' She clasped her bosom, rolled her head aghast in the accustomed fashion.

Father buried my head in his hands. He suspended me against the wall while my feet dangled freely for several moments. I could clearly see the two rows of his stained stumpy teeth and the spume on his enraged lips. My consciousness ebbed to a white pinprick behind my eyes. Sensing an inconvenient case of child murder, Father let me drop.

'I'm heart sick of you,' he said, unnecessarily, his legs astride my foetal crumple.

I looked for Mother to defend me. She did not. Her thoughts were elsewhere. Her hands were resting on her stomach and she was smiling, benignly.

'I think I felt him kick,' she said.

Eleven

We were several decades on and budding new life was kicking her again; a fresh-faced young tumour this time, in her lung. I took her back to the hospital, to see the oncologist, Dr Ryford.

'Dr Jaffar has outlined the nature of the treatments. I've told you the good news and the bad in terms of possible benefits and side effects. Is it all clear?'

'Yes,' she said.

'Is there anything you'd like to ask me?'

'No.'

'You've thought it through?'

'Yes.'

'What's your decision?'

'I won't be having chemo.'

He nodded, smiled. He was deflated. You could tell in the way he picked up his pen, balanced it, let it drop aimlessly into his open palm. Chemo was his star prize. She had turned it down.

The old man had turned it down too, ten years before; the fags, of course, him and her. Father and Mother, they each knew the price. They'd seen it paid by other people; smokers, rasping and retching, they knew all right.

'I'm too old,' she said, by way of explanation. 'It would

132

be too much for me; too severe. I know my own body, its limitations.'

'It's your choice,' he said.

He placed his pen back on the desk. She had given him no-where to go. You could sense him moving on mentally, looking over her shoulder toward that ever-moving escalator that would trundle in the next luckless, wheezing victim.

My mother sat with her jaw set, hands clasped. She'd said what she'd come to say; she hadn't thought beyond it. I had.

'I have a question.'

He brightened, momentarily. 'Oh, yes?'

That's when I asked the oncologist a thing that's troubled me, haunted me really, ever since. My mother wouldn't ask any questions, you see, and I wanted information; we live in an information era, right? It's what we demand; we're falling down on the job unless we glean all the meat from the bone of those suckers in authority and plenty of it. The oncologist was thin, fair-haired, late thirties. He looked like my agent, sounded like him too; a clipped air of educated competence. I leaned forward and asked him straight out:

'What are her prospects?'

He looked at me. I'd put him on the back foot and wanted to keep him there.

'What I'm asking is – how long has she got?'

He glanced to my mother, looking for a steer. He was un-comfortable about whether or not to answer in her presence. She just sat implacably, staring back. He had no choice but to pick his words with care. I don't now remember what they were, those carefully chosen words, but there were statistics, skilfully arranged, on a verbal silver salver from which he in-vited us to help ourselves. I swept his statistics away, pressed on:

'But what are her chances? You're the boss man, take an educated guess.'

I thought my mother had wanted to know, you see, had just been too coy to ask; I'd assumed that with her being old the vestiges of mythical power still clung for her to the hem of the healer's godly raiment. I hadn't realised that so long as the question remained unasked then my mother had control; she would retain the choice, in the future, however long or short that might be, to know or not know her conceivable fate. Once the question had been asked, you see, it could never be unasked and the knowledge imparted by the answer could never be unknown. I'd thought I was giving my mother something but I was actually taking something away.

Dr Ryford went over the same statistics again, slowly, softly. He was telling us, her, anything from one to four years, is what it all meant; four being the dizzy Everest of optimistic possibility. When he'd finished he sat back in his chair, blinked rapidly.

There, I thought, pleased with myself. I've coaxed it out of him. She knows now how long she has. I congratulated myself on a job well done.

Ryford didn't look comfortable; in fact he looked downright unhappy. These young doctors, some of them are more sensitive than their patients; more sensitive than some of their patients' sons anyway. It's quite a job, being an oncologist, maybe even more so in Glasgow where we're as aggressive as our tumours.

Outside, in the fresh air, my mother lit up.

'You hear that?' I said, doing the-glass-is-half-full acting. 'There's a whole lot a person can achieve in four years.'

She didn't say anything; just sat in the passenger seat with the safety belt twisted. She was looking straight ahead and breathing hard. I felt my energy drain. I looked to the hills.

From the car park you could see Ben Lomond.
It's a lot smaller than Everest.

You could see Lomond too, from the playground of Dreichstane Primary School. I know this because I remember standing alone in the tight Victorian playground, my overlong Caledonian Tailor's blazer matching my overlong face as I watched groups of other people's friends laugh and joke comfortably with each other, catching up after the long summer break. They used unfamiliar words: Dreichstane words like 'seeven' for 'seven' and 'luckin' for 'looking'. They spoke of unfamiliar landmarks like the Needle and the Brandy Burn. I felt keenly the awkwardness of the outsider and looked around for the succour of fellow misfits of comparable status. I saw none, only those half asleep, mouth breathers from the planet Dim, who seem to hang around, immobile as toadstools, in every school playground.

Among other fears, I was anxious not to draw attention to myself, lest the hanging dog scandal had remained fresh in the public imagination. Many of these boys were bigger than me and I couldn't risk making enemies. When the bell rang, I joined the appropriate line, looking as meek as possible, and when we entered our allotted class, I chose a desk by the far wall, well away from the searchlight of the teacher's eye. Solitary as I felt, I need not have worried; an old friend, the threat of violence, soon placed me in its care.

'You, boy!'

I glanced around, timidly. Mr Dowie's harsh gaze was focused straight at me. 'Me, sir?'

'Yes, you, sir!'

Mr Dowie, or 'Clucky' according to his nickname, was a man of medium height but gigantic temper, thin of frame and straight as a ruler. He wore a shambling brown suit and a nylon shirt in one of those vivid, unknown colours for which the spectrum has no name. He was long since bald but had refused to concede follicular defeat and would wet his hair and plaster it forward in the manner of its former glory. Under the classroom lights his few strands would dry out and stick up like hen's feathers. Hence his waggish nickname, 'Clucky'. He was mildly psychotic and had a moustache to prove it.

'Yes, you – that old trick, eh? Slinking into the room and picking a desk by the wall – get out here now! And bring your schoolbag!'

The sound of mockery, like a flock of wayward sheep, ran around the room. The harsh bark of Mr Dowie rounded up and safely penned it.

'Silence!'

I stood frozen at the front of the room, my panicked face scanning my new classmates, not one of whom I could call friend. Certainly not Arthur Run-with-the-Buffalo. Anticipating the awkward judgement of my look, Arthur had positioned his head discreetly to one side so that it became masked by the girl in front of him, a hulking item with an optimistic blonde bob and cheeks like a squirrel's pouches in chestnut season. In an agonised silent prayer, I asked only two things – that Mr Dowie did not reveal I was an incomer from Glasgow and that he did not mention the *Gazette* incident. I can report that God answered my prayers.

'So you're the dog strangler from Glas-gow, eh?'

A collective gasp of self-righteous, scandalised horror rippled around the room.

Mr Dowie stood looking down at me. He had said 'Glasgow' in the way many people did in those days, like it was a turd and he was poking it with a stick; in this case, a dog turd.

'I was warned you'd be joining my class,' he said in a low

growl. 'Did you do what they say you did?'

'No, sir.'

'You didn't hang a dog?'

'No, sir.'

This prompted another mass gasp of showy disgust.

'Silence!'

'Sir . . .'

'Speak up, boy!'

'*No, sir!*'

In my nervous state, the words had issued forth in a bellowing blast. My increased volume raised a subversive titter. Clucky gave a warning touch of the leather strap he kept under the shoulder of his jacket and the titter skittered away.

'Are you being insubordinate?'

I did not answer. I could not. I did not know what 'insubordinate' meant.

Mr Dowie, fearing ridicule, grew wary. 'I'll be watching you,' he said – 'sit!'

I made to walk off.

'Not there!' He snapped his fingers. 'Go to the middle, where I can see you. Change desks with Chalfont.'

Limpy collected his belongings and, muttering about the unfairness of existence, lugged his gammy leg once more to the right wing of life, not unlike Garrincha.

By playtime, I had become an object of curiosity. Normal boys, God-fearing boys, wholesome and straight of limb, wandered up to ask me what it was like to hang a dog. Did it cough blood? Did its eyes pop out? Did dogs beg for mercy or only for sweeties?

I answered each question with the authority of a neuro-specialist addressing a first year intake of students. No, a hanged dog does not cough blood, though at the point of maximum throttling, it does bite its own tongue off. I had retained the tongue, I explained, and sent it to the Museum of Natural History in London, though I had yet to receive the courtesy of a reply. As for the eyes, I reported that they had not popped out; a single eye only having leapt from its socket to trail in gruesome fashion down a hairy cheek. Summing up for the benefit of my students, I concluded that a dog does not beg for mercy as it does not understand the concept; though doubtless if mercy were to come shaped like a fruit pastille, it would probably get the hang of it, so to speak, quite quickly. It was a fine performance by me, confident and relaxed. I proved a veritable font of medical wisdom for my interns. I had done everything but rap their chests with my fingers, testing for TB.

By the end, the boys were calling me 'Mossy'. I was exultant. I had a nickname. I belonged. Unfittingly for a dog murderer, I purred with pleasure. To compound my success, I could see Arthur McDonald, no longer running with the buffalo, but standing on the fringes of my spellbound audience, kicking a pillar of the school shed, looking chagrined and tearful. How could he contradict my version of events when he'd denied ever having taken part in their execution? I hoped McDonald might learn a valuable lesson – honesty may be the best policy, but dishonesty is its own reward.

As the bell sounded, the brilliant young dog dangler, Dr Ivan Moss, made his way into line, flanked by a cordon of his appreciative acolytes. Within moments, Dr Moss's arm was up his back and his distinguished, aquiline profile was kissing the crumpled crisp bags and sweetie wrappers that littered the playground gravel.

'Liar!'

I could not look up, or turn round, but I deduced that a rival specialist had elected to challenge my medical findings.

'Ya fucking wee wank – what are yi?'

'A wank,' agreed Dr Moss.

The unidentified counter-theorist gave a renewed and vigorous tug at my arm. 'What kind of wank?'

'A fucking wee one,' I expanded.

'And a liar – shout it out!'

'I am a lying wank!'

The bell sounded, saving me, and the theorist removed his knee from my back. I remained prone on the ground for some moments so he might reason his business to have been satisfactorily concluded and his victory to have been comprehensive. When he had gone, I rose and did my best to resume the role of distinguished doctor, smiling confidently and dusting myself down like a man who has emerged invigorated from the heady to and fro of intellectual discourse. I watched my assailant stroll to the front of our line, untroubled by any obligation to queue. A presence sidled up and came to rest by my side.

'You've messed with the wrong guy there, Moss,' said Arthur. 'That's Dunt Vernon.'

I frowned. 'I didn't see him in class earlier.'

'He's always late on Mondays.' Arthur paused for effect. 'He's got a milk round.'

The penny dropped. 'Ah.'

With grim satisfaction, Arthur added, 'He's the leader of the Mad Jappa.'

My assailant looked back and showed me a fist.

It was a fist that said – 'I'm not finished with you.'

I experienced the melting of the bowels and desire to whimper that is common among eminent men of learning.

For an image of Dunt Vernon, picture Kirk Douglas in *The Vikings*, but wearing grimy flannels and work boots. Forget Black Blob, I was the one hanging now, from a rope of trepidation.

My brief moment of glory had arrived and passed. Thereafter, Jimmy 'Dunt' Vernon waged upon me a nerve-jangling campaign of psychological and physical terror. If Clucky Dowie left the room or stepped into the cupboard to smooth his head plumage, Dunt would turn and pelt me with missiles. There'd be thumps in the back in the dinner hall queue, followed by gobs of spit in my soup. My school life became a study in misery. Inevitably, my work suffered; once comfortably slothful, I now resorted to the desperate expedient of study.

This was a severe price to pay as it aroused resentment from my fellows. They relied on sluggish idlers like me to prop up their own position in the league table of under-achievement.

In studying, my aim was simple – to gain a change of desk position and find refuge toward the back of the room, among the intelligentsia, safe from the relentless eye of Dunt. As a result of my cowardice, I became temporarily bright and was accorded the accolade of a seat in the second back row. This ought to have brought some measure of relief. Unfortunately, as I left one hostile eyeline, I blundered into two more.

Shona Burns and Janet Gooding were best friends. They stood in queues together. They ate their meals together. Where Shona went, so did Janet, and vice versa. It followed, therefore, that they would always sit next to each other in class. In other words, they were inseparable – until I separated them. Or rather Clucky did, by tearing them apart to accommodate me.

I took Janet's desk, Janet took Limpy's. Hostile glares were exchanged like pennants at a grudge match as I positioned my unwanted form between Shona and Janet. I was trapped then, between Shona Burns and Janet Gooding. If Shona and Janet wished to whisper to each other – which they did, frequently – I'd be poked with a ruler and urged to arch myself backwards like a gymnast on the brink of a reverse somersault. If they

wished greater concealment, I'd be poked again and signalled
to crouch forwards, like a minion being presented to royalty, so
that they might conduct their whisperings behind the wall of
my body.

Being naturally intelligent, both Shona and Janet were un-
fazed by the notion of learning. If Mr Dowie demonstrated a
mathematical proposition on the board, both girls had the ability to absorb, consider and replicate what they had seen. Myself,
I was not so fortunate. Each day, I'd attempt to set my mind
like a steel trap, determined to snare and pacify each wild, un-
fathomable concept and commit it to the larder of my brain.
Always, I'd be distracted by some fleeting impression: autumn
shadow falling across an abandoned syllable on a carelessly
wiped blackboard; a breeze from an open window wafting the
bracing pong of the milk crate shed toward unguarded nostrils;
the dance of dappled sunlight at play on the dubious stains on
Clucky Dowie's ancient flannels. And always the ominous, lurking leer on Dunt Vernon's face as the clock told two, then crept
forward toward the agony of three. These things and others
I'd attempt to set aside as I leaned, sweating, over my exercise
book, straining to maintain my perilously held position among
the intelligentsia.

On the day Dunt Vernon smashed an egg over my head and
tried to make it into an omelette with a Bunsen burner, I decided
to speak to my father.

He was at the table, eating his stew.

'Father, I need to talk to you.'

He looked at me, warily. 'Is it about money?'

I shook my head. He relaxed.

'Speak.'

'I'm being bullied at school,' I said.

'Who by?'

'A big boy.'

'Is he a tough nut?'

'Yes, Father. He copies my homework and boots me up the jacksy.'

Father considered this information. He bent me over and studied my jacksy for signs of misconduct. From between my legs I watched him ruminate, his jaw muscles flexing and clenching in earnest concentration. Occasionally, there would be the squelch of gristle grinding between molars. Having considered, Father straightened me.

'Right,' he said. 'There's only one way to deal with a bully – you stand up to him. *For bullies are all cowards at heart.*' Father assumed a resolute expression. 'Come with me,' he said, beckoning with the crook of his finger. I followed him out of the house.

'I did some boxing in the navy,' he explained, 'now's the time to put it to good use.'

My heart gladdened. 'Are you going to fight him, Father?'

'No,' my father said, 'you are.'

He opened the gate and stepped into the garden. I followed, my glad heart already sinking.

For my instruction, Father demonstrated his boxing skills.

'I'll start with bobbing and weaving.'

Father danced around our baldy lawn, circling a rhododendron and ducking imaginary punches from non-existent opponents. He made puffing noises to simulate the avoided blows.

'You see how I present a moving target at all times?'

'Yes.' He still hadn't changed out of his work suit. I watched his shabby trousers yoyo up and down on his braces.

'Now – footwork. Watch carefully, I learned this from the great Dick McTaggart.'

'Did you fight Dick McTaggart?'

'Not exactly,' admitted Father, shiftily. 'But I've studied his style closely on television. Are you paying attention?'

'Yes.'

I wasn't paying attention. I was thinking of easier ways to deal with a tough nut – like running away or, better still, my old friend suicide.

'Ivan!'

Father's voice shook me from my escapist reverie.

'Footwork can baffle an opponent and render him at your mercy. Are you ready?'

'Yes.'

'Hup!'

I watched Father's legs become an enthusiastic blur of white calf and grey flannel as he executed a dainty pirouette and turn. The movement was marred by a footwear accident.

'You've lost a slipper,' I said, pointing. 'It's stuck in the mud by the rhododendron bush.'

Father affected irritated disdain. 'Details!'

He continued springing up and down, his fists peppering the air, his exposed sock growing long and floppy as he squelched nimbly on the damp sod.

'You see? Now you try! Up on your toes – come on, come on!'

I failed to move, making him growl.

'Ivan!'

Father was in the warrior zone, the old magic flooding back.

To humour him, I shuffled reluctantly round the garden, the thin white streamers of my arms wafting gently in the air.

To my alarm, I noticed a crowd starting to gather by our undernourished privet hedge. Small children at first, then bigger boys – men of respect: the Mighty Elk, Freddie Fallon, Jim Leston, the McIlhones, Dan and Eddie. I knew these bigger boys would begin to jeer, once they had seen the lie of the land.

'Now try and peg me with your right,' urged Father. 'Go on!'

I made a half-hearted flapping motion, provoking scorn.

'That arm movement wouldn't flag down a bus – put some brawn behind it!' Father was playing to the gallery now. 'Like this!'

Inflamed by the old magic, the warrior zone and the roar of the crowd, Father thrust a spirited jab to my chops. Startled, I let out a howl.

The bigger boys took this as their cue for mirth.

Father rounded on them, clenching his fists and flashing a severe look. The severe look had little effect as each of the boys stood several inches taller than Father, who was what they call in my country 'a smout'.

To save his face, Father slapped mine a couple of times with the flat of his hand.

'Jab and run,' he prompted, 'jab and run!'

Exhausted, I was saved from further humiliation by Mother. She stepped into the garden holding a plastic tray with two mugs of orangeade and a chipped plate of Abernethy biscuits.

Seeing her swollen belly, the bigger boys laughed and made crude comments behind their hands. The Mighty Elk, being his own man, made a bovine bellow, signifying lust. He pawed the ground in a scurrilous motion, drawing the acclaim of the watching herd.

I hung my head in shame.

Father made an emotional appeal. 'Leave the boy in peace,' he shouted at our tormentors. 'He needs to learn the art of self-defence.'

'Ivan's a Jessie,' sneered Dan McIlhone.

'Maybe so, but you know your literature – "If you pricketh a Jessie, doth he not bleed?"'

The statesmanlike compassion of this utterance silenced the crowd. Flattered at having their better natures appealed to, they began to disperse.

'Come, Ivan.'

Father led me indoors. My face was still crimson. He allowed me to drink both glasses of orangeade and to eat all the biscuits, as an aid to my recovery.

'You need the sustenance,' he explained. 'You've a grudge fight coming up.'

I nodded. Father gripped my shoulder in resolute support.

'What do you have to do?'

'Jab and weave,' I said, 'jab and weave.'

That night I sweated over my homework. Afterwards, as a treat, Mother made me swallow a raw egg whisked in milk, explaining that this was what top sportsmen drank. On finishing it, I realised why top sportsmen seldom smiled.

Twelve

Next morning, there was a mean look in my eye. I knew this, because I had put it there myself, in the bathroom mirror, while brushing my teeth. Just the one eye. I had tried the mean look in both eyes but discovered this to be hazardous, following a narrow miss by a bread van on the walk to school.

I knew what would happen on this morning and I was ready. Father's stirring mantra from the night before resounded in my mind. 'If you stand up to a bully he will run away – *for bullies are all cowards at heart.*'

I was resolved to stand up to Dunt Vernon. If I did not, the beatings would never cease and would only grow in severity. I pictured myself with my pension book in hand, being pursued from the post office by an octogenarian Vernon, our flashing walking frames sparking off the pavement, as he hounded me, asthmatically, toward the relief of my grave. Well, let him come, I thought. I'm ready.

I flexed my knuckles, and heard them give a reassuring crack. I had been honed. I had been tempered. More than this – I had seen the films. I knew the template. Wasn't every hero obliged first to suffer at the hands of his dastardly nemesis before crawling away to lick his wounds, be tended by a loving woman, then coached in warfare by a disillusioned, grizzled veteran? That's the way the movies and, therefore, real life worked. The grizzled veteran would administer a couple of instructive kickings to the hero – who would then, having finally absorbed the lessons, one day turn the tables on his master. At this point, the grizzled veteran would give a startled smile, rub his chin, wrinkle his world-weary eyes and mutter, 'You learn well, my young friend – you are ready.'

This was how, more or less, it had gone the previous night with Father. After our session in the garden, we had repaired to the living room. Here, as he'd stooped to drape his wet sock over the fireguard, I had applied the gift of footwork to the flannelled dangle of his bollocks, buckling his legs before the grate. The eyes of the grizzled veteran, my father, did not wrinkle wryly. Instead, they'd bulged in his startled head as he'd wheeled round, ready to exact revenge.

'*What the fucking fuck . . .?*'

Mother, assessing the situation, had slid quickly to my defence, shielding me with her body – her two bodies, to be strictly accurate, being pregnant. Faced with the unseemly prospect of picking a fight with his own foetus, Father took himself off to the kitchen to cut a calming wedge of cheese.

'You've a habit of playing with fire,' said my mother.

'It wasn't me that married him.'

She thought about a whack, but demurred.

After all, I had a point.

Next morning, I stood alone in the school playground. I was fantasising that I was standing alone in the playground, even though I was, weirdly, standing alone in the playground. My homework was in my satchel. My satchel was at my feet. The flashing pistons of my fists were ready.

'*You want my homework, Vernon? Well, come and take it!*'

'Hey, Moss-Toss!'

The clothes of fantasy fell in rags at my feet. I was standing alone in the playground all right, and I was naked of spirit too.

'I'm talking to you.'

Dunt Vernon had taken to referring to me as 'Moss-Toss'. He had hoped others would too. As a sperm-based nickname, it had not, so to speak, stuck.

By way of greeting, Vernon punched me in the chest. I did not react.

'Have you done your dictation?'

'Yes.'

'Gimme – I want a copy.'

'I can't,' I said. 'If you copy it, we'll have the same answers. Then Clucky will know we've been cheating.'

Vernon gave me an incredulous look. He spoke to his acolytes, mimicking my voice.

'Then Clucky will know we've been cheating.'

Sniggering ensued, dutifully. Vernon snapped his fingers. 'Homework – give!'

I heard my voice say, 'You want my homework, Vernon? Well, try and take it.'

He did not move. None of the acolytes spoke. They looked to Dunt Vernon. He blinked, baffled.

'What?'

Father's words had given me strength and courage: 'If you stand up to a bully, he will run away – *for bullies are all cowards at heart.*' Seizing my moment, I rose to my toes and peppered the air with jabs. 'Come on then!' I yelled.

I followed this up with a creditable demonstration of the great Dick McTaggart's footwork.

'Come ahead, Vernon!' I shouted.

I kept up a steady bombardment of blows into the chill morning air. I swayed and dodged, stuck and ducked; I was slippery as a conger eel, presenting an ever-moving, elusive target. I was waiting for Dunk Vernon to take to his cowardly heels, his bluff having been finally, exultantly called. I waited for, oh, quite a long time, before my energy began to dissipate and I started to wane, gradually, winding down like a steam train to a final panting halt, the pistons of my fists hanging weary and docile at my sides.

'Come on then,' I said again, feebly. But my old menace, which was to say my new, recently acquired menace, had departed, taken to its heels and fled. Unlike Dunt Vernon.

Dunk looked at me, stonily.

'E for Effort,' was all he said.

And he hit me.

I stayed hit for, oh, quite a long time, lying prostrate in the playground while the lassies skipped ropes around me and the bigger boys conscripted my stricken form for use as a corner flag. My satchel had been rudely ransacked and my dictation homework snatched. By the time I recovered, my burst top lip had started to congeal and I sat dazed on the ground, packing away my books. A scrunched ball of paper bounced from my head. I picked it up and opened it out. It was my dictation homework.

'If you'd given me a copy in the first place,' said Dunt Vernon, standing over me, 'you'd have saved yourself that fat lip.'

I looked up at him, hopelessly. The bell sounded and everyone formed lines. I folded the dictation homework and placed it back in my bag. My feelings were of terror. Someone, Vernon or one of the acolytes, had scrawled an obscenity across its length. What would I tell Dowie?

In class, His Cluckiness was at his tetchy worst. His head

strands stood stiff and alert like the crown of an angry cockerel.

'Pass all homework to the front – now!'

I watched Dunt Vernon pass his exercise book forward then turn to savour the apprehension on my face.

'Has anybody been unwise enough *not* to have done their dictation homework?'

Clucky's glare swept, routinely, around the room. None but a fool would have dared defy him.

The fool, having no choice, put his hand up.

At first Clucky did not see me. Not expecting to encounter defiance, he had failed to notice it.

I thought about taking my hand down. But had I failed to own up on the spot, and waited instead to be unmasked by Clucky at a later juncture, how much worse might that be for me? In any case, Dunt Vernon would not, I felt, allow me to deny him his sport. He'd tell Clucky for sure. And Clucky would go berserk. I kept my hand in the air for what seemed, oh, a long time.

'Please, sir.'

Perhaps if I were to own up, do the decent thing and tell an honest to goodness lie, Clucky might show clemency. After all, I had become lately, had I not, a model pupil? I was encouraged in this delusion by the fact that I was the only transgressor. Had there been either two of us, or many, Clucky would have felt it necessary to quell the rebellion by force. With a mere one, well, a little light sarcasm, a few prods with a goading finger and who knows, perhaps I might be permitted to defer my dictation homework until the morrow. Oh yes? And what if Dunt Vernon took it from me again? I didn't dare think so far ahead.

'Moss? You?'

'Yes, sir.'

Clucky Dowie looked at me. His belting shoulder twitched, like a gunfighter making ready to draw. He reached under his cloak to adjust the infamous twin-tongued special – the leather strap that was reputed each summer to remain sealed in a vat of pickle in Mrs Clucky's pantry in order to rejuvenate its viciousness for the following term.

'Stand up.'

I stood up. My face ran pale; my fingers grasped the sides of the desk for comfort.

In the music room next door, I became aware of Mr McLeod plink plonking 'The Road to the Isles' on the piano. It sounded so normal, so free from fear that I felt giddy.

'Take your hands off that desk – stand up straight!'

I attempted to do his bidding.

'I said *straight*, boy,' boomed Clucky. 'That's not *straight!*'

'Sir.'

It should be understood that 'standing up straight' was not a reasonable demand to be made of a child in those days. From entering school, and before, it had been drummed into us that 'children must be seen and not heard' and that one must never, ever 'cheek your elders'. In fact, whenever 'your elders' visited, children would be banished to the other room, if one existed, and instructed not to reappear until the guest elders were ready to depart. 'Cheek' was defined as the expressing of any opinion that deviated, however mildly, from that of the elders. It followed that since self-expression was a punishable offence, it became, in a child's mind, a sin. By definition, a good child was a silent, invisible child. In such a climate, how could a child be expected to 'stand up straight' when the very foundation stones of his self-confidence had been thumped loose by the sledge-hammers of disapproval every day of his young life?

In attempting to render it erect, I succeeded only in giving my body a Pisa-like tilt in the opposite direction. This produced an apoplectic scream from Clucky.

'*Straight!*'

Next door, 'The Road to the Isles' ceased abruptly. Mr McLeod was that rarest of individuals in those days, a sane teacher. I pictured his hands hovering poised and startled over the piano keyboard, while he wondered what to do. A psychotic teacher was like a violent neighbour – you didn't like to get involved.

I stood briefly, uncertainly, straight.

'You'd better have a good excuse, Moss.'

'I do, sir.'

That was my first mistake.

'Hah! An excuse is not a reason, boy! Do you have a reason?'

'Yes, sir.'

'Then go ahead. *I'm all ears!*' He made an imperious, sweeping gesture with his arm. '*We* are all of us all ears – *aren't we?*'

Everyone agreed that they too were all ears.

'Well, what is it?'

I had no idea what excuse I might offer. I had a reason, yes, his name was Dunt Vernon, but if I pointed the finger of accusation, it would be the worse for me – and, if I didn't, the teacher would punish me. I was caught, pinned and wriggling.

'Speak up!'

My throat had gone dry. I opened my mouth to speak and found my upper lip adhering to my gum, creating an unflattering harelipped effect. I heard my wavering, cracking voice say, 'Sir, the reason I never did my dictation homework is that I – I'm lazy – and I couldn't be bothered.'

The lunacy of this answer created a release of tension so vast that a hysterical mass guffaw ensued. Next door, Mr McLeod, mistaking the nature of the guffaw to be harmless high spirits, resumed his sprightly gallop to the Isles.

Clucky said nothing. I had committed a calamitous error. I

had not, to his mind, paid him the compliment of lying through fear. Therefore, an example would have to be made. He reached under his cloak. He took out the strap, stroked it and thrashed it across his desk. With a jerk of his thumb, he beckoned me out.

I shuffled down the aisle, a condemned boy, a yoke of despair across my fearful shoulders.

Clucky, determined to build me into a worthy adversary, pointed, accusingly. 'See how he swaggers toward the front! *He deserves everything that's coming to him!*

Some years later, the belt would become banned from schools on the grounds that its use constituted a violation of the rights of children. Ergo, by an extension of this legal logic, any child who has been belted has had his rights violated. I look forward with interest to the first test case of retrospective litigation brought by some opportunistic or embittered former pupil, who once suffered at the hands of his educators.

'Move, boy!'

Clucky's voice thrilled with expectation. He worked the strap between his hands to supple it. Smoothing some hens' feathers over his crown he threw back his cloak to free his shoulder for serious swishing.

'There!'

Wretchedly, I stood upon the indicated spot and extended my arms, palms flat and layered, in the customary fashion, one atop the other. As Clucky had adjusted his cloak, so I had taken the opportunity to tug my jumper cuffs down to protect my wrists. This too was an established practice – a lash to places not cushioned by fat produced welts that burned for days. Clucky was having none of this humane, if tacit, convention.

'See how slyly his mind works!' he sneered to the class. 'Push that jumper up over your arms!'

Out-slyed by the deranged maestro, I did as instructed.

Being belted in those days was, above all, a piece of theatre –
a treat for the audience and an opportunity for the performers
to shine. The belter, of course, enjoyed star billing. His responsibility was to initiate the action – the beltee's to react to it. The
success of the drama was dependent on the creative interaction
between the two. Some belters favoured the Shakespearean approach, bestriding their classroom stage in Colossus-like fashion;
roaring, bellowing and rolling of eyes being de rigueur. Their
mean straps would be brandished like pronged daggers. This
oversized sort of performance, a traditional favourite of the
Scottish Thrashing Industry, allowed the beltee, in his turn, to
find a variety of accommodating notes that he might play; perhaps 'cowering with exaggerated fear' or 'stylish impudence'. As
a result of this formalised, if unspoken conspiracy, the Scottish
Theatre of Belting had become increasingly ritualised. The
more subtly understated 'realist' or Lee Strasbourg school of
thrashing, in which the physical pain of the beltee is not only
matched but superseded by the spiritual anguish of the belter,
had yet to find mainstream acceptance. Soon, earnest young art
teachers in daring Hush Puppies would champion the showy
angst of the Method approach, egged on by their miniskirted
staff-room girlfriends, who loved them madly and accepted their
infidelities because life was crazy as we were all living under the
shadow of the bomb.

But not now, not yet.

If the speeches of a beltee in those days were essentially feed
lines of the 'yes sir, no sir, I forget, sir' variety, there yet remained
some gifted victims who could be relied upon to inject light,
wit, and a charming gaiety into the mundane business of being
whacked indiscriminately by an under-achieving baldy schizoid
in a scabby suit.

Alas, I was not one of those gifted few. I could not feign cheery imperviousness to pain for I resented the unfairness of the contest. I was to be bullied by Clucky Dowie for having been bullied by Dunt Vernon. Where was the justice? My life seemed hopeless. As I extended my hands, waiting to be struck, the thought of Harry Crawgie flashed through my mind. As you sew, so shall you reap – which was a lot of sewing, if you wore net curtain underwear.

The stroke came down hard, catching me on the fingertips and thumb knuckle. I had cupped my palm at the critical moment to present a smaller hitting area – a cunning ruse employed by the wilier, which is to say more cowardly, beltees. The resulting hollow in my palm had augmented the sound of the blow, making it satisfyingly startling, so that a collective intake of breath had thrummed around the room. I exaggerated the keenness of the pain, wincing and rubbing my hands. Since the pain was genuinely keen, I would have been obliged to rub my hands and wince anyway. It was a tactic, of course, a diplomatic olive branch, aimed at the saving of face, both the belter's and the beltee's.

The implied subtext to this minuet was: 'Look here, old chap, you're a sadist with a fearsome reputation to uphold – I'm a sacrificial victim who has to share a playground with my fellow lackeys. What say we come to a gentleman's agreement – I'll register enough pain to keep intact your top billing as a violent psychotic, and in return you go easy on me and call it quits at a single monstrous hit? How does that sound, old boy?'

Clucky, of course, was alert to the complicated nuances whereby genuine responses were indistinguishable from faked ones – and of the unspoken horse trading that flitted between eye and gesture. He lowered his belt and addressed the class.

'I will not tolerate insolence – it doesn't matter whether it comes from the front rows or the back, you'll all be treated the same.'

Assuming the matter to have been concluded to our mutual satisfaction, I turned toward my desk.

'Where do you think you're going?'

'Sir?'

Clucky looked at the class, assuming the exasperation of the thwarted man of reason. 'You see what I'm up against? Blind indifference! *This is a boy who never learns!*'

The blindly indifferent boy who never learns felt his heart give a fearful leap as Clucky barked – 'Hands up!'

I presented my hands for the second time. He whacked them, making a grunt, his knee bending on impact, his scuffed brogue tiptoeing with the effort of the extra force. His eyes glinted. His head gave a little tremble.

'Again,' he said.

'Sir,' I said.

I tried to steady my affronted hands. He hit them a third time. He was into his belting groove now and keen to continue.

'Again.'

'But, sir—' The shaming hint of grovel cracked my voice.

'Again!'

A fourth stroke.

'Again!'

I felt sick. I held my hands up. They were shaking visibly. What perky resistance I had mustered had drained away – it was survival now. I'd forgotten the audience, even if Clucky hadn't, it was him and me, and him winning, hands down, or rather up. And through the throb of palms, the fright, the reddening wrists and face, through the inner sense of chaotic injustice, I prayed he'd have the self-control to stop at six. That was the law, or so we vaguely thought, as laid down in Magna Carta at Runnymede in 1215: 'Hereinafter let it be known that no psychotic of ye kingdom, however venerable, shall belt ye fuck out of a child above that of syx strokes – syx being a number more than fyve but less than syven – of his majesty's finest lashes.'

'Again!'

Again? Jesus Christ. Even King John knew when to put the tin lid on it, and he was a medieval tyrant.

'Sir?'

'*Again!*'

From a teacher who couldn't 'draw it' five was a sore thing. And Clucky could draw it. His intention was obvious; he wanted me broken as an example: 'Let this message go out to all in my realm of Cluckiness – that my will shall reign supreme.' I would be broken soon, I knew that. After which, there would be the scarring shame of tears. But lo, hear ye this, as I didst think this thing, raising my flayed hands yet again, a curious event came to pass.

'I said – again!'

As I obeyed, Clucky raised the belt high in executioner's mode to deliver yet another ferocious stroke. My eyes shut, instinctively. I waited. The stroke did not come. I made my eyes open. Clucky had halted, unsteadily, in his action. He was frozen in the act of watching me, watching him. He gave a little gasp then, by degrees, began to crumple, in a sort of wafting motion, gently down onto his knees. Once kneeling, he pitched forward until his back arched and his forehead rested on the dusty wooden floor before me. The few strands of his hair stood out like tiny brush strokes, as if Adrian Hill had inked them in for *Sketch Club*. I could see some fading freckles on his scalp amid cranial bumps and the gathering flakes of his dandruff waiting to be harvested by the thresher of his comb.

I did not know what to do. I looked to the class. Some of the class looked back at me. Others were straining, cautiously, out of their desks to see. The boys were mostly curious and the girls mostly aghast, or pretending to be, their hands held in appalled fashion over their mouths.

Nobody dared move too far, fearing it was some treacherous ruse and that Clucky might spring up with an 'Aha!' to entrap any wayward souls. But Clucky did not spring up. He sprang down.

The class let out a strange shriek. He had keeled onto his side and was lying with his eyes open. His lungs let out a low hiss. I looked back to the class.

'What'll we do?'

Shona Burns had moved to my desk to get a better view. She and Janet were holding hands. For the first time I noticed how pretty they both were; the rich dark lustre of Shona's hair, the shorter, more silken fairness of Janet's. There was a knock at the door and everybody rushed, like a flock, to retake seats with backs straight and hands neatly folded in plain view. Mr McLeod came in and looked around, self-consciously.

'What's all the noise? Where's Mr Dowie?'

'He's here, sir,' I said. I indicated the recumbent heap and stepped aside to clear his view.

'My goodness.'

'What is it, sir?' somebody asked. 'What's happened?'

That voice spoke for all. This was a thing beyond our knowing. We all looked to Mr McLeod for a diagnosis and an explanation. After all, he was a teacher and was therefore omnipotent.

Mr McLeod kneeled over Clucky. I don't know what we expected a music teacher to do. Perhaps he'd inject an aria or two, repair a ruptured sonata, he'd have Clucky up on his toes and giving it 'The Skye Boat Song' in no time.

Mr McLeod tensed, looked up. 'Somebody fetch the headmaster – and fetch the janitor too. And *run!*'

The prospect of licensed sprinting drew many volunteers.

'Me! Me! Me!'

Arthur was first to the door.

Mr McLeod held Clucky's wrist between thumb and forefinger.

'Is he dead, sir?'

'Will we get a day off, sir?'

An unruly burst of scandalised laughter stampeded round the room.

Mr McLeod said nothing. He removed his jacket and covered Clucky's stricken face.

Clucky Dowie was dead.

From a stroke, while giving out strokes.

Apparently, the Silent One had a sense of humour.

Thirteen

At four o'clock, like everyone else, I galloped from the classroom and sprinted home in exuberant spirits to report the sombre news of Clucky's demise. Disappointingly, there was no answer when I rattled our door knocker.

I sat on the step outside the close, wondering what to do. I heard a window open and a voice call to me.

'Ivan?'

I looked about. It was our upstairs neighbour, Mrs Moidart.

'Your mammy's not in, son,' she said. 'She's been taken into the Thornhill hospital. To have her wee baby.' She smiled inanely and made a simpering gesture with her shoulders to convey the miracle of birth.

I said nothing.

A taxi pulled up outside the close. Father paid the driver and stepped out.

'Father, guess what,' I said.

'Not now, Ivan,' said Father, glancing up at Mrs Moidart. She took the hint from the gravity of his expression and shut the window. Father ushered me back into the close.

In the living room, he sat me down.

'I'm hungry,' I grumbled.

'Later.'

Father had, he said, a grave announcement to make. I wondered why the announcement could not as easily be made while I chomped on a slice of malt loaf.

'Your mother might . . . lose the baby.' As he said this, Father leaned forward, his broad forehead resting on his hand. He began massaging his brow with his fingertips.

I weighed his information for emotional gravity. It held none.

To fill the silence, Father let out a moan. '*Why?*' he implored, feelingly. '*Why?*'

I let him run out of steam with the *why*s then I hit him with the news about Clucky.

'Who's Clucky?'

'My teacher.'

Father shrugged his shoulders in an irritated fashion. 'Don't bother me with trifles, Ivan. My newborn baby could be lying dead soon on a mortuary slab.'

Father eyed me, slyly. I knew which way he was heading.

'That poor child!' He raised his eyes in stoic fashion against the cruelty of the world. 'I forgot to find out the hospital visiting hours,' he announced, slapping his thighs and rising. 'I'll go to the Hazel and telephone from there.'

'You don't need to go to the pub,' I said. 'Mrs Moidart will let you use her phone.'

'This is a personal tragedy and she's a nosy old bag. The two things don't go together.'

'What about our tea?'

Father reached into his pocket. He took out a tin of Spam and threw it to me. 'I'll be back within the hour.'

'What if you're not?'

'Start without me.'

I finished without him, too. I fell asleep on the couch. When

I woke up, I could hear him in the kitchen, blundering about.

I stood in the living-room doorway, rubbing my eyes against the light. 'How was Mother?'

'Oh, the same.'

'The same as what?'

'She's not good. I'm at my wits' end. Where's that Spam?'

'If she's not good, that's not the same.'

'The same as what?'

'The same as the same.'

Father eyed me, warily. 'You're right.'

He found the remains of the Spam. 'I'm trying to protect you because you're young and vulnerable,' he said. I watched him smear a doorstop of bread with margarine. 'That's the burden a parent must carry. Your mother's in a bad way.'

'She is?'

'Heart rending.'

I clutched the hem of my pyjama jacket, for comfort.

Father saw my distress. 'There, there,' he said, with a satisfied smile. He slapped a rind of Spam onto the doorstop slice, took a bite.

'What did the doctor say? How bad is a bad way?'

Father ignored my enquiry. He pressed on. 'Do you know the Lord's prayer, Ivan?'

'The what?'

He pouched some masticated debris in his cheek to create some speaking room. 'The Lord's prayer – do you know it?'

'Yes.'

'Then forget about asking questions. God hates lip. Try dropping to your knees and praying – that's how bad your mother is.'

I was alarmed. 'When is she coming home?'

'Depends. The harder you pray, the faster she'll recover. So it's up to you. Her recovery is in your hands.'

I got down on my knees. 'Will you pray with me, Father?'

'I'm an atheist, God would see right through me. A few extra devotions from yourself would balance up the family books and chuff him to bits no end.'

Father pulled on his jacket, headed for the door. 'I'm going to the hospital. Put out the light when you're done,' he said.

'Yes, Father.'

I heard the front door shut.

I kneeled in the middle of the room, so God could see me better. This meant being abject on the threadbare patch of carpet so that its exposed fibres bit into my knees. I prayed as speedily as I could, squeezing in extra yards of ardent blank verse as I drove my tongue hard and fast round the corners of devotion – sometimes slurring my words at high speed along the way and slamming the odd kerbstone of a noun; but thanks to God's will and simple bloody-minded effort, I managed to ratchet up the mileage on my spiritual clock. Having prayed like a crazed demon, I straightened my legs with difficulty and stood, breathing hard. I was freezing cold and my chafed kneecaps looked like a pair of bloodied waffles.

I knew that Father had not been heading for the hospital. And he knew I knew. And the Lord knew too, though he said nothing being, as usual, silent. I didn't begrudge the Lord his prayers, reasoning that I owed him for striking down Clucky. I'd thank him again, if he'd do the same to Dunt Vernon. It was gratifying to have paid off my account with the Lord and that night I slept like a baby.

Like most babies, that is, but not Mother's. Few children howl from an incubator.

Stan did.

* * *

We were not permitted a day off following Clucky's demise. In those days there was no such thing as trauma. If the word didn't exist in a spelling book then, in the eyes of the education authority, neither could the condition.

A young male supply teacher was jetted in from exotic Paisley. Disregarding the fact that we were fragile beings who had been through a wounding experience, he comforted us by dishing up reams of written exercises and thrashing the desk with his belt. He would brook no cheek.

'Your last teacher might have tolerated insolence – but there'll be none with Mr Niven!'

Given that our last teacher had died while attempting new peaks of physical assault upon my person, this came as a disquieting message. That the new man referred to himself as 'Mr Niven' should have further stoked our concern. People only refer to themselves in the third person when they doubt the validity of their first person. If it remained a troubling time for all, it was worse still for me. I had been marked down as a deviant. In class, Mr Niven knocked the spirit out of me and in the playground Dunt Vernon kicked the shit out of me.

I tried another prayer. God was silent.

Business as usual.

Mother returned home. She looked pale and drawn but tried her best to be cheery.

'Hello, Ivan.'

'Hello, Mother.'

She tried to hug me. I pulled away. It felt odd. She'd been in hospital a fortnight, which was the longest I'd ever gone without seeing her. Father entered, holding a small shawl bundle in the cradle of his arms.

'Have you been a good boy?' Mother asked.

'See for yourself,' said Father, answering for me.

'What do you mean?'

To forestall awkward questions about his own conduct, Father was drawing attention to mine.

He nodded to a copy of the *Gazette* that lay open on the table.

Mother picked up the paper. A headline read – 'Teacher Dies Belting Dog Throttle Monster Boy'.

Alongside a photo of Clucky's stricken widow, I again appeared giving my cheery thumbs-up.

'Alleged Puppy Killer Ivan Moss . . . A much-loved and dedicated teacher . . . town sees troubling rise in teen rebelliousness . . .'

Mother threw down the paper. She shook her head. 'We should never have come here,' she said. 'This town is jinxed.'

'There there,' said Father, thrusting the bundle toward her. He turned to me. 'Now see what you've done,' he said, with satisfaction.

I looked at them. Thin light drew warm smiles. The two protective stalks of their bodies bent over the tiny bloom of Stan. It was his turn to have his lip thrummed by Mother and to infuriate Father by saying 'uff-uff'.

My child work was done.

Dunt Vernon had also read the *Gazette* article. Inflamed by my celebrity, he attacked me with renewed venom. He snatched my gym shoes from my bag and choked a cistern with them, thus forcing their retrieval and condemning me to squelch about the gym floor, making embarrassing noises to mass amusement, as I attempted scissor leaps.

In bed that night, I thought of the morrow. The familiar gnawing black hole of dread took hold of me and I pulled the covers to my ears, so that my soft moaning wails could not be heard. I had begun to accommodate Dunt Vernon in my life as a permanent and terrible affliction, like a hunchback or a peg leg. It did not occur to me that I could ever be free of his dominion. A child can see no future, because he has very little past; without a past there can be no reflection and thus none of the self-awareness that comes from lessons learned. We had yet to pull on our Afghan coats and read about the Eternal Now. Instead we had the eternal nowt, in all its terror and hideous boredom. How could we children have known that all things must pass, whether we want them to or not; the bad and the good alike?

The bullying ended.

Dunt Vernon was to become the victim of what is best called poetic justice.

It happened like this:

We had taken our morning desks as usual, not daring to chat too loudly. If Mr Niven could hear our racket as he approached down the corridor, he would exercise his authority on entry with a vigorous display of swishing. Except that Mr Niven did not appear that morning. Instead, an elderly crone entered the room. She stood before us.

'Boys and girls, I am your new teacher. My name is Miss Andrews. Please stand and say "Good morning, Miss Andrews."'

We rose and assumed that stilted sing-song lilt: 'Good morning, Miss And-rews.'

'Good morning, boys and girls,' returned Miss Andrews.

We eyed her, curiously. Miss Andrews had blue hair, brown brogues and a white glove on one of her hands.

'There are two things you should know about me,' explained Miss Andrews. 'I don't like using the strap, but use it I will, and severely. I also use this.'

She picked up a blackboard pointer, allowed us to gaze on it, before slamming it down without warning on Limpy Chalfont's desk. Limpy gave a slight jump, but pretended not to have done.

'The second thing you should know – and you will already have noticed this – is that I have a false hand.'

Miss Andrews held aloft her false hand for our admiration. It was slightly smaller than her real hand and the fingers were curled, as if frozen in the act of clutching a bunch of flowers, or holding a sheep's head by the ear.

Tempted by his own wit, I heard Dunt Vernon's sotto voce whisper – 'That's a good shape for giving a wank.' This drew some localised tittering from Dunt's acolytes and a smattering of others who wished to be seen, for reasons of fear, as payers of homage. I did not join in, on two counts: first, I refused on principle to share a joke with Dunt Vernon and second, though I answered to the name of being one, I had only the vaguest notion of what a wank actually was. Dunt's jest was, of course, an outright challenge to the authority of Miss Andrews and we watched with interest to see if and how it might be repelled. Miss Andrews paused briefly then pressed on, pretending not to have heard Dunt's taunt. That was it then – she was just a mouse, with a voice that squeaked marginally less than her brogues.

Let anarchy commence.

'You will take out your English exercise books,' she instructed.

In our own sweet time, we took out our books.

Miss Andrews patrolled up and down the aisles.

'You will turn to page fifty – the poem, "Widecombe Fair".'

We found the poem.

'We shall read it aloud. Wherever my pointer falls, that person shall stand and will read two lines.'

The pointer duly fell on the desk of Janet Gooding. Janet stood to read.

'Tom Pearce, Tom Pearce, lend me your grey mare, all—'

'Wait!'

Janet waited.

'This poem is also a sung ballad – it has a very definite metre.' Miss Andrews demonstrated the very definite metre, bashing it out on a desk, with her gammy paw.

'*All* along, *down* along, *out* along *lee* . . .!' She looked at us. 'What does that metre remind you of?' We looked back at her, blankly. She enlightened us. 'Why, it's a horse, trotting, isn't it!'

Scales dropped from eyes, or in the case of our denser comrades, onto them.

'We need a strong boy to demonstrate for us – a strapping boy – a boy man enough to handle a galloping horse!'

That sort of guff cut no ice with me and I inched sideways into partial eclipse behind the beefy shoulders of Doreen Sumpter. There was no need for this precaution. Miss Andrews knew exactly which strapping man-boy she had in mind.

'You – what's your name!'

'Vernon.'

'Vernon, *miss*.'

'Vernon, *miss*.'

'You're the class leader, the number one boy, aren't you?'

Dunt affected bored modesty.

'I can see you're big and strong. You will demonstrate for us. Out you come!'

Bemused by the stealthy camouflage of flattery, Dunt sidled onto the floor, into our collective sight, self-consciously grinning.

Miss Andrews tapped her pointer. Janet Gooding resumed reading.

'For *I* want to *go* to Widecombe Fair.'

'Excellent! Next reader!'

Miss Andrews tapped another shoulder. She began cajoling Dunt with vigorous instruction. 'Ride that mare, Vernon, ride it!'

Dunt Vernon rode the non-existent mare, bobbing up and down, uneasily. Miss Andrews cantered alongside, keeping him company.

'Next reader!'

Shona Burns stood. 'With Bill Brewer, Jan Stewer, Peter Gurney, Peter Davy, Dan'l Whiddon, Harry Hawk—'

'Clutch the reins of that sturdy steed, Vernon! Make it spring! Up and down! Up and down! See it bound along the Devon countryside – ride! Ride!'

Dunt rode, rode, his face reddening.

'Wonderful! Your seat is superb!'

Dunt looked wretched. The penny had dropped. He clip-clopped up and down the room, stuck in a fly trap of sticky, unaccustomed praise. His face was locked in a fixed smile but the hot coals of his eyes warned his watching audience – 'If you laugh, ya cunts,' those eyes said, 'I'll kill you one and all!'

'And *Tom* sat *down* on a *stone* and he cried . . .'

'Sit, Tom! Sit!'

Dunt squatted on his hunkers, looking gratifyingly foolish.

'Let's see some crying, Vernon – cry!'

Dunt, having no choice, boo-hooed, to order.

Limpy Chalfont took up a couplet, then the Garry twins, which took ages since they were illiterate, all of which time Dunt Vernon was obliged to cover with an orgy of tearful wailing.

'Next reader!'

I stood. 'And all the long night he heard skirling and groans . . .'

'Groans, Vernon, groans!'

'*Oohhh . . . Oohhhhhh . . .*'

'From Tom Pearce's old *mare* in her rattling *bones* . . .'

'Rattle those bones, Vernon, rattle!'

Dunt rattled, wretchedly. He had cantered over the Fields of Embarrassment, performed dressage in the Gorge of

Humiliation and had now galloped over the top into the realm of Fixed Class Legend.

He was ridiculous.

'Now – everybody!'

Everybody – which meant every last one of us, except Dunt Vernon – boomed out the words, with exhilarated glee.

'*Old Uncle Tom Cobley and all, old Uncle Tom Cobley and all . . .!*'

We fell silent.

'Thank you, Vernon, you may sit down.'

Dunt sat down.

In our eyes, he never quite rose again.

Fourteen

I felt uneasy over my handling of the Dr Ryford consultation. It had begun to dawn on me that in my headlong rush for so-called 'knowledge' I might have closed a door in my mother's mind, rather than opened one. In a spirit of self-flagellation, I rang Stan.

'You spoke to Ryford?'

'Yes,' I said.

'You pressed him for details, for facts?'

'Facts and details, Stan. One to four, that's his best offer.'

'We're not selling a house.' It was a reproach but mild. He was mollified that I had acquired hard information. Stan liked facts.

'At least now we know,' he said.

'That's what I thought.' I was relieved. Stan wasn't berating me for my insistence on showing Mother her ticking meter, he was paying me a grudging compliment. I realised the unpleasant shiftiness of my own position: I was more concerned that my brother should think I'd done the right thing than that I'd forced the bloodied corpse of our mother's stunted life to be held up before her own agonised gaze.

'So you think I did the right thing?' I shouldn't have asked him outright. My brother immediately sensed weakness.

'Why are you asking? You think you did the wrong thing?'

'Not wrong.'

'But not right. What's on your mind, Ivan? You're sorry you told her?'

'Not sorry.'

'For God's sake—'

'Tell me I'm being airy fairy, an old hippy or something, but I wondered if . . .'

'What?'

'Well, if she'd have been better not knowing.'

I gave a cowardly little chortle as I said this, like it was a trivial thing, pre-empting someone's life; happened every day between emptying the garbage and ironing a shirt. I was fearful, at this heightened time, that my blundering action might solidify into lifelong legend: 'There he goes, Mother freezer Moss; cut her life short; chilled her to death with hard mean facts.'

'Why do you say that?' Stan asked.

'Not knowing gave her hope.'

'Hope? Or self-delusion?'

'Whichever, that was her business, Stan. No one has the right to take that comfort away. If that's what helped her, made an intolerable situation bearable.' I was arguing hard against my own position, I had to be careful. I began to soft pedal. 'I mean, whatever gets you through the night, Stan. Religion. Ouija boards, you name it.'

'Now you sound like an old hippy.'

I gave another chuckle, trying to keep the tone light. 'I mean, ask yourself – would you want to know when exactly you were going to die?'

He thought for a moment. 'She has one to four, that's not exact.'

I couldn't keep up the pretence. I had to say it. I said it.

'Stan, I'll come clean. I have a horrible fear I've put a full stop on her life.'

There was a silence.

'Stan?'

My brother said, 'Yes, yes, I heard. I was thinking. I see.'

'What do you see? Stan? What?'

'You're asking me if you did the wrong thing in making Ryford tell her?'

'No, not wrong. I'm asking you if I did the right thing. You know . . . the thing which is right.'

He didn't speak. I thought I'd lost him this time for sure. 'Stan?'

'Yes, I'm still here.'

'Say something.' I needed him to let me off the hook.

'You did the right thing.'

'Good.'

'You did what you thought needed to be done.'

'Thanks, Stan,' I said, 'that means a lot.'

'But from here on in, your action is between you and your conscience.'

'Stan?'

'I have to go. I have a productivity meeting.'

He put the phone down.

Me and my conscience looked at each other. Having nothing to say, we put the kettle on.

I carried my cup into the dining room. I sat down and opened the laptop.

I climbed in and shut the lid.

It was Sunday afternoon in Dreichstane. I was attempting homework at the kitchen table. I did not feel well. *Two-Way*

Family Favourites cloyed on the radio. Clothes were drying and the air was fetid with the stench of boiling sprouts. Father was polishing the skip of his old officer's cap, as he had taken to doing, increasingly. Mother grunted as she heaved a washing basket full of damp clothes onto the table. I ground my teeth. Elbowing some freshly boiled underpants aside, I drove my pencil forward. I did not see the approach of the hand that whisked away my school jotter.

'Give me that!' I protested.

'What is it?' Father asked, fending me off.

'Homework,' I said, 'an essay.'

'What is the subject?'

'Travel.'

'Travel to the back green,' said Mother, seizing her opportunity, 'it's a good drying day. A bit of help from you both with hanging this lot out wouldn't go amiss.'

We looked at her as though at an alien being, speaking in an unknown tongue. Father perused my essay and began quoting, in an amused way.

'*In conclusion, the country I would most like to visit is Hungary, as it has the highest suicide rate in Europe, which appeals to me, as I am always depressed and . . .*'

Father's voice droned on. Stan whined in his pram. Mother used tongs to slurp a dripping jumper into the sink. On the radio, Jean Metcalfe sent love to all those back home in Pontefract from a dear son serving in München.

Father continued: '*Being Scottish, I am heartened by the idea of self-destruction but lack the nerve to commit the act, as I have not yet been tormented enough by the English, as they are too nice. I pray that one day Scotland will be invaded by Russian Red Army beasts, so I will have an excuse to do away with myself and . . .*' Father stopped reading, abruptly. I had taken things too far.

On the radio, Pearl Carr and Teddy Johnson were into the chorus of 'Sing Little Birdie'.

Father turned them off. His face was stern with disapproval. 'Russia is a failed social experiment,' he said. 'Are you telling me that life under the boot heel of a tyrannical world power is a condition to be admired?'

'Not admired,' I explained. 'But it would cheer me up. At least then I'd know who to hate.'

Father grimaced. 'Hatred hates the hater most.'

Mother was in quickly. 'I blame you,' she said. She was again using the tongs to load a drenched jumper into the sink. 'You filled his head with that Russian rubbish.'

Father cursed. The radio was turned back on. Pearl and Teddy were still at it.

I felt faint, claustrophobic: the rowing voices; the intrusive screech of the singing; the crowded kitchen; the putrid vegetable stink. I stood up. As I did so, my knees buckled and my brow fell forward. Father caught me by the scruff before my chin could hit the table.

I came to with my head between my legs.

'He needs air,' my mother was saying.

'There's air in here.'

'Fresh air. Take him for a walk.'

'Where would we go?'

'It's a walk – you don't need to go anywhere.'

'He doesn't want to go for any walks.' Father looked me, accusingly. 'Do you want to go for a walk?'

My head still swam. My eyes were clearing.

'How would you know what he wants?' chivvied Mother. 'You hardly even speak to him.'

This news surprised Father. Mother leaned in close. Her breath smelled of fags and tea.

'Ivan, do you want to go for a walk?'

'A walk, yes, maybe.' I said, woozily. 'I'd like to see the Brandy Burn.'

Mother swivelled, triumphantly. Cornered, Father turned his gaze to the window and screwed his eyes against the dazzling sun. 'Looks like rain,' he said.

Everyone I knew had been to the Brandy Burn. To avoid social disgrace, I had pretended to know it well.

'Go on, take him,' said Mother. 'It would get you out from under my feet.'

'*The Cruel Sea* is coming on the television.'

'God almighty, how often have you seen that film?'

'Men died,' rebuked Father sternly, by way of avoiding an inventory.

They let the subject of the Brandy Burn drop.

So that they would pick it up again, I said, loudly, 'Forget it!'

Back to my old self, I clumped huffily to the living-room window. I made my shoulders droop in a wretched fashion, signifying disappointment. Outside, Limpy Chalfont hobbled past. He flicked the double Vs in greeting. I showed him my fist, discreetly, while continuing to look dejected, a masterpiece of dual role-playing that left me drained and emotionally exhausted.

On the radio 'You Need Hands' had succeeded Pearl and Teddy. Father shuddered at Max Bygraves' nasal whine. 'Fuckit,' he said, rising. 'Ivan, fetch my shoes.'

'Ye-es!'

It took us much travelling time to locate the mythical spring and we traversed the vast, flat plains of Sycamore Avenue before braving the gruelling slope of Maple Drive and turning our faces eastward into the heart of the sun. Weary of foot, we slumped on a garden wall near the fringes of the wood. Father wafted his damp armpits, gratefully.

'Are you sure you wouldn't rather have an ice pole?' he asked, his voice sagging with forlorn hope.

I pointed up into the trees, in steadfast fashion, indicating a distant clump of bushes. 'The Brandy's up there,' I urged. 'I'm sure of it.'

I looked at Father.

'Come on,' he said, and rose wearily.

At last, after much toil, we arrived at the fabled Brandy Burn. My heart sang and my spirits soared. In the heady dazzle of the scented air, sparrows became golden eagles.

'What do you think, Father?'

He was silent. I assumed him to be seeking out the bon mot that might encapsulate the fragile beauty of the moment. He found it.

'I've come out without my fags,' he said, rummaging through his pockets.

I forced his attention back to the rolling hills, the small yet verdant valley, at the foot of which bubbled the clear and lively waters of the burn. I watched the breeze waft the thinning quiff of his hair.

'Ivan?'

'Yes, Father?'

'What is it that makes a boy your age want to kill himself?'

I felt myself blush at my earlier confessional outburst. I backtracked, hastily. 'It's not that I want to kill myself, I just . . .'

'Of course you do,' my father said. 'Every intelligent man wants to do away with himself from time to time. It's a fact of life.' Having blundered onto the dreaded subject, Father had no option but to continue. 'Speaking of which, you do know the facts of life, don't you?'

I nodded.

'Thank God for that,' he said. 'Now, where were we?'

'Suicide.'

'Ah yes!' Relieved to be on safe conversational ground once more, Father pursued the subject with gusto. 'People do away with themselves when they're unhappy.'

'Yes, but what is it that makes us unhappy?'

'Living.'

I considered this. 'Then we're trapped,' I said. 'Life makes us unhappy, yet it's all we have.'

'No,' my father corrected. 'There's a distinction. I said living, Ivan, not life. There's nothing the matter with life, it's just the way that we live it that's wrong. Living is a hard business.'

We looked at the hills. The unfamiliar sun was easing our clenched shoulders, straightening the drooping stems of our backs. 'Come on,' the sun was purring, 'let down your guard. I'm the lucky old sun, you can trust me.'

'What about life, Father?'

'Life is just a fucking mystery,' my father said.

'Yes,' I agreed.

I wanted the present to remain vivid, that moment, there and then, in the scented air, standing alongside my father, under the purring, the lucky old sun, talking about the fucking mystery of life and the hard business of living.

I wanted to hold the present, so I recalled the past.

'Father, do you remember when we lived in Govan?'

'Of course I do.' He gave me a squinting look. 'I can remember a time before you were even born,' he said. 'Can you imagine that?'

I tried to imagine that. 'What was it like, before I was born? You know; the war?'

Father sighed, nostalgically. 'Chaos. Destruction. We squeezed whole lifetimes into a single day.'

'Were you happy?'

Father assumed a tone of gentle rebuke. 'What is this obsession with happiness? Happiness is a fleeting condition, Ivan, not an ongoing state of being.'

'When you talk about the past, you seem happy.'

'The past is always happy, because what's past is no longer a threat.'

'What about the present? Are you happy now?'

My father frowned. 'If I could make my past my present, I might be happy.' He took a breath, loosened a mental button. 'There was a woman I knew once before I was married. She . . .'

Puzzled, I spoke too soon. 'What woman?'

My father frowned, composed himself, tidied away things past. 'What did we agree about living?'

'That it's a hard business.'

'Is it a happy business?'

'Fleetingly.'

'Indeed. And do you remember the proverb? The fine old Russian proverb?'

'Yes,' I said.

'And what does the fine old Russian proverb tell us that life is not?'

'Life is not a stroll across an open field.'

'Correct.'

I frowned. Father smiled. He seemed happy that I was not happy as we looked out across the open field that life is not a stroll across, even though we had just strolled across it to be where we were.

I was confused. 'Father?'

'Yes?'

'I think dark things. How am I to live?'

My father stooped down to my level. It was not a far journey, as he was, as I have said, a smout. 'Find a thing you love to do,' he said, with feeling, 'and devote your life to the doing of it.'

'What do you love, Father?'

'The sea,' my father answered, without pause for reflection.

Love seemed a daunting aspiration. 'What if I never find a thing to devote myself to?'

'Then you are in for a long and troubled life,' said my father.

'What if I die tomorrow under the wheels of a bus?'

'Your life will still have seemed too long.'

I considered. 'You're right, Father.'

'Fulfilment, Ivan. That's all there is. Try to find it.'

I looked at him. He stretched his back, uncoiled the taut spring of his rangy five foot seven.

'Are you fulfilled, Father?'

'Do I look fulfilled?'

'No,' I confessed. 'In fact, it sometimes frightens me . . . thinking that my life might one day end up like yours.'

'It frightens me too, my life one day ending up like mine . . . But things change.'

'When will they change?'

'Soon.'

'How change? In what way? And how fast is soon?'

My father did not answer these questions, which was, of course, his answer.

We stood together in silent thought. Yes, we Mosses had rolled far. With a single bound, we had escaped to a magical land of inside toilets, outside coal bunkers, private gardens and planned estates, unbounded by the blackened walls of tenements. We were living in the Promised Land. No doubt about it; sheep, cows, trees, home boilers for white clothing, the lot. A place like the Brandy Burn disturbed your sense of self. It seemed alien, because pretty. And because alien and pretty, you felt like you were on holiday, and light of heart. And your father was standing next to you, doing things with you, like a proper boy and his father did. I noticed a strange thing had happened to my face. My mouth had creased and my eyes had narrowed.

I was smiling.

I was happy. Luckily, it was only fleeting.

'Father—'

'Shush,' said Father. 'Listen.'

'What is it?'

A cloud blotted the sun. Father shivered and spat some phlegm onto a cow pat. Fat brown flies lifted, scattered.

'There it is again,' said Father.

We listened. Sure enough, we could hear a tinny sound, punctuated by jagged voices and the occasional echoing crack.

In the adjoining field, a clump of boys, big bad boys, were making a racket. One was jabbing a cow's udder with a sabre. Another was chanting, 'M. J. Ya Bass!'

I knew what this stood for – The Mad Jappa. I was fearful and looked at Father.

'Yes,' he said. 'It's time to go.'

On our way back, it started to rain. Father bought a *Sunday Mail*. We halved it and made paper roofs for our head houses.

Fifteen

When we arrived home we could hear voices from the living room. Having arrived unexpectedly, Granny and Grandpa Moss were taking tea. In those days, few people had a phone in the home, so an unannounced visit was a common occurrence. These excursions were somewhat of a lottery. It was not unusual for a traveller to embark on long bus journey, only to discover that the intended recipient of the visit had gone out, emigrated, died or was hiding in the back room behind the bed cabinet so as to elude the visitor's attentions. This was how Granny Moss had located Mother, spotting her through a gap in our hastily drawn curtains.

'That's a lie!'

'Tell me then,' demanded Granny Moss, 'what exactly were you doing crouching behind a tallboy?'

'I told you, I was changing Ivan's bed clothes.'

'You changed them yesterday,' I reminded Mother, stupidly.

'You see!' said Granny Moss. 'Damned out of her own mouth!'

Granny Moss gave Father a satisfied look, like a prosecuting attorney who has produced a surprise bombshell witness.

Mother made an impassioned appeal. 'Tell her, Ivan – tell her to keep her big nose out of our marriage.'

Father did not tell Granny anything of the sort. He stood in the middle of the room, glowering to hide his confusion. I felt for him.

'Bloody old witch! Speak to her, Ivan!'

In lieu of decisive action, Father removed his paper hat.

I detected a gluey aroma.

In a far corner, Grandpa Moss sat quietly, assembling some component parts of an Airfix model.

He saw me looking.

'It's a Heinkel . . . a Heinkel . . .'

'Bomber?' I supplied.

'Yes. In . . .'

'Deed?'

'Correct,' said Grandpa Moss.

I was impressed. 'Father and I tried to put that together,' I told Grandpa, 'but we couldn't do it, could we?'

'No,' my father admitted, 'it was too fiddly.'

Mother rounded on him. 'Is there anything in life you *can* do?'

Grandpa Moss kept assembling the little grey pieces of aircraft. His detachment looked blissful.

Mother wouldn't let it rest. She turned to Granny Moss. 'It's you,' she said. 'You're a vile, poisonous old bitch hag of a woman.'

Granny Moss affected disdain. 'I'm not going to rise to your bait!'

'And I won't sink to your level!'

While the women were busy with not rising or sinking, Father had slithered along the wall and turned on the television set. *The Cruel Sea* had just started. Father perked up. Out of emotional delicacy, he kept the sound muted. The *Compass Rose* appeared on screen. It had not yet sunk. Together, Father and I recognised the much-loved scene.

'Snorkers – good-oh!' we parroted to Stanley Baker's moving lips. Father gave me a pleased smile. I had learned well.

Seeing us, Mother picked up her cup and saucer and hurled them against the wall.

Granny made a show of shock. Rising, she slapped Mother's face. Mother retaliated with a hair tug. Father sprang up and wrestled them apart. Grandpa Moss left the room quietly and entered the lobby cupboard.

I followed him, turning on the light. We made a sofa out of a defunct oil heater. I felt calmed by the silence and the musty smell of hanging coats. As he continued his work on the Heinkel bomber, Grandpa felt obliged to entertain me.

'I can name you the Rangers team of 1928,' he said. 'The one that ended the infamous twenty-five year Scottish Cup—'

I waited, out of politeness for, oh, a long time. Then I said, 'Final?'

'No.'

'Drought?'

'No. Bit like . . .'

'Hoodoo?'

'Yes, hoodoo.' He fixed me with a look. It was a long look. He did not move for the duration of the look. I waved my hand in front of his face. He stirred. 'I hadn't died,' he said. 'I was . . .'

'In a coma?'

'No.'

'Swooning?'

'No.'

'Thinking?'

'Yes, thinking.' Grandpa coughed the smell of coats from his throat. He made his voice sound grave, like Neville Chamberlain declaring war, or like the men who announced the teams at

football grounds, in the days before disc jockeys. He began to intone: 'T. Hamilton, Gray, R. Hamilton, Buchanan, Meiklejohn,
Craig; Archibald, Cunningham, Fleming, McPhail and . . .'

Grandpa hesitated. I assisted.

'Morton?'

'Yes.'

Even I knew Morton.

It had been only eleven names, but each one had represented
a slow step down into the dank cellar of boredom. I looked at
him to see if he had stopped speaking. Mistaking my look of
relief for admiration, he continued.

'I expect you would like to hear the Celtic team of that
legendary.'

'Day?'

'No.'

'Afternoon?'

'Yes, afternoon. Here it.'

'Is?'

'Yes.'

He composed himself, began the same routine, slowly, slowly. 'J. Thomson; W. McStay, Donoghue; Wilson, J. McStay,
McFarlane; Connolly, A. Thomson, McGrory, McInally and—'

'I'll never get that one,' I said.

'McLaine,' said Grandpa.

I opened my mouth to speak. Grandpa held up a restraining
hand.

'Referee, Mr William Bell.'

I fell silent.

'You're waiting for the linesmen,' he said. 'But I do not know
the.'

'Linesmen?'

'Yes.'

He inserted a tiny Luftwaffe pilot through an open plastic window and sat him down on his sticky glue bottom. Having done this, Grandpa flicked the cockpit window shut with a fingertip. He held up the beautifully neat, meticulously assembled plastic miniature of a Heinkel bomber. Together, we savoured its impressive majesty. The Heinkel was perfect in every possible detail, save one. The wings were on back to front.

Grandpa appeared not to notice this blemish.

'Uh . . .' he said.

'Huh?' I added.

'Yes,' he said.

Affecting a dour look and grunting, the way Scots do when attempting to disguise a kindly act, Grandpa presented me with the gift of the bomber.

I flicked on my smile and gushed, dutifully. 'Thank you.'

The cupboard door opened.

'So that's where you are,' Father said. He looked flushed and agitated.

'What's the matter?'

'Never you mind. Hold Grandpa's hand and run down to the bus stop.'

'Where's Granny?'

'She walked out in a huff and forgot to take him.'

Father turned away. I helped Grandpa on with his coat.

Even from the street, we could hear Mother and Father arguing in the living room. I was concerned that Mrs Moidart might call the police, as she had on occasion threatened to do, and felt uneasy on the walk down to the stop. Near the Clock Café at the top of Thorn Brae, we caught up with Granny. Having returned Grandpa to her like a mislaid umbrella, I ran all the way home.

I was sweating and panting. One or two small boys stood giggling by the garden. I ran into the house. The screaming was loud enough to drown out the shouts of oily sailors in the water around the *Compass Rose*.

'A real man stands up for his wife – a real man doesn't kowtow to his mammy!'

'Quit your nagging, you shrew!'

'I should've married Tommy Fintry!'

'And I should've married Maria Tomlin!'

'She didn't want you. She dumped you! You were too much of a—'

Mother was unable to proceed with her reflections on Father's character, for Father had interrupted her narrative flow by grabbing her and squeezing her windpipe.

I saw him lunge, watched the enraged hand on its journey, heard her startled 'ooh' and gurgle as Mother arched back over the sideboard, feeling instinctively for her skirt to shield her modesty. She lay slumped, making little moans. Father loomed over her, hands twisted in frenzy. Mother gouged her nails down his face.

'I wish you had married that Fintry bastard – if you had, it would've saved me a lot of fucking . . .'

As he had done at the Brandy Burn, Father searched for *le mot juste*. Before he could locate it, a voice from the television interrupted. The voice said, 'Here is a newsflash.'

My parents broke off, straightening in curiosity. Newsflashes were rare and prized events. A picture of a blonde woman appeared on the screen, interrupting Jack Hawkins who had been in his cabin savouring a consoling drink. The blonde woman was glamorous looking. She had fat red lips. Though not, at that moment, as fat or red as Mother's. A newsreader with a posh accent spoke in a stately monotone. He said: 'The film star Marilyn Monroe has been found dead in her apartment in Los Angeles. Police are at the scene. The cause of death is at present unknown. Further details will follow in the evening bulletin. That is the end of this newsflash. We return you to *The Cruel Sea*.'

But we did not return. Father was too shaken by the news and turned off the set. Seizing her opportunity, Mother picked herself up from the floor and fled to the sanctuary of the bathroom.

To cheer us all up, I took my Compendium of Games from the sideboard and set it up on the table. I rattled the Ludo dice invitingly in its plastic cup.

My father shook his head. 'Marilyn Monroe's just died,' he said. 'The lights have just gone out again, all over Europe.'

We heard a shattering crash. The going out of lights included the bedroom. Mother had just lobbed a standard lamp out the window. Outside, by the privet, the gathering of small boys yelled and hooted.

Out of respect for Marilyn, Father swished the curtains, shutting them out. 'Fucking women,' he said, from the heart.

As he himself had said, it's not life, it's the way that we live it.

Sixteen

Eager to atone for my error, I made a bucket list for my mother, which comprised exciting, worldwide adventures: to the swaying frond and fruit-laden cocktail land of Hawaii; to Thebes to ponder the twin mysteries of the pyramids and Egyptian driving; to Switzerland for the expensive oxygen and cocktails, then on finally to Venice, in bittersweet mood, where lovers have either a first holiday to nurture their romance or a last in an effort to revive its dying bloom. I wanted my mother to rekindle her love affair with life. I was not clear why I felt obliged to do this. It would seem a cruel and heartless thing to stimulate a desire for living that death would soon deny, but I reasoned that illness is a spiritual thermometer not only for the dying but the living. My mother had a last maternal obligation to reinforce her own sense of life and therefore mine too by refusing to fill her yawning casket unless dragged toward it by the ankles while screaming and scraping her reluctant fingernails down the ravaged sod. Only then might I be reassured that I had not broken her will and that this inexplicable in and out breathing racket we call living might still, to her, be worth the admission ticket. Our modern culture demands a relentless and noisy yea-saying in order to drown out our doubts and mask the unpleasant reality that life for many people is a vapid, unfulfilling and daunting thing. I would have taken my mother anywhere in the world she might have wished to go. Or rather I wouldn't, my wallet would. I had delegated the tedious chore of actually accompanying her to my brother, Stan. Any longer than a day in the presence of my mother and I'd have throttled her, which would have represented poor holiday value and done little to expiate my guilt.

We were in the living room. I had a notepad on my knees. Though it wasn't cold, my mother sat hunched over the electric fire, smoking.

I started in. 'I've made a few notes,' I said.

She looked up. 'What sort of notes?'

'Of fun places to see and visit.'

'Hospitals?'

'No, other places. Distant places. Around the globe.'

She thought about this. 'Is this what they call a bucket list?'

'Not at all. Just a few fun places to see and visit.'

'Why would I do that?'

'You have one to four years, a good chunk of time. We have to crowd a lot into it.'

She thought about this too. 'Why?'

'All right, it's a fucking bucket list. What's wrong with that?'

She shrugged, took another draw. She hadn't set foot over the doorstep since receiving her prognosis. The dutiful son, I was patient yet persistent.

'There must be somewhere or something that would tempt you outside again; wherever it is, I'll take you there.'

She considered. 'Anywhere?'

A bite. Progress. 'Anywhere.'

'Okay.'

An hour later we were standing in the queue of a newsagent's shop on Paisley Road. I had offered her the world and she had chosen the sub post office to collect her pension.

'There's been a spate of muggings,' she explained. 'Your aunt Tina is nervous about going for me now.'

'I could have collected it for you.'

'You wanted me to go out,' she said. 'I'm out.'

Her logic was faultless but I questioned its parameters. 'Out is quite a big place,' I reminded her. 'This place isn't even on out's doorstep. There's much more to out than this.'

She ignored my breezy tone.

Three times, withered crones in beige raincoats enquired about her health. Each time she made the same guarded, coded reply. In the lift returning to her flat, the same thing happened a fourth time. Emerging onto the landing, she turned to me.

'That's why I don't go out,' she said.

We went in.

It was strange being in with my mother. I realised being in with her felt the same as being out; her condition having shackled our minds and blinkered our perceptions, narrowing down life's infinite possibilities to a steady progression toward an inevitable single conclusion. She was not recoiling in cowardice or shrugging indifferently at the external world, but had begun clearing a mental and spiritual path toward her demise. Stan reported to me a conversation he'd had with a taxi driver. He'd told the driver his mother was ill with cancer.

'What variety?'

'Lung,' Stan had replied.

'She'll be dead in a year,' the driver had responded, matter of factly. 'My sister had it. That's all most of them ever last with lung.'

Our mother, of course, had seen others, many others, many times, in the same predicament as she now found herself. I might try to pull the wool with fanciful talk of exotic locations, but it was over my own eyes; my mother's own eyes gazed fixedly ahead. She had begun her withdrawal and was packing her bags, preparing for infinity; you can't go much further out than that.

She had agreed to radiotherapy treatment. I think she did it to appease Stan and me. One day I took her back to hospital, where they ran off an X-ray plate to determine the effects of the treatment. She had been complaining of shortage of breath.

'The trouble is,' said Dr Ryford, 'radiotherapy kills off healthy cells in the area as well as bad ones. The good news is the tumour hasn't as yet grown any larger.'

He'd tried to slip in the 'as yet' but I pounced on it.

'I can't give you any assurances,' he said, 'other than we're doing our very best.'

My mother rose and made one of those elderly person grovels of thanks. By way of counterbalance, I offered a grunt. On the way along the corridor she stopped.

'What's the matter?'

'There,' she said, 'that waiting room.'

'What about it?'

It was an old drab waiting area, like all the others.

'I remember it,' she said. 'I sat there with Stan when he was a baby.'

'Ah yes,' I said. I had a vague recollection of Stan being sickly when young.

She looked up at me. 'That was back in the old days,' she said, 'when I was useful.'

'You're still useful,' I told her. She wasn't listening. She had shuffled on, leaving the waiting room behind. Or so she thought. I made a prudent mental note to return her to it that night.

Memories are valuable; if you leave them lying around, they

disappear like a dropped wallet.

That night we talked of the past.

Young Stanley, like his father, was highly strung and troubled. As a baby Stan had the disconcerting habit of lying back in his pram and freezing solid. To lie cold and rigid in your shawl at eighty is one thing, but at eight months, quite another. Without warning, his body would stiffen and his blue eyes stare sightlessly ahead. I took this to be some form of infant protest, but Stan turned out to be suffering from mild epilepsy, for which medication was prescribed.

If Father's mercurial spirits had been uplifted by the birth, they were overflowing thanks to the illness. Mother would surely be quiescent now she had a baby with a dodgy nervous system in tow. But in his cunning machinations, Father had overlooked a further fact; babies cost money. His parental responsibilities had doubled, but his pay packet had not. Effectively, it had shrunk. Ergo, both parents would now be unable to climb from the un-happiness well since each remained tethered at the bottom by the twin shackles of duty and poverty. Being myself above such humdrum considerations as love and money, the change in our family circumstance did not, at first, impact on me. Gradually though, pocket money became a haphazard treat then stopped.

To ensure a steady supply of funds, I took to scouring the bins and workmen's huts for 'gingies' – refundable bottles. On one occasion, while liberating an Irn-Bru vessel from the pocket of a hanging jacket, I noticed a wage packet. Inside was a sin-gle pound note, probably the 'skim' that the workman had slyly pocketed before handing over the housekeeping money to his wife. In a precocious gesture of support for women's rights, I pocketed the note.

In the chip shop later the proprietor, Leno, gave me his

customary greeting. 'Hey! Izza Ivan! Yi working, Ivan?'

'No.'

'Ach, izza no working? A wee minute for chips.'

'Right.'

Chips, even in those days, were never ready in a chip shop. In these establishments, customers always arrive as a sort of surprise. Leno was middle-aged with, fittingly, a salt and pepper moustache. He leaned his arms on the polished silver surface of the counter and entered that mild unseeing trance, peculiar to all who work in chip shops, as they await the sizzling conclusion of their art. As if in response to some secret chip maker's dog whistle, he snapped out of his trance and into action. He gave the chips a vigorous shake in their mesh holder, making the hot fat hiss angrily like a wild animal.

'So – izza not working?'

'No, Leno, I'm not working.'

'How not?'

'I'm only eleven.'

'Age izza nae excuse! Just chips?'

'No. A fish supper please, Leno.'

'Ooh, a fish supper, is it?' Leno pulled an uncomprehending face. 'Well, izza no fish suppers in Leno's shop – think again.'

I reconsidered. 'A fiss supper then please.'

'Ah – a fiss supper! Atsa better awthegither!' Leno turned to the sullen girl who was wiping the counter. 'Teresa, put a fiss in for Andrew Carnegie here.'

In the west of Scotland there remains no 'h' in the words 'fish supper'. How this anomaly of speech came about no one knows. Perhaps losing the 'h' began as a wartime economy of diction – if a busy housewife could save on her *h*s then this might afford her more free hours to devote to munitions work or knitting socks for the trenches. All we know for sure is that it is a wonderful old tradition that nobody understands, but one which is fervently upheld wherever working-class Glaswegians gather in bus shelters at closing time to clog their arterial passages with grease.

'Salt 'n' vinegar?'

I nodded. Teresa wrapped my purchase in its *Daily Record* swaddling coat.

'One fiss supper – one and fivepence.'

I handed over the pound note. Leno raised his not inconsiderable eyebrows.

'You sure you're no' working?'

'I'm not working,' I said. 'If I was, I'd have noticed.'

Teresa glowered in censure at this cheek. She counted out my change onto the greasy service counter in severe clunks.

'Izza justa wee funny man,' defended Leno, generously.

Outside, I savoured the exquisite decadence of a fiss supper in mid afternoon.

I watched the midday sun highlight smears of oil on a stagnant gutter puddle. The sun had a troubling effect. It eased my mind from its habitual frozen crouch and made it think lovely thoughts. In a working-class household, a lovely thought is like receiving the gift of a giraffe; it may be exotic but it is a useless burden. A drowsy numbness filled my senses as I bit into the juicy, murderous batter. I had eighteen shillings and seven pence in my trouser pocket. If only life could always be like this.

It couldn't.

When I arrived home, my parents were waiting. I had been seen leaving the workmen's hut. In a rare display of co-operation, Father held me by the ankles while Mother beat me like a carpet. Big, delicious coins rolled to the floor and, when I was safely away and sobbing, Father gathered them up. Later, he claimed to have returned them to the workman. Unless the workman owned the Hazel pub, I doubted that.

One day, soon after, Miss Andrews rapped the gavel of her false hand against the desk top.

'Class!'

We looked up.

'Moss!'

'Yes, miss?'

'Does the course of your future rest on gazing idly out of the window?'

'No, miss.'

'Then pay attention. The eleven-plus is just ahead. This exam will determine your future. Your marks, Moss, have gone downhill rapidly.'

This verdict dismayed but did not surprise me. Something had happened. The coiled inner spring of fear that had propelled me up the intelligence ladder had slackened with the downfall of Dunt Vernon. I could no longer rely on his invigorating morning battering to pep me up for the day ahead. Dunt had lain low after his humiliation and had taken to playing truant, or dogging it, to use our vernacular. After a while, glamorous stories of car thefts and break-ins began to filter back to us at our desks, where we sat bored, quietly parsing dull sentences. As a rebranding exercise, Dunt's career change proved a public relations triumph, as he acquired fresh mystique in the eyes of his peers.

'Moss!'

'Yes, miss?'

'I'm speaking to you. What does your father do for a living?'

'Miss, he's a sales director with a well-known city provisions merchant.'

Limpy Chalfont translated, helpfully. 'Miss – he sells Spam in a grocer's shop in Govan.'

Tittering ensued.

Miss Andrews gave us a severe look. Raising high the baton of her false hand, she silenced the room. She continued with her attack. 'I hope you'll do better for yourself than cutting Spam,' she chided, 'but at this rate, you won't even be the man your father is!'

'Yes, miss.' I affected a downcast look, for show.

'See me at three o'clock,' Miss Andrews said. 'I'm giving you a letter to take home to your parents.'

I grew alarmed. 'Please, miss . . .'

Her eyes narrowed. 'Yes?'

'Nothing, miss.'

After tea, I presented the letter to Father. He perused its contents, made a disapproving grunt. In the letter, Miss Andrews had tracked the waning trajectory of my dying academic star. Father frowned and gnashed his teeth. I eyed him, warily. Teeth gnashing was a signal that he had begun stoking the boilers of his paternal love. It would be tough love, of course, involving thoughtful blows to tender places.

'Did she say anything else?'

'No,' I croaked. A tactic occurred to me, slimy as usual. 'Yes,' I said.

'What?'

'She said I won't be the man you are.'

I watched as Father swelled from the inside out. From his threadbare rump invisible feathers sprouted to form an exultant peacock fan.

'Did she say that indeed?'

'Indeed she did.' All I had done was to omit the word 'even' from Miss Andrews' assessment. Perhaps it was a trick I had picked up from Grandpa Moss. It's amazing what can be achieved when you don't finish a. In diminishing myself, I had made Father great. Incumbent upon greatness, I hoped, would be a display of magnanimity to the vanquished.

'Wait here,' said Father.

He returned minutes later with a wobbling armful of elderly books. He sat the books in a crooked pile on the table and turned to me. 'I read these books at sea,' he declared, pointing. 'Here are some of the finest philosophers known to man.'

I looked. The finest philosophers known to man stood next to a bowl of plastic roses that Mother had collected free with Oxydol tokens. Evening sunlight caught the dust that had gathered inside the lifeless petals. They reminded me of the grime inside Norrie Garry's ears.

'Have you heard of the great ones? Plato? Aristotle? Plautus?'

'No, Father,' I said.

Father pointed to the sages, reverently.

I couldn't help noticing the great ones had been augmented by a Neville Shute and a couple of Mickey Spillanes. My concentration was restored by a blow to the head.

'Dostoevsky!' said Father. 'Chekhov!' Goethe!' One by one, he bounced the fabled names of world literature off my skull.

My literary instruction at an end, Father sighed, exasperated. He stroked the remainder of the toppled books like they were a faithful old family sheepdog.

'I had high hopes for you once,' he said, 'that's why I saved these works for your instruction. What good's come of them, eh?'

I did a spot of head hanging for show. 'No good, Father.'

He gave a disgusted snort, in the manner of a wealthy patriarch who has lavished great sums on a dissolute offspring so that he might be educated at the nation's finest palaces of wisdom.

'Unless you buck your ideas up, there'll be trouble.'

To indicate the sort of trouble he had in mind, he gave me a stern poke in the chest. The matter dealt with, he set off for the Hazel with a spring in his step to play the role of disillusioned intellectual; the Joseph Conrad of Spam.

Thereafter, I tried to be frightened so that I might regain the interest necessary to make me go on learning things in which I had no interest. It was hopeless. Try as I might to paint a mental picture of Father as a low-bred, unfeeling ruffian with a flinching aesthete for a son, I knew that neither portrait was fair or accurate. Most men of the time were uncouth. They beat their children with bare hands. Father was a cultivated man and beat me with volumes of Chekhov.

One day, another incident occurred, which proved momentous.

I was standing at my desk reading aloud my essay. Miss Andrews had given us free rein to express our personalities. The rein had been short, however, and tethered to the granite monolith of 'Why I Love Scotland'. Unwisely I had chosen the path of sarcasm in my offering. Thus, my mocking observations about 'The White Heather Club' and Andy Stewart, a white man in a kilt who did Louis Armstrong impressions, were admired by my teacher but not appreciated. I was instructed to sit. Doreen 'Shoulders' Sumpter was invited to rise.

Miss Andrews had announced that the most improved essayist would be rewarded by reading his or her work aloud to the class. For the first time in her school career, Doreen Sumpter found herself a prized exhibit.

Encouraged to bask in her triumph, Shoulders appeared stricken with disbelief. Finally, after brisk encouragement, she rose onto her substantial trotters. I was seated behind her. My sprawling gloom at being runner-up was shielded by the enormous grey-skirted Sumpter arse.

From the heave and swell of her back it was obvious that Shoulders was all agog with herself.

Off she cantered.

'"Scotland and Why I Love It" by Doreen B. Sumpter . . .'

Her voice started as a panting wisp that swelled unsteadily into confidence. The sweat of effort dribbled from every earnest pore as on she gibbered about Sweet Afton's gently flowing waters and Scotland's misty valleys and how the far Cuillin hills were pulling her away. In truth, it would have taken a cattle truck to have borne a breathless lump like Shoulders anywhere, then a ten-foot pole to prod her up the ramp into the cage and off to the slaughterhouse where she belonged. I felt her essay to be a shameless playing of the race card, the chest-thumping, hairy-kneed guff we'd all seen on the telly – a land of men in kilts doing Highland dancing and singing in public school accents about crofts in Skye while living in stylish bungalows with pebbled driveways in Bearsden. Not that Shoulders could be blamed. We children thought this was who we were because it was who we were taught we were, even though accepting this myth meant denying the evidence of our own plain eyes. *true for once*

Finally Miss Andrews said, 'Well done, Doreen. Thank you for an excellent essay.'

'Yes, miss.'

'And your handwriting is improving greatly.'

'Thank you, miss.'

Doreen sounded like she was about to faint from sheer giddy pleasure. This was understandable. The Land of Praise had always lain far beyond her dreams, more distant to her than Brigadoon. The citizens of Praise tended to occupy the high end of the evolutionary scale – slim, pretty lassies with wholesome smiles and creamy complexions, and tall boys with nice blazers and high foreheads who sang their hymns straight, not the sniggering dirty versions like the rest of us.

'Let's all show our appreciation for Doreen's essay with a round of applause.'

Doreen remained standing as we clapped, dutifully.

I had become aware of a writhing in her bodily movements that I construed as shyness in the face of so much unaccustomed approval. But it was more than that. These movements were accompanied by a faint whimpering that, because of my close proximity, I alone could hear. They were, unmistakably, sounds of distress. I puzzled, but briefly. Glancing at the floor, I watched a liquid snake arrow its way through a tangle of feet toward the blackboard.

Doreen's wretchedness became apparent.

'What's wrong, Doreen?' asked Miss Andrews.

Poking my head round an elephantine flank, I attempted levity. 'It's Afton's sweet waters, miss – they're gently flowing!'

Miss Andrews looked to the floor then raised her head. 'Doreen,' she said, simply, 'you are excused. You may leave the room.'

Shoulders Sumpter left her desk, clumping in a one-woman stampede to the door.

Miss Andrews sent Limpy for the janitor. She pointed her false hand at me in a *j'accuse* fashion. 'Moss! Come out here!'

I did so and stood before her.

Her voice was angry and she was unusually distressed. 'Do you think it's clever to go around making smart remarks?'

The correct answer to this question, logically, was 'yes'. I chose the path of discretion.

'No, miss,' I said.

I threw in a little head hanging for good measure – just enough to give her the idea that I thought her big and powerful.

I was back on stage, you see. When you were out front you had to put on a show for your people.

'Tell the whole class what you said about Doreen Sumpter's accident!'

'I said—'

'Louder, Moss!'

'I said Afton's sweet waters were gently flowing, miss.'

The class tried out a tentative titter; it swelled into a confident guffaw. As a humiliation tactic Miss Andrews had this time miscalculated. Moments before my little remark had been of merely cult status, heard only by a chance few; now it had crossed forever into the mainstream.

Miss Andrews knew what she'd done. Her face was now puce with annoyance, both at herself and me. She fixed me with a look, her adult eye hard and intelligent. Her look said, 'You silly, cruel boy – you just don't know what you've done.'

I felt mild shame. It showed on my face. This seemed to satisfy her.

'Return to your seat, Moss.'

Being adult, she knew, as we did not, that what we had all just witnessed was not a routine accident, but a defining moment in a small existence. For the rest of her life, Shoulders Sumpter would bear the disfiguring scar of having humiliated herself in class – and at the moment of her greatest triumph. The message extracted from this unfortunate tangle would not be a hard one to discern. Wherever she went, whatever she did for the remainder of her life, Doreen Sumpter would be careful never again to do anything well.

At three o'clock, packing my bag, I felt a tap on my back. I turned. Shona Burns proffered me one of her secret notes. I made to pass it on to Janet.

'No,' she said quickly, 'it's for you.'

'Me?'

She half smiled, turned.

I opened the note. It read: *Dear Ivan, I like your essays. They are very funny. S x.*

There, I told you it was momentous.

That night, I felt a curious tingle all over my body.

Next day, I stole a look across at Shona Burns. Her head was down over her exercise book. An S of dark, lustrous hair curved along her smooth, flawless cheek.

At interval time, I sat in a toilet cubicle. In my hands was the note Shona had passed me the day before. No matter how many times I read it, my head still swam and my body still tingled.

I took a pen from my bag. Finding a clear space on the wooden door, I made my declaration:

> *Flow gently sweet Afton, amang thy green braes;*
> *Flow gently I'll sing thee a song of wet claes.*
> *Big Sumpter's asleep by your murmuring hiss,*
> *Flow gently sweet Afton, she's soaking in piss.*

Please understand that in matters of the Scottish heart, it's seldom about what we say and more often about what we don't.

Seventeen

The eleven-plus arrived. Having nothing better to do, I had worked hard in preparation.

Father perused my results. I stood by his side, awaiting his judgement. I did not stand too closely, as he had his jacket off. We had entered the age of poplin and his underarms exuded the pungent guff of sustained use. A clean shirt could last a working week in those days and we were on a Thursday, so the aroma was heady.

Father took his time. He was scouring the document for negatives.

'You can't take it away from him, Ivan – he's passed his eleven-plus,' said Mother.

'Yes,' agreed Father, grudgingly.

'He deserves a reward,' prompted Mother.

Father stiffened at this suggestion. His eyes swivelled. Since the birth of Stan, he had taken to patrolling his wallet the way a goalkeeper would his six-yard box.

'I'm not made of money,' he explained, unnecessarily.

'When your sister Celia's boy passed his eleven-plus, he was given a new bike.'

'Graham deserved a new bike,' Father shot back. 'His marks

were exemplary. He's going to Glasgow Grammar on a bursary.'

'You should encourage your own son, never mind other people.' Her dislike of Granny M had seen Mother's anger erupt and ripple outwards, to include the entire Moss family.

Exasperated, Father reached into his pocket and threw a handful of coins into the air. 'There!' he said.

I was on my knees, counting them into piles, before they'd hit the floor.

'You're pathetic,' said Mother.

Father cursed, wounded by this judgement. He turned toward Mother. She lunged for the ornamental companion set and unsheathed the poker. 'Don't even try it!' she warned.

Stan made himself small behind the standard lamp. My parents glared at each other. Father took a step. He ducked as the poker sailed through the living-room window.

Around fifteen minutes later, two policemen arrived. Mrs Moidart, upstairs, had snapped at last. My parents were chauffeur driven to the station in Ludovic Square, to cool off.

To entertain Stan while they were gone, I made him put on his shoes and we walked around the garden in the dark, which he liked. The living-room window lay in slivers on the lawn and Stan and I made a game, in the blackness, of cracking the bigger shards under our feet. Impelled by guilt, Mrs Moidart brought down mugs of soup and urged us to go back indoors. We were asleep by the time our parents returned, but I stirred on hearing their muffled voices.

The battle was not renewed. Neither was there much talking and Father went soon to bed.

A little later, our bedroom door opened and I heard my mother's voice call softly.

'Ivan.'

I did not stir. I knew what she wanted. I was to fulfil my

appointed role as a sympathetic listener while she perched in the hearth, chain-smoking and pouring stewed tea, all the while holding forth in one of her impassioned, weirdly hypnotic streams of unedited invective. I was to nod sagely and approvingly while Father's character was nailed to the wall and lacerated into a bloodied mass of damning faults. Each of these would be illustrated by examples which would highlight his pitiful shortcomings and ineptitudes both as parent and husband. Every vitriolic story or coruscating report would end with the same stock attempt at restoring fair-minded balance: 'But I don't want to poison your mind against him, it's up to you.'

'Ivan?'

I feigned slumber. When she had gone I opened my eyes and, as usual, stared into the dark.

We started at the big school, Dreichstane High. We were new boys; myself, Neth Skillet, Bo Divney, Tonga McIninch, Limpy Chalfont, Jim Leston. Stripped of our status as elders of Dreichstane Primary, we huddled in a timid circle against the bounding, fifteen-year-old giants who loped among us, bellowing and guffawing, claiming the playground with easy confidence for their stampeding football matches. We were the small boys now.

The main body of the school was old and forbidding. Around the periphery of the playground, temporary outbuildings lay scattered haphazardly, as if dropped from a van by delivery men who were running late. These units comprised the science lab, the gym, the domestic science department and the woodwork shop. Across Floors Street, posturing at the margin like a renegade outsider stood the art department.

On our first morning we were parted, the boys from the girls, for the purposes of religious instruction. I do not know why we were parted. Perhaps God wanted to show us that he hadn't lost his touch since his Red Sea triumph. Our teacher was Miss Leaming. She was a popular dispenser of religious instruction in that she never required us to open a bible. On completion of the morning register, she would turn both cheeks to face the *Glasgow Herald* while we copied each other's homework.

Duly instructed, a bell would sound and the boys would join the girls for classes. There were exceptions. In those days, woodwork, technical drawing and domestic science were judged gender-specific subjects. Thus, no sweaty boys in aprons ever fretted over flan cases, and no aspiring female joiners with chisels down their drawers ever hacked away at crude-looking toothbrush holders. Nor did we wear "drawers", but - navy knickers.

While gathered together in the maths class, we were paid a visit by the headmaster, Mr Thornton. Though he surely stood no taller than five foot seven, he was known as Big John. In Scotland where, as I have said, the cloud level hovers at a perpetual five foot eight, five seven is considered a quite sufficient height. That was not the reason for Mr Thornton's nickname. Though modest of stature, Big John had a very large and formidable presence. Instinctively, as he entered, we all breathed in. He took purposeful steps in squeaking black shoes that preceded his arrival like a police whistle. His grey hair lay prostrate across his scalp, presumably out of sheer terror, and his eyebrows, or rather eyebrow, was a thick, unbroken line of peppery foliage, like a ridge of jagged rough fringing a particularly daunting golf bunker. He appeared to regard clothing as a sort of character test: his starched white collars bit his neck like a vampire's teeth. His suit seemed woven from bracken and came with a tightly buttoned waistcoat, thrown down like a gauntlet against ordinary human comfort. His hairy socks could have kept the woodwork room in sandpaper for several terms.

Big John stood before us and delivered a short, stern lecture. He told us what we could expect of him and what his school expected of us. Limbo dancing and beach parties appeared to play no part in the curriculum. Having said his piece, he departed; possibly to meet his tailor in the forest, where they would cut saplings together for a new suit.

When the door closed on Big John, Mr Nockiss, our maths teacher stepped forward. He had a pale face topped by thinning red hair. From a distance he retained a patina of youthful joviality, which meant that we smiled up at him, trustingly. When he stepped closer and indicated the belt under his cloak, we realised he was strictly old school and that his grin was sardonic. He too gave us a short, stern lecture. Because children are adaptable and catch on quickly, we were disappointed by his offering, finding his delivery arch and theatrical, lacking the growling intensity and sureness of touch of the master, Big John.

Mr Nockiss attempted to court our favour with a jest. In silence, we watched his joke clunk to the floor and roll under his desk to wheeze and die. It was a tiny victory, but a welcome one.

In the playground, we stood huddled in the cold.

'I'm having a birthday party next month,' said Bo Divney, brightening our spirits. He prodded a finger around our little circle. 'You, you and you can come. But not you.'

Limpy Chalfont grinned anyway, proud to have been singled out for the distinction of rejection.

'A party?' said Tonga McIninch, cautiously. 'What, you mean with lassies and that?'

'Yes. There'll be lassies.'

Tonga was silent. His silence spoke for us all. Though we were some distance from being men of the world we were experienced enough to know that girls were not boys. Looking at boys did not give you an erection, unless you were Smiling Peter, who drove the ice cream van for Paglianni's.

Bo looked amused. He could afford to be. He was already a louche playboy. Legend had it that Lizzie Mather had allowed him to grope her left breast one sultry Sunday evening in the bluebell woods. From a modern-day perspective of sex traffickers, pole dancers and teenage grandmothers, this may seem an unremarkable occurrence. But to us, at our age and in that era, a girl's breast was as distant as outer space and to touch one was a staggering accomplishment on a par with handling a moon rock. Thinking of girls filled us with dread and excitement.

'Tell us again about that Sunday in the woods,' implored Neth, for whom the meddlings of Eros were a constant thrill and torment.

'Well . . .' said Bo, teasingly.

As we gathered in close, Bo told his tale. We turned as one to look at Lizzie as she skipped rope with her friends. She saw us leering: mentally pawing the ground, our hot tongues steaming on the gravel. She gave a sort of glowering shudder and glanced away.

'I've got a stonner,' said Neth.

'Me too,' said Tonga.

'And me,' I admitted; a stonner being local vernacular for an erection.

Like my friends, I had finally crossed the metaphorical Rubicon that saw a boy child become an adolescent – I was now a time-served wanker. In former years we had called each other wankers without ever understanding the mechanics of the enterprise. Stumbling upon the practice by an accident of instinct, I had quickly become a slave to the freedom of self-abuse. I cursed the fact that it had taken me so long to uncover this delicious secret and sought eagerly to make up for lost time. I could have wept, Proust-like, at the memory of all the erections

I'd wasted down the years – *À la recherche de stonners perdus*.

Yes, erections were delicious things. They were also trouble-some. By the domestic science wing, Shona Burns was standing with Janet Gooding. Shona was looking at me. When I looked back, she turned away. Girls, too, were troublesome things. The thought of Lizzie Mather's body might stir my loins but even in her drab uniform of grey skirt, white blouse and black shoes, it was Shona who made my heart sing and dance.

Father was eating his tea at the table, spooning greasy broth from a chipped bowl. Mother stood by the sink, wiping Pyrex plates that had gone filmy with age, like cataracts over old folks' corneas. *cataracts form within the crystalline lens – are not externally visible - twit*

'How is your new school?' Father enquired, mildly.

I was flexing my shoulder for show. It was stiff from having lugged home a haversack stuffed with freshly issued textbooks and jotters. I was harbouring resentment.

'It's not a new school, it's an old school.'

'The age is immaterial.'

'Then why did you call it new?'

Father gripped his spoon tighter.

'There's a ban on short trousers,' I told him, untruthfully. 'I was the only one wearing them.'

'There's nothing healthier than shorts. They let the air about your legs.'

'Why don't you wear them?'

'Don't push it!'

The spoon became a dagger which Father wielded, menacingly. A length of soggy leek clung to the underside; seaweed on a greasy silver hull. I looked to Mother for support, in vain. Having sensed the threat of financial outlay, she busied herself with giblets.

'I was fifteen before I'd my first pair of long trousers.'

My eyes narrowed. 'I thought you were in the navy at fourteen?'

'I was. They kitted us out in tropical shorts.'

'For New York?'

The spoon became a rapier, jabbing the air by my face. 'Be very careful.'

The twin shackles of poverty and sea legs on dry land had begun to madden Father, loosening what remained of his reserve.

Having betrayed me by her silence, Mother sought craven-ly to lighten the mood. 'What lessons did you do at your new school?' she asked.

'Old school.'

'At your new old school – what lessons?'

'Algebra. French.'

'Say something in French.'

'*Mes pantalons sont très petit.*'

'Enough!'

Father's spoon hull slammed the broth ocean. Greasy splash-es flecked the plastic tablecloth.

'He's got trousers on the brain!'

'No wonder! I'm at a new school and I'm wearing my old school's uniform!'

I was gratified to find a self-righteous catch trip my voice. I inclined my head to showcase a single tear that glistened at the corner of my eye.

My parents brooded. Mother signalled Father into the privacy of the living room. I sprang forward and put my ear to the glass partition so as to hear their muttering. When they stopped talking, I sprang back to the table and on their reappearance looked dejectedly up from my empty plate.

'Your father and me have been talking,' said Mother, taking the lead. Father lurked behind her, awkwardly. I took this as a positive sign. It meant Father had, so to speak, changed his position. 'We're going to take out a Provident Loan. You're to have long trousers.'

They stood beaming, as if anticipating a great fanfare, perhaps from a Greek chorus or Eddie Calvert, the man with the golden trumpet. They were still years off forty, the pair of them, yet weary from the grinding worry of children and habitual debt. If Mother made it from one Friday pay packet to the next with sixpence left in her purse, it had been a successful week.

I proffered no thanks. Sensing their crumbling resistance, I attacked with full vigour.

'And Chelsea boots?'

Mother groaned. Father was puzzled. 'What in God's name are Chelsea boots?'

'Pointed shoes,' explained Mother.

Father stared; he blinked, uncomprehending.

'Shoes that come to a point,' elaborated Mother. 'With elastic at the sides.'

No coin dropped into Father's mental register.

'Beat groups wear them – Freddie and the Dreamers.'

I flinched at this gruesome lapse of musical taste.

'John Lennon wears them,' I corrected.

The Beatles were sun gods. Television had filled our homes with their radiance. Until the Beatles, people on television were honorary undertakers who appeared on Panorama, in dark ties, looking grave. The Beatles were impish, but only Lennon had the whiff of anarchy. Being repressed, youth adores anarchy. Father continued to grapple with the original concept.

'Shoes that come to a point?'

Mother nodded.

Father's eyes writhed at the heretical notion. Here was yet another flagrant breach of proper Scottish standards.

'Only a buffoon would wear things like that. It's a school, not Charlie Cairoli's fucking circus!'

I recoiled like a sensitive young aesthete on the threshold of his dream. It worked.

'Don't shout, Ivan,' said Mother. Father nodded, compliantly. They were in a state of harmony over the trousers; a leg each, so to speak. I saw Mother's fingertips reach out to him. He took her hand and squeezed it; right there, in my sight, the first time ever.

My father said, 'We'll see.'

We saw.

On the Saturday, we went up the town to Arnott's and I was bought my first pair of full-length trousers.

Father disappeared to McSorley's Bar twice during the simple transaction. This worked in my favour. Exasperated and angry, Mother marched me and Stan to Gordon's shoe shop in Stockwell Street where we splashed the last of the Provident line credit on Chelsea boots.

In the shop, Stan pointed at the pointed shoes. He jumped up and down, giggling. I put them on and that night wore them to bed with my pyjamas.

Reporting for school on the Monday, I felt manly and mature. At every opportunity I'd hoist my new trousers above my ankles to flash the elasticised gussets of the Chelsea boots.

At playtime I ran close to Shona Burns and stooped to pull up my sock, ensuring she received a chic and sexy eyeful of white calf and elastic. In the doing of this, we each upheld strict court-ship etiquette. I looked at her but she did not acknowledge me. I knew that her lady-in-waiting, Janet, in accordance with ancient custom, would convey news of my look to Shona.

The renewing of contact, now that we were in a strange new

environment with our desks far apart, had become to me a matter of urgency. If I could summon up the courage, I would invite Shona Burns to Bo Divney's birthday party. Such a step, however, of speaking to a girl, with my mouth, using words, would be a tortuous one. Even thinking of it made my heart race and my stomach clench. I looked to my shoes for confidence. I had the world on my feet.

The sixties had begun. Youth ruled the world. Not in Scotland.

'Quiet!'

We were in class; Mr Nockiss indicated a novelty item standing beside him. 'This is the school's visiting nurse, Sister Galloway.'

The nurse, a granite-faced woman of middle years, was clad in a white coat with matching joyless shoes. She stepped forward, her hands clasped at her stone vagina. Our insolent gaze dribbled off her like urine down a war memorial. Mr Nockiss continued.

'You will be medically examined by Sister Galloway. You will do exactly as she tells you – if you do not, there will be trouble!'

To illustrate the manner of trouble he had in mind, Mr Nockiss thrashed his belt in showy fashion across his desk, creating a small breeze. In the updraught, a pile of papers loosened from their neatness and began fluttering to the floor, pleasing us.

'Quiet!'

We were segregated, the boys being led away to line the corridor outside Sister Galloway's temporary station in the janitor's office. In the queue, we spoke in excited mutters. We thrilled at the marvellous worlds of opportunity that were opening up before us. Newspapers and documentaries had begun identifying the dangerous new phenomenon of the 'teenager', a sociological group we were on the cusp of joining. Teenagers were rebellious, out of all parental control; they lived for pleasure, cheeked the police and spent their huge discretionary income on pep pills and razor blades that they'd sew into the lapels of their bespoke mohair mod suits in readiness for epic battles with greasy bikers; again, not in Dreichstane they didn't.

'What are you doing on Friday night?' asked Neth Skillet.

'My father is making me join the Boys' Brigade,' said Bo Divney.

'So is mine,' said Tonga.

'Mine too,' said Limpy Chalfont.

'And mine,' I said.

A new division, the Third Dreichstane had been inaugurated in a church hall on Elm Drive. Like most Protestant fathers ours had, in their youth, been members of the BB. With their lives now blighted and embittered, they wished to pass on the great ankle chain of tradition by inflicting the Brigade's uplifting miseries upon us, their sons.

'Next!' called Nurse Galloway.

It was my turn. I stepped, routinely, into the office. When I stepped back out, my world had been turned upside down.

There was no known cure for my affliction.

'You have what?' asked Father that evening after school.

'I have a heart murmur.'

Mother clutched her own chest, dramatically. Father was less distressed.

'I bet I know what it's murmuring,' he said, adopting his waggish tone. '*I want a button-down shirt! I want a mop-top haircut!*'

He was lounging in his battered leatherette armchair. Stan was picking at the strips of black insulation tape that concealed its rips and gouges. The Provident incident still rankled. Mother ignored Father, pressed on.

'What else did she say?'

'I'm pigeon-toed. I have an inward turn on my right foot.'

'That'll be your feet leaning in to hear what your heart's murmuring.'

Father was making a cabaret out of my misfortune.

'Story, Daddy, story!' pleaded Stan.

Father picked him up, sat him on his knee. 'Once upon a time, there was a boy with a heart murmur and pigeon-toed feet—'

'That's enough, Ivan,' chided Mother.

She alone looked concerned, with good reason. Were I to die, it would almost certainly involve the spending of money.

'What did the nurse say we should do about the heart murmur?'

'Nothing,' I said. 'She said we should wait and see.'

This prognosis brought relief to Mother. 'You hear that, Ivan – we wait and see!'

Father grunted his approval.

Emboldened by the lack of need for financial outlay, my parents snapped into furious action and began waiting and seeing, straight away. Mother reached for a cigarette from the packet up her cardigan sleeve and lit it.

Father held up a languid hand and Mother threw him one too.

Stan giggled. He jumped up and down, trying to put his head through Father's smoke rings.

I steeled myself.

Eighteen

'The heart murmur isn't the bad news,' I said.

They looked at me. I felt faint as I prepared to divulge the awful truth. Trepidation must have registered on my face for Mother clutched her throat at once.

'Ivan, what is it?'

'I failed the eye test too.' My voice trembled as I said, 'I need spectacles.'

Mother gave a low moan of fiscal pain.

Father's jaw twitched, menacingly. 'Christ almighty,' he said, 'more money!'

I was filled with woe.

In those days, spectacles were an aesthetic handicap to a child, on a par with a calliper or harelip. The wearing of bins would cast me forever adrift on Leper Island with Limpy Chalfont as my hobbling Man Friday.

The timing was hideous; Bo Divney's party was approaching. I slumped over the Long John sideboard, swathed in gloom.

Father took the lead. 'How bad is your eyesight?'

I looked at him. As usual, he appeared blurred. I was used to people appearing blurred at the edges. In my parents' case, it seemed a symptom of their personalities. In this instance,

I could see straight through them both. I knew what he and Mother were thinking – if I had managed without specs this long, why not longer? It was the 'wait and see' philosophy applied to my vision. In their eyes, so to speak, I might, with luck, graduate from myopia to total blindness, thus saving any interim outlay on spectacles.

'I don't know,' I replied at last.

'Then let's find out,' said Father.

My parents moved about the room, waving random hands, holding up ornaments for me to identify and subjecting me to a battery of improvised tests in an attempt to assess the extent of my visual impairment. Mother pointed to some inky squiggles on the wallpaper, the doodled handiwork of Stan, and invited me to describe them.

'What squiggles?'

'The ones on the wallpaper pattern.'

'What wallpaper pattern?'

'Damn!' said Father.

'We've no choice,' wailed Mother. 'We'll take him to the optician on Saturday.'

My father looked at me. 'Trust you,' he said, bitterly.

In bed that night, Stan spoke in the dark. 'What are you doing?'

'Nothing.'

'Yes you are, you're talking to somebody.'

'No, I'm not.'

I was, though. I was praying. I didn't mind having a heart that murmured. Since I alone would be inconvenienced by its conversation, it followed that my heart could prattle away to its, well, heart's content. If I wasn't interested in my heart's repartee, I'd just button my shirt to muffle its sound. Pigeon toes, too, were no problem. They matched my pigeon chest. But spectacles were beyond the teenage pale. Spectacles hooked themselves behind your ears and leaned on your nose; they were walking sticks for the eyes. Specs never went out at night and lived in a case at the side of your bed; they were the sartorial equivalent of pensioners' sheltered housing. Above all, specs were passion killers. The Montagues and Capulets need never have fallen out if Romeo had worn reading glasses, for Juliet wouldn't have looked twice at him.

Thus I offered my short, grudging prayer to the Silent One, pleading for the miracle of restored sight. I was not optimistic. Given his past record of puckish jocularity, I expected to wake up next morning with an extra eye in the middle of my forehead.

I was wrong.

The following day, at breakfast, I picked up Father's paper. On the front page a miracle gleamed forth. It was a picture of his Holiness, John Lennon. He stood posing awkwardly with 'his lovely wife Cynthia'. This wife was so lovely he'd apparently kept her in a locked room for some years, like Grace Poole – presumably so his adoring female fans wouldn't catch lovely fever and switch their affections to Paul or George. That wasn't what had arrested my attention. What I saw made the paper shake in my hand. There, astride that already famous pointed nose, His Eminence, Mr Alpha Male incarnate, was wearing a pair of spectacles. Not demure specs, with apologetic semi-frames, sidling onto his face, hoping you wouldn't notice their presence. No, these specs were black horn-rims – bold and resolute, planted upon the ridge of his proboscis with the proud authority of a Union flag atop Mount Everest. They were an unmistakable fashion statement, redolent of the fifties jazz cellars and beat poets that his Supreme Holiness was reputed to love.

In my mind's ear, above the prattle of my murmuring heart,

I could hear every scrunch-eyed loser in Britain rise up as one to salute the bright new read-a-car-licence-plate-at-twenty-five-yards dawn. What we beheld, written on an eye chart carved on tablets of stone, was a truth divine; specs were hip. We, the bleary worshippers at the shrine of the fuzzy alphabet, were the chosen ones. I peered closer and checked. Yes, there was no mistake. My-opia was John's opia too.

Specs were cool.

So it was that the members of the Moss household gathered in a small cluster outside Penman's Optician's in the high street.

'What's wrong, Stan?'

'The noise is hurting me!'

Spooked by the rackety traffic, Stan was hopping up and down, clutching his ears. I felt troubled too, and our parents looked tense – maybe we should all have been hopping together, as a family.

In the window, the spectacle frames were displayed on a revolving spindle. Their positions were fixed according to price, with the most expensive frames at the top while below, in descending order of monstrousness, skulked the lowlier specimens. I knew what I wanted. The black horn-rims sat atop the mound, looking chic, shiny and assertive. I strode buoyantly, but alone, into the shop. Turning, I saw my parents outside the window, hunkered down, knees on chins, earnestly perusing the NHS section; the lowest dregs of the spectacle-maker's art.

Finally they entered the shop and began a guarded conversation with the optician. They emphasised the relatively minor nature of my ocular defects, reasoning that the thicker the lens, the higher the price. They were hoping to browbeat the optician into overturning the findings of the school nurse. To have a son staggering around spec free and blundering into the furniture was, to them, the least costly of all possible options and therefore the one to be pursued.

My parents explained their point of view. The optician nodded. 'I understand,' he said, enigmatically.

I was led away to undergo tests. An enormous pair of hulking metal frames was placed on my face and assorted lenses slotted in and out to ascertain my visual limits.

The optician shone a light into my pupil. 'Hmm,' he mused, as we stared into each other's eye. I watched the veined rivulets of my massive orb offer a flickering reflection. 'Right,' he said.

The light was flicked off and I was lead back into the body of the shop.

Mother and Father moved forward involuntarily, like loved ones in a film, awaiting the outcome of a mining disaster.

'Well?' Father asked.

'He has an astigmatism.'

Mother clutched her purse. 'Is that expensive?'

Father pulled a tetchy face, as if it were my fault. Remembering his decorum, he checked himself and turned his grimace into a concerned pat of my shoulder.

The optician weighed up the situation in wily fashion. 'Have you seen anything he fancies?' he enquired.

'Yes,' I said, leaping in, 'he fancies these!'

I pointed to the horn-rims atop the spindle. Crow black, they sat; bible black; Beatle black.

'Ah, yes,' said the optician, reaching. 'Would you like to try them on?'

'No, he would not,' countered Mother, swiftly.

The optician's fingers were left clawing the air. He glanced at me, then at my parents.

'Perhaps something else?'

'Well . . .'

There was no perhaps about it.

Down and further down the spindle went our gaze.

'Those?' enquired the optician.

'Lower,' said Father.

The optician kneeled to retrieve the selected pair. I heard his knees crack at the unaccustomed depth of his squat. He sat the cheap brutes on my face. Instantly, I looked about fifty. They made the metal hulks from the test chamber seem the epitome of Paris chic by comparison.

'What do you think?' ventured the optician.

'Are they under a pound?' asked Mother.

'I was speaking to your son.'

This was boldness of a high order. Permitting a child the right to feelings, thoughts and aesthetic judgement was considered, well, it wasn't even considered – it was a strange thing yet to come like voyages to Mars or croissants.

'I like the black horn-rims,' I protested, feebly.

It did not matter what I thought. The monsters were affordable, so it was already a done deal.

Outside, Father prodded me in the back. 'Forget pop stars,' he urged, 'these are the spectacles top politicians wear.'

I said nothing. I had stepped into the shop hoping to look like John Lennon. I had stepped out resembling Sir Alec Douglas-Home.

In a playtime huddle, we discussed strategy for Bo Divney's forthcoming party. None of us had ever been to a party before, including Bo, who would be hosting it. We emptied out the drawers of our collective imagination looking for clues as to what was required for such an event. Girls had already been established as a prerequisite. A further brainwave arrived when someone suggested 'Music'. We pounced on this suggestion.

Tonga's older cousin owned a Beach Boys album. It had

songs about parties; albeit beach parties. These parties involved buggies, surf boards, Pacific breakers, dollars, beer, lean tanned men, leggy blonde girls, guitars, sunshine, barbecues, and above all, a beach. Since we were pale, stumpy, west of Scotland schoolboys, reared in perpetual drizzle, who could not easily lay hands on a biro, let alone an ocean, the problems became quickly apparent. Our party balloon, not yet fully inflated, had begun to hiss and droop. We were raw adolescents, without money or experience – and yet. It was Neth Skillet who found words to tap the elemental exuberance at our core.

'Who cares,' he said, 'all we need are lassies!'

The tension dispelled and we laughed like drains. We kept the mirth going longer than was strictly justified because we liked the shared feeling of being together and in on something new.

'We'd better get busy with the invitations,' somebody said.

'Who should we invite?'

A delicious terror gripped my belly. My eyes, newly sharpened by the magnifying windows on my face, roved around the playground in delirious yearning.

And I saw her . . .

My mother had agreed to radiotherapy treatment. She wasn't convinced but did it to appease Stan and me.

I'd take her to the Beatson clinic for treatment and so would he.

I'd sit in the waiting room making notes, her shopping bag next to me, while she was spirited off to one of the side rooms, through the wall, to be blasted with radiation. Down the weeks, through the sessions, she continued to look well fed, in fact like her old self, if a little haunted in the eye, and I began to wonder if there hadn't been some medical miscalculation, that maybe this thing could have a happy outcome after all. I should have known better.

One day I was in the clinic, sitting in the waiting area with the rest of troubled humanity, street people, work people, strangers so ordinary you couldn't tell the sick from the healthy; all slumped with our sports sections and four-fingered Kit Kats, waiting for word. From the corner of my eye I became aware of a trolley being pushed into the room by two porters. They sat the trolley over by the far wall while they went away to make enquiries, fetch paperwork, or feed the Klix machine, something. As I looked, I became aware there was a creature lying on this trolley, a living thing, her white face caught in the glare from the window. She was an old woman, this creature, very old and bone thin, her eyes closed, so still and white that her skin and presence were almost lost among the bedding she lay in. Still and far away, in the privacy of her bed, in this most public of places, this creature lay; a piece of human debris awaiting collection.

A blue-clad nurse came into the room with the two porters. The nurse had a clipboard. She leaned over the trolley. 'Christine,' she called out, gently, firmly. Nothing. 'Christine?'

This time the old woman's eyes opened sharply. Her eyes were alert with fear, with wariness and intelligence. I'd come to know that look soon enough.

She was at the end of her life this woman, this Christine. I hadn't wanted to stare but, of course, did. In this waiting room of the sorely troubled, I was mesmerised by the creature's distant otherness. I was struck by the thought of her parents, long dead, who had crouched over her crib all those decades before, right at the beginning, two long dead people maybe trying out names and discarding them before they found the one, the perfect fit that stuck: Christine. Was she alive? She was alive all right, but on a different plane from the rest of us. She was in that place we all intuit sometimes, when we wake alone in the small hours, heebie jeebied and terrified, with the room cold and the world indifferent and our fingers groping for a light switch. That place, she was there; the realm of the long goodbye.

My mother appeared, her coat buttoned, looking anguished and breathless, yet relieved too.

'Okay?' I asked, rising.

'Yes,' she said and fiddled with her belt. She was wheezing.

I heard the swing doors dunk and, turning, saw Christine's bed manoeuvred out of the room to disappear down the corridor to who knew what.

In the car, I did upbeat acting. 'This treatment – it's still doing some good, right?'

'Yes,' she said.

'Then that's all that matters. You'll see, in time—'

'No,' she said, firmly. 'Don't.'

'Don't what?'

'Talk to me about time. I don't want to know about four good fucking years, art exhibitions, concerts, foreign travel, bungee jumps or anything else, you got me?'

'I'm only saying that—'

'No,' she insisted. 'Let it go.'

I let it go. We didn't talk for the rest of the journey.

And that's the way it settled. She'd let us take her for treatment but she didn't want to walk to the corner for a paper, let alone go white-water rafting. When the last of the radiation treatments had taken place, number thirteen, she promptly stopped eating. No matter what I bought her, whatever she liked, it would be nibbled half-heartedly and abandoned on the tray. A person has to eat, right? One night I went over, rang the bell. When she didn't answer I let myself in. She was lying on the floor, her legs having crumpled beneath her.

I tried to lift her up, different ways, but they all hurt, caused a sharp pain in her back. I rang NHS 24, plumped each of her cushions, sat down. It was weird her lying there on the floor, us making routine conversation, waiting for the ambulance. I tried to find something positive to say.

'At least you beat the smoking,' I said.

She had quit smoking. Not a one, for weeks. It was control, of course. At the end people crave control more than anything, more even than tobacco.

'I didn't give it up,' she said. 'It gave me up.' She didn't want to take any credit; she knew if she'd done it years earlier, maybe back in Dreichstane, she might not have been in her ultimate predicament. Lying on the floor had given her a new perspective on things. 'Get a broom,' she said.

'What?'

'There's a spider's web in the corner, it's annoying the hell out of me.'

There's a plus in everything.

The paramedics came, a man and a woman. In seconds they had my mother upright.

'What happened?' the woman paramedic asked.

'She was on her way to the bedroom,' I said, 'and her legs gave out.'

'My legs didn't give out,' my mother corrected. 'My son doesn't know me. I actually tripped.'

The man paramedic looked at my mother, her emaciated, stricken condition, then he looked at me. 'Maybe you should think about moving the bed into the living room.'

I didn't say anything.

Afterwards, I rang Stan with the update. It was late. He was worried. 'Thank God,' he said, 'I thought you were going to tell me it was the worst, that you'd gone in there and she was lying, you know . . .'

'Dead?'

'Yes.'

I thought about it. 'Would that have been the worst, Stan, would it really?'

We let it hang in the air, but over the next few months we both had time to consider that question.

I moved her bed into the living room.

One night we talked; discussed options. The crumbling legs incident had given Stan and me a nasty turn and we'd begun to feel a sense of inadequacy and foreboding when we thought about our mother's future. We agreed that I would raise the subject; test her reactions. When I did she remained adamant that she would never allow herself to be admitted into hospital. She wanted to be at home. I asked how she felt about a hospice.

'How'd you mean?'

'Just to visit.'

'Who visits a hospice?'

'For help,' I urged, 'you know, support.'

'They support you on the way in, carry you on the way out.' Amused, she allowed herself a grim laugh.

'No, look, that's a common misconception. I spoke to some- one . . .' I was aware my cheeriness sounded faintly ghastly. 'Wendy something; Wilma. No, it was Wendy.'

'A hospice?' she repeated. There was scorn in her voice, the only healthy thing about her.

'You don't need to stay in there,' I assured her. 'Wendy told me you can go for a look, as a social thing, people visit there.'

'What sort of people would visit a hospice?'

'Hospice people,' I said. 'Customers.' Yes, I called them customers.

I wanted to make the word 'hospice' sound drop-in and cool, a sort of adjunct to a trendy gym or wellness centre where you popped in for a foot spa and reiki massage before dashing off for tennis lessons or a chai latte.

She gave me a look. Her voice came out deep.

'You tell Wendy I'll go when I'm fucking ready.'

She looked at me. I felt shifty.

We understood each other.

Nineteen

I too was fucking ready.

I was wearing my pin-collar shirt. I had oiled my hair. It was the night of Bo Divney's party.

Hoping to sneak out of the house without comment, I'd stumbled into Mother and Mrs Moidart at the front door. Having recovered from the froideur caused by the window incident, they had resumed their habit of gossiping on the stairs. One Friday night, I'd interrupted a discussion about sock thefts from the washing line in the back green to bear them the news of the Kennedy assassination. People tell you where they were on that night. They never tell you what drivel they were gibbering.

'That's him off to his first party,' said Mother. She patted my greased head. Mrs Moidart smiled at me in a cloying way, making me twitch for Oswald's rifle.

By leaving early, I'd wished to avoid detection. Aware that a first party was a rite of passage, I'd feared being cheered along the street to waving hankies, like a ship being launched down a slipway. I watched the night's early drinkers, heading for the pub. Scowling loners with turned-up collars; stolid fathers and their apprentice sons, being mentored in the long tradition of weekend alcoholism.

I pitied them all. As I walked on air past the ruined stump of Dreichstane Castle into Tower Road, I pitied anyone who wasn't me.

My liberal use of the hair cream had proved a questionable decision. I had applied it on impulse, naïvely thinking it a mark of respect for a man to grease his head for a lady. There were houses on one side of the road and thick woods on the other, so that on my promenade, the hardy remainder of late autumn's insect life had found itself attracted by my sticky, fragrant head.

Turning a corner, I found number 6 and rang the bell. As I waited at the door, I took stock. Theirs was a nicer road than ours; their homes, unlike ours, were not flats, but proper houses. Still council though, so I held onto that at least. The garden was a thick, luxurious square of grass, spick and span and neatly trimmed. The garden intimidated me. There was more dirt on our living-room carpet than on their front lawn.

'Yes?'

Her father was a standard issue Protestant of the time: short, severe, splinters of flint for eyes. He had the look of Shona, except I'd sooner have squeezed her breasts than his.

'Hello. I'm Ivan Moss.'

He looked me over.

'*Sho-na!*'

She appeared in the doorway, springing out from behind the coat stand. She had her smart pale grey raincoat already on. Like me, she'd been anxious to avoid the awkward agonies of chat with the parents and wished to make a speedy getaway.

We walked down the path. It was a short path but a long walk. Words had become suddenly as large and heavy as paving stones to me and it was some time before I managed to spit out even a modest, 'Cold, isn't it?'

Glancing, I saw her mother at the window, fiddling with a

curtain tie-back that had become suddenly troublesome.

'What's that on your hair?' asked Shona.

'Brilliantine.'

'Not that; it's some kind of insect, let me see.'

I lowered my head. She picked my scalp clean of flies. As an ice breaker it was cheaper than champagne cocktails.

'I like your glasses,' she said.

'You do?'

'Yes. They look really fab. They make you look special.'

I blushed. 'You mean like Sir Alec Douglas-Home?'

'No, like John Lennon.'

My head swam. It was the taste of flattery that did it; she'd held up a great big dollop and I'd licked it off the spoon – straight onto my starved and eager taste buds.

When she took my arm on the walk to Bo's house, I all but swooned.

Everyone had aided the music effort by bringing along what records they owned or had liberated from the collections of relatives: early Beatles, Stones and Manfred Mann eked out Frank Ifield's novelty yodels, assorted sugary dirges by the Bachelors, and sanitised mambos from Manuel and His Music of the Mountains.

I myself possessed a solitary record, even though there was nothing in our house to play it on. I had purchased this disc in a fever of enthusiasm and would fondle it regularly for the thrill of ownership. I cherished this article. I had brought it along, dutifully; writing my name in ink near the hole, for safety's sake.

We played Switch. This was a sturdily sexist game in which chairs were first positioned in a circle. The 'men' would then occupy the chairs while the 'women' perched on their knees like ventriloquist dummies. A song would then blast tinnily from the Dansette. The men and women would kiss each other relentlessly

231

until the record ended. Each girl would then rise, move on in a clockwise direction to the next set of knees, re-perch herself, and the exercise would be repeated in time to the musical cues.

I was positioned at one end of the room with Neth Skillet next to me. By an unfortunate quirk, Shona found herself, as the game began, on Neth's knee. As I kissed a random set of lips, I counted the chairs that would have to be endured before I had my go with Shona. They numbered a biblical twelve. I suffered. I ached. I endured. By the eighth chair I was oozing stigmata and was considering putting myself up for canonisation. The Dansette was reloaded. The ninth chair finally arrived, followed by a painful tenth. At the eleventh hour, my plans were shattered, damningly enough, by myself.

My record had come on. It was 'Pasadena' by the Temperance Seven, a droll homage to twenties oompah swing. A collective howl of scorn at this stylistic monstrosity brought the game to a premature halt. People stood up and stretched their aching backs. I was dismayed. Not only was my musical taste the subject of scorn, but every male in the room had kissed my date, except me. Even Limpy Chalfont, who had been invited late, through pity.

After Postman's Knock, where I was again unlucky, we broke for air. A cold description of early teenage behaviour may seem wanton and sluttish, but our kissing was chaste – you could clamp lips with a girl for whole days and it wouldn't occur to you to place your tongue in her mouth or let a hand stray onto her knee. We treated kissing as though it was an extension of the school curriculum – much better than physics but not as good as playing football for the school team, unless it was only the second eleven.

On the way to the bathroom, I bumped into Shona. She smiled at me. I glowed back, but only on the inside. On the outside, my face remained stoically dour and unyielding. I still had eyes though, and eyes are harder things to hide. She had eyes also, I noticed, two of them; and hands which, somehow, we held. There is the closeness of wanton kissing. But a hand resting in a hand it has long yearned to hold is closeness of a different order.

As Shakespeare put it: 'Young men's love then lies not truly in their hearts, but in their eyes.'

Not hitting the spot? Try doing this:

Sing the first verse of the Beatles' 'I Wanna Hold Your Hand' to yourself, up to and including the chorus. Done that? Yes, I know how naïve those words are. But if you haven't felt the feeling they're describing then the loss is yours.

We turned toward the window and leaned on the sill.

'Look,' she said, pointing.

'Yes,' I said, 'the moon . . . lovely.'

'Lovely' was suspect, but I had divined that women liked moonlight, so I'd dressed my vocabulary up in its good Sunday suit. To impress, I told her something of the Temperance Seven. In fact I told her everything I knew about them which was, roughly speaking, about one hundred per cent more than she'd wanted to know. It was my mouth, you see. It wasn't mine any more but that of a lunatic DJ who'd escaped, frothing and in chains, from the cargo hold of Radio Caroline.

'Are your specs for reading or distance?' she asked at last.

'Distance.'

'You don't need them for anything close up?'

'No.'

She was looking at me. She continued to look at me. The penny dropped.

'Oh.'

I removed the big specs and felt curiously weightless. She

stood waiting for her cheeky chap to do something. I wasn't cheeky, I was a nervous fawn.

Not that nervous though.

I kissed her.

Arriving home, I discovered that an incident had occurred. Father had a towel swathed round his head as an improvised bandage. Mother had locked herself in the bathroom. Stan cowered in the bedroom. Father was wiping his own blood from the living-room walls. The poker lay, tellingly, in the fireplace.

'Aren't you going to ask me what happened?' queried Father.

'No.'

'Your granny Moss is in hospital. She's suffered a heart attack.'

'Ah.'

I looked around the living room. Broken ornaments and thrown saucepans littered the floor.

I wondered how an assault on Granny's heart could have resulted in a trashing of our living room. Father answered my unasked question.

'Your granny does possess a heart, contrary to what a certain party might think.' He shouted this so that the certain party, who had slunk from the bathroom and was now cooling off in the kitchen, might hear. 'Speaking of parties,' continued Father, 'how was yours?'

'Better than yours,' I said.

In the bedroom I took off my shirt and slept with it under my pillow. Waking up from time to time, I'd take it out to smell Shona's scent.

We went to other parties together. We walked, too, in the bluebell woods, though I never achieved a grope, not once. All the same, the soft warmth of her breasts as we clinched would swell my ardour.

'Stop that pressing. I know what you're doing.'

At school, I'd cheek the teachers to catch her attention. I'd write essays, of course, taking elaborate pains to show off by making them puckish and entertaining, always squinting from the corner of an eye when I read them aloud to check if she was smiling.

I was invited to Shona's house for tea. After Battenberg and savoury biscuits, her father took me into the hall cupboard to show me his woods.

'These are my woods,' he said. There were three shiny bowls, in a string bag. I admired them, dutifully. 'Have you ever played?' he asked.

'No.'

'Would you like to play?'

It was a test. I felt dazzled under the fierce searchlight of his scrutiny.

'Yes.'

The next day I found myself on the municipal bowling green. All around were potbellied men, with breathing difficulties, in yellow sleeveless pullovers and lightweight white caps. I blended in nicely in my drainpipe trousers and army surplus combat jacket, the one with the swastika and 'Waffen-SS' inked whimsically in three-inch lettering on the back. Entering into the spirit of good-natured competitiveness, I launched a smooth trundler and loped up behind it in the prescribed bowling manner.

'Quite good for direction,' conceded Shona's father.

He looked awkward. Something was troubling him. He handed me a pair of plastic shoes.

'You forgot to put on your galoshes.'

From a turret, like a lookout post in Auschwitz, a puce-faced greenkeeper gave an enraged shout. He was frothing and pointing. I looked. Behind me, a neat path of indentations, in the shape of Cuban heels, lead from the rubber mat, up the green, toward the jack.

For me, the war was over.

Despite this hiccup, I had the sensation of life beginning to accept me. Life, as always, wore a checked shirt, cavalry twill trousers and smoked a pipe. Life threw his big homely arm around my shoulders while Life's wife was in the kitchen baking a wedding cake. It would be ready in, oh, five years or so.

This sensation seemed not at all fanciful, but preordained, sure of foot and correct. We were little people, you see, small-town people. Our papers for the future were in order and had been officially franked. In those days, there was nothing stronger than the tribe. It felt born in us to stay close to home, not to run away to different places chasing new partners, or our own tails which usually, in the end, turned out to be the same thing. Of course, local marriages are as problematic as any other kind. The difference is, for some reason, they last better.

Not all of them.

As if to prove the point, Granny Moss keeled over one night putting out the milk bottles.

I was awakened by a loud rapping at the door.

When I peeked out into the hallway, Mother and Father were already up and half dressed. Mother was handing Father the poker, just in case. Father opened the door, poised for action. Two policemen stood before him, looking grave. They removed their hats. I listened while a short, murmured conversation was conducted at the doorway. The policemen left.

'What was all that about?' I asked.

'She's gone,' he said.

'Granny Moss,' clarified Mother, for my benefit.

'When you say gone . . .?' I pressed.

Mother chose, this time, the delicate approach. 'You know the kind of gone where you don't come back?'

'Yes.'

'That kind of gone.'

Next morning, at breakfast, Father put down his tea cup and lifted his jacket from the back of the chair.

He left the room. Mother turned to me.

'He's heartbroken.'

Father returned, badgered a pound from her purse and left the room again.

'Bastard,' said Mother.

I had never been to a real live funeral before and was looking forward to it. We gathered at Aunt Celia's house for cups of tea and, since it was a death, Skirling Jock's Luxury Assortment. Because there was no drink, people were tense and when Father cracked a mild joke, we all laughed gratefully until Grandpa rapped a spoon off a side plate for silence.

'At the service,' he began, 'I'd like a few . . .'

'Prayers?'

'No.'

'Hymns?'

'No. To say a few . . .'

'Words!' we blurted, all guessing as one.

'Look who's here!'

Aunt Celia was standing in the doorway. At her side was a squat man dressed in a naval uniform that had braided cuffs. The man's complexion was swarthy and tanned. His eyes were beady and amused. He was smoking a cigarette that jutted, more or less exotically, from a shiny holder. From the papoose of his pocket, the neck of a whisky bottle peeked out from its tissue paper shawl. The man might have been a shady émigré bar owner, distant kin to Sidney Greenstreet in *Casablanca*. Except

237

that he was only my uncle home from the sea.

'Rolf!' shouted Father, springing up. 'I didn't think you'd make it!'

'Neither did I,' said Uncle Rolf, as they stood, pumping hands. 'Train up from Southampton – taxi from Central Station.'

'It's so good to see you!' I had rarely seen Father like this, thrillingly animated, his eyes shining with delight.

'You too – how's the old fella doing?'

'See for yourself,' said Father.

We all looked.

'Yes,' said Grandpa. 'A few . . . a few . . .'

'Drinks?'

Grandpa nodded.

Uncle Rolf unscrewed the cap of the bottle. 'Celia, bring some glasses.'

The assembled guests looked suitably disapproving. You took a drink after a funeral, not before. But they all graced the occasion with a nip, anyway, to pass themselves in company. So long as you appeared not to be enjoying it, you were covered.

During the service, Grandpa Moss said a few. Aunt Celia stood by his side, filling in the blanks. The minister was heartened, he informed us, to see the whole family rallying round Grandpa in his time of need. We all nodded, in a self-satisfied fashion, as an organ played and the velvet curtain jerked uneasily shut along its crooked runner. When the curtain re-opened, the coffin was gone and I looked around to see whether it was good form to applaud the unseen magician's sleight of hand. Afterwards, by the parked cars round the garden of remembrance, the minister went about, shaking our hands warmly. When Father dropped an envelope containing a bung into his pocket, the minister feigned surprise.

'Goodness,' he said.

After thanking us, once again, for our support of Grandpa in his hour of need, the minister departed. His timing was impeccable, as he was spared the sight of Grandpa being hustled, struggling, toward a white council van for transportation to the care home where he would henceforth live.

We watched the carers press Grandpa by the head into the back seat and the van scrunch off, at speed, down the gravel. Undefeated, Grandpa wound down the window and leaned out.

'You bunch of . . .'

'Shits?' offered Tessie, Granny's sister. She shared her dead sibling's wry humour.

'No.'

'Swine?'

'No.'

'It's for the best,' sobbed Aunt Celia, as Grandpa bawled out, 'Traitors!'

It was an unsettling spectacle, evoking dark thoughts which had to be stifled. We retired to the Quo Vadis for a drink and a sing-song.

Despite unease from Mother, Uncle Rolf came home with us. On entering the living room, he tripped on the hole in the carpet and took a flier, chin first, into the drop-leaf diner.

'Christ, Ivan,' he said. 'I've rounded Cape Horn four times without missing a step, but that carpet of yours is like the Bermuda Triangle.'

Mother laughed with gusto, sensing an opportunity to spin this criticism into support for some new Axminster.

'Sit down, Rolf,' she said.

'I will, Kathleen, when I find a seat I can trust.'

He shook an armchair on a wobbly leg to illustrate his point. Mother tittered, obligingly. Maybe there was a three-piece suite in it, too. She went into the kitchen to fetch glasses. Uncle Rolf opened his suitcase and threw me something.

'What's this?' I asked.

'A mango.'

He turned to Father and winked. 'Not quite the old Turkish proverb. Do you remember the old Turkish proverb, Ivan?'

Father remembered the old Turkish proverb. He looked alarmed. 'Don't recite it, Rolf.'

But Rolf did, being that kind of uncle. 'A wife for duty, a boy for pleasure, but a melon for ecstasy!'

Uncle Rolf chortled – a confident chortle, guttural and dirty. Father tried to copy it, to cover his embarrassment. He was uneasy at the prospect of more fruit-related proverbs being aired in my company.

Mother returned carrying the special occasion glasses, the tiny ones with the lone piper motif.

'What's that stuff hanging from your teeth?' she asked me.

'Mango,' I said.

'It looks disgusting.'

'Think yourself lucky – it would have been a melon but it wouldn't fit in the case,' said Rolf, and he gave Father a look.

Intrigued, I made for the bathroom to savour the spectacle of my own repulsiveness. I did horse teeth into the mirror. Straightening one of Mother's kirby grips, I passed a gratifying twenty minutes dislodging the more fibrous deposits.

When I returned, Uncle Rolf and Father were grappling, grunting, on the floor. Mother was waltzing round the living room with Stan to her own rendition of 'Bandit of Brazil'. The grapple was a friendly one, it transpired, springing from filial high spirits. Whereas Mother's song, I divined, was born of tipsiness, loneliness and neglect.

When they had all calmed down, each drinker sought to

entertain the company. Since I was the company and the hosts were all drunk, I was careful to keep an indulgent smile strapped to my face in case the mood turned ugly.

'Ivan, it's your turn,' urged Uncle Rolf. 'Favour us with a song.'

'No, no,' said Father, bashfully.

'Go on!'

'Not tonight.'

'*Please!*'

'No, no, no.'

'Ach, away, you semi-precious clown,' taunted Uncle Rolf.

Father bristled, cleared his throat.

'*Red sails in the sunset, way a – out on the seeeea . . .*'

My father seldom sang. When he did, his voice took wings. But they were tiny, paper wings so that he would crash heavily to earth, bringing the sombre tombstones of his melodies with him.

'*Oh, carry my a-loved one, home safely to a – meeee . . .*'

Mother and Uncle Rolf applauded. 'Thank you, Ivan, that was lovely.'

'*Swift wings you must a-borrow . . .*'

'Oh, there's more – sorry.'

The red sails of sunset were finally hauled in around sunrise.

In between times, Father and Uncle Rolf reminisced, fought, wept and made intermittent visits to the Hazel. At dinner time, which is to say, at breakfast time, I found myself sitting alone with Uncle Rolf at the kitchen table. Mother and Father were in the bedroom, shouting. Mother was trying to make Father clothe himself for work but the attraction of slicing corned beef had, that morning, lost all allure.

'Never marry,' said Uncle Rolf.

'What?'

'You heard me. If you must marry, make it to a deaf mute – a beautiful deaf mute with magnificent haunches.'

Uncle Rolf rolled his eyes. He weighed the deaf mute's invisible haunches in his hands and made a moaning sound. Disposing of the haunches, he picked up his bacon sandwich and took a deep bite. I watched the dribbling fat cool and harden on his plate.

'I'm a buttock man, your father's a tit man.'

I feigned prudish deafness and spooned my porridge.

Uncle Rolf leaned over and rapped his knuckles, making a door of my head. 'Don't worry, I know you're in there,' he said. 'I've never met a male Moss yet who wasn't in thrall to his cock.'

The tips of my ears tingled. I had a Latin textbook propped on a sauce bottle. My eyes bored into it, in busy translation. Yet again, happy boys were carrying arrows to a country house.

'Did your father ever tell you about the exotic dancer in Tangier?'

'No,' I croaked.

'The one with the dog?'

'No.'

'But you know that story anyway?'

'Yes. I overheard Granny Moss telling it to Grandpa.'

'Your granny ruined your father's life. But don't tell him I said so.'

'I don't need to – my mother tells him that every day.'

'Your mother's a good woman. She should have married me.'

'Why didn't she?'

'I don't want a good woman. Not yet anyway. There's plenty of time to be bored out of my cranium.'

'Will you stay at sea?'

'For five more years. Then I'll buy a house in Ayr and campaign for the Labour party. Market towns are a lost cause, but when I'm on a soapbox looking all keen-jawed and resolute, I'll have my pick of any widow I want.'

'Is that why you're going into politics?'

'Yes.' His uniform jacket was draped over the chair. He took a half bottle from a pocket and emptied the dregs into his tea. 'Your father and I are both socialists. Your father has a clever head but the nature of a fool.'

I dismissed Father's clever head. I wanted to know what the nature of a fool looked like. I had my own reasons.

'You can't be a romantic and a socialist, Ivan. Romanticism is decadence, a state of mind predicated on glamorous despair. Socialism is vibrant and forward-looking; it represents the highest flowering of man's potential.'

Uncle Rolf considered his own words. 'Christ, that's shit of a fast-flowing order – but don't let it obscure the sense.'

He was bullish in build, rather than stocky, with coarse features: a ruder, more confident version of Father.

'And you, Ivan, what about yourself? You'll leave this town, of course?'

'Why of course?'

'A home town is like a too-tight pair of shoes. You've got to get out and waggle your toes a bit.' He leaned in close. 'You like waggling your toes, don't you?'

He made it sound like something unspeakable, toe waggling. As I fumbled in my mind for words, he treated me to a burst of song:

'*She was delicate as porcelain, her saucer eyes were blind,*
but her arse was big and hairy so I took her from—'

He broke off as abruptly as he'd started. 'Don't make the mistake your father made. Don't stop waggling your toes too early.'

I remembered Fred-Up-the-Stair. 'What about my mother? She has toes too.'

Uncle Rolf narrowed his eyes. 'Women like a tight shoe,' he

said, cryptically.

'Look, Rolf!'

Father was standing behind me. I turned. He was beaming, self-consciously.

'Remember this?'

Father was wearing his old radio officer's uniform. Mother came into the kitchen, carrying toast on a plate. She was not impressed. 'Take that clown suit off and get into your overalls.' She turned to Rolf. 'He wants to go back to sea, Rolf. I hear this every other week.'

'This time I mean it.'

'I hear that too.'

Father kept his resolve. 'My uniform still fits. It's an omen.'

He brushed his shoulders, stood erect. 'What say you, Rolf?'

'Tell him, Rolf,' said Mother, 'for God's sake talk some sense into him.'

Uncle Rolf considered. 'You might still fit the uniform,' he said. 'But does the uniform still fit you?'

Father frowned. Uncle Rolf gave me a knowing look. I gave him one back, though I wasn't sure what it was we both knew.

He did, though.

Uncle Rolf returned to sea and to his life as a full-blooded, roistering sailor. Enthused by his example, Father joined the Naval Volunteer Reserve. He became a part-time roisterer – a roister-ette. He would roister on Thursday evenings between the hours of seven and ten and then have a condensed roister four weekends a year on a training ship in Portsmouth. The rest of the time he would work in Dunne's grocery shop and roistering would be left on the shelf with the tinned peaches.

Or it should have been. The trouble is that once disturbed, the sediment of excitement is slow to settle.

Twenty

Father seemed liberated by Granny Moss's death. As part of his new racy image, he bought what could best be described as a car. It was a black effort, elderly and dented, with patches of brown rust gaily decorating the wings. Father posed before it proudly, wearing his mildewed naval uniform, while Mother took a picture with a box Brownie. I declined an invitation to augment the composition with my presence, on the grounds that doing so would constitute 'a beamer', which is to say a red face induced by a humiliating experience.

Father smiled grimly while Stan clambered on the bonnet. The moment duly recorded for posterity, Father changed out of his uniform and into a lurid nylon shirt and khaki summer flannels.

'Let's have a run,' he instructed.

We weren't keen, but Father's eyes had flashed amber, signifying caution, so we pulled our coats dutifully on. The run proved a more literal enterprise than intended. The car ran us to the foot of Vine Crescent and we, in a spirit of collective fair play, ran it back up again. Or rather, pushed.

'Can you not take it back to the shop?' suggested Mother.

'I didn't buy it from a shop,' replied Father, wiping oil from his hands on the duster of his old underpants. 'I bought it from a man in Paisley.'

'How much did you pay for it?' Mother demanded.

'Thirty pounds,' muttered Father.

'That means forty,' I counselled Mother, helpfully.

The standard of my cheek had improved and my barbs could draw metaphorical blood like a sarcastic midgie.

Father applied the handbrake and locked the car. The Hazel beckoned. If things went well for Father, he rewarded himself with drink; if they went badly, he consoled himself with it.

The car lay abandoned where it stood for some weeks until sufficient funds could be raised for the purchase of a reconditioned battery. With the first shudder of the car's rebirth, Father's enthusiasm reared up afresh.

'We've had a run,' he declared. 'Now we'll try a holiday.'

We shrank back, defensively. We had holidayed before. Father had once pushed Stan all the way from Govan to the Broomielaw for the Rothesay ferry, when the old Silver Cross pram was too big to fit on the bus. We pushed that pram, all three of us, along the road to Ettrick Bay on a day of rare Scottish warmth. Stan had lain back, kicking his bare feet in delight at having them tickled by the lucky old sun, grinning sleekily up above. Out of simple, trusting contentment, Father had sung a nonsense song as we walked.

'*Mares eat oats and does eat oats and little lambs eat ivy . . .*'

Mother was so happy she smoked only three fags the whole walk. We had felt nourished, you see, inside and out. Obviously we had to pay for our happiness and next day, Scotland being what it is, whatever it is, the sun had gone in and the rain had come out. Uncle Rolf pitched up off the Waverley ferry and drink once more dictated our emotional climate. In Scotland, drink is sunshine on demand.

'Where are we going, back to Rothesay?'

'No,' teased Father.

'Dunoon?' ventured Stan.

'Neither of those,' said Father, grimly. 'Blackpool.'

I saw Mother flinch.

In those days, to polite eyes, Blackpool was not a seaside town, but a squalid byword for low pleasures and base appetites. The very name sounded like a shameful disease, a sort of impetigo of the spirit. 'Please excuse Ivan for not attending school. He had a mild touch of Blackpool for which the doctor has prescribed penicillin. Yours faithfully . . .'

'Mrs Moidart went to Blackpool,' said Mother, darkly. 'She said the people were dirty. Her landlady cooked the porridge with sugar, not salt. It was disgusting.'

Father gave her a resolute look. 'Did she eat it?'

'Of course she did – she'd paid for it.'

I chortled.

'What's wrong with that?' Mother asked, indignantly.

I jumped up and down with glee.

You had to be there.

The old bitch, my mother, had no intention of dying. Let me rephrase that: she would oblige us by doing so, but at her own pace and on her own terms. Using the broad Olympian overview, my mother had quickened the pace toward death to a point where it was hard for Stan and me to keep up.

However, on the nitty-gritty, day-to-day level it appeared a different matter. Minutes can feel like whole days when you're sitting by a bed in your mother's living room and spring is outside and your own flesh and blood is sniping at you, eyeing you suspiciously like you're plotting to kill her off by poisoning the soup that you're spooning to her lips in order to keep her alive.

'Why would I want to kill you?' I asked her, terminally exasperated.

'It's sunny out.'

'So?'

'If I was dead, you could sit in the park with your notebook.'

'You've got a point. Maybe I will do you in.'

Death too, like everything else in life, is about control. A sick person may be helpless, but one thing she can have dominion over is what food or medication goes or does not go into her mouth.

One day the doorbell rang. From a drowsy torpor, Mother's eyes flashed open. 'Who's that?'

'Why don't I go see?'

I knew who it was. In a few seconds I was making introductions. 'Mother, this is Wendy Friel from the hospice. Remember I told you about Wendy?'

'Hello,' said Wendy. Her voice was a languid drawl that nuzzled the air in practised empathy.

People talk about hospice workers in reverential tones; the term 'angels' being a common compliment. My mother was not so impressed.

'What do you want?'

I opened my mouth to sweeten the pill of Mother's gruff rudeness. Wendy gripped my elbow; a thoroughgoing professional, she *understood*.

'I just want to see how you are. If there's anything we can do.'

Mother didn't reply. She continued eyeing Wendy like she was a Mormon or someone offering to transfer all her debts onto a single easy to pay loan. Wendy had chosen to dress in black, which wasn't a good sales pitch. If I worked in the compassion industry, say maybe for Hospices-R-Us, I'd send a conjurer round in a clown suit or maybe a cheerleader with pompoms, a little levity on the way to the grave being a fine and welcome thing.

Gamely attempting a spot of rapport building, Wendy switched to the intimate approach. 'How about your pain, dear? Are they managing it successfully?'

'They were up till now,' said my mother.

I shuffled awkwardly where I stood.

Wendy clicked on a smile, flashed it at me. 'People are affected in different ways,' she said, by way of reassurance. She wheeled back to Mother, tried again. 'Kathleen?'

'Fuck off,' said my mother, turning her face to the wall with finality and pulling up the duvet.

Wendy straightened. Her lighthouse smile beamed on with stoic beneficence.

'Do you get a lot like her?' I asked, for something to say.

'The odd one,' Wendy confessed. She raised her voice a discreet but telling decibel for my mother's benefit. 'But I won't give up though.'

I saw my mother's thin frame tense under the duvet.

At the door, Wendy the hospice woman told me one useful thing. 'When it's time,' she said, 'keep talking: hearing is the last sense to go.'

I wondered, vaguely, how she or anyone else might know this for sure but it seemed, well, unseemly, to enquire.

'Thanks,' I said. 'I'll bear that in mind.'

And I did.

On our first day at the caravan site, I bought a blue denim cap and a mouth organ. In the brewing folk war between Dylan and Donovan I'd backed our local boy, Mr Leitch from Maryhill. I did this with the same unerring instinct by which I'd proclaimed the Temperance Seven a greater pop group than the Beatles. As history freely concedes, I was right, both times.

Because Donovan had a wasted leg due to an infant bout of polio, I took to hobbling. I limped out of sight round the back of the Windy Harbour campsite and blew, heartily, into the harmonica. When no tune came out, I had the naïve audacity to be disappointed. I'm not sure what I expected to hear – 'Moon River' perhaps or, at the very least, the middle eight from Manfred Mann's '5-4-3-2-1'.

To me, purchasing the instrument was somehow synonymous with having the ability to play it. I'd vaguely expected skill to come as part of the package. After all, if you bought a washing machine, you wouldn't anticipate having to weave your own clothes on a hand loom before you could use it, would you? I gave the harmonica a couple of hard, petulant taps on my palm and, sticking it into the junk cupboard of my back pocket, hobbled away.

I could hobble very well, entirely self-taught; no lessons.

'What's up with your leg?' Mother asked.

'Nothing.'

She was hanging out washing. At home, Mother would hang out washing in a shared concrete yard. Because she was on holiday, she enjoyed the luxury of hanging it out on a shared grass yard. Thanks to enlightened breakthroughs like these, working women all over Dreichstane were now taking jobs as female astronauts or directors of merchant banks.

In the cramped gloom of the caravan, I took a silver locket from a brown paper bag. I had bought it for Shona from a jeweller's shop near the beach. Now I was unsure. Why was I unsure?

The night before I left, I'd walked with her in the bluebell woods.

'Stop that.'

'Stop what?'

'I've told you before. That thing with your hips, I don't like it.'

I apologised. But I didn't mean it. Neth Skillet had already had his finger in Joanne McPhail. I hadn't even had tits yet. We walked on a little more. I reminded her I was going next day to Blackpool, inserting a note of drama as if suggesting myself as a gallant young officer on his way to the Somme. I asked Shona if she'd wait for me. I was aware that many relationships foundered during the twin uncertainties of world war and the holiday fortnight.

'Of course,' she said, squeezing my hand.

I felt that good feeling again when we held hands, the one we'd had at Bo's party, when the world seemed to open up, hinting at a clear sure road ahead, all the way from where we now stood to the horizon's distant glow. I was myself again, not that overheated fellow of a moment ago trying to wangle a dry ride.

I walked Shona out of the woods and across the street to her door.

'I'll send you a postcard.'

'Okay.'

I gave her a kiss, right there on the pavement. My heart, a tartan whippoorwill, ached at leaving her, yet sang for the gladness of my knowing her.

A hundred curtains twitched and I was proud.

Walking home along Tower Road, Neth had given a shout and ran up to me.

'Where have you been?' he asked.

'Out with Shona.'

'How'd you get on?' He was breathless.

'All right,' I said. 'I like her . . . I like her a lot.'

It took a lot for me to say 'a lot'.

'How about you?' I asked.

His face was flushed and gleaming. 'I can't say it.' He beamed, wondering how he could say it. Apparently, he couldn't say it. He said it anyway.

'Look.'

He opened his palm. He was holding a packet of Durex. One was missing. It had been used.

'That's what I can't say,' Neth said. 'I promised Joanne.'

I looked at him.

'Now you can't say it either.' He stared at me, earnestly. 'Not a word, right?'

I nodded.

He laughed.

Catching a passing cloud, he rode it up the hill home to Maple Drive.

I tried to keep hold of my whippoorwill. It had morphed into a duck that quacked mockingly at my ankles.

Nothing pains us like the success of our dearest friends.

So what I'm saying is that it felt odd, looking at this locket. My emotions were confused, sun and shadow playing across my heart. When I thought of giving the locket to Shona, a sense of warmth and security filled me. Yet when I looked at my parents' marriage, or considered my own inexperience and frustrations, the sun went in and I felt empty. I intuited that this was the way love started out, a dainty minuet, a game of holiday trinkets and fine feelings. Gradually, the feelings run out like sand from an egg timer until a couple has nothing whatsoever left to say to each other and are thoroughly exhausted by the relationship. Then it's time for them to marry.

On top of which, Neth Skillet had broken his duck and I hadn't.

You can't underestimate these things.

To kill time on our holiday, I'd walk the five miles into Blackpool town centre. Once there, I'd mooch along the prom alone in what people describe as the typically sullen, teenaged manner. If this behaviour was typical, I did not see many other examples of it on display. I longed for other teenagers to be typically sullen with, but found none. I marvelled at other holidaying young people, northerners mostly, who formed packs, with males and females mixing in a free and familiar way. They'd hog the pavements wearing daft hats and begging bites, in loud voices, from each other's toffee apples. At that time in Scotland, if a man were to wear a daft hat in public, he would risk, as a first offence, a stern rebuke from the police. If he persisted with the practice and went on to be say, for argument's sake, kicked to death by an enraged gang of citizens, then most Scots of the time would have agreed that this was an excessive response, but that there were mitigating factors of incitement to be considered, in that the victim had been 'asking for it' by wearing a daft fucking hat in the first place.

Entering the caravan, I was surprised by the stench of whisky and the sight of unknown, grinning faces.

'This is my son, Ivan.' Father looked up at me. His eyes swam like two newly cracked yolks in a frying pan. He was wearing a smile that appeared stitched to his face.

'Hello, young man.'

'Hello.'

It was the afternoon and Father was drunk.

'This is Frank and Edie.'

'I'm Frank,' the man said, 'that's Edie – in case you're wondering!'

Everybody laughed.

'Frank and Edie are from Yorkshire,' said Mother, trying to bring me in.

'Huddersfield,' specified Edie.

253

There was a brief hiatus which Father filled. 'Ivan's been down on the prom, eyeing up the talent.'

This drew a faux-saucy exclamation from our guests. I felt my face flush.

'He's a good looker,' said the blonde woman. 'I quite fancy him myself.'

Mother tried to laugh, but I could see her squirm on her chair at the thought of her teenage son being ogled.

Edie had blonde hair, bobbed short. She had her feet up on the little couch. Frank, an older man with bristle on his upper lip and a stained blazer with a silver button missing, was squashed next to her, massaging her toes. I had never seen toes being massaged before but, after all, this was England. If these people could put sugar in their porridge then they were capable of anything.

The man, Frank, had a regimental badge on his breast pocket that depicted crossed swords and cannon. The yellow thread had grown grubby and was starting to unpick itself, leaving a tiny dark pouch whenever Frank leaned over to charge his glass, which was often. Frank was evidently the joker sort of ex-serviceman.

'I call her the little woman, Ivan, but *little*? I mean, look at her, just look . . .'

Father obliged, eyeing Edie cautiously.

Mother gripped her glass tighter.

'All the same, mind you, all the same . . .!'

Frank gave Edie's rump a playful slap.

'That's enough of that in polite company,' said Edie, affecting a tone.

My father and mother tittered. Father squeezed Mother's knee in an awkward fashion, to show he too could do bawdy things. Everyone but Mother was drinking Haig from plastic picnic cups

Every so often Mother would turn to Stan and murmur, not quite quietly, 'What's the matter, son, are you tired?'

Edie took the hint and moved her generous arse. When she rose, I noticed her skirt had creased under her, so that she revealed a good measure of thigh. I noticed Father noticing too.

'I'll water the horse before heading back to barracks,' said Frank, waggishly, at the door.

My parents laughed dutifully.

'How about tomorrow night?' asked Frank.

'I don't know if . . .'

'Ivan will look after Stan,' said Father, instantly. 'You're on.' He didn't dare look at Mother. My parents saw Frank and Edie for the remainder of the holiday. Mother never seemed comfortable and would sit clutching her small sherry while the others quaffed and laughed.

On our last night, I was lying in the bunk bed with Stan. Mother was asleep, having come home early from the site's social club, leaving Father there alone, talking to Frank and Edie.

I heard Father's key turn in the lock. He started fumbling in the tiny built-in wardrobe, rooting in his sock drawer. I knew he kept things other than socks in his drawer. He kept his condoms there. I knew, too, that it was very late.

When a boy hears his father rummaging in the sock drawer at dead of night, he knows the gloves are off. I felt the shock of fresh air, then silence, as Father stepped back into the darkness and shut the door.

Next morning, he was still hungover as he loaded our battered suitcases into the boot. He caught Mother's disapproving look and his eyes narrowed. 'What's up with your face?'

Mother shook her head. She helped Stan on with his jerkin.

'One holiday a year,' Father pleaded, 'I'm entitled to have some fun.' Mother gave him a look. He batted it straight back.

'You've had your fun here too,' he said, accusingly. 'Don't act like you haven't.'

Mother didn't bite. She was biding her time.

Father turned to me and Stan. 'Get in the car,' he ordered.

By the time we'd hit Preston, Father had already made four stops; three to refresh himself and another to relieve himself of his refreshments. His mood did not mellow with the drink. We knew there was trouble ahead. On a country road some-where in the Lake District, the car gave a sudden lurch as Father wrenched up the handbrake.

'Out of the fucking car!' he screamed. 'Get out, the lot of you!'

We did as instructed, lining up against a dry dyke wall as if waiting to be shot for treason.

Father rounded on Mother. 'You slut! You whore!'

The hills glistened with drizzle. Farmyard animals eyed Father warily as he ranted.

'You accuse me, but you let that creepy cunt touch you!'

'He didn't.'

'He did! On the leg!'

'It was you,' she protested. 'You told me to be friendly.'

'Not that fucking friendly.'

Teeth were bared and clenched. Faces reddened.

'It's all right for you, I suppose, to take that fat hoor behind the partition curtain?'

'Don't change the subject,' said Father.

'What's good for the goose is good for—'

Stan stood shivering, watching our parents. I could see his brain struggling to process the monstrous information from his senses. I steered him by his hood toward the diversion of a hedgerow and offered him a fruit gum.

'I don't like shouting,' Stan said.

'It's okay,' I said, 'don't worry.'

Over by the car, Mother gave a shriek. I watched my parents' hands choke each other's windpipes as their reddened heads keeled out of sight down the radiator, grimacing, like a ghastly double sunset.

I averted Stan's gaze toward the uplifting pastoral majesty of the Lakes. 'Look,' I said.

We gazed at the craggy, majestic slopes. It would have been a humbling experience, except that we were already as humble as they came.

'What's that?' asked Stan.

'What?'

He pointed at my hand.

'Nothing.'

I had the silver locket in my palm. I closed my hand into a fist and tossed the locket high over the stone dyke, into the mud, among the other penned, lowing beasts.

It seemed the right place for it.

On our return, I avoided Shona. I had my reasons for doing this and, though I did not know what they were, I was sure they were valid. Perhaps I wasn't ready to settle down. In Scottish terms, this was immaturity on my part, as I was already fourteen. Undoubtedly, I would succumb to the misery of happiness at some future time but not now, not yet . . .

Twenty-one

'So, are you or aren't you?'

I considered Neth Skillet's question. We were in Flogger Petrie's house, corner of Cherry Place. Flogger was our classmate, a big-built girl from Fife. She had a pretty face and a gentle nature, but because she was as large as any yeoman and had an accent that made you think of ploughboys, we considered her an honorary man. Flogger had been enjoying some purloined afternoon sherry with her friends Linda Doyle and Rona Brockley when they'd noticed Neth and me lurking outside and invited us in. Once inside we had become quickly bored by the girls' conversation and had excused ourselves to enter the garden shed where we might discuss weighty matters of state. Here it was that we squatted, in frank, confessional discourse.

'Yes,' I said, finally. 'I'm still a virgin.'

Neth sighed, shrugged. 'I knew it.'

I felt a pang of resentment at the loucheness of his tone.

'Are you still getting it from Joanne McPhail?' I asked.

'Yes,' he said.

I burned inside. There was a vast gulf between us. How vast? Penis length.

I steered the conversation onto more favourable ground.

'How about jokes? Is Joanne McPhail a good laugh?'

'No. How about Shona Burns?'

I shook my head. 'I don't think being a good laugh is a girl's thing.'

'You're right,' he agreed. 'A good laugh is a great thing; it's the dibs.'

I felt heartened, glad to be back on common ground. If you couldn't shoot your gun a laugh was a close run second best. The reasons weren't hard to fathom. At school, we laboured under the regime of teachers; at home our parents chivvied and bullied us then at weekends, for a treat, we would be oppressed by the officers of the Boys' Brigade.

'Com-panee by the right . . .' would intone our captain, Mr Farrelly – 'queek marrh!'

And we'd queek marrh around the perimeter of the small church hall in our ludicrous uniforms. The more rebellious of us would tilt our pillboxes at rakish angles and push our belts down from the no-nonsense requirement of just below the nipples onto our hips, so as to look more like gunslingers rather than bellboys in unfashionable Doris Day and Rock Hudson films. Round and round we'd marrh; wheeling, doing about turns and forming fours.

On those evenings I made a pair with Neth. For some time he and I had cultivated 'It' – a brand of superior humour or foolish piffle, according to taste, that pleased us and a few select others. This was how we judged people; on whether or not they had 'It'. With 'It' imaginative word play was prominently to the fore, thus: 'She moved with the grace of a Brumpton Yappa', or 'Please parsley my bogle with your thrum.' As we clumped in endless echoing circles round the church floor we'd note a squat wooden packing case that stood, in permanent isolation, on a raised stage. We would goad each other with whispers; attempting to excite illicit sniggering with entertaining speculations as to what the box might hold; the more outlandish the suggestion, the better. I once offered 'a supple tribesman with a foldaway spear', but Neth trumped this with the superior 'a tiny jockey riding a kitten'. Admittedly these jests look foolish on the page but to extract their full value try turning Protestant, having nothing in your pocket but your balls and marching round a drill hall for hours on end on a rainy Friday night.

In Flogger's shed, Neth continued, 'If you were to say Cardinal Limpy Chalfont to a woman, they'd just look at you like you were daft.'

'Yes, yes!'

I nodded manically, a man possessed. I took up the theme and ran with it. 'Whereas, in actual fact, Cardinal Limpy Chalfont is an exquisite example of the mirth-maker's art.'

We giggled, delighted. As a phrase, 'mirth maker' had 'It', as did 'Cardinal Limpy Chalfont'.

Following a timeless, leg-kicking, belly-clutching guffaw, Neth grew serious.

'You need to do the deed,' he said, resolutely. 'With Shona or another, you need to break your duck.'

'Yes,' I said. My mood grew fierce. 'Whether she's a good laugh or not, that duck needs a good breaking.'

'It's necessary. Do whatever it takes – okay?'

'Whatever it takes,' I said, through clenched teeth.

We shook on it. We thrilled, the way explorers do. We hunkered down, side by side, young and pink; a pair of Bykovskys orbiting inner space in our *Vostok 5*, the Dreichstane satellite of a garden shed. The door opened. Flogger stood before us looking flushed.

'You've just missed it,' she said.

'Missed what?' I asked.

She was smiling in a peculiar way. 'Come into the house,' she said, beckoning.

In the living room, Linda Doyle stood grinning coyly.

'It's your own fault,' she said.

'What is? What have we missed?'

'Show them, Rona.'

Rona Brockley did a twirl. 'Notice anything?'

We looked at each other. No, we had not noticed anything.

The girls giggled.

'We took all our clothes off,' said Linda.

'And we put them back on again,' continued Rona.

I looked at Neth. His thoughts were at one with my own.

'How do we know that?'

'Easy,' teased Linda.

She indicated the tiny flags of labels, bearing washing instructions, on open display outside the girls' dresses.

'We put them back on outside in.'

'Or is it inside out?'

They giggled again.

'Look.'

All the girls showed us their labels.

'If you'd been here, you'd have seen us naked,' said Rona.

'With nothing on,' added Linda.

I didn't blame her, it merited repetition.

I walked home with Neth. We didn't speak. All the time I'd been in Flogger's shed, promising Neth I would do whatever it took to do it, I could have been in Flogger's house, with naked girls, possibly doing it.

Obviously, there was a moral to the tale. I didn't want a moral.

I wanted an immoral.

* * *

261

Not long after, a girl gave me the eye. Not just any girl, but one of the Mellish twins, a notoriously wild pair of temptresses. Together with her sister April, May Mellish did not only enjoy but relished her reputation as our town's premier hell hound in a school blazer. The Mellish sisters were almost blonde, totally good looking, ridiculously sassy and academically suspect. Each twin trailed an admiring posse of thinner-blooded, aspirant bitch queens in her wake.

Was it my imagination? No, May had flicked a grin at me as she and her disciples had crossed the playground. This wasn't any coy, lily of the valley simper, but a full-on 'Hey you, I'm looking right at you' eyeballing, lock-on stare. I'd never encountered such confidence in a woman before and had practically blushed and dropped my lace hanky.

To make myself appear bohemian, I'd procured a used jacket from an Army and Navy store that made me look like a brigadier inspecting troops on a parade ground. I had taken to walking the town with a notebook in my breast pocket and would make jottings; musings and similes or, on a bad night, I'd practise my autograph. The act of scribbling, in itself, made me feel deep and bohemian.

A fairground had come to Shanks Park. One night, I wandered in. I was looking for the place where the bad people went. The previous day, two bad people had entered Booty Lowe's shoe shop in Houston Square. Booty was elderly and had the habit, when business was slow, of dozing in his chair behind the counter. While he had slept the two bad people had strolled in and staggered back out again, carrying his till. Rumour had it that those two had been April and May Mellish.

Over the metallic pops from the rifle arcade and the screams of girls holding down their skirts on the waltzers, the Animals were singing 'Don't Let Me Be Misunderstood'.

May was over by the slot machine arcade. She was talking to some greasy-haired biker fellows. I could see their motorcycles lined up provocatively by the coconut stall. I smirked; bikers – how clichéd. Still, she was just a kid, she had to go through that phase; the wild men, the wind in her hair, the raucous, high octane parties, until finally, one day, she'd grow up enough to fall for a battered, complex type like myself; a guy who'd kicked around the block of the human heart a few times. I tossed away the stick of my toffee apple like it was the butt end of a Disque Bleu and reached, in world-weary fashion, for my notebook. I had nothing to say, I just wanted to be seen, posing against the landscape, reaching in a world-weary fashion for my notebook. I stole a peek to see if she was fascinated. She was; but not by me. A large biker was steadying her aim as she shot pellets at some playing cards.

Having mimed a few deep thoughts, I turned and headed homeward up the Rannoch Brae. Ah, that May, she just wasn't ready for me yet.

'Hey!'

I heard the heavy crackle and rasp of an engine and turned. May Mellish was riding toward me. She slowed, struggling to steady the heavy motorbike, and rested her foot on the pavement for leverage.

'Where are you going?'

'Home.'

'What for?'

'It's where I live. I go there often, it's a habit.'

I still felt raw from the earlier snub.

'I'll give you a lift.'

'No thanks.'

I walked on. She roared forward, performing an unsteady wide arc before doubling back to face me. She was on the wrong side of the road. A red Western bus had to pull right out to negotiate her. The driver did incredulous shaking of the head.

May didn't look at me. She wasn't shy, she just couldn't be bothered. I watched her eyes cover the sloping shoulders of Ben Lomond, the distant lights of far-off roads, the bluebell woods, all in a single inscrutable sweep.

'Get on,' she said.

I was doubtful. She was still wearing her school blazer.

'Get fucking on!'

After a brief, wobbling struggle against gravity, we roared away. The wind smashed my face into a melting halloween mask as we zoomed past hard-working citizens queuing at bus stops and bone idle ones returning from ice cream vans in their squalid carpet slippers.

'You okay?'

'Yessssh,' I said.

'You like it?'

'Itsh great!' I lied. The wind had pared back my lips. My sensitive molars ached from the cold. 'Wow,' I said cravenly, feigning wild enthusiasm.

'Hold on!'

I clamped shut my streaming eyes as we sped in a blurring rage round Dreichstane's humdrum circumference. When we passed my street at high speed, I tried to shout out.

'What? What did you say?'

I tried again. The blast scattered my words like confetti thrown from a racing car. I gripped May hard. My nose was a running font; my panicking fingers were splayed white epaulettes draping her slim, girlish shoulders.

At the cusp of Sycamore and Vine, May stopped the bike. 'Get off,' she said.

I was stiff with cold.

'Get the fuck off! I have to get this bike back!'

I dismounted the pillion, in ungainly fashion.

'It's my brother's,' she explained.

I felt rejected, used. I never wanted to see her again. 'May?'

'What?'

'Can I see you again?'

She shrugged, nonchalantly. I watched her roar away, leaving me perplexed and mystified. Lying in bed, later, I suspected I'd failed my audition. I always felt that way with May, even though I must have passed because, thereafter, we met many times.

During school or, more accurately, when she'd deign to attend school, May would ignore me. In the evenings, if we didn't have the bike, we'd walk to the woods where we'd built a den from tall ferns and scraps of old door frames abandoned by tinkers. We found a rusting garden gate that formed a grill on which we'd heat bacon or sausages stolen from home. Sometimes I'd skip school too and we'd spend the day roaming around Paisley, shoplifting, before tramping back over the Gleniffer Braes to the woods where, exhausted, we'd lie among the ferns in the den, enjoying our spoils. We would huddle together for warmth and I would feel her hard bony body under her tight jeans and chunky knit jumper. If she was wearing her school skirt, I'd attempt liberties. We rarely overburdened each other with conversation. I recall, rather, a lingering sense of awe at the ferocious energy that was somehow contained, perilously, in the frail vessel of May's body.

I asked her once about the future, how she saw herself; told her I pictured myself as a hermit, in a cave with other hermits, in a hermit club. This abstraction drew an exclamation of disgust. She clambered up a nearby tree, as though to gain distance from the stale fug of my introspection. I realised I somehow both attracted and repulsed May.

We relieved an off-licence in Linwood, one day, of a bottle

of Emva Cream and fled back to our den to guzzle it. Later, we petted heavily, though she would not let me enter her. When I pressed her for a reason she told me it would happen in its own sweet time, if it was to happen at all and that I should be content, for now, with the intrusion of my finger. I complied with this wish. Our den was the Blue Angel Club and May, who was a year older than me, Lola-Lola to my naïve and repressed Professor Rath.

I would lie awake, thinking about her. It dawned on me that I was not cut out to be truly bad or, to be more specific, like her, a creature of instinct. Hearts like May's, crazy hearts, by no means unattractive hearts, beat to a different rhythm. Those hearts knew that life is no quiet stroll across an open field as we, the faint hearts, out of fear, delude ourselves it is. Life was a desperate charge against hostile forces, with invisible assailants shooting poison arrows at you from both sides. If you were hit, you snapped off the shaft of the arrow and kept running, full ahead, without stopping to agonise, physically or otherwise. For those hearts, a question is a form of moral stasis and an answer a blanket the weak pull over their heads to cover unease. To reason is to move too slowly, to encumber oneself with a backpack filled with doubt. The bad didn't reason, because they knew the answers already, instinctively, not despite running at speed, but *because* they ran at speed; fleet of foot, or on a Norton motorcycle, their senses heightened and alert, fine-tuned to the blathering nonsense of existence.

I thought out some of this in words over a few weeks and felt the rest.

At last, I suggested we set fire to the den. We did and it burned with a stink. I think we both felt regret, though we laughed to cover it. Why had I suggested it? Following May's cue, I had felt that nothing should last too long.

Not long after, Bo Divney approached me in the playground.

'I'm sorry about May.'

'What do you mean?'

'You don't know?'

'No.'

He told me.

'Oh.'

There is always one person in every school who dies prematurely in a motorcycle accident. It ought to be a formalised ritual on the school noticeboard, on a typed slip of paper, headed 'Volunteer Required'.

Rejuvenated by their holiday, my parents now fought with added vigour.

I interrupted Father's throttling of Mother one evening to ask whether I could borrow his aftershave. Familiar with domestic violence, I had grown to be its weary witness.

'What for? You don't even shave!'

'I don't vote either, but I still hate Alec Douglas-Home.'

Flogger Petrie was having a house party. I was keen to go. Shona might be there.

Mother tugged herself clear and gave Father's face a hard slap. Father winced. He turned to me. 'I'm out of aftershave,' he said.

As he walked away, I watched Mother, enraged, rush at him with a potato peeler. As she lunged toward the kidney area, the handle fell off and the slatted metal stem dropped harmlessly to the floor. Father looked startled. So did Mother. This was a new, exciting breakthrough in mutual degradation.

I stooped and picked up the peeler.

'How about hair oil?'

'What?'

'Hair oil: oil for hair.'

'You said hair oil was old hat.'

'It is.'

'Then why do you want it?'

'To use as aftershave.'

Father gave a flattish snort, signifying amusement. I handed the peeler back to Mother.

At the door, I turned back to see Father sitting on the couch, his hands on his knees. The patches of black insulating tape masking the gashes in the couch had, like the rest of us, given up all ghost of pretence. The settee's wounds, like ours, were laid bare. Father put his head in his hands. The collar of his shirt was frayed. I was surprised by the size of the bald patch on his crown. Mother was in the kitchen, clattering our remaining plates. In the hallway, I found Stan standing shivering. He was naked, but for a vest and was clutching his dick for comfort. He had bronchitis.

'Go back to bed,' I said. 'Everything's okay.'

He started to jump up and down, shouting, 'It's not okay – everything's horrible! Horrible!'

He coughed, in phlegmy, eye-bulging rasps. He was still coughing as I strolled out the door and down the crescent, reeking fragrantly of Vitalis.

In Elderslie, we entered the pub, Neth Skillet being first to the bar. 'A pint of heavy,' he said, decisively.

The barman, a sweating middle-aged human barrel in concertina flannels, eyed him warily.

'How old are you?'

'Twenty-two.'

Nonplussed by the sheer brio of the lie, the barman reached for a glass.

We sat at a table, sipping our pints, speaking in over-loud, confident voices, hoping not to retch on the harsh taste of the beer. I watched wisps of smoke like small beacons rise from all sides of the bar, to converge in a thick rancid fug that hovered just above our heads. In those days, eyes did not smart from smoke, nor clothes stink, because the world and everything in it smelled of tobacco smoke. I watched older men with overhanging bellies wheeze and rasp, their abrasive curses filling what had once been air. Occasionally, one of them would slump to the floor and be borne away by willing friends. The bus shelter outside the pub was a sort of sin bin where fuddled drinkers would sit propped and muttering until a bus appeared or until they were able to stagger back inside the pub and demand more drink. Occasionally, drunks would be robbed and beaten in the shelter while they slept. This was a considerate practice by the mugger in that it confined criminality to a neat, purpose-built, civic unit.

'Let's go,' urged Bo Divney.

'Yes,' I agreed. It was getting late and I was eager to see Shona.

'Careful,' cautioned Neth, 'we don't want to arrive too early.'

'We're too late to be too early,' said Tonga.

'Ah, but . . .'

Neth had two sisters, one older, one younger, and as a result was a master tactician. 'You can't arrive really late, or else the room's so loud your entrance isn't noticed. The trick for us is to arrive just as they're worrying we won't come.'

'Neth's right,' I said, keen for us to move. 'We've got to surf the wave of expectation.'

This metaphor won approval. There was an appreciative collective purr as we oiled our mental surfboards and headed for the door.

A car horn tooted. We looked. Father's rusting monstrosity of a vehicle wheezed alongside us. He tried to wind down the window. The crank came off in his hand. He cursed and opened the door.

'What's up?' I asked.

'Get in,' he said.

Mother was sitting in the back, with Stan.

'I'm going to a party.'

'No, you're not – get in.'

I looked at my friends. They were already edging up the street, heading toward the world of girls, drink and music. And Shona Burns.

'Tell him, Kathleen.'

Mother leaned forward. 'It's an emergency,' she said. 'A boy on a bike brought a telegram. He came all the way from Glasgow.'

'What emergency?'

'Grandpa's gone missing.'

Like Harold McMillan, we were all at the mercy of events.

The care home was on the south side of Glasgow, in a residential area. The residents of the residential area had objected to the building of the care home. This was puzzling, as they themselves seemed indistinguishable from the people in the care home. Elderly, medicated souls gazed forlornly from institution to residential tenement and back again, one upon the other. Perhaps it was this very similarity that discomfited the residents of the residential area being, in every sense, too close to home.

We were shown to the dining area of the care home. Grandpa had climbed out of a window while eating his evening porridge. His spoon lay embedded in his congealed food, exactly as he'd left it. Mother asked why the plate hadn't been cleared away. A fat woman, the night attendant, her beefy legs toasting at a single-bar electric fire took a drag at her fag and said, 'I thought the police might need it as evidence.' I looked around the dining room. She had been diligent in the matter of evidence. There were puddles on the floor, scorch marks on the ceiling and crusted food round the gas rings of the cooker; she had left no stone turned.

The local police having received no tip-offs about a renegade pensioner in carpet slippers with a wanderlust, we took it upon ourselves, as a family, to track down Grandpa. Using ancient hunting skills handed down from our highland ancestors we walked around the local park calling out his name and when that failed we headed to a café for chips. Replenished, we galvanised our efforts and decided to seek out those places to which Grandpa might have felt himself sentimentally drawn. Bravely, Father volunteered to scour the pubs. His search was thorough. As a last resort, we drove slowly but erratically past Grandpa's old workplace, the sewage plant, lest we should discover him crouched in a foetal position hugging a turd, for comfort. When Father finally uttered the words 'It's useless, let's go home', we sighed in collective relief.

That night, lying in bed, I felt cold. Noticing the curtains billowing, I rose. I closed the window, though I could not remember having opened it. The window lock had lain broken, ever since Father had fixed it following one of his clambering-in-drunk-at-three-a.m. incidents.

I stood for a moment, considering. Acting on instinct, I walked into the hallway, opened the door of the cupboard and turned on the light.

Grandpa was sitting on the old paraffin heater, shivering. His trench coat was muddy and his pyjamas were torn at the knees where he'd shinned down the drainpipe during his escape.

'I fought in two world . . .'

'Cups?'

'No.'

'Ballroom dance championships?'

'No.'

'Wars?'

'Yes.'

And he had, he had fought in two world wars. Too young for the first, he had lied that he was older in order to be accepted. For the second, he was too old, so had lied that he was younger so as to enlist. On both occasions, he maintained he'd only done it to get away from Granny Moss.

'Is there anything I can get you, Grandpa?'

'I would like a . . .'

'Cup of tea?'

'No.'

'Sandwich?'

'No.'

He held out his hands.

'Hug?'

'Yes.'

We hugged.

Father drove Grandpa back to the care home.

He was dead within the month.

The funeral took place the week before Christmas. As a wheeze, I suggested Stan and I be allowed to post our Santa lists up the crematorium chimney.

Uncle Rolf, once again on compassionate leave to bury a parent, managed a quip as the velvet curtain droned across Grandpa's coffin. 'Death comes in threes,' he said to Father. 'What say we bludgeon the minister to take the heat off the rest of us?'

Father, three pints in, laughed louder than he had wished. 'Sorry.'

The minister pretended not to have heard but crashed his eulogy through the gears, in order not to risk a repetition of the scurrilous outburst.

At the purvey in Ibrox House, Father hit the whisky. While we sat, spearing our chips, he held forth on the subject of his frustrated life. The passing of Grandpa had seen another constricting bond broken and wistful talk of the sea began anew.

'That's where I should be. And one day, by God, I'll do it!' He flashed Mother a look and added a dash of lemonade to his Bell's.

'Do it then,' said Uncle Rolf, quietly.

Father adopted a resolute air as he took hold of his glass. 'I will, don't you worry,' he said and took a big slurp.

Uncle Rolf wouldn't let it lie. 'I'm sailing from Liverpool on the *Patrician*,' he said, leaning forward. 'I know for a fact they need another sparks. Take the train down with me.'

He gripped Father by the arm, squeezed for emphasis. 'Don't be a part-time sailor.'

'If only it were that easy,' said Father, starting to squirm.

'It is,' Mother said.

Uncle Rolf raised his eyebrows. 'You see? Kathleen wouldn't mind, would you?'

Mother shook her head. 'I've been telling him for years.' She turned to Father. 'If it would make you happy then, for God's sake, go!'

Father's glass hovered uneasily at his lips. We were all watching him. 'All right then,' he announced, 'I'll go!'

He sank his drink.

Everyone fell silent.

'He won't go,' said Stan.

And he didn't.

Something was building, though; you could feel it.

Twenty-two

I was stooping over the bed, trying to persuade my mother to take a pill. She kept her mouth clamped shut, moved her head from side to side, puppet fashion, leading my chasing palm a merry, maddening dance.

'Why won't you take it?'

'Because I don't know what it is.'

'It's a painkiller.'

'I'm not in pain.'

'You're not in pain because you take painkillers.'

'Let me read the bottle.'

I gave her the bottle. I watched her eye the label suspiciously, peruse the contents list close up, scrutinise the directions for use.

'If I wanted you dead,' I said, 'I could hit you with a hammer.'

'Too messy,' she said, in all seriousness. 'You'd be caught.'

Some days I'd had it with her. This was one of those days. Anger gave me the confidence to raise again the subject of a hospice.

'Why do you keep on about these places?'

'They'd know how to look after you.'

'I'll admit myself when I'm ready, when the time is right.'

'How about hospital?'

'No way. I'd sooner go into a hospice.'

'When will you go into a hospice?'

'When the time is right.'

She had, of course, no intention of ever going into any hospice. Her own bed would be her last resting place. She knew this would be unmanageable for Stan and me, or any two people with anything resembling lives to lead, so was doing her best to die quickly. She'd stopped eating, pretty much entirely. You'd see the skin of her thighs hang in horrifying folds when you helped her up onto the commode. All her life she'd been too modest even to own a dressing gown; you'd always see her fully clothed. Now Stan and I were emptying her shit from a pail.

One day, in a brief respite from her morphine-induced paranoia, she summoned Stan and me to her bedside. She apologised for the 'inconvenience' she had been causing us. We told her looking after her welfare was the least we could do.

My knuckles were torn and my ribs hurt. Stan covered his bleeding nose with a Handy Andy, making it look like the snot of grief. Seconds earlier, we'd been in the kitchen conducting a policy discussion. In a bold new initiative, I'd tried to ram Stan's head into a non-existent gap between the fridge and tumble dryer. He'd countered this resolution by lashing out with his Caterpillar boots, which accounted for my aching rib cage and the ridged print on my snazzy summer shirt. Looking after our mother was truly the least we could have done but it was also, by a long way, much more than we were capable of doing. The tension we felt resulted in these violent squalls; often fist fights, always within earshot, as we debated the best interests of a patient who could be, by turns, contrary, obstinate, vindictive and conciliatory.

Because she was at home, the apparatus of the state kicked in: home helps, district nurses and GPs. As fast as any remedial equipment could reach us from occupational therapy, her condition would deteriorate too rapidly for it to be of use. The home helps or care assistants visited three times a day; their maximum caring availability, maybe ten minutes of care per visit. This left plenty of care gaps through the day and night for Stan and me to try and plug with our unique brand of family tenderness.

One night we were changing shifts. I was going over the book with Stan. We kept detailed notebooks, as instructed, on the amounts of medication discharged, nuances of patient condition, and any progress which might have been made over the administering of food or drink. As we spoke, our mother was demanding to be lifted onto her commode.

'I need to go. I need to go right now.'

Needing to go would be undertaken around twenty times a day. All occasions were urgent, matters of 'right now'. On around half of these 'right now' occasions nothing, not a meagre dribble, would result.

Stan listened to her carping wail for a moment then grabbed me by the elbow.

'What is it?'

He hauled me into the kitchen before speaking. 'I can't take this any more,' he said. His voice was a low murmur. He had his hands held at his face. I noticed his thumbs were tucked into his palms.

'It's not for ever,' I reassured him.

'If I take any more time off I'll lose my job.'

'You hate your job.'

'I like eating. Unlike you, I don't have choices.' He looked at me, his expression both resolute and appealing. His hair appeared to be thinning. His eyes were red as if they itched. 'You know this is too much for us,' he said. 'We're on our own and we need help.'

'Yes,' I admitted. He leaned on the draining board, sank his head into his hands. I gave him a little nudge to help him with his train of thought. 'What kind of help?'

He looked up; thought about saying it; made himself say it. 'There's a nursing agency in Paisley.'

I opened my mouth to speak. Stan anticipated what he thought would be my objection. 'I know,' he said, nodding already in empathy, 'it'll cost money.'

I didn't care. 'Fuck money,' I said. 'At this rate we'll be dead before she is.'

I was startled by my own words. I felt liberated.

I watched the strain lift from Stan; plainly, visibly, you could see it already leaving his being. He thought about hugging me. I tensed. He changed his mind. A thought occurred, making him frown. 'Thing is, we don't know how long this could go on.'

'Exactly,' I said. 'All the more reason to do it.'

He nodded, eagerly. Not knowing whether to laugh or cry, he did both.

It had gone quiet in the living room. I went in. She glared at me, a steady look, defiant, watched me walk around her bed, clumpitty clump, step by step.

I threw back the covers. The sheets and duvet cover, clean on, would have to be washed again.

'I told you I needed to go,' she announced, with a victor's smile, 'but you wouldn't listen.'

I looked at Stan. 'Make the call,' I said, with feeling.

It was nearly Christmas. I was lying on the couch, reading about how Rudolf Hess would spend his festive season in Spandau: Hess's torment; Hess's loneliness; Hess's stoicism at sitting in his cell wearing a paper hat with nothing for company but a chipolata; the hand-wringing of civilised liberals at holding a decent, God-fearing Nazi in limitless incarceration. In the accompanying photo, Hess was smiling and strolling around a garden the size of Kent. He looked like a schools inspector about to retire on an index linked pension.

In the free world of Dreichstane, Christmas was on full lavish display. Santa rode a three-legged Rudolph up the soot-stained wallpaper over our fireplace. Above my head, spider legs of faded decorations sagged outward from the light shade to probe the gloomy corners of the living room. The television was on, ads for toys flashing relentlessly. Stan was sitting cross legged before the screen, in clean vest and pants, his face gleeful in anticipation of the imagined bounty that lay ahead. He was old enough now to imagine. I didn't want to disillusion him.

Father's key turned in the lock. There was a slurred grunt as he attempted a jovial greeting, followed by a meaty thump as he keeled over onto the hall floor. Mother moved, at speed, to assess the situation. I rose from the couch and looked out into the lobby.

Father lay on his back, squirming like an upturned crab. We watched him.

'Fuckers!'

He closed his eyes, stopped struggling.

Stan tugged at my arm. He was doing his trembling thing. 'Is he dead?'

'No,' Mother reassured him, kneeling. 'Daddy's been awful busy at work. He's having a wee lie down.'

I ushered Stan into our room, then returned. Father was dozing peacefully, his feet sticking out the front door onto the communal landing.

'Help me, Ivan.'

Together, Mother and I dragged him into the bedroom and onto the bed.

'I hate my life!' yelled Father, festively, before resuming his somnolent torpor. From the television in the living room, Andy Williams sang a sugary falsetto of seasonal goodwill.

'*Have yourselves a merry little Christmas, let your hearts be light . . .*'

That night, out of uneasiness, I rallied my raiding party, Stan, for a swoop. As our parents slumbered in their different ways, Mother fitfully, Father dead to the world, we reconnoitred cupboards, the outside coal closet, even our own bedroom, looking for Christmas spoils, but to no avail.

In the kitchen, my eye chanced upon the pedal bin by the sink. A tangle of carrier bags, carelessly disposed of, thrust out from under its plastic lid.

I walked to the food cabinet and pulled down the flap on its sliding hinges.

We stood side by side, marvelling at exotic liquids; yellows, browns, intriguing ochres. I picked up expensive bottles and held them, with reverential awe, for Stan to touch and stroke. Together, we made acquaintance with the different textures of the glass; some smooth, some chunky, others dimpled and burnished. I whispered aloud the variety of exotic names on the labels – Martell, Warnink, Tia Maria, Bertola Cream, Glenmorangie, Bell's and Babycham – a global guide to grape and grain, a world of unattainable advertising delight, now ours to have and hold.

Mother appeared at the door in her curlers, sans teeth. She confirmed my suspicion.

'That's the overtime you're holding,' she said. 'He spent it on drink. Every last penny.' She looked at us, the jury. 'I ask you, how can anybody work with a man like that?'

Stan and I looked suitably grave. Mother's tone had been flat and defeated, yet with the raised, telling hint of incredulity. It was spectacle, after all. And spectacle is exciting. The Charge of the Light Brigade would have been entertaining, viewed safely from a Parker Knoll, through binoculars.

'He wants to go back to sea,' mourned Mother, over her shoulder, on her way back to bed. 'But first he's going to burn his boats.'

Stan, having assimilated all the relevant information, looked up at me. He was hoping I'd tell him he had misunderstood, had grabbed the wrong end of the festive stick. A no-present Christmas was unthinkable, wasn't it? Life didn't work that way, did it? Presents were a child's right, enshrined in the Declaration of Arbroath of 1320, weren't they? 'It is in truth not for glory, nor riches, nor honours that we are fighting but for selection boxes – for that alone which no honest child gives up but with life itself.'

I looked again at the food cabinet.

There they stood, all in a row: fancy bottles, well-bred bottles; delicate liqueurs and exquisite tinctures. Each one a flash of defiance from somewhere deep in Father's soul, or to give it a more accurate name, his wallet. It was the shame, of course. He had shirked the challenge of returning to sea and so had asserted himself by stuffing his money confidently down a drain. These were the sixties, the decade of ideas. The middle classes might wrestle with 'cogito ergo sum', but in our house Father's pay cheque did the thinking for us. There was only one evaluation that solved the problem of being or non being: 'I earn therefore I am.' Ergo, the less I earn, the less I am. On twenty-five quid a week, Father must have felt like the Invisible Man.

Until then it had never occurred to me that my parents had any sort of independent existence. I assumed them defined by their allotted roles of 'Mother' and 'Father'. Father's tether was straining at the capstan. Soon we would all pitch and roll on the unruly swell.

The next day, after Father had roused himself, Mother snapped into desperate action.

Following a free and frank exchange of views, Mr and Mrs Claus effected an eleventh hour agreement. White-bearded old Father Provident was summoned. He opened his sack and handed our parents a credit line, franked and stamped, with compound interest accruing festively.

At the breakfast table on Christmas morning, I looked at Stan. He was wearing boxing gloves, a cowboy hat and trying to eat Maltesers with his knife and fork. He was happy.

Our parents sat opposite, looking wearily middle-aged and, in every conceivable sense, spent.

I watched them dunk their burned toast into singed, greasy eggs.

It was the best of times. It was the worst of times.

It was the last of times.

'Moss?'

'Yes, miss?'

'Stand up.'

We were in Miss Greer's English class. I stood, as instructed. In the ritual manner, I gripped the sides of my desk in a comfort posture, simulating the nervousness of the humble pupil who expects reprimand or punishment.

Old Miss Greer, a tiny figure, was studying the three A4 pages of my essay, flicking them back and forth between spit-moistened fingers. Chalk dusted the shoulders of her gown like icing sugar. She peered at me over her big, old woman glasses.

'This isn't the first time you've done this.'

'No, miss.'

'Nor the second.'

She was building up to a roll. I knew a spectacular little rocket shower was headed my way. I stood back mentally to allow her room to light the touch paper.

'It's really very good. In fact, I've decided to enter your essay for a National Scholarship Award.'

On the word 'award' a laconic 'ooh' sasheyed around the room before trailing its feather boa out the door and down the corridor. Being fifteen, we didn't 'ooh' any more, unless with irony.

'Step out here and read it aloud.'

I performed a modest 'Must I?' raise of the eyebrows, not too high though, in case she changed her mind.

'Pay attention – Ivan Moss will read us his modern folk tale.'

With monstrous humility, I shuffled down the aisle. I took the pages, read aloud, savouring each carefully wrought sylla-ble. In truth, the essay had sounded finer in the silent sanctum of my inner ear, having been written in dense, conscientiously packed prose; not in the robust strut and swagger of the spoken word. There were, however, a couple of passable drolleries and the odd well-executed verbal pirouette. I contrived to end on a shaky epigram, which drew a round of applause, albeit after a spirited kick-start from Miss Greer.

As I stood, beaming modestly, I sought out Shona. Our eyes met, and as they did her cheeks reddened and her gaze dropped to the ancient, suddenly important inkwell on her dilapidated wooden desk. I watched lovely strands of that familiar dark and lustrous hair, rich shoots of vibrant plant life, conceal those dark brown eyes and shield her feeling heart.

She had never forgiven me for going off with May Mellish.

If I could festoon that feeling heart with dazzling word petals, perhaps she might try.

I could always hope.

As Uncle Rolf had once said, a small town is like a tight pair of shoes. Except that you wear them inside your head. Drink loosens your mental laces.

My colleagues and I had become partial to a particular brand of what could, at that time, be legally termed British sherry. On television this beverage would be promoted in adverts depicting stiff-collared butlers bearing silver trays and crystal glasses for important dignitaries in elegant drawing rooms. Lacking a drawing room, my fellow courtiers and I would gather in the gents convenience in Houston Square. Over aperitifs at the urinal, we would discuss the future. My friends, my very dear, close friends, Bo, Neth and Tonga, startled me by making declarations of clear intent; they spoke of apprenticeships, of college courses and career paths. I was stunned. Where had I been while they were making those choices? I recalled no guidance over the future.

Our teachers had been unable to convince, or inspire. Since they lived in the same small town as us, with the same narrow horizons, this was hardly their fault. The only difference between our teachers and ourselves was that they were paid forty quid a week for sitting on one side of the room looking at us, while we sat on the other, looking at them for free.

'My da will speak for me,' said Bo. 'He'll put my name down for a tool-making course.'

'I couldn't work in a factory,' Neth admitted. 'I fancy a sales position in an office.'

'I'm aiming for a college place,' said Tonga, 'to study commercial art.'

Bo Divney turned to me. 'How about you, Ivan?'

At a loss, I could only blurt out, limply, 'I haven't really thought about it.'

Looks were exchanged. I felt myself eased out from our secure little refuge, armed only with a dole card, to face a dangerous night of marauding bosses and glum apprenticeships.

Until then, I had thought my friends' view of the world to be similar to my own. Having watched the example of my parents, I'd deduced the future to be a prison camp and work an unfortunate conditioning of the brain. You stepped into the camp a free man. Once in, they handed you a wife, two ungrateful children and a brown overall. Sentence served, you stepped back out with a peptic ulcer and a thinning quiff, dragging your prospects behind you in a hand cart.

I knew there was more to life than my tiny town, because drink had watered the summer flowers of my brain and told me so. On the other hand, I loved my tiny town and the people in it. As a result of the conflict between head and heart raging on the battleground of my growing soul, I was often left completely drained.

Not only emotionally.

Late one night, I took off my vomit-soiled shirt, rolled it into a tight ball and stuffed it behind the lawn mower in the back shed. Composing myself, I entered the house. The living-room door was slightly open. I could see Father's slipper jiggling back and forth on his foot. His voice was a strangely coy murmur and I realised he was on the phone. I tiptoed toward the door and listened.

'What makes you and I tick?' he enquired, in a fawning simper. The answer must have pleased him, because he let out a brief chortle, not an open and vulgar chortle, but a cooing, purring chortle, fetid with intimacy. I knew my mother could not possibly be on the receiving end of a chortle of that order.

'You see, sweetheart, with people like us . . .' He broke off. He had seen me. He covered the mouthpiece.

'Ivan?'

'Who's that?'

'I'll call you back.' Putting down the phone, he went on the attack. 'What kind of time do you call this?'

'Time for a true socialist government,' I said, resenting his seizing of the high ground.

'What do you mean?'

'I had to wait an hour for a bus. In Cuba they'd bring the bus to me.'

'Why didn't you walk?'

'Because the streets are rife with crime; capitalism has failed us.'

We stood, looking at each other. Years before he'd have given me a clip for such lip. Since I was now as tall as him, or rather of equal shortness, he could no longer risk violence. He gave the air a bracing sniff. 'Have you been—'

I didn't wait for him to finish. It was my turn. I went on the offensive. 'Was that Mother on the phone?'

'No. It was your aunt Celia.'

He rocked up and down, guiltily, on the balls of his feet.

'Was it hell,' I said.

His nostrils twitched. He was flailing around for some authority. 'Have you been sick?'

'No.'

'You've been drinking. Have you been drinking?'

'No.'

'Then why aren't you wearing a shirt?'

'I went out without one.'

'Are you sure you haven't been drinking?'

'If I'd been out drinking, I'd have been wearing a shirt, wouldn't I?'

He let it pass. I didn't.

'Who is she?'

He eyed me, beadily. 'Who is who?'

'The woman you were talking to on the phone.' I took a breath to steady my voice. 'The one who isn't Aunt Celia.'

'You're mad.'

'I'm not blind though. I've got specs. Enormous great hulking specs – you bought them for me, remember?'

'I've had enough of this.'

'Where's Mother?'

'She's gone. We had a fight.'

'What about – your girlfriend?'

He gave a dismissive snort. 'As if I could afford a girlfriend.'

'That's not an answer.'

I watched him scrabble around in his brain.

'We fought about money.'

'You haven't got any money.'

'Exactly. You'd think having none would solve the problem, apparently it doesn't.'

Finding a nugget of self-pity flashing in his pan, Father immediately staked out his claim. 'She took Stan with her . . . my son, my boy.' He leaned against the door handle for support. It gave way. He was pleased. He saw it as a symbol for his disintegrating life.

I considered the inconvenience of having my own life split asunder. 'Get her back,' I said. 'Bring Mother home.'

'She won't come home. It's over.'

'What?'

'You'll have to do it,' he said.

'Me?'

'If you want her back, do it yourself. I've had enough.' He shrugged, uselessly. He was feigning the exhaustion of a decent man run ragged by a headstrong wife.

I watched him pick up the wedding picture from the sideboard. A thorough-going professional, he made his lower lip tremble and his Adam's apple thrum pitiably. I pressed on.

'Who is she?'

'Who?'

'Her – your hoor.'

'I don't know what you mean.'

'Sure you do.'

'Don't get above yourself.'

'Does she live round here?'

'That's none of your business.'

'She does exist then, you admit it?'

'Who?'

'Your other woman, your girlfriend.' I remembered the word he'd used on the phone. 'Your sweetheart.'

He struggled. His lip flickered. He blushed. His mouth surrendered to a tipsy, lopsided grin.

My father had become a bashful schoolboy.

He wanted to tell me all about it, you could see. He thought himself a man of the world because he'd found some old trout who'd given him a poke.

'What's her name?'

He smirked. He laughed. I started smirking and laughing, too. I wanted a jovial mood, so my father's eyes would be filled with stardust. I wanted him to know what it was like to walk on air, to trill like a linnet about his newfound love, to canter through fields of sunflowers whistling 'Edelweiss' for the benefit of me, his son, his appreciative audience.

'So, what's her name? You can tell me.'

'You'll tell your mother.'

'No I won't. We're all boys together, aren't we?'

He thought about it; our being boys together. You could see his mind goading him, daring himself to lay down that load, that heavy tangle of guilt and nerves. He wanted to set it down right there on the living-room carpet to quiver and steam, for the world to see and share. I saw his lips part, sensed the rapid rise and fall of his chest with the anticipated rapture of confession. My own lips moved silently, willing him on. To speak this word, this name, would be to change his world, and therefore ours, for all time, for better or worse.

The air seemed to sing, like the wind in the wires, on a lonely road, under a threatening sky; it sang like that.

'Maria.'

'What?'

'You heard.'

Things clicked into place. This was what it had all been about: the reckless excess of the Christmas booze incident; the inexplicable mood swings; the relentless raiding of mother's purse. I looked at him.

'Maria, like in *West Side Story*?'

'Yes, like in *West Side Story*.'

'Not like Maria von Trapp in the *Sound of Music*?'

'Not like that, like the other one.'

'*West Side Story*?'

'Yes.'

We looked at each other. There now, it was spoken. We were each relieved, in our different ways, and exhilarated. My father and I wore the same fixed, slightly demented look.

'You've done it now,' I said.

'Yes,' he said.

And we laughed; a cold laugh, and hard.

Twenty-three

Mother was not at home, said Granny Cairns.

Granny looked guilty about keeping me standing on the doorstep but felt obliged to send back a withering signal to the enemy, my father.

'Where is she, Granny?'

'In Govan – she took Stan down to the swings.' Granny had built up a little spite, needed to discharge it. 'Your father's a no-user, I said that all along.'

I did nodding gravely acting, then turned. She called me back.

'It's the drink,' she explained. 'You'll never drink, will you, son?'

I shook my head, dutifully. Looking at me, she started to melt. Here I stood; a young boy, my life before me, the weight of the world on my frail shoulders et cetera . . . She lifted my hand and I felt the exhilaration of folding money being pressed into my compliant palm.

'Thank you, Granny.'

In those days, a pound bought you eight pints.

There was a swing park at the foot of McKechnie Street, by the river.

'Ivan?'

I had surprised my mother. She was sitting by the railings, near the ferry point.

'What are you doing here?'

'Looking for you.'

Stan had left the roundabout to slink along the railings. He was confused at seeing me in Glasgow; his own brother, here at the ferry landing; he couldn't work it out, whether I was now his friend or an evil enemy like his father. I offered him a sixpence. His hand snaked out and the strangeness evaporated.

I turned to Mother. 'Father sent me.'

She pulled a face.

Stan shouted for me to watch him. He hurled a stone into the water. It made a chunky sound as it burrowed deep into the sleek river flesh and Stan jumped with glee, laughing. We were not laughing, my mother or I. Mother looked out at the river and so did I. The river was deep; wide and strong. We watched it pass us in silence, as though it was some fierce thing that might growl if we moved. My mother shuddered.

'Let's go,' she said.

We went.

In the Lyceum Café we conducted business.

'He wants you back,' I lied.

'Does he now?'

She was fiddling with the wrapper of her tea cake. Stan had a dish of ice cream and a long spoon.

'Stop kicking the table, Stan,' my mother said.

'Yes,' I said, 'he knows he's made mistakes.'

'Mistakes' had drawn the raise of an eyebrow. 'Is that what he calls it?'

I wondered if she knew already, about the other woman. But how can you tell what another person knows unless you ask them? And I couldn't ask her. I pressed on.

'You should see him,' I said. 'It's all he can do to wash himself.'

'No kidding.'

I shrugged, pitiably. 'A clean shirt's a thing of the past,' I said. 'I've to very nearly drag him to the soap dish.'

On and on I went with the molasses and the treacle. That's the thing with lies; they start out as a drip, drip, then gather momentum. Next thing you know, you've a raging cascade on your hands and you've no choice but to paddle blindly, shooting the rapids of your own bad faith as you carom toward the waterfall.

My mother didn't budge. 'And you,' she said, 'how are you?'

'Fine.'

'You don't look fine.'

'I'm still fine.'

The word hadn't volunteered itself. I'd had to drag it out, pull it from my throat like a tapeworm. 'Hunky dory.'

Hell, I wanted to spill my secret, cough my guts about my father's mistress. There was a knot in my stomach. The trouble was, I'd thought about this moment: were I to tell my secret, it might change everything. My secret had made me think about the word 'for ever'. If I were to tell my secret, our mother might hate our father, for ever. Stan might hate me too; for ever. Would sixpences still work when he was forty? Probably not. So you see, my burden, a thing of immensity, my immense burden, lay on my shoulders. My mother removed it from me without effort.

'I won't be coming back,' she said. 'Not this time.'

I looked at her. She knew.

'I know,' she said. 'About the other woman. Do you know about the other woman?'

'Yes,' I said.

I told her how I'd come to know about the other woman. When I did so I felt the strain leave my mind and lightness fill my spirit. Our lives had been ripped asunder; what a relief.

291

'How did you find out?' I asked my mother.

'He told me.'

'He told you?'

'In so many words; he's been telling me for years.'

'Her name's Maria,' I told her. 'I overheard them talking on the phone.'

My mother nodded. 'I know,' she said, 'Maria Tomlin; his lost love.' She giggled as she said 'lost love'.

I was puzzled by this; wondered if this meant something. Didn't laughter equal levity? Perhaps she was being sophisticated. I'd read about sophistication in the Sunday tabloids; perhaps continental chic had come unexpectedly to Dreichstane along with fitted carpets and Sacha Distel records. Had couples begun to accommodate each other's needs and peccadilloes as though we were fully formed, tolerant creatures and not the stunted, vindictive, unforgiving Scottish poor?

They had not.

'His jacket smelled of that cheap whore's scent, so I shoved it under his nose.'

The confrontation, it seemed, had not resulted in a civilised exchange of views between the two opposing parties. In lieu of detached diplomacy, Mother had hurled an Irn-Bru bottle at Father. He had ducked and the bottle had shattered against the wall. Within minutes Mother's case had been packed and Stan had been swaddled in as many clothes as he could wear and still remain mobile.

'How long has he been seeing her?'

'I don't know,' said Mother, with finality, closing the subject. 'And I don't want to know.'

The portents for reconciliation were not, as you may have deduced, hopeful. I tried, nonetheless.

'Please,' I said. 'How about it? Will you come home?'

It was my last attempt at rescuing the vestiges of our old life.

My mother sighed; a resolute, if defeated, sigh. 'I can't fight the past,' she said. 'She's haunted him all his life. It's too strong.'

I thought about Father and me that day at the Brandy Burn. The half-formed confession he had begun to utter: 'There was a woman I knew once, before I was . . .' Ah, the ridiculous banality of other people's love lives. Fuck them all, I thought. I was young, you see, and unhurt.

Stan had finished his ice cream. He was kicking the table again. My mother told him off. She made to sip but didn't. The tea had gone cold. No sense drinking cold tea. She put her cup down.

The waitress brought the bill.

There's always a bill.

I never went back to school. Since I'd turned fifteen, nobody seemed to mind, or even notice, including Father. Not to be outdone, he took to visiting the GP. Having had himself officially diagnosed as depressed, he began to cheer up. Clutching his certificate of official gloom, he romped in the clover of his condition, feeling himself at liberty to behave as randomly as he pleased. Celebrating his fortieth birthday, he lost the tip of a finger to a slicing machine. Such was his state of inebriation, he hadn't even noticed until an elderly widow let out a shriek on receiving the unexpected bonus of a digit end atop her quarter pound of Spam. [*no — Spam came in a tin. You mean chopped pork & ham.*]

Father had what he'd always craved; falling for the temptress had given him the courage to be selfish. With Stan and Mother now living safely out of view with Granny Cairns, he was free to make his moves. Nightly, he would slip out for pokes with his new muse. In the mornings, he would return, shirt tail flapping, padding woozily up the street like a sated satyr. The neighbours knew what had happened and, while they didn't ignore him, they kept out of his way. Not that he cared. He had a plan.

One night the temptress drove him round to our house to collect his remaining clothes. I was curious to see her. I had always assumed, vaguely, that he had picked her up on one of his weekend naval visits, while docked at some exotic island, like a part-time Fletcher Christian. In the event, Maria Tomlin was not a dusky-skinned beauty in a grass skirt from a distant land of pagan ritual, but an overfed, twice-widowed beauty consultant from Cranhill. They had met, or rather re-met, not on a sun-drenched Tahiti beach, but in the Stroll Inn; a sticky-carpeted, telly in the corner, soulless guzzling hole a mile away. She'd been in Dreichstane for a year, having moved, as we had done earlier, on the ever-flying magic carpet of the slum clearance programme. From Mother's desertion, stray clothes pegs and crumpled carrier bags still littered our floor.

'Your father's been doing some thinking,' said Maria Tomlin, the Ttmptress.

'Not enough, or he wouldn't be with you,' I returned.

Unwilling to further engage, she gave Father a prompting nudge. He made himself speak. 'You need to move out,' Father told me. 'This house is only ours till the end of the month.'

He looked to the temptress for reassurance. She nodded.

She didn't look like the stuff of mythology, but who does? She was older than him: flopping breasts and a businesswoman's pencil skirt; patent shoes; asthmatic too, another bonus. Every so often she'd produce a Lady of the Camellias wheezy flutter to retain his attention and his sympathy.

Father's eye had a faraway look. 'I'm going back to sea,' he told me, gazing mistily toward the living-room wall.

'No you're not,' the temptress corrected, bluntly. 'We've been through that. You're staying on terra firma.'

Father nodded. 'I'm staying on terra firma but from a place that overlooks the sea.'

'There's a mobile grocery shop for sale in Cape Wrath,' said the temptress, looking me in the eye for the first time, 'and a crofter's cottage at a diagonal to the Shetlands. It's as far north as you can go without falling off the edge. It's what Dad's always wanted.'

She called him that – 'Dad'.

'Except you can't actually see the sea,' Father said.

'Even if it overlooks it?' I seized the opportunity to drive a thin wedge between them.

The temptress narrowed her eyes. 'If you stand in the attic and put your head out the dormer window, then yes, it overlooks.'

Father turned to me. 'You can see the sea,' he said, drolly, 'if you've a touch of the giraffe.'

In other circumstances, I'd have paid up with a smile.

The temptress gathered our dirty cups and click-clacked on the bare floor to the kitchen. It was hard to hate Father. I could see his life unravelling before my eyes into a long, drawn-out balls-up.

'Where will you stay?' he asked me.

'At Granny Cairns'.'

'There'll be no room.'

'We'll make room. It'll be like the Lonnie Donegan song – we'll sleep in the kitchen with our feet in the hall.'

I wanted him to feel shitty and feckless.

For a moment, he looked gratifyingly wretched. I wasn't going backward to Govan though, I couldn't. I was moving onward, to London, to hang out in the Horn Rim club with Michael Caine and John Lennon; to shake my fist and shout 'Smash the System' at Tariq Ali speeches I could barely understand.

The temptress reappeared from the kitchen. She was wiping

her hands, showily. There was a look of distaste on her face. I could sense what she was doing. By implying a lack of hygiene on Mother's part, she was exonerating herself from the responsibility of stealing another woman's husband on the grounds that she, the said lawful wife, was a slatternly bitch. Three marriages in, she probably saw herself as a freedom fighter for the cause of grubby husbands. Luckily, she didn't say anything directly or I'd have been obliged, out of chivalry, to have picked up some clothes pegs from the floor and hung her by the tits on the washing line, in defence of Mother's honour.

The three of us stood, feeling awkward, for our different reasons.

'What will you do for a job?' Father asked me.

'I don't know.'

'I have good contacts in the grocery trade.'

'Yes,' I said. 'If I ever go off my head, that's exactly what I'll do.'

There was a silence. I wonder if my father felt what I did: the sharp tug of life moving on; our aching inability to connect at this last and critical moment; no ship to shore dots and dashes, no international distress call, just the ancient tacking sail of nature and desire sweeping us both in different directions on their endless, shifting, troubled currents.

'Well then . . .' my father said at last, shrugging.

'Yes . . .' I said.

The temptress stood at his side, playing the sensitive onlooker while failing to stifle a satisfied smirk. She linked her arm through his and he didn't protest.

My father held out his hand. I wouldn't touch it.

I knew where it had been.

The day before I left Dreichstane, I was walking down the Linn Brae. I followed the curve of the dry stone wall that skirts the municipal tennis courts and putting green before the road winds on to Ludovic Square and the high street.

I became aware of a squeaking noise, some way off, behind me. Glancing round, I saw Shona. She was pushing her toddler brother in his buggy pram. Thirsty for oil, a wheel was signalling its distress.

As I looked, I hesitated, not knowing what to do. I wasn't sure why I was unsure but I knew I should have stopped, I realised that much. I thought about stopping, about waiting for her to catch up but somehow I couldn't; a shyness thing. Truly, I wanted to wait and walk with her but didn't, somehow, dare, being still without her forgiveness; so a shyness and pride thing. We walked on separately, her behind, me in front, the squeak of the buggy wheel in our mutual ears, working like some kind of mating call, some kind of reproach, maybe both, I didn't know. I could feel the taut wire of expectation between us, so I supposed Shona could too. Approaching the foot of the Brae, my shoulders tensed, my breathing had become nervous and shallow. I kept walking, I don't know why. I was on a road, I suppose, and my feet knew no other than to keep moving forward. Feet were forever walking on, not doing what you required of them; they could make life difficult, feet. I'd make mine stop though, establish an important principle. I'd show them, for good and all, that I could take control. Once stopped, I'd wait and force my head to find those thoughts, those words my mouth would need to find; the courage to speak.

Ahead of me was the little railway bridge by the canal road.

I'll wait there, I thought. That's where I'll stand and wait for her. I'll say the things that will make the difference; that will make everything better, the way it used to be, before it's too late.

We'd smile, Shona and me, dallying a while then, as we talked, me professing guilt, wringing hands, we'd walk on. Once forgiven, we'd laugh together under the canal bridge rafters, our voices echoing in the dank chill as we picked our way through the crusting piles of pigeon droppings. There was a swing park, corner of Dimity Street. Maybe we'd sit there, minding her little brother as he played on the roundabout. There was something I had to ask her, you see, a matter of deep importance, though some might call it a trifle, all right, a trifle of deep importance, that needed nonetheless to be resolved: was it love we felt or not? That was my question. Yes or no. Simple enough, you'd have thought. To ask it, all I had to do was stop.

So I stopped. I looked behind me. Shona was no longer there. I couldn't see her, then did. She had taken the cinder track into the tennis courts through the wooden gate at the bottom of the brae. I hesitated. I stepped forward. I stepped back and hesitated again. I might have followed her but it felt wrong, going back. We had missed each other. I had waited too long. It was a freak accident of timing. To pursue her would have looked weak; desperate men always lose their women.

Next time, I thought, cheering. There'd be a next time, of course there would, and I'd ask her then.

It can keep until a better time, I thought, much better that I wait.

I hitch-hiked to London the next day. I never saw her again. But I didn't forget her either.

There would be a next time; I'd make sure of it. There's no statute of limitations on a muse.

'*Flow gently sweet Afton . . .*'

Twenty-four

'Mr Moss?'

'Come in.'

Our private nurse, Mags, had pitched up from the agency. She wasn't the demure little thing in a rustling white coat I'd vaguely hoped for, whose thighs I'd idly ogle while she bent over to administer the morphine.

'Just go on through.'

'The living room?'

'That's it.'

Had she been single and attractive I might've kicked my mother out of bed and climbed in myself, allowing her to play Catherine Barkley to my wounded Frederic Henry.

She leaned over to take a peek at my mother. The duvet was pulled up to my mother's nose; two flinty eyes gazed back, unblinking.

'Would you prefer I called you Kathleen or Mrs Moss?'

Kathleen, Mrs Moss, didn't oblige with a preference. She could ignore both approaches with equal facility; the formal and the informal.

'Call her Kathleen,' I said.

'Mrs Moss,' said Kathleen, my mother. 'Now get me up, I

need to go, I really need to go – right now.'

'Fine.'

Mags had a touch of the heifer, being tall and big boned. She had Mother sitting up, lifted, debriefed and in a startled pissing squat on the commode before she'd had time to say, 'Call yourself a nurse – you don't know what the hell you're doing.' Mags knew exactly what she was doing; she was born for the job. A tang of antiseptic seemed to follow her as though she dabbed Dettol behind her ears. The floorboards tended to rattle when she crossed them. Her movements at all times were swift and decisive and gave the reassuring impression she'd been well trained in the art of stewarding infirm travellers to the banks of eternity, or the local crematorium, depending on spiritual outlook.

Back in bed my mother feigned sleep, possibly to avoid the new nurse and her brisk ministrations.

'You've thought about hospital?' Mags asked.

'Of course,' I said, 'she won't go.'

'I won't go,' rasped my mother and went back to sleep.

'Hospice?' whispered Mags. 'There's a woman, Wendy something – Wendy Friel?'

'Yes,' I said. 'She's been coming around offering succour but I'm not sure my mother wants any succour.'

'What gives you that impression?'

'Last time she was here my mother told her to stick her succour up her arse.'

'That's an unusual reaction.'

'My mother can be an unusual woman.'

We both turned to look at her. The unusual woman had her teeth in a glass, her mouth hanging agape.

'Wendy will be back,' Mags insisted. 'They're always grateful. She always wins them over in the end.'

'The end?'

'Yes,' Mags said, nodding. 'Judging by her condition, it won't be long now.'

'I see.'

I looked suitably sad, but a mean little part of me knew there was a nursing meter running, so it was reassuring to hear the end was on the nigh side.

'There's a camp bed in the other room,' I told her, 'that's where I or my brother listen for her when she calls.'

'No,' said Mags. 'I prefer to stay close.' She cast her eye around the room. 'I'll sit here.'

'Okay.'

She moved a motorised armchair that I had bought and that had cost hundreds into position. My mother had managed to use it once, for ten minutes. It was just one more well-intentioned item among a flurry of shower seats and walking frames that were redundant before they'd even arrived.

It was always a relief to hear Mags's ring at the bell and she was never late.

I would finish my own caring shift feeling torn; guilty at leaving yet cock-a-hoop to quit the house of gloom for the regular world with all its myopic, selfish and life-affirming trivia.

Three of us shared a new rota of night duties over the week and we were able to augment this with volunteers from charities like Marie Curie.

Though my mother hurried the process of dying as best she could, it can, nonetheless, take a substantial amount of time to conclude the act. I came to realise that carers can be as trapped as those they care for.

I'd sit in the motorised armchair in the small hours feeling, selfishly, like a prisoner in a cell. I'd try to read under the thin shaft of the halogen bulb but my mental discipline would crumble and eventually I'd slump in a dazed torpor staring out at the dwindling lights in the tower blocks opposite, watching them snuffed, one by one, as time crawled by and the immense rolling blanket of the night sky slithered off to be replaced by morning grey.

Humdrum misery takes place unseen; the thickness of a wall, the vastness of a world away. Every day, unsung people perform small heroics for little money and no praise. Home helps were the dibs; people slaving for a pittance but who weren't above washing my mother's arse or changing her soiled bed. Death can meet life in a kind word, a thoughtfully propped pillow or water held to a parched, cursing mouth when stick arms can no longer reach for themselves.

I met volunteers who'll come around to sit with and tend to dying strangers. Why they'd choose to do this rather than sinking a Pinot Noir in Òran Mór or bagging baguettes in Subway I don't know. They'll administer medication, if the dosages are ready and made up in a proper medical pill box. You spend a lot of time making up these doses, checking and rechecking, scared you've made a mistake. Whoever's on shift, whether you, your brother, an overnight charity volunteer or a paid nurse that person or persons will monitor in a notebook the patient's actions; the patient's food and liquid intake; the patient's comfort and medicinal feeds.

One afternoon, I was changing shifts with Mags. As a final errand, I'd to visit the chemist on Paisley Road to collect a prescription for Liquomorph. I was gone no more than half an hour but when I returned a police car and ambulance were parked outside the communal entrance.

Jesus, I thought, stifling a relieved and guilty thrill. Brace yourself, this is it – she's humped.

Emerging from the lift on the fourteenth floor, I was met by a female paramedic leading a wobbly Wendy Friel by the arm. Wendy was wearing a head bandage and a shell-shocked expression.

'What happened?'

'It's all under control,' the paramedic said. 'The police are inside.'

Recognising me, Wendy gripped my arm. Her eyes were wide and ointment smeared her forehead from a cranial lump under the bandage.

'Don't forget,' she said, resolutely. 'Keep talking.'

'What?'

'Hearing is the last sense to go. So what must you do?'

'Keep talking?'

'Correct.'

Mags appeared at the door.

'What the fuck . . .?'

'There's been an incident,' said Mags.

'Don't forget,' called Wendy Friel.

'I won't,' I said, all at sea.

'Forget what?' asked Mags.

'To keep talking,' I told her. 'Apparently, it's the law.'

Wendy waved her arm at me in a slow arc as her stricken face vanished behind the squeaking door of the closing lift.

In the living room a young PC was sitting by my mother, looking nonplussed. He had his notebook open but he was sucking his pen. He took it out to speak to me. 'Mr Moss?'

I nodded. I was trying to make sense of things. 'What's going on?'

Mags stood by the door. She was gripping the edge of the sideboard for comfort. 'Wendy stopped by just after you left,' Mags said. Her voice was trembling. 'She asked your mother if she'd changed her mind about entering the hospice.'

'The answer was no,' said the young PC.

'I could have told her that,' I said. 'What happened?'

'Wendy kneeled by the bed,' said Mags. 'That's when it kicked off.'

'What did?'

'Your mother took exception to being prayed for. She clumped Wendy across the head with a Lucozade bottle.'

Mags and the PC looked at each other, gravely. He turned to look at me. 'As this is a case of assault,' he said, 'I should take a statement. But Miss Friel was very understanding. And in the circumstances . . .' He motioned diffidently in the direction of my mother.

'The bottle was full,' Mags explained, 'hence the damage.'

'Yes,' I said, 'she doesn't really like Lucozade.'

'I don't really like Lucozade,' my mother said, drowsily.

'Too gassy,' I explained.

'Too gassy,' she agreed.

The PC closed his notebook.

Afterwards, driving home, I found the episode curiously uplifting and morally instructive. My mother's action was confirmation that she had indeed, and to my personal relief, retained her zest for life. Additionally, she had expressed her religious reservations in characteristic fashion through the precious gift of violence.

Unlike the Silent One, my mother did not work in mysterious ways.

The next day had been one of irritation and tetchiness, on my part as well as my mother's. Once home, though, I had been unable to settle, my emotions unaccountably churned up. On an impulse, I had abandoned the plate of food I had prepared and climbed back into the car.

Mags looked up guiltily from *Heat* magazine when I entered. 'Did you forget something?'

'It's okay,' I told her. 'I'm not staying.'

My mother was propped up in bed, wheezing. Her teeth were out to let her breathe easier. I stooped by her ear and spoke.

'You've had a bad day today,' I told her, 'but you'll have a better day tomorrow.'

She didn't open her eyes. 'Tomorrow,' she said.

I was wrong.

At home, next day, I sat writing at the big dining-room table. Emily's black bags of clothes and books still sat on the Windsor chair. I knew what I'd be doing with them now, they'd be thrown into the boot of the car, to be scattered like so much designer-labelled seed corn, feeding the charity shops of Byres Road. I was still mulling over Emily's comment; the one about my being free without her, to live my life exactly as I wanted. In fact, I was thinking about it when the phone rang.

'Mr Moss?'

It was Mags. My heart sank. I was enjoying myself, lost in space, working.

'Hi, Mags, what is it?'

'I think you'd better come over.'

'Why, what's up?'

'It's started.'

'What's started?'

'Cheyne-Stokes breathing.'

'What's that?'

'Just come over, please. Would you please come over?'

'Okay.'

'And bring your brother.'

'Uh . . . Okay.'

Yes, it had started. No – it's nearly the end.

Her eyes were closed, her breathing scary with congestion. Stan and I sat either side of her bed and did the hand-holding thing. You keep talking, telling them it's all right, it's okay to go; some of us, apparently, need permission to quit this earth, we need to know all debts have been settled and it's time to close the account. We'll all have our accounts. I'll have mine, you'll have yours.

She gave a little extra puffing gasp of breath. White spume, a last over-boiled saucepan, coursed down her lower lip. I reached for a wipe.

We sat looking at her, still talking her away on her journey. What we didn't realise was that she had already arrived. It was hard to tell what had just happened because it appeared that nothing had just happened.

My mother's account was closed.

Finally, I turned to Stan. 'Fancy a cup of tea?'

He nodded.

The making of tea seemed the most natural, most welcome thing in the world. I started to rise but Stan beat me to it.

'I'll get it,' he said, heading for the kitchen.

I sat looking at her and thinking. What? That what we think and feel can't be deduced while it's actually happening. There's too much crowding in on us; business to be done; people to be informed; arrangements to be made. Feeling comes later, absently, through muscle memory; the picking up of a phone to dial a number that's been discontinued. The turning of your car, mistakenly, into a street where someone you knew once lived.

She was still sitting half up, dead, with her eyes open. I turned the spindle on the bed mechanism, lowering her down from the lively chatting position to the more taciturn prone. When she was flat, I tugged the wedding ring off her finger and put it in my pocket. I thought I should try to close her eyes, having seen it done in films. After a few clumsy attempts with my lumpen fingers, I managed. I rang Dr Semple and reported the death. I then rang the district nurse and left an explanatory message on her machine. I was still waiting for the tea.

'Stan?'

There was no answer; no clatter of cups or roar of warming kettle.

'Stan?'

I started to rise. As I did so, I heard the nostalgic sound of shattering glass. I walked into the kitchen to find Stan standing, looking pained and sheepish. He had punched his fist through the kitchen window, in a kind of grief frenzy or some such. Blood trails doubled back along his forearm and slurped onto the flower-patterned floor tiles.

'Look at the mess.'

'Sorry,' he said. 'I'll get a cloth.'

Like mother like son.

My mobile chirruped. 'Hello?'

It was the district nurse. She offered her condolences and asked if it would be convenient to send a van round in the next hour or so.

'Why?'

'I need the air mattress returned that our department loaned you.'

'Right.'

'We have other patients, you see. Our work goes on.'

'I quite understand,' I said and put down the phone.

Cunt, I thought.

Generations of Mosses and Cairns have been cremated at Craigton; it's our Wounded Knee. If you're from Govan, a

Craigton drop off is pretty much the law. Not for me though, I've stipulated otherwise. I'll take anything: a burial at sea; hell in a handcart, bin bag, you name it; I just don't want to join the family herd of lowing ghosts clogging up those dreary iron-gated acres.

The minister said a few words. Good words, homely and plain. He spoke the twenty-third Psalm. I found myself nodding, approvingly, seduced by the euphony of biblical cadence. Afterwards, I took the lectern and read William Blake's 'The Smile'; a dark, savagely ambivalent, ultimately affirmative poem, with no unhealthy reek of the church. My mother might have disapproved but she was in no position to object, being otherwise engaged.

Stan took the ashes home.

Twenty-five

Not long after, the landline phone rang. Sometimes people keep tugging at you and you don't know why.

'Ivan?'

'Uh huh.'

'It's Tom. Tonga. Tom McIninich.'

'Oh, hi, Tom.'

I'd tried my 'I'm a reclusive artist and you're interrupting' tone but Tom, Tonga, didn't back off. He made his pitch. He told me Bo Divney's condition had worsened and that he had been taken into a hospice to see out what little time remained. The word 'hospice' lay like a brick in my stomach. It was too soon.

Tom left a pause for me to ask which hospice. What else can you do?

'Which hospice?'

'The Canterbury, in Paisley. You want to see him?'

I tried a little slippery writhing. 'Maybe Bo would prefer the sanctity of solitude, the quiet contemplation of . . .'

'Fuck off,' said Tom, not in the mood for dicking around. 'Just do the right thing for once.'

'And break the habit of a lifetime?'

'The man is dying, Ivan.'

'We're all dying.'

It didn't sound good. I remembered my mother.

'That came out wrong,' I admitted.

By blinking first I'd let him off the hook so Tom, Tonga, moved in for the kill. 'So are you coming or aren't you?'

'Sure,' I said. 'A dying guy in bed – I can't wait.'

'You don't have to come.'

'I'm coming, I'm coming!'

'You mean it?'

'Yes!'

Tom's mobile Biffy Clyroed in the background.

'It's Bronagh,' he said to me. 'I have to take this.'

Bronagh was Bo's wife. I held on while Tom spoke to her.

I felt harassed and put upon. I really wasn't ready for more round the bed visits, the Sisyphean drudgery of pushing the good cheer boulder uphill. Tom came back on the line.

He said, 'You're off the hook.'

'What do you mean?'

'You don't have to come to the hospice.'

'Why not?'

'That's the bad part – Bo's dead.'

'Shit.'

I heard Tom, Tonga, catch his breath. 'I can't speak any more,' he said. 'Let me call you tomorrow.'

'Any arrangements yet?'

'Ivan, he's still warm.'

'Of course.'

'Speak soon. Stay strong, mate.'

'I will.'

I put the phone down, took a bottle from the wine rack and poured a settler. I found it surprisingly easy to stay strong. I did this by accentuating the positive. A funeral might be grim but it was easier to deal with than a sick bed; or, for that matter, one of Tom's, Tonga's, parties. I made a resolution; if I was heading for a second, unwelcome blast of fancy syntax and Gabriel's trumpet, I wanted a joyous reward. I needed to change the rules. There had to be something in this funeral for me.

I knew exactly what I wanted in it for me.

I wanted Shona.

But how?

Here's how.

We sat there, talking fast. Every so often we'd break off to grin and look at each other.

'Nuts!'

'Crazy!'

From time to time we'd remember the sombreness of the news that had brought us together and utter a platitude, or joshing reminiscence, to Bo's memory.

It had been decades since I'd seen Neth Skillet. How many years, I could only guess. I knew he worked for a local data company and had tracked him down, over the course of a morning, through the web. Next day, easy as that, there we were; Neth and I, half a lifetime down the line, sitting in a café bar in Linwood. We were near the factory unit complex where Neth worked. It was his lunch break. He looked prosperous, had put on weight. His cheeks were pouches filled with too many homely dinners and naughty puddings. He was still Neth, though; glint-eyed and manic. When he was into a story his excited voice was loud and sharp all over the café. Tonga told me Neth loved Westerns. At home he'd stick in a John Wayne DVD, get good and drunk, and ride the arm of the couch like Trigger until hauled off to bed by his wife. We talked of Bo Divney, and of this and that

1) short legs   2) wrong horse.

memory; a spill-over of events and minutiae we'd sucked up over the years and which was now slopping out and running down the sides of our life glass. It was like old times with Neth, but we only had an hour and time was passing fast. I thought I'd better get to the point; the real point. I bent my head over my skinny latte and asked if he'd ever heard anything of Shona.

'Shona?'

'Shona Burns.'

'Oh, yes.' He turned it over in his mind. 'Yeh, I heard something.'

'What? When?'

'Oh, years ago.'

'What did you hear?'

'She divorced.'

My heart leapt. 'Shona divorced?'

'Yeh. Then married again.'

My heart stopped leaping and slumped back in its armchair.

'She had a kid, I think, late in life, a girl, no, maybe a boy.'

I gave him a look.

'Doesn't narrow it down much, right?' He thought again. 'She went to Canada. Or was it Carlisle?'

'You tell me, Neth.'

'I can't remember. Somebody mentioned her in a bar, long time back. The music was loud, I couldn't hear. Teardrop Explodes, or Tears For Fears; something with crying and snot. We're talking the eighties here, you know?'

I nodded. He must've recognised the look on my face. What he saw amused him. What's more he understood it and he grinned. When he grinned he looked like the old Neth again, which was to say the young one.

'I could find out.'

'You could?'

'If it helps, I know where her mother lives.'

My eyebrows went on alert. 'You do?'

'Yes, I do.' He held the grin; paused for effect. 'And so do you.'

I was puzzled. 'I know? How?'

He continued with his inscrutable sphinx-type thing.

I ran it over in my mind. I got it. 'She's still in the same house?'

'Very same house.'

'Christ almighty.'

'Same street, same house.'

'You're kidding me. You're yanking my chain.'

'It's true. So help me.'

'Nobody lives in the same place for forty years. Not these days. It doesn't happen.'

Neth pulled a face. 'We're talking Dreichstane, remember?' He did a Chinaman voice. I don't know why; maybe he was still being inscrutable. 'Dreichstane no likee change.'

I nodded. I was stunned, in turmoil, curiously excited, confused too. I tried to stumble out a sentence. Neth read my mind.

'You going over there to see her?'

I shrugged. 'After all this time? It wouldn't be right.'

He leaned back in his chair. 'You really want to go over there and see her, don't you?'

I shook my head. 'It's been too long; it wouldn't be sensible.'

'Sensible.' He gave a little yap of mocking glee, leaned forward, his folded elbows on the table. 'Listen,' he said. 'You remember what Berti Vogts said? We meet everybody twice in life. You're either going over there and seeing Shona's mother or you're going to wipe her from your mind. Which one is it?'

We looked at each other; him with his sprite grin, me frowning.

'The first one.'

* * *

313

Dreichstane Castle stands in Tower Place. It was the former home of the Houston family. The Houstons were descended from an Anglo-Saxon nobleman called Hugo Fitzalan de Padivan whose ancestors came to Britain with William the Conqueror. As a reward to his allies after the Battle of Hastings, William dug deep into his glittering treasure chest of British lands. By the time it came to Hugo's turn, William must have been reduced to fumbling for loose change in the pockets of his chainmail because all he tossed him were a few stubbly acres by the banks of the River Cart. Centuries ago Dreichstane Castle crumbled, but in a distant burst of civic image rebranding some visionary local committee had fired an 'e' and hired an 'a' for the town to become known as Dreichstane.

I'm telling you this because I drove around those same castle remnants six or seven times as I summoned up the courage to carry out what I'd come to Dreichstane to do. Sure, I'd been back a couple of times down the years but each time I'd done that I was a man in transit, mentally heading somewhere else, eyes blinkered and fixed on some imagined horizon up ahead; always working on that script, this series, that house or woman. My feelings, too, on those occasions had somehow been suspended. I had been like a man swimming underwater, holding his breath until finally he made it out the other end.

This was the other end.

As a gentle rehearsal I'd driven the car up Vine Crescent and stopped it right outside the old house. That old house; our house, the one with the garden where Father had tried to show me how to box; the one Stan and I had picked up shards of window glass from following one of Mother's Kristallnachts when she'd gone berserk; our garden, the square of shabby grass we'd cultivated and that had been other people's for forty years since the divorce bomb had blasted apart our threadbare but cohesive little world.

I sat outside the close in the shiny steel and glass box of my car. I didn't move, just let things course through me, in and out. After a minute or so of this, I let rip at the top of my voice. I shrieked and howled, out loud, like one of Bacon's screaming Popes.

When I'd composed myself, I started the car. Minutes later, suitably poised and affable, I'd rounded the castle, turned off the hill and was standing outside number 6, a bunch of cheap flowers in one hand, package in the other. The square of lawn was still trim and neat. It was like old times. Except that forty years earlier I didn't need a lumbar support on the car seat or have a bald patch on the crown of my head.

A small woman with tidy white hair opened the door. I smiled, warmly. I was trying to pass myself off as a respectable citizen so as not to spook her. Strangers make pensioners nervous and I wanted her relaxed. Only if things went really badly would I bludgeon her to death and steal her savings book.

'Mrs Burns?'

'Yes.'

'It's Ivan. Ivan Moss.'

She looked at me, uncomprehendingly. To help smooth my approach I affected a gentle, question-marked inflection, hoping to put her at her ease and jog her memory. 'I lived round here a long time ago? Do you remember?' It came out slightly sinister. I felt like a suspect vicar with an ankle tag doing a meet and greet with new parishioners. She was trying, though. I saw the 'hold' signal in her eyes while her brain riffled through a lifetime of obscure, forgotten acquaintances, trying to dig out my file.

'I was friendly with Shona.' I used the term 'friendly' in a loose sense. Generally speaking, friends don't stick their tongue down your throat or give you body heat at parties. The S word clinched it; a wary recognition dawned.

'Oh yes, of course – Ivan. Now I remember you.'

She looked at me, not quite drinking me in.

'You went bowling with my husband.'

'Yes,' I said.

Her eyes narrowed. 'I remember.'

In order to slither out from under the bowling incident I handed her one of my books: a verification of my worth and identity, but especially worth; one with my picture on the sleeve. I wanted her to think well of me; to demonstrate myself as a successful local boy who had made good, not only good but glamorous and dangerous; in short, I wanted to be Heathcliff in varifocals. It was chest beating, of course; showboating. Roughly speaking, the subtext was – 'I give you this trophy. Now bring unto me your daughter.' I was hoping she didn't know the book had been remaindered.

'You're looking well,' I said, lobbing in a greasy pearl of shameless flattery.

'You too. How's your mother?'

I gave an almost imperceptible sigh and allowed my eyes to become dewy; lit by the wan radiance of recent loss.

I related the bare bones of the story; not too much detail. Old people have heard these tales of fleshly woe before and many times; maybe lived them too. Death wearies and frightens them.

'You've heard about Bo Divney?'

'Yes,' she said. 'I'm friendly with his mother. Poor boy. A tragedy, isn't it?'

I nodded in seemly fashion before reaching my hands into the pay dirt. 'How's Shona?'

'Oh, she's fine. She was so sad to hear about Bo.'

I concurred, playing the man of feeling. My real feeling was shiftiness. I wanted to ask; managed to ask; made it sound as matter of fact as possible. 'Is Shona coming to the funeral?'

'I'll pass on the arrangements when I have them. I'm sure she will, if she can.'

'Of course,' I purred. My hands were clasped solicitously, at cock level. Mentally, I felt the flutter of the black ribbon on the back of my undertaker's top hat.

She began to relax a little. I stood there on the step, watching myself drink in every word of our all too brief conversation. How long? Maybe ten minutes. I brushed her words delicately, like an obsessive etymologist, searching for hidden layers of meaning and subtext. She had been guarded; I understood that. After all, some guy comes lurching out of the past, with a bunch of flowers in his paw and a leer on his face asking about your daughter, you're going to be cagey, right? New lives and relationships had been formed in the intervening decades; new partners found, new loves cemented; homes had been bought; grandchildren raised; Christmases and landmark birthdays had been enjoyed with more jolly times ahead, beckoning; these are the ties that bond and bind us.

Or so they tell me.

A lot of old faces turned out for Bo's funeral: Neth, Tonga, Freddie Fallon, Eddie McIlhone, the Mighty Elk. A whey-faced guy with buck teeth stepped out of a Volkswagen Passat and, when he saw me, flicked the Vs for old times' sake. It was Limpy.

He motioned us over to show us the controls of his car. The clutch was built up to accommodate his withered left leg. I noticed the brake had been built up too and asked him why.

'I met my wife at a Polio Society dinner dance. She has a gammy left leg, with me it's the right. Some day we'll afford two cars. Until then, we're driving this fucking pedalo.'

We laughed. A little pulse of boyish electricity thrummed

around our group. Somebody asked the time and we fell quiet.

For the service, Bo had prepared a last, puckish surprise. A titter of appreciation rippled the church as his coffin slid behind the velvet curtain to 'Ring of Fire'. From our spot in the circle, my face scanned the gathered mourners, hungrily. I was searching for a face. Not just any face, that face, her face. Neth saw me looking and smiled.

At the bar of Bo's old bowling club, we gathered for beer and sandwiches.

A section of the lounge had been cordoned off with a line of chairs for us mourners. We pushed together some Formica tables and sat in two lines facing each other. It was like we were back drilling on a Friday night in the BB church hall on Elm Drive. We had been boys then, our lives a field of endless clover that lay ahead, waiting to be romped through. At least that's how you think of it with hindsight, though at the time it didn't seem so hot to me, the future.

People told their stories. Predictably, everyone had married young from the crop of females close to home. Everybody was a hard worker, a steady guy. As I looked around, I realised I was the only one at the table who wasn't married with at least two grown-up children or a logo beside his name on Friends Reunited announcing proudly, 'I'm a grandparent!'

There were casualties, of course. We spoke of some who had never got to grips with the world, who maybe had a bad break too many, were now leaning too heavily on drink, maybe divorced and jobless; back living with elderly mothers and pulling the weekly shop home from Spar in a tartan trolley; or sitting around the house in dressing gowns, waiting. Those are the ones who didn't show for Bo's funeral. We, on the other hand, were the lucky ones, who didn't feel obliged to hide a private sense of shame. My own inner life was public; my stock in trade.

Afterwards, I stood on the pavement with Neth Skillet. We'd had a few drinks. We were each waiting for our lifts home, in our different directions.

Neth came straight to the point. 'Shona didn't come then, uh?'

I shook my head.

'Did her mother say she'd come?'

'No. I thought she might though.'

'For you?'

'For curiosity. For the past.'

'Some people don't care about the past. Want me to put out feelers?'

'No, it's all right.'

'I could try.'

'It's okay,' I said. 'It's a closed door.' And it was. I felt foolish and slightly disgusted at myself for having tried to open it.

Neth nodded. 'You're right. Let it go.' He shook his shoulders in his coat to loosen them.

I looked around at these strangers, my friends; the grey men, us, the boys, hugging and pumping hands. Some would laugh at themselves for having to push their specs onto their foreheads and squint as they tried to jab new contact numbers into mobile phones. Others slunk away into family cars, discreetly, having paid their respects, done what they'd come to do. You could see the relief on those faces as they clunked car doors, clicked into safety belts, warmed engines, eager to escape this collision of worlds, the living death that is old friends.

The hour, as they say, was getting late.

'Remember "It"?' Neth asked me, suddenly.

'Yes,' I said. And I did. I'd never forgotten It; our own brand of humour. 'Remember Pope Limpy?'

'Cardinal Limpy,' Neth corrected. 'He never made pontiff.'

'That's right, they froze him out, those big hat bastards.'

'Just because he was a Protestant.'

'Discrimination.'

'Right. A disabled Protestant Pope in the Vatican, you're talking breakthrough.'

'They weren't big enough people!'

'Not big enough people!'

At that moment, Limpy hobbled round to the boot of his car, to show Eddie McIlhone his new golf clubs.

For a moment, we were our old selves, our young selves, laughing, slapping our thighs.

'Remember Flogger Petrie's shed?'

'Yes, yes!' I said.

Neth gave me a look of searching intensity. 'Man, we talked that day! *We talked!* Life, sex, death! Anything and everything!'

'The whole shebang,' I said.

'The whole shebang.'

It started to drizzle. We stood, looking at each other, smiling.

Neth was dapper in his blue wool overcoat; his jaunty, light-weight suit subdued by the sartorial necessity of a black tie. He still wore the same hair shirt though, that had maddened him all through his life. When he looked in the mirror, Neth's clothes told him he was a businessman. His reflection handed him a rule book of conduct to which he attempted to adhere. Those eyes, though, still glinted, crazed.

Drizzle gathered on our shoulders, sparkling.

'You left us for a long time.'

'Yes,' I said. 'I came back though. In the end, we all do.'

Neth looked up at the swinging sign above the doorway of the bowling club. It was as though he was talking to someone else, himself perhaps, not me.

'It comes back to me all the time,' he said, 'it never leaves me.'

'What doesn't?'

His voice was a sort of startled, embarrassed blurt. 'The past,' he said. 'All of it, everything; a sight here, a sound there and zap, I'm back through time, seeing it, living it again. I can't seem to shake it off.'

'Try,' I said. My voice was cold and hard. I was sick of the past: a picture frozen in time and lost souls trying to climb in through the frame; fuck it.

A silver Audi swung into the narrow car park. A woman in a trouser suit with light piping on the lapels opened the driver door and waved at us, at Neth.

'Your wife?'

Neth nodded. 'Elspeth – she's a teacher.' He corrected himself. 'Deputy head.' Neth waved back to Elspeth, the teacher, the deputy head.

'Would I know her from the old days?'

'No,' he said. 'You wouldn't know Elspeth from the old days.'

'Good,' I said.

He turned to me. 'You're right,' he said.

'About what?'

'What you said earlier. We're different people now.'

'Yes.'

We stood nodding wisely; two stately, greying figures, different people once again.

Twenty-six

I met Stan at Paisley Cross and he drove me home. We didn't speak much on the journey; he was still rankled over my behaviour during the last days of our mother's illness.

'You wouldn't even sing "Bandit of Brazil",' he said. 'She asked you and you said no.'

'She was raving – zonked out of her skull.'

'Our mother's last wish.'

'She had lots of last wishes. Most involved sitting on the commode.'

'One song.'

'I couldn't do it, Stan – that shite and onions big heart sentiment, that's your bag.'

'Sing to me, our mother said!'

'I froze! Gimme a break!'

My feathers were ruffled. I had ruffled feathers and I was yelling.

'No wonder you can never hold down a relationship,' my brother said.

I didn't bite. I was narked though. 'Stan, do me a favour.'

'What?'

'Take a fit.'

'A what?'

'You heard. For old times' sake; a fit, if you'd be so kind.'

'You're sick.'

'Please. I need cheering up.'

'Stop it. People can't just fit on demand. I'm driving, he's telling me to take a fit.'

'Well, if you won't do it then shut the fuck up.'

'You're the pits.'

Stan didn't shut up, he shut himself down. He had ammunition for a new fresh huff and was eager to use it.

I wanted to be quiet with my thoughts. The day had been demanding; I felt depleted and, at the same time, overloaded.

'What about the ashes?'

'What?'

It was Stan. He was asking about our mother's ashes.

'I still don't know what to do with them,' he said. 'I don't want them in the house.'

'We'll think of something,' I told him. 'It'll come to us.'

Our mother's ashes were still in the boot of his car. I still had her wedding ring at home. We'd give it to Stan's daughter when she was old enough. We'd had no clue what to do about the ashes though. We were driving along, skirting Govan, when it came to me.

'Don't go through the tunnel,' I told Stan.

'What?'

'Too much traffic. Take the slip road by Lidl, we'll head west over the Squinty Bridge.'

'There'll be a bottleneck at the Squinty Bridge; it's too close to town.'

'I'm older than you, I'm pulling rank.'

I'd had an idea about the ashes.

It was a detour and Stan wasn't pleased. I offered him a piece

323

of gum which he took to pretend he wasn't in a sulk.

We passed through the rump of Govan; the shell of Harland and Wolff, the old police cells on Orkney Street, the fire station on Govan Road, the ghost of the public bath-house by the Town Hall, now the Film City production studios. They'd kept the water warm there, at Summertown Road Baths; it was always colder at Harhill Street Baths, back of Harmony Row.

We neared the basin of the old dry dock. Ahead stood the strange silver hulk of the Science Centre, isolated on a barren lunar landscape, as if waiting for some astronaut to climb out and plant a flag, claiming it for some distant galaxy or maybe to ask the route to Venus, avoiding the city centre. I thought about Mother's ashes in the urn bumping around in the back with the spare wheel and the car maintenance manual.

I thought too about how, a few years before, Stan had, in a gesture of healing, invited our father to his wedding. He'd come, put in his appearance, even though the temptress hadn't been pleased. It had been a timely move as he was dead by the following summer. We Mosses are built for the sprint not the marathon.

We were on the Squinty Bridge, the Arc.

'Pull over, Stan,' I said.

'On the bridge? Are you kidding, there are double yellow lines – there's a bus lane.'

'Pull the fuck over,' I told him, 'and open the boot.'

'We should have gone through the tunnel.'

'There was more traffic at the tunnel. I did us a favour.'

'That's not an argument, that's just grabbing the last word.'

'Stan.'

Stan pulled the car in left, smack on the bus lane, flashed his hazard lights. He sat clenched, staring ahead, blinkered against the rasps and snarls from the other drivers. Finally, he saw me.

'What are you doing?'

I didn't answer. I was out of the car.

I took the canister, the ashes, from the boot.

'Ivan?'

I walked to the rail of the bridge.

'What's going on?'

'Watch,' I said.

I threw it off the bridge, the canister, the ashes, down into the water. From the promenade of the Quay Café, a few diners, eating al fresco, watched it hit the river.

I watched it too, from the parapet of the bridge, planting my feet against the bluster of cross winds edging me this way and that.

The canister plummeted then bobbed, resurfaced. I saw it float away from me; down past the dry dock craters and the unsold duplex flats hastily thrown up by the developers during the boom years. We were all going to sit on river balconies eating croissants. The Clyde isn't a chic river. You might live on a houseboat on the Thames or Seine, but you wouldn't in Partick or Linthouse for fear of being mugged and beaten to death with your own anchor. No; you'd die of hypothermia

I don't know what I'd have done if those ashes hadn't sunk, but sink they did.

I climbed back in the car and shut the door against the traffic, the noise, the blaring horns of other drivers.

'Well?'

I waited for Stan to do something, maybe hit me, perhaps weep, or threaten litigation. He didn't do any of those things. He said, 'How'd you know that's what she'd have wanted?'

'She wouldn't have wanted it,' I said. 'But that doesn't make it wrong.'

We sat for a moment. We didn't speak.

Up ahead, the lights blinked amber.

'Go!' I yelled.

Stan didn't need telling. He roared away, cutting people up, trying to beat the lights.

It was out of character.

'Ignore them,' I said.

We ignored them. We were entitled; it was our moment.

I'll say something for the word racket – there are times when you can surprise yourself. There are days when you can hold your own past and present in your head at the same time. This balance, this holding of past and present, may be what poets refer to as a transcendent moment. I don't know if plumbers feel transcendent moments, or property magnates, or cab drivers, or the African women we drove past that day, in their too-bright clothes, lugging bags of shopping to council flats once built for the sons and daughters of sixties Govan.

If we try, we can rise above ourselves.

Up there, among the A4 white paper clouds, you feel free.

You come back down again, though. We all come down.

That's the deal.

Now, if you'll excuse me, there's a bottle of Merlot with my name on it.

Keep talking.